Marcelle Bernstein wa
Manchester and later w
on *The Observer* Colou
Page and the *Daily Mir*
She now lives in Brighton with her husband, Eric
Clark, and their three children.

Of this marvellous prizewinning novel, she comments:
'Many of the characters in SADIE are based on relatives I
knew or had heard of from family stories; my maternal
grandmother, who was very much of the inspiration for
Sadie, was a great horder of trivia – love letters, old
photographs – as well as being an incredible raconteur.'

By the same author

Nuns (non-fiction)

MARCELLE BERNSTEIN

Sadie

GRAFTON BOOKS

A Division of the Collins Publishing Group

LONDON GLASGOW
TORONTO SYDNEY AUCKLAND

Grafton Books
A Division of the Collins Publishing Group
8 Grafton Street, London W1X 3LA

Published by Grafton Books 1984
Reprinted 1984 (three times), 1985, 1986 (twice)

First published in Great Britain by
Victor Gollancz Ltd 1983

ISBN 0-586-06228-9

Printed and bound in Great Britain by
Collins, Glasgow

Set in Times

For my mother

Acknowledgements

I owe a debt of gratitude to the many people who helped me over the last three years with their time and their knowledge. I particularly want to thank Bill Williams of Manchester Polytechnic's Jewish History Division, Ward Rutherford for his advice on military matters, and Alannah Buckley. The staff of the Archives Department of the Manchester Central Reference Library and the Jewish Chronicle provided fascinating material. Mrs S. Josephs gave invaluable guidance on Orthodox practice and members of my family and friends remembered so much of the past for me. Finally, I thank South East Arts for the Writer's Bursary they awarded this book.

Marcelle Bernstein
Brighton, May 1983

Chapter One

The carpet was a faded pinkish-grey. Sadie knew that if she stared hard at its yellow scroll pattern she would be able to make out the shape of a strange bird: it was a secret she cherished. Only today her mother's foot, in the funny cloth slippers they had all put on specially, obscured part of the design. She wriggled uncomfortably on the low wooden stool and leant behind her mother to look at her sisters. Miriam and Flora were trying to sniff back tears. Her mother was silent, eyes dry with despair as she stared unseeing at the group of men who stood in a semicircle, their heads bent in prayer. Sadie had watched in horror as earlier in the day, her mother had made a long rip in her best dress, which she wore now. As she cut Sophie had said something in a low voice about a righteous judge, and then Grandma Diamond had started weeping again.

Sadie sighed and twisted round so that she could see the flowers painted on the black cabinet in the corner. She loved this room, with its special smell of floor polish and old books. She was only rarely allowed in, for Sophie was afraid her boisterous six-year-old would smash the few treasured objects she kept on the mantelpiece, on the narrow strip of maroon velvet fringed with silk. At either end stood a silver candlestick, Sophie's gift from her parents when she married Saul. Displayed in an ebony frame inlaid with mother-of-pearl was the photograph of Sophie's brother Mark and his bride. Then there was the carved cowrie shell Sadie loved to handle, admiring its purplish sheen. It was a memento of her parents' brief honeymoon: underneath it bore the inscription 'Lytham 1883'. Just then Sadie heard them say 'Saul'. It was the only word she could make out in Hebrew, and she wondered what they were saying about her father. She glanced up at the men. They all wore creamy silk prayer shawls banded with deep blue or black. That afternoon Sadie had seen her mother go to the drawer in the sideboard where Saul had kept his own *tallis*, and take it out very carefully. She had shaken it open while the others watched and smoothed it with the palm of her hand. Picking up one end, she had deliberately torn off part of the heavy silken fringe. Then she had buried her face in its folds and started making a choking noise. Grandpa Diamond had become very upset and hurried the children from the room.

Sadie fidgeted and turned her attention back to the group of men. They were rocking gently back and forth, the way her father did on Saturday mornings in *schul*, and their voices were low and quick. The Hebrew defeated her again, and she transferred her gaze to the mirror over their heads. This gave her a shock. Usually she could see reflected in it the big picture that hung on the wall. This had a frame of beaten copper and showed two immensely old people sitting in a dark cottage before a fire. Underneath, on the frame, was a rhyme Sadie knew by heart.

> Some would eat but ha'e nae meat
> And some could eat that want it.
> But we ha'e meat and we can eat
> And praise the Lord that sent it.

She liked the rhyme but the picture frightened her, so she only ever looked at its reflection. But today the glass was draped in a black cloth, a blank eye gazing at her. Seeing that, she knew something was really very wrong indeed and she started to cry herself, wildly. Grandma Diamond leant over and picked her up, and took her into the kitchen where they had a cup of tea and played cat's cradles until she was better. When she came out everyone was leaving. Her mother was still sitting on the low bench and one by one the people were coming up to her and pressing her hand, saying something about the Almighty and comfort you and Jerusalem. Sophie looked at them and nodded, but did not reply.

Morning and evening for seven days, Sophie and her daughters sat upon the low stools and ten men came into the house and made their prayers for Saul. By the end of that time even Sadie knew by heart the *Kaddish*, the mourners' prayer. Grandpa Diamond had told her what it meant and she liked the sound of the words: it made her feel important to say it with the others.

> And hereafter, when all shall have ceased,
> He tremendous, alone shall reign; who was and
> is, and ever will be in glory. He is
> without beginning, without end; to him belong
> majesty and dominion.

It was years before she learnt just how her father had met his death. Although he was not a big man he was strong – he could pick up all his small daughters together and carry them laughing round the kitchen. He was used to handling the great boxes of fish he bought wholesale at the market. But that November day in 1895 the freezing dawn air had turned the wet cobbles to ice. Saul's foot must have slipped as he shouldered a box up on to the cart. He twisted to support it, stumbled beneath its weight and, falling, said the men who worked with him, struck the side of his head against the cart tail. They had rushed to summon Sophie, but he was dead before she reached his side.

For a month after the *shivah* period ended there was *sheloshim*. Sophie kept the curtains drawn in the front room during this time of mourning and although the morning and evening prayers ceased, she would recite the *Kaddish* twice every day. The girls did not go to school, and the only work done was to clean the house and cook occasionally. Every day someone from 'The Society' came with food already prepared. Real life was suspended. It was as though nothing more could touch them. Sadie remembered that time years

9

later, when she had reason to do so. What remained clearest in her mind was her mother's pure grief, running through the dark days like gold seaming a nugget of earth.

Number 12 Locket Street, in the North Manchester suburb of Cheetham Hill, was part of a row of terraced houses, indistinguishable from its neighbours, notable only in that it possessed a stunted lilac, one of the few trees in the street. The patch of front garden had enough grass for the children to play on and in the summer was brightened with lupins and love-lies-bleeding. In the stone-flagged back yard was an ashpit and a small building for rubbish.

Inside, the house was unremarkable with the exception that the front room boasted a glass-fronted bookcase filled with solidly bound classics – Carlyle and Tennyson, Goethe and Schiller. Sophie and the children spent their time in the kitchen, which the range kept warm. From it ran the scullery containing the mangle and the copper for washdays. Sadie marvelled that in so short a time, home could have changed so much. She was used to hearing her mother singing, her father arriving home at odd hours: 'Where are you, *bubeleh*? Am I in time for a cup of tea?' Now no one turned up the gas in the front room, and the smell of cigar smoke that she had so relished after lunch on Sundays was gone for ever.

Sadie could not know that the ferocity of Sophie's anguish astonished even herself. Suddenly the newly-made widow saw no future for her and her three small daughters, only a past that had been torn from them. Saul Browne had been everything to her. He had arrived in Manchester as a small child when his own father, Israel Bronowski, left Borisov in 1863 to avoid forced conscription into the Russian Army. Israel changed his name in deference to his adopted country and eventually built up a business in the Manchester fish-market, the only work he could get with his practically non-existent English. Saul had, in time, worked with him and eventually the two went into partnership. That was to

10

celebrate Saul's marriage to Sophie Diamond. He was twenty-three, she was seventeen. Three children were born to them within the first seven years of their union: Miriam, a plump, round-faced child, shy and submissive, pretty as a peach. Sadie, completely different, a restless, thin little girl with hair the colour of dark copper and curious changeable eyes. Sophie would compare her unfavourably with Miriam and sigh privately to herself. The child was no beauty, that was certain. And between the two came poor Flora, with her slightly bent spine and her passion for books. 'We'll have to find a *yeshiva bucher* for Flora,' her father would say, and he and Sophie would exchange a look. Perhaps she would turn out better than they dared hope, perhaps some unworldly scholar would like her . . . 'She's the best-natured of you all,' Sophie claimed, and this was true.

As soon as the official period of *sheloshim* permitted it, Sophie started rising before dawn. The knocker-up would tap on her window as he made his rounds. Shivering in the January darkness she would go out, following the lamp-lighter as he doused the gaslamps in the streets, down to do her husband's work, walking to the fish-market to buy and sell and haggle with the men. At first the auctioneers watched out for her and let her buy at favourable prices, but she learnt fast and by the spring she was holding her own. The grandparents and neighbours helped by giving the children breakfast in her absence and seeing them off to school. As soon as she could afford to do so, Sophie sent for Aunt Rebekeh. She was the youngest sister of old Israel, living still at Borisov. A spinster, she came eagerly to housekeep for Sophie, but she was too old to learn the ways of a new country. She always spoke Yiddish to the children, who answered her in English, and one of them would have to accompany her when she went shopping.

With Aunt Rebekeh in the house, Sophie was independent. They baked their own bread and kept a permanent stockpot of soup simmering on the range. On festive days, such as *Purim*, Aunt Becky produced rare delicacies like *Hamantashen*,

11

the tiny spiced cakes called Haman's ears which the children adored. Sophie made all their clothes on the old treadle machine her parents gave her from their workshop, working late into the evening. Only on the Sabbath did she stop. On Saturday no one so much as stoked a fire. One of the girls would fetch over the *shabbos goy*, the delivery boy from the greengrocer on the corner, who would bring coal for them. And if he was out, the grocer came himself.

All the children went to Jews' School at 78 Cheethim Hill Road. Sadie started on her fifth birthday. It was a vast place by her standards and she held Miriam's hand tightly. Sophie had braided her hair close to her head and she wore one of Flora's black pinafores. The children gathered in small groups in one high room which smelt to Sadie of chalk and strangers. The middle-aged woman called 'Miss' was making out the new register of unfamiliar names: Polly Applebaum and Bella Blum, Samuel Fengelstein and Adam Knopf. Sadie was to share a desk with Betsy Farachi and Octavia Tischler. The other two struck up a friendship based on the exclusion of Sadie, but fortunately she had the support of her sisters at playtime, and also of one of Miriam's friends. Leonie Samson was a strapping redhead, an only child who enjoyed Sadie's dependence. The two formed an unlikely alliance as Leonie taught the younger girl how to do cross-stitch and find caterpillars. Sadie absorbed what the school taught her: learning by rote, writing by copybook, arithmetic by monotonous mental drill. Never an academic child, she preferred drawing and sewing, of which there was a great deal. 'Woman's chief resources', as it was described by the School committee. Many of the pupils had foreign parents, immigrants who had fled Eastern Europe and the growing anti-semitism there. Harriet Weiss and Sonya Goldenkrantz, two of her classmates, were regarded with some disdain by Sophie, since they did not speak English at home.

They lived, most of these families, on Red Bank, a high sandstone ridge falling away to the valley of the Irk. It was

12

made up of streets which were largely unlit, occasionally unpaved and often unhealthy. The tenement houses in Fernie Street and Verdon Street were roomy and cheap, and the immigrant Jews moved in and operated them as both homes and workshops. Others set out as hawkers, peddling cheap trinkets, sewing needles, matches and stationery, though the majority – men and women alike – were slipper-makers, tailors, or cap-makers, the last two trades helped vastly by the introduction of Isaac Singer's lockstitch sewing machines. Many of these immigrant women did not even know that their children were expected to attend school, and an attendance officer came round to convince them that the law required them to be educated. Sophie, who read the *Manchester Guardian* and had never needed the free suits and dresses provided by the School Clothing Society for needy children 'whose parents are proved to be unable to afford getting them', looked down on these newcomers. It was a snobbery she shared with her own mother. Riva Diamond considered the rise in her family's status considerable, and with good cause. If now they had little enough, it was under their own roof – more than her father had managed in the whole of his life.

Gershon Gershonovitch had left Russia in 1860. He took with him his pedlar's pack and nothing else at all. Not even his name. At the German frontier post the guards informed him the patronymic would not be sufficient for documentation purposes. Peering at the tawdry trinkets in his pack one of the guards suggested 'Diamond'. The pedlar and his wife did not see the sneer and would not have cared if they had, wanting only to be gone. The name was written laboriously into the permits by the guard, who misspelt it.

As Sophie's girls grew older, her anxiety about them increased. She had not had much from her own parents but she could give her daughters even less. The Diamonds lived nearby and both still worked hard in their dark workshop, turning out boys' and men's caps on their old machines, straining their eyes in the gaslight as they struggled to fulfil their orders. Old Diamond put by all he could, knowing that without dowries his granddaughters stood small chance of finding husbands.

When Miriam was seventeen, the *shadchen* called upon Sophie. Mrs Mandelberg had contacts with Jewish communities throughout the country and knew of many young men anxious to marry, looking for some money, perhaps, to start a small business. Sophie laughed. The girls would have a trousseau, nothing more. Nonetheless, Mrs Mandelberg persisted. Sophie spoke to her father, and at last a match was made for Miriam with a young man in Bristol. Caspar Weinstock was in trade with his father, who owned one of the only two kosher butcher shops in the town. In time it would be his. Miriam would never have a better offer. In three weeks the matter was settled.

Sadie missed Miriam. Flòra was not a companionable girl and with one exception their neighbour's children were nowhere near her own age. The exception was Bella, daughter of a very Orthodox family who held themselves apart from the less rigorous Jews in the community and even, it emerged, from the Brownes. One evening Sophie had asked if Bella might have supper with them. Mrs Chrystal had patted the headsquare she always wore in the house and given a small smile. 'You know, Mrs Browne, you are very kind. But we keep our daughters close.'

'Close!' Sophie had exclaimed as soon as she was out of hearing. 'Under lock and key is more like it.'

Sadie turned more and more to Leonie Samson. Leonie had green eyes and an ample body even at fourteen and Sophie did not wholly approve of the friendship. Leonie was older than her daughter, and her parents were not quite respectable. The father gambled. The mother, it was said, had once been an actress and the fights in which they frequently indulged were an endless source of irritated speculation among the neighbours. Leonie, though, admired Sophie, and in the years following Miriam's departure she came to spend more time in their house than her own. She was a voluble, noisy girl and her open adoration won Sophie over. For Sadie, Leonie was an inspiration. She was the only person she knew who had huge ambitions for herself, quite outside the usual girlish longings for a husband, a home and children. These things seemed to hold no charm for Leonie. 'I'm a good guesser,' she would say cheefully, 'and good guessers never marry.'

Sadie, awed by her self-confidence, asked wistfully, 'But what will you do?'

It was a ritual question, which she asked often, and Leonie always had a different answer. She would become a woman doctor – this was just after Sophie had read to her a report in the *Manchester Guardian* about the new Elizabeth Garrett Anderson Hospital in London. At sixteen she spent two days immersed in her mother's copy of *Under Two Flags* and informed Sadie that she was going to follow Ouida's path as a writer. For the next month she swept her hair up on top of her head and spoke in a soft purr. On this occasion, however, she sounded more determined than Sadie had yet heard her.

'I'm going to be a dancer. I'm going to join the Ziegfeld Follies.'

'What on earth's that?'

Leonie gave her a withering look. 'Don't you know anything? He's an American impresario and he puts on extravaganzas, with hundreds of girls parading about the stage wearing wonderful clothes.'

'In *America*?'

'Why not?'

'You can't go there. It's too far.'

'Of course I can. You make it sound like something out of Jules Verne. I'll just get a boat and go.'

'Leonie, you can't. For a start, how do you know this Ziegfeld man will give you a job? You haven't any experience of dancing.'

Leonie shrugged. 'He needn't know that, need he? I'm

15

starting lessons next week. But don't tell my father.'

'How will you be able to pay for them?'

Leonie gave her a conspiratorial wink. 'I'm going to sell programmes at the Hulme Hippodrome. I start on Monday.'

Sadie gasped. 'Leonie, you can't!'

'Stop saying that. I can. I *can*. And I will. Just watch me.'

'But it's not . . . I've never heard of anyone doing that.'

'You mean you've never heard of anyone you know doing that, don't you? Well, I'd sooner sell programmes than sit in a workshop, wouldn't you?'

Sadie nodded reluctantly. 'Yes, I suppose so. But people will think you're . . .' she hesitated, not wishing to offend the older girl.

'I know what they'll think and I don't care.'

'Won't your parents stop you?'

Leonie gave a short laugh. 'Not them. As long as I'm out of the way they don't care what I'm doing. And if I'm earning my keep they won't say anything.' She got up and looked in the glass, carefully flicking her eyebrows. 'Anyway,' she went on, her back to Sadie, 'I'm more worried about what *your* mother will say.'

When, that evening, Sadie told her mother about Leonie's plans, Sophie listened in consternation and remained silent. Sadie was washing up, and when she turned to see her mother's reaction she saw that Sophie was close to tears.

'That poor girl,' she said. 'That poor child. You realize what this means, don't you?'

Puzzled, Sadie shook her head.

'It will finish her for a good match, that's what. No decent boy will want her now.'

'Ma, that's ridiculous. Why shouldn't they? She's not going to become a different person just because she sells a few theatre programmes.'

'That's just where you're wrong. She will, it'll change her. She's already old for her age and this will turn her into a woman when she should still be a girl. She'll see too much, she'll know too much, and she'll be spoilt.'

Sadie protested, 'Leonie knows how to behave herself.'

Patiently Sophie tried to explain. 'Look, I know that. You know that. But it's what people will think of her, don't you see? The truth doesn't make any difference. When they look at Leonie, they'll see an experienced woman, not a fresh young girl. And when a Yiddisher fellow looks for a wife, that's not what he wants.'

'Perhaps she isn't interested in a Yiddisher fellow.'

'What else is there for her, I'd like to know? A home, children, what more do you need, you girls?'

Sophie sighed and winched down the airer from the ceiling. She had been worried for some time that Leonie was putting ideas into Sadie's head. The girl had been getting moody and difficult lately. She ought to give her more to do around the house, make sure she was fully occupied. Mrs Chrystal was right after all. Keep your daughters close.

That was not the solution, though. Sadie was fourteen. She would be finished school in a few weeks, there was her future to think of. For poor Flora it was different, but one day Sadie would have to be spoken for. Though God knew how that was to be managed without a dowry worth mentioning. It was a miracle they'd seen Miriam so well settled, for all she was so pretty. Still, Sadie was a good girl. Sophie finished smoothing the sheets on the wooden slats of the airer and hauled at the rope until the contraption rose to the ceiling. She knotted the rope firmly through its brass wall ring and dried her hands on her apron, eyes fixed, lost in thought.

A pity.

If only the child had been a beauty.

Chapter Two

In the summer of 1906, pregnant with her third child, Miriam sent a despairing letter. She had been ill; she felt terrible. Sophie worried for a week. She was too busy to leave the business even for a few days; and she wanted to travel to Bristol later on for the birth. Caspar's elderly parents were unable to cope with the energetic children. There seemed to be no solution. It was Sadie, finally, who begged to be allowed to go. Sophie was against it.

'I couldn't make the journey with you, and you can't travel alone. You're not yet seventeen.'

'I will be in November. Bristol isn't so far, and it would be so exciting. Please.'

'And what use would you be to the poor girl when you get there? I know you, you'd be off somewhere dawdling about, daydreaming, just like you do here.'

'No, I wouldn't. I'd be a help, really. I could help shop, and I can cook. And I'll look after the babies.'

Finally, reluctantly, Sophie agreed. Three days later Sadie was on her way. She travelled to London with Mrs Mandelberg, who was visiting a relative there and who had promised to see Sadie to Paddington and aboard her train. Sophie turned a deaf ear to Sadie's protests. 'This way, at least I know you're almost there. Wire me immediately you arrive, please, and make sure you look after Miriam. Don't talk to anyone on the train, will you? Keep yourself to yourself.'

Sadie had not visited Miriam before, and the long journey through the lavish West country pleased her. At Bristol she was met by Caspar who took her home to where the terraced villas crawled out of the harbour up the hillsides, the front gardens bright with marigolds and

18

hollyhocks. Yiddish jargon was scrawled on the walls and on shop windows and Miriam's kitchen smelt richly of potato *lutkes* and hot salt beef. Miriam turned from the stove, brushing back wisps of hair. 'How lovely that you're here! You look so grown up and what a pretty outfit, who made it for you? How's Ma? And Flora?'

Laughing, Sadie said, 'Just a minute, one thing at a time. Let me see the children.' Sarah was trying to tell her about her doll and little Isaac sat in the middle of the floor, thumb in mouth, watching her with solemn brown eyes.

Within a week, Sadie was looking after the children most of the time. Miriam, in the fifth month of her pregnancy, was heavy and uncomfortable and very tired. Every afternoon, when the housework was done and the evening meal cooking, she would sleep. Meanwhile Sadie wheeled the bassinette with Isaac crowing happily and Sarah hopping busily along at her side. They walked for miles. When Sarah became tired she joined the baby and Sadie pushed them both. One day she found she had almost reached the top of the town. Up Black Boy Hill she went, her arms and legs aching from the pushing, the sun hot on her back. She was wearing a silk blouse of faded rose, her favourite, and the exertion had heightened her colour. At the entrance to a little park she stopped, drawn by the greenery. As she hesitated, uncertain whether they could enter, or if it was private, a man approaching the gates smiled at the children. Sadie said, 'Excuse me, but can we go in?'

He glanced quickly at her, then stopped, surprised, 'Why, sure,' he said in a quiet voice with an accent strange to Sadie. 'I guess so. It's open to everyone.' He was looking at her hard, and Sadie blushed. She was suddenly conscious that she was unchaperoned, that he sounded odd, and that she was sweating from the heat. Embarrassed, she wiped the back of her wrist across her forehead and then stopped, mortified at her unladylike behaviour.

'Thank you,' she replied, and went through the irion gates into the park.

They stayed for nearly two hours. Sadie sat on a bench under the heavy chestnut trees, and Isaac lay in his pram and slept in the shade. Sarah roamed to and fro, collecting daisies and bits of twig, lost in a private world of green houses in the tall grasses. They had a picnic of the ginger beer Sadie had bought on the way, and the cakes Miriam had put into a bag before they left. Sadie was giving Isaac water in his bottle, absorbed in the baby, when she glanced up to check where Sarah was playing. The child was not in sight. She called softly, 'Sarah! Come here, I can't see you. Sarah, Sarah, come out!'

No response came and she felt a pang of alarm. She put the baby back in his bassinette, realizing suddenly how late it was. The air was cooling, the shadows lengthening across the grass. The friendly park, the welcoming rhododendron bushes where Sarah had been playing suddenly seemed menacing. Most people had gone, she saw with a shock. She called again, more loudly this time, and began to run, pushing the bassinette, hurrying frantically around the paths. 'Sarah! *Sarah*!'

Apprehension chilled her: someone might have taken the child, she could have wandered out of the park unnoticed. How long had she been gone? Five minutes, ten? An elderly woman, seeing her rush past for the second time, offered to help and separately they made a further circuit of the paths. When they met on the far side, still with no sign of Sarah, Sadie was white with anxiety. Thrusting the baby at the woman Sadie began to run back the way she had come, her voice hoarse as she called the little girl, until a man's voice halted her.

'Excuse me, is something wrong?'

She turned, recognizing the accent before the face: the man who had directed her earlier. She explained, breathless and distraught, and he immediately took charge. 'We'll search together.' He swung round, swiftly scanning the park. 'Have you been through those bushes?'

They found the child ten minutes later. Unconcerned, Sarah was sitting cross-legged in a clearing, singing to herself, a tuneless crooning nonsense song. Ranged in front of her were broad leaves, each holding a heap of grass seeds. Seeing Sadie, she said, 'Auntie, it's tea time. You want a nice cup of tea with me?'

Weak with relief, Sadie replied, half-laughing, 'Oh, Sarah, why didn't you answer me?' She picked the child up and hugged her, and Sarah struggled crossly to free herself.

'It's *tea*-time,' she repeated firmly. 'You just be good.'

Obediently, she crouched down and accepted a leaf plate. Over Sarah's head she looked up at her companion. They smiled at each other, both touched by the child's innocent absorption.

'Thank you,' said Sadie.

He made a little bow. 'It was nothing. Really. Will you be all right now?'

'Oh yes. I'll take them straight home.'

'Then I bid you good-day.' When he lifted his hat to her, Sadie scarcely noticed: she was coaxing Sarah back to the path and the waiting bassinette.

That evening, she told Miriam in detail about the incident. 'So,' she finished miserably, 'I don't think I ought to take them out again. I might have lost her.'

Miriam was indignant. 'Nonsense, it could have happened to anyone! She hadn't run away, she just hadn't heard you. Don't worry about it.'

'Well, I don't think I'll go to the park again.'

'I don't see why not. Another time, just make sure you sit in the open, so she's always in sight. That's what I do.'

Caspar, finishing his meal, said firmly, 'Miriam's right. Sarah's a little pickle, there's nothing for you to blame yourself over. You found her quickly, no harm was done.'

Sadie, helping Miriam clear the table, said, 'All right then, but I think I'll keep her on a chain!'

Drying up the china, alone, she found herself thinking again about the man with the odd accent who had helped her earlier. She hadn't really thanked him: he had gone out of his way for her, and she had barely spoken to him once Sarah was found. He looked pleasant, too. It had been rude of her. Her mind busy, she had forgotten all about him a moment later.

When she had put everything away, she opened the kitchen door quietly. In the moment before they heard her, she saw Miriam and Caspar together, unaware of her presence. Miriam was sitting in a straight-backed chair. She had been sewing for the new baby: the small garment had fallen unheeded to the floor. Caspar was kneeling by her chair, arms round her waist under the shawl, his face pillowed between her breasts. Miriam held him tightly to her, lips in his hair.

Watching them in the brief moment before she turned away and they, hearing her, moved apart, Sadie felt a sudden fierce jealousy of Miriam. She had so much: a man, children, a home. Sadie would be going back to Manchester, her mother's house and an uncertain future.

In bed that night she saw again the harmonious embrace she had interrupted. It was the first time she had ever witnessed so intimate a scene. She had been only six years old when her father had died, and since then Sophie had been, except for relatives, very much alone. The girls had grown up in a household where affection was mostly feminine: the quick hugs of a sister, the brisk fondness of a busy mother. Her grandparents were devoted to each other but undemonstrative. Nor did she ever see any displays of affection in the houses of her friends. On her occasional visits she would be aware of a father somewhere in the background, usually working in the shop, doing his accounts, or perhaps in the evenings reading beneath the gaslamp. Only Polly Applebaum's father emerged as a personality. A vast, jovial man, he filled their kitchen to bursting point with his presence, teasing Polly about her braids, telling Sadie he liked her pinafore. But his wife, a faded creature, would respond only with a tired smile to his jokes.

Sadie and Leonie occasionally discussed whose parents occupied double beds, and whose single. Bella Chrystal's parents, for instance, came into the latter category, like the other Orthodox Jews the girls knew. Neither of them would so much as shake hands with any one of the opposite sex, nor would they touch each other in public. Before their children also they preserved this modesty, and even to kiss goodbye when Mr Chrystal left for the tailor's shop where he worked, they would go into the hallway alone.

These facts were imparted with much importance by Leonie, who listened to her mother and her friends gossiping. Sadie had not been able to understand why anyone so old as Bella's parents would want to kiss anyway, and had paid scant attention. Now, suddenly, she began to realize that marriage had a side to it of which she had never been aware. She remembered that when Miriam had left home she had pestered her sister to discuss Caspar. Miriam, reticent, would say little beyond 'It'll be your turn one day.'

'And what good is that?' Sadie had wailed later to Leonie.

Now she lay in the back bedroom, Sarah safely asleep in the truckle bed beside her, and wondered what Bella Chrystal's life would be like. Despite her mother's vigilance Bella managed to be a talkative girl, and just before Sadie left Manchester Bella had imparted the information that she was to become engaged. Sadie had been thrilled: Bella, like herself, was only sixteen, and the first of her friends to be married.

'But where did you meet him?'

Bella looked complacent. 'The *shadchen* arranged it. He came with his parents from Leeds yesterday.'

'What's he like?'

'Nice, I think. Very quiet. He's called Morris Rosenberg.'

The mother had done most of the talking; the boy had said almost nothing at all. They would live in Leeds where Morris worked as a *sofer*, a calligrapher writing on fine parchment the Hebrew script for the small oblong *mezzuzahs* which adorned every Jewish doorway. He was, even by Mrs Chrystal's rigorous standards, highly Orthodox. Bella would defer to her new husband in everything: he would dictate what books she might read and what information she should receive about the outside world. He would enter and leave rooms before her, and when they walked out together, Bella would take her place on the outside, between him and the road.

Sadie could make no sense of this. 'But Bella, you're a woman, he's supposed to walk on the outside to protect you. Everyone knows that.'

Clearly quoting her mother, Bella replied, 'God will protect me.'

Sadie could only look at her in wonderment. 'Yes. But why can't Morris protect you as well? Why don't you receive the same consideration that the men do?'

Bella had been quite unable to follow Sadie's argument. For her there was no questioning these attitudes. 'Because,' she had answered matter-of-factly, 'because men are higher than we are.'

Accustomed as she was to the strict moral codes of Orthodox Jews, Sadie was nonetheless alarmed by this glimpse of Bella's future. And Sophie, when told of the conversation, had literally snorted her irritation. 'I've no patience with them. I *know* it's important to preserve tradition, I *know* the values are good ones. But this isn't the religion, surely, to live as if they were still in the *shtetl*! I can't see why these women put up with it.'

Sadie had agreed with her. But now, lying in the dark, she saw again Caspar's head on Miriam's breasts, and her sister's rapt face. Stirred by this glimpse of emotions to which she was a stranger, remembering Bella's calm acceptance of her role, Sadie found it difficult to reconcile the two. Would Bella feel what Miriam so clearly felt? Would Morris Rosenberg abandon himself to his bride as Caspar had, kneeling there beside Miriam? And what would it be like? Would it ever happen to her, Sadie? She knew there was almost no money for her dowry, and Sophie had had trouble enough in finding a husband for Miriam. Her mother had told her so often she was no beauty that she had no vanity at all. Would anyone want her? Sadie had never before seriously considered what the future held for her. It was as if until today she had been a child, and now she was one no longer.

She supposed she could always earn a living. She could become a dressmaker, or she could work in one of the garment factories as thousands of other young women did. She shuddered at the thought. It would serve for a while, if it became necessary. That was all. It was not what she would choose. She knew those dark factories, where the women sat in long rows over their work, hour after hour, gossiping and singing, working their machines with one hand, guiding the cloth with the other, eyes straining in the poor light from the high windows, too cold in winter, too hot in summer. Or she could go with Sophie, buying fish at the market in the early dawn, to sell again to the local shops. But Sophie wouldn't let any of her daughters help her. 'It's bad enough for me to have to do it,' she would say, 'I'm not having you there too.'

Sadie lay flat on her back and the tears of self-pity slid down into her hair. Silly fool, she told herself, it's not as terrible as that. She got out of bed, padding quietly past Sarah to the door. She went downstairs in the dark, feeling her way against the wall. In the kitchen she poured a glass of water from the jug they filled at the standpipe beside the back door. Perched on the edge of the table in her long white nightdress, drinking the tepid water and sniffing back her tears, she decided that there was only one thing to be done.

She would find herself a husband.

Sadie took the children to the park again the following week. As she walked up Black Boy Hill she noticed a couple on the other side of the road. The woman was taller than her companion, who Sadie suddenly recognized as Sarah's rescuer. Without thinking she called out 'Hallo'. He stopped, turned, and then smiled as he raised his bowler to her.

'Good afternoon. I'm pleased to see you all again. How's the little girl?' He said to his companion, 'This young lady and I met the other day when her charge evaded her in the park.'

'She's forgotten all about it. But I haven't. You were very kind. Thank you.'

'It was a pleasure to be able to help.' He waved and moved off after the tall woman. The couple entered one of the tall Georgian houses opposite the park.

An hour later, when Sadie glanced up from making Sarah a daisy chain, she saw that the sun had gone and a low black cloud darkened the sky. Even as she gathered up Isaac, smoothing down the skirts of his dress and fastening him in the bassinette, heavy drops of rain began to fall. She caught up Sarah under her arm and pushed the bassinette under the trees. After fifteen minutes the children were restless and the rain heavier than ever. She decided to go home: she could cover the children with a blanket and she would dry. By the time she reached the park gates her fringe was sticking to her face and her pleated silk blouse was soaked. As she stopped, panting and wiping her eyes, a pleasant voice said, 'May I rescue you again?' He was at her

26

side, holding an umbrella. For a moment she hesitated. The memory of her mother's many warnings came into her mind. She had thanked him now: it was not done to speak to strangers. A low rumble of thunder shuddered across the sky and made up her mind for her. In her predicament it was absurd to worry about formal introductions. Just then he added, 'Or are you not speaking to me?'

She said, with relief, 'Oh yes, please.'

'I'll see you home then, if I may.'

She paused. Instinctively she did not want him to see Miriam's little house, and she knew her sister and Caspar would disapprove strongly of her being accompanied by a stranger.

He looked at her carefully, so that she lowered her eyes in case he could read her thoughts. Evidently he could. 'If you prefer,' he went on easily, 'I'll just walk with you till the rain stops, shall I?'

His assurance made her feel nervous and gauche, and to her annoyance she found herself stuttering slightly. 'That would be very – civil of you.'

Holding the umbrella over her he asked, 'Would you feel better if I introduced myself? My name is Nathaniel Laurence, of Chicago, at your service.' Then seeing her puzzlement he added, 'Chicago is in America.'

'Good gracious! Is that why you speak so strangely?' She clapped a hand to her mouth, suddenly aware of her rudeness. 'I mean, I've never met an American before.'

'Have you not? Well, there's a lot of us around, but perhaps not around here. Have you always lived in Bristol?'

'I'm only staying here with my sister. I'm from Manchester. Do you live here . . .?' she stopped, suddenly self-conscious. She had never held a conversation such as this with a man before, and she was surprised to find him so easy to talk to.

He held her arm to guide her round a large puddle, and then, glancing down, said, 'Look at your dress. You're soaked.'

'I know. I can't hold my skirt up and push, that's the trouble. But it's warm rain, isn't it? I don't really mind.'

As they approached the centre of the town he started to tell her about himself. He was an engineering architect working for a firm in Chicago. A Bristol partnership, Foster and Wood, had invited a member of the American firm – famous as pioneers of the new method of building with concrete – to come over for a few months as an advisor.

They were approaching the angle of Broad Street and Vine Street where they could see Christ Church when Mr Laurence exclaimed suddenly, 'Wait a minute. Don't move!' He had pulled his watch from his pocket, and obediently she halted. After a moment two strange, brightly-coloured figures lurched forward on a gallery high on the church tower. They raised hammers and struck two bells beside the ornately canopied clock. Sarah shrieked her excitement. 'The quarter Jacks,' explained Mr Laurence, 'striking the old bells. Aren't they something?'

Sadie manipulated the perambulator over a kerbstone. 'Does your wife like it here?' she asked, feeling very daring and grown up.

When he did not reply she glanced round at him and saw the odd expression on his face. He made an effort to pull himself together.

'The lady I was with earlier today is not my wife, I'm afraid. My landlady.' There was a pause, then he asked, 'Does that make walking with me better, or worse.'

'Oh, better. I mean, worse.' She blushed.

'You know, you haven't told me your name yet,' he said. 'Since you do not volunteer it, I evidently must request it. Might I know whom I am addressing?' He was regarding her gravely, and as she told him her name she found herself thinking he had a pleasing face, broad and strong. His eyebrows were heavy, and his eyes had a directness that disconcerted her. When he talks, she thought, he smiles less

28

than most people do. He watches. As though giving him her name had been too great a revelation, she suddenly felt she must escape. 'Look,' she exclaimed, 'the rain's stopped. I must rush home, the children will want their tea. Thank you so much, Mr Laurence.'

'Will I see you again?'

'Please excuse me, I must go.'

She gave a brief smile and hurried away. He stood looking after her. With a sigh, he shook the rain vigorously from his umbrella, closed it and walked briskly away.

Sadie assiduously avoided going to the park again. She had found the encounter pleasant. Too pleasant. This was the first time in her life she had spoken to a man like this. He must be at least thirty, she thought. Old. For the next month she was kept too busy to think of anything but the family: Miriam's child arrived earlier than expected. In the excitement of welcoming the little boy, and looking after her sister, Sadie almost forgot Nathaniel Laurence.

Chapter Three

On the morning of the eighth day after the baby's birth, he was circumcised. The house was filled with relatives and friends invited to the ceremony: the women subdued and slightly anxious, the men making wry jokes among themselves. Caspar's father dominated the group. A corpulent, red-faced man who worked in his butcher's shop with his son, he stood foursquare in his best dark suit in the front room, addressing uncles and cousins Sadie had not seen since Miriam's wedding. Sophie went in to offer them all some tea and heard Mr Weinstock saying, in his low boom, 'So I said to the *mohel*, I hope you know the difference between a boy and a bullock . . .' One of the uncles cleared his throat warningly, and he swung round to see her.

'Ah, Sophie, we were just saying . . .'

'I heard what you were just saying, Harry,' she replied tartly. 'Don't let Miriam hear you, that's all I ask.'

Miriam had come downstairs for an hour for the occasion. She looked rested and apprehensive; the baby in her arms was half-awake, questing softly for food, nuzzling towards her.

Sadie asked, 'Are you going to feed him now?'

'No. I'll wait – it's best afterwards.'

The sisters looked at each other.

'Oh dear,' Sadie said.

'I know. But it's got to be done, or he won't be a good little Jewish boy.'

'Won't it hurt him, though? He's so tiny.' Sadie looked at the minute hands, flexing and curling helplessly on the soft wool of the shawl.

'No,' Caspar patted her shoulder reassuringly. 'He

doesn't know what's going on, don't worry. It only takes a few seconds and it'll all be over. And our little *boychikel* will have the seal of God.'

She shuddered and Caspar laughed at her and pinched her cheek. 'You'll have to be braver than that when it's your baby, you know. You've got all this to look forward to.'

Sadie glanced round, and saw Sophie standing behind her, listening. She met her daughter's eyes and shrugged slightly. Sadie knew what she was thinking: she'd have to find a husband first, and how were they to do that, with things as they were?

Precisely on time the *mohel* arrived with his black bag. A plump, elderly man in a long black silk coat and wide, fur trimmed *shtreimel*, he was deferentially introduced to the family by Caspar. He did not shake hands with the women, but bowed gravely. The baby he watched with gentle, pale blue eyes, and he patted Miriam's arm with an unexpectedly fine-boned hand. All the men not already wearing them had donned *yarmulkas*, and the *mohel* led the way into the dining room, where Sophie had spread a large white sheet on the table.

'Who is to be the *sandek*?' he enquired. Caspar's brother, the baby's godfather, went forward and the *mohel* seated him on a low chair and arranged a cushion on his knees. Caspar took his son from Miriam – exchanging with her a look Sadie could not interpret – and whispered comfortingly, 'We'll have him back in a moment.'

The men had now all gathered round the chair and Sadie, waiting outside with the women, could just see on the table the open box, and laid beside it a small, curved silver knife and a silver goblet for the wine. Loudly the *mohel* said, 'Blessed is he who cometh in the name of the Lord.' His voice fell to a gabbled murmur, broken only by the response of the men. Suddenly there was a sharp cry from the baby and a long drawn out wail. The women gasped, and Miriam blanched. The cries stopped after a moment. 'The *mohel*'s giving him

31

sweet wine on his finger,' explained Sophie, then Sadie heard the *mohel* saying in Hebrew, 'This child, son of Miriam, shall be named Joel.'

There were more prayers: 'May the lad grow in vigour of mind and body, to a love of Torah, to the marriage canopy, and to a life of good works,' and at last the *mohel* appeared, holding the squirming baby tenderly, soothing with little murmurs as though the child were his own. He placed him in Miriam's arms. She, receiving him thankfully, hurried upstairs to feed him while the guests busied themselves with the wine and sponge cakes Sophie and Sadie had made.

Later that day, when the guests had left, her mother packed Sadie and the children off for a walk so that Miriam and the baby could sleep. After half-an-hour she found that she was on her way to Black Boy Hill and the park. As she walked, she wondered whether it had been an accident. She was wearing her best for the festivities, her hair was washed and shining, and her hat was new – a rare treat for her. Under the creamy straw, she had seen in the glass as she set out, her eyes were shadowed and smokey. In the park she sat on her usual bench and pushed the bassinette forward and back, to Isaac's delight, and talked to Sarah as the child pottered around with bits of twig and buttercups. The only people around her were elderly women or nursemaids with small children. She was conscious of a feeling of disappointment, of emptiness. When she heard a church clock chime four, she got to her feet and walked to the gate. She was well on her way down the hill when she heard hurrying footsteps, and Mr Laurence's voice.

'Miss Browne! Miss Browne, please, slow down!'

He was beside her, hatless, buttoning his jacket. 'I saw you from the window and rushed out. Forgive me,' he gestured at his clothes, 'but I wanted to see you.'

''Allo, man,' Sarah waved at him from the bassinette where Sadie had perched her. 'What he do say?' she demanded, and Mr Laurence laughed.

'I do say, will you come and see my house?' he replied. 'It's all right,' he went on hurriedly, seeing the look on Sadie's face, 'Mrs Winter, my landlady, whose house it is, is there. We would not be alone. Do come in for a moment, and then, if I may, I'll walk you home.'

Sadie hesitated, looking across at the white house where Mr Laurence lived. It looked well-kept: Mrs Winter had been beautifully dressed. She didn't think anyone would mind if she accepted. And, after all, they need never know. Sarah's chatter would make no sense to Miriam.

Shyly she said, 'Yes. Thank you.'

'Splendid!' He put a hand under her elbow and guided her across the road, helping to push the bassinette. He picked Isaac up easily, tucked the child comfortably under his arm, and took the key from his pocket. The little boy, who generally yelled at strangers, was reassured by the competent handling and remained quiet. Mr Laurence noticed Sadie watching him.

'I like babies,' he said in explanation. He looked as if he was going to add something, but at that moment Mrs Winter appeared, and he made the introductions.

'Mrs Winter is more a friend than a landlady. Her husband works with us – that's how I came to be here. They look after me rather too well.'

Mrs Winter smiled and took Isaac from Nathaniel's arms. 'And we love having him here. Would the children like a drink?'

'Thank you, yes, I'm sure they would.'

'Come to the kitchen with me and we'll give them a glass of milk while I make some tea. The cook's out, so we have it to ourselves.'

Sadie had never imagined a kitchen such as this. She was used to the cramped, dark room in Locket Street where Auntie Becky ruled and the whole family ate, except on *Shabbes*, while above their heads clothes were continually drying on the airer. This room seemed vast. Copper pans were ranged on big shelves and plates gleamed on the wooden dresser. She watched Mrs Winter open the larder door to get biscuits. In the long cupboard she saw endless rows of jars: bottled and preserved fruits, dried foods, jars of jam and pots of pickles. Strings of onions hung on hooks, a basket on the floor was piled with apples. Mrs Winter brought out a jug covered with a beaded muslin cloth and poured milk into two cups. While the kettle on the gas stove came to the boil, she turned to Sadie. 'You're very young to be in charge of these two, aren't you? My daughter could never manage.'

'I'm almost seventeen,' Sadie said defensively, helping Sarah on to a chair. She sat beside her and gave Isaac his drink with a spoon. The woman watched her, and said, musingly, 'Nathaniel's over thirty.'

Sadie, unable to see the relevance of this remark, made no response.

After tea Nathaniel suggested they take the children into the garden, and sat on the grass with them. Sarah and Isaac, revelling at being the centre of attention after their eclipse by the new baby, scrambled over him.

'You'll spoil your suit,' Sadie protested, trying to bring her charges under control.

'You demonstrate a truly housewifely concern, Miss Browne.'

She liked the way his voice drawled, and wished she could say something amusing in response. She could think of nothing and the silence lengthened until Sarah placed the daisies she had been picking on Nathaniel's head. Sadie burst out laughing, and Sarah joined in delightedly.

'Women!' Nathaniel Laurence exclaimed, brushing the daisies out of his short beard and pulling Sarah on to his knee.

'Am I not good enough unadorned? Or do you wish to cover up my ugly face?'

'It's not ugly.' Sadie had spoken before she thought. He

sat up and looked at her, his eyes thoughtful. And as he did so, she experienced a sensation completely new to her. She felt – although it was not a word she had ever used – flirtatious. She bent her head so that the cream straw hat, its brim pricked with dozens of tiny holes, hid her eyes. She knew very well what Sophie would have called her at that moment. A flibberty-gibbet. Just as she always said Leonie was 'flighty'. Despite the knowledge that she was behaving outrageously, Sadie could not resist tilting her head very slightly so that she could see Mr Laurence. He was still watching her.

'We must go,' Sadie said, after a long moment. 'I must get the babies home.'

'Will you take tea with me again?'

'I . . . thank you, but I don't think it will be possible. My mother has to go home next week, and I'll go with her.'

He got to his feet, helped her up and, in spite of her weak protests, accompanied her down to the town. On the way he asked, 'If I wrote to you, Miss Browne, would you reply?'

She was shocked. 'Oh, that wouldn't be possible. My mother would not allow it.'

'You may not have correspondents?'

'It's not that.' Confused, she saw the trap coming but could find no way to avoid it.

'Then – why not?'

'She would want to know who was writing to me.'

'Am I so improper as to be unmentionable?'

Embarrassed, Sadie said, 'No, of course not. But my mother would think so.'

'Because she hasn't met me?'

'No. Because you're not a Jew.'

There was a silence. His face wore an expression of comical disbelief. 'I don't follow.'

Patiently Sadie tried to explain. 'My mother isn't particularly religious. But she wouldn't want me to meet

35

people who were Gentiles. It's not that they aren't nice, it's just that they're – different.'

He considered for a moment. 'Well, there must be a way round it. If your mother didn't know, would you write to me? I'm not suggesting that you deceive her, merely that you do not inform her.'

'It's the same thing, isn't it?'

'Yes, I suppose it is. But I can't see that a letter need hold any fears for your family. Couldn't I send them to a friend to keep for you? Please?' He held out a hand towards her, palm up. Looking at him, she thought suddenly she could give Leonie's address. Impulsively she said, 'I'll write it down for you.'

He handed her his little black notebook and a pencil. Quickly, she scrawled the address. 'I must run,' she said, breathlessly. 'They'll be waiting for me. Thank you for tea and the walk.'

She held out her hand. He took it between both his own, and pressed it.

'I'll write to you tomorrow so there is a letter waiting when you get home.'

Surprised, Sadie stared at him.

'You won't have anything to say so soon.'

He did not smile back at her. He merely answered, 'But I will. Goodbye, Miss Browne.'

She started to push the bassinette through the crowded street.

He stood, watching her, until she was out of sight.

Chapter Four

He was as good as his word.

When Sadie arrived home, there were already two letters
waiting for her. Leonie had rushed round as soon as she
knew Sadie was back, her face bright with excitement so
that Sophie, glancing at her, said, 'You look very full of
yourself this morning!'

Sadie stiffened in anxiety and Leonie caught the movement. Smoothly she explained that she had found a post at
the Theatre Royal. She would be selling programmes at
first, but she intended to be on the stage before very long.
Sophie had clucked her tongue with disapproval and sighed
to herself. She had heard it said that Leonie's mother had
been an actress, and though she didn't know the truth of
the matter, there was no smoke without a fire. Sophie liked
Leonie for her ebullience and her down-to-earth common-
sense. At barely nineteen she looked like a mature woman
with her tonged curls and ample bosom. On her way out,
Sophie patted her on the bottom.

'Just you be careful, Miss,' she said affectionately. 'Mind
your Ps and Qs, and don't be too flighty.'

The girls looked at each other meaningfully.

'Well, little Sadie,' asked Leonie, when Sophie had gone.
'And have you been minding your Ps and Qs?' She put her
hand into the pocket of her pinafore and pulled out two
letters.

'These suggest some clandestine correspondence to me. Or
else why were they not sent to your home address? Oh, no!'
She held them high as Sadie grabbed for them. 'In my role
as pillarbox I must exact a small penalty.'

Sadie looked startled. 'What on earth d'you mean?'

'You can buy my silence. You must tell me who he is, and

just a bit of what he says.'

Crossly, Sadie said, 'I don't know what he says, do I? You've got the letters, not me.'

'Aha, you're touchy about them. A good sign. It must be serious.'

'I don't know. I don't quite know how it all happened. I just met him by accident and then before I knew it, we just seemed to know each other.'

'What's his name?'

'Nathaniel Laurence. He's an American.'

'American! Is he Jewish?'

Sadie shook her head.

'I thought not. Hence the secrecy. Oh, Sadie, whatever have you been up to?'

'Nothing at all.' She spoke with asperity. 'I lost Sarah in the park, so he helped me find her. Then there was a thunderstorm, and he had an umbrella. And we had tea once, but his landlady was there.'

'He sounds – effective.'

'Yes.' The thought had not occurred to Sadie before. 'That's exactly what he is. He was there just when I needed help.'

'Lucky you. Knights in shining armour . . .'

'A brown bowler, actually,' Sadie interjected.

'. . . rarely turn up in real life. When they do,' Leonie looked knowing, 'the thing is, to get them off their horses.'

'Leonie, you have a wicked mind. Now please, can I have my letters?' Leonie handed them over.

'I will tell you about them, but I'd like to read them by myself, if you don't mind.'

These were the first letters Sadie had ever had from a man. She did not know what she expected, but she found Nathaniel's both touching and amusing. He was very formal. 'Dear Miss Browne,' he began (it was to be two months before it became 'My dear Miss Browne,') and he told her of his work, of a play he had seen. She answered them quickly, talking of the return to Manchester, the greyness of the light there after the soft west country summer. 'I miss the park,' she wrote, and next time, 'I miss our park.'

Nathaniel wrote to her of his family, and in return she told him about Sophie, and her father, her sisters and her grandparents. She described Locket Street to him, and how she spent her days.

At first they exchanged one letter a week.

Soon, it was two.

In December Nathaniel wrote that he wanted to come to Manchester to see her. No, she replied, I can't see you, it is not possible. He persisted. Meet me somewhere in the town, he begged, I will be wherever you say, at whatever time. I want to see you again.

She showed this letter to Leonie, who was as thrilled as if it had been written to her. 'You must go, you must see him. Are you made of wood? Look what he says. "I want to see you again." My God, I wish someone were writing that to me.'

'Where could I go? Ma would be suspicious.'

'Look, you're not a baby any more. You must tell her you're coming to see me – tell her anything you like, only get out of the house. Arrange to meet him at the Midland Hotel, why don't you?'

Sadie gasped. 'I wouldn't dare. I'd be terrified to go in there.'

'I'll go with you.'

'Have you been in, then?

'Yes.'

'Who with?' Sadie was curious.

'Well, if you must know, with someone who bought a programme off me – oh, it's all right,' she protested, seeing Sadie's face. 'He's a perfectly respectable man. We just went

39

in and had some coffee one evening. And a brandy.' She watched Sadie for her reaction. 'Don't worry,' she added hastily, 'you don't *have* to drink a brandy. You can have tea there, you know. All perfectly nice and respectable, with Gentleman's Relish in the sandwiches and a silver-plated teapot.'

So Sadie agreed to see Nathaniel. On the following Wednesday afternoon she set off for town. She had spent an hour getting ready, carefully pinning up her hair and ironing her blouse. She wished she had something less shabby to wear than her handed-on grey coat with its high fur collar and unfashionable cut. But she brushed it thoroughly and decided that in the end she looked quite presentable. When she walked into the foyer, fifteen minutes early because she was afraid of missing the omnibus, she found Mr Laurence already waiting, broad and serious, hurrying to meet her with evident pleasure. 'I was so afraid you wouldn't come after all.'

'After you travelled all this way? I would not be so rude.'

'Thank you for being here. It's wonderful to see you again. I'd forgotten your eyes were grey.'

'And I'd forgotten . . .' she stopped, suddenly pink. 'I'd forgotten how much I liked the way you look,' she had been going to say, before realizing how compromising it would be. Instead, she dropped her eyes modestly.

'Come into the Alexandra Suite and have some tea.'

When she glanced nervously around he said, reassuringly, 'Don't worry. Everyone here is very busy about their own business. They're not watching you.'

For the two hours they spent together Sadie found she was far more shy than she had expected. After the correspondence, she had thought she would be able to talk to him as freely as she had written, but in the face of his direct gaze, his concerned questioning, she became almost monosyllabic. He seemed not to mind the long silences, but rather to enjoy them.

'I'm sorry,' she said, flustered and apologetic at one point, 'but I can't think of anything to say.'

'Why do you have to say anything?' he asked. 'I'm very happy just to be sitting with you. Besides,' he went on, 'it is up to me to entertain you, not the other way around. Beautiful young women are not supposed to do anything other than look decorative.'

'You shouldn't . . .' she began to say, then stopped, self-conscious.

'What should I not?'

'Make fun of me.' She spoke in a low voice.

'But I'm not. Whatever do you mean?'

She made a dismissive movement of her hand.

'I know I'm not pretty. It's all right, you don't have to pretend.'

He leaned forward, his face grave. 'Perhaps no one had told you before that you are?'

'No.'

'But you are, you know. Extremely pretty. There's something very special about you.' Then, seeing her embarrassment at his intensity, he started to talk about himself. He had spoken before of his family, in his letters, but now he told her of his time at college.

'Then what did you do?' she asked.

His face darkened. 'I . . . got married.'

She said nothing. She was deeply shocked. So he was married. Quickly, she gathered up her gloves, started to pick up her handbag. She could not stay with him another minute. He caught her arm. 'You don't understand. Please sit down. Let me finish.'

Something in his face made her subside into her chair.

Speaking heavily, he said, 'I should have told you before, but I didn't want you to think I was—' he stopped, searching for words – 'playing for sympathy, I suppose. I'm a widower.'

Sadie pressed her hand to her lips. 'I'm sorry,' she said in a low voice. 'I misunderstood.'

'She died eight years ago. A lifetime ago. Since then, I've been very much alone. It would have been unbearable if it hadn't been for Alice.'

'Alice?'

'My daughter. She's nine. She lives with my brother and his wife in Chicago. She's very happy there with their own family, and I live there too, now. It's a big house, we get on well. The perfect solution, really. But I'm beginning to want a home of my own again.' He paused, and looked at her. 'Do you mind?'

'Of course not. I'm pleased you told me.'

'No. I mean, do you mind that I've been married, that I have a child?'

She looked puzzled. 'Why should I?'

'Will you go on writing to me, knowing all this?'

'Of course I will. What difference does it make?'

'I don't know, I just thought . . .' he stopped, looking relieved.

When Nathaniel had returned to Bristol they continued to write. On paper, Sadie found her spontaneity returning. From two letters a week, they began to write three. Over the weeks, he began to write to her almost every day. Sadie replied. During the course of those weeks, on the pages of those letters, Sadie came to know love.

Then again, Mr Laurence wrote that he wanted to visit Manchester. This time she agreed without demur. The Midland Hotel did not awe her so much on the second visit. She turned up half an hour early, and sat in the foyer to wait for him. Knowing he would shortly be with her gave her confidence. She sat very erect, enjoying the unfamiliar luxury: the thick carpets and deep chairs, the brilliant lights reflected in many mirrors and the hum of conversation around her. Occasionally, she thought that people shot her curious glances. I am waiting for a man, she told herself, and crossed her ankles demurely. She saw Mr Laurence before he caught sight of her. The doorman brought in his suitcase and she was impressed by the ease with which he dispensed tips, and the deference with which he was treated by the clerk at reception. Clearly, this was a world in which he was very much at home. Oddly enough it had not crossed her mind before to wonder if he had money. Looking at him now, in his dark coat with its fur collar, at the heavy leather case, she realized that at least by her standards, he must be a wealthy man. Before she had time to pursue this thought further he had glanced round and seen her. His face lit up and he hurried over to her.

'Hooray, you're here. I hope I haven't kept you waiting.'

'I'm early. Hallo.'

He looked at her with his usual gravity. In the silence, they both began to speak at once, and laughed together.

'Now,' he said, 'let me just go up to my room to wash up after the journey, and I'll be with you directly.'

He looked round and caught the eye of a bell-boy. 'Get a waiter, would you, and ask for tea for two to be served in the Alexandra Suite in five minutes.' He turned back to Sadie, 'You go along in and I'll be there in two shakes.' He hurried away.

Last time, he had poured the tea. Now Sadie said, 'May I?'

'Please.'

She gave him his cup, and then asked, 'Will you be staying here long? You didn't say you would take a room.'

'No. I didn't want to make you anxious. And I'm not sure how long I shall be here. It rather depends on you.'

Sadie choked slightly on her scone, but said nothing.

'However,' he went on. 'Perhaps we may return to that later. But first, tell me how you are, and what you've been doing.'

She did her best, conscious that, as before, she found it harder to be amusing in person than on paper. But when she was telling him about Sarah's latest exploits – she

43

forgot herself completely, and he watched her with real interest. Finally he said, 'I've been in the train for hours, and could do with a walk. Would you like that?'

She hesitated, suddenly afraid she might be seen, that someone would tell Sophie. Yet half of her – she could not quite understand this – found the prospect of walking with Nathaniel in public oddly exciting. She assented, and they left the hotel and crossed St Peter's Square in front of the Town Hall. Mr Laurence looked up, a comical expression on his face. Sadie, following his eyes, saw nothing but the elaborate façade.

'Do you like it?'

He winced. 'It's not that bad, I guess. Back home we have a lot of buildings that look just the same: it's the self proclamation of a big provincial city.'

'You sound as if you're laughing at it.'

Instantly tactful, he replied, 'Don't think that. I'm not.' He caught her arm, halting her in her stride. 'Just look carefully at this place. At the shape of it, the size. What does it all say to you?'

'It's – impressive.'

'Yes. But *why* does it impress you?'

She studied the turrets, the stone tracery, the arched windows and carved arches, the massive clock tower. Finally she said, helplessly. 'It's so old, I suppose.'

Nathaniel beamed at her. 'Just what you're meant to say. Now, look at it again.'

Obediently she followed his pointing finger. 'See that? And that? And that? And those doors? Detail like this tells you it isn't really that old, only pretending to be. It was finished about thirty years ago. A pseudo-Gothic monstrosity, that's what it is.' He sighed. 'People are mad.'

Puzzled, Sadie said, 'It looks nice to me. Do you have this style in America?'

'Heavens, yes. Plenty of it. Only Americans, with their well-known passion for taking things to extremes, have

44

gone even further. We had a Greek revival, and a man called Robert Mills made our public buildings in Washington look like a setting for *Julius Caesar*.'

'What's wrong with buildings looking like that?'

They started walking again, towards King Street.

'It infuriates me,' Nathaniel continued, 'because turning to the past for inspiration when you design a building is all wrong. Grecian pillars were right for the Greeks, and Gothic arches suited medieval times. But what relevance do they have now? A building – especially a public one – should express its own civilization, not a dead one.' He banged on the pavement with his cane to emphasize his point, and Sadie watched him, absorbed in what he was saying.

She thought that if her father had been alive he might have told her things like that. How would it have been? she wondered, and quite consciously placed herself in the position of a dutiful, listening daughter. She lifted an attentive face to him and he, half aware of her deference, was both amused and touched, and set himself to interest her. I'm listening to a clever man telling me things I've never heard of before, she said to herself. This is the most exciting thing that's ever happened to me. They were nearing King Street before Nathaniel stopped talking and saw with surprise how Sadie's politely interested manner had gone. She was looking up at him with delight and astonishment.

Impulsively she took his hand. 'No one has ever spoken to me like this before. I'll always remember the town hall because of what you've been telling me. And,' she added simply, 'there is so much more, isn't there?'

He smiled. 'I could tell you a good deal more, Sadie, about a great many things. There is always so much more.'

He was stirred and elated by her intent, listening face. You're a fool, he told himself. She's a girl who's grown up without a father. She's eager to learn: that look would be turned on anyone who talked to her like this. He did not want to believe that: he knew that he loved her and yet feared to speak. She seemed to him so utterly innocent, would she understand what he felt for her?

They reached King Street. The lamps were being lit as they walked down, and they watched the sudden blue flare against the dusk. In their companionable silence he found his indecision about this meeting hardening into resolve. What was there to lose? When he spoke, it was to say, 'You know, we're still very formal. Do you think we might begin to use first names after all our lengthy correspondence? Or is our lack of formal introduction an insuperable barrier?'

She tipped her head to see him. 'It *is* a bit ridiculous. I hadn't thought.'

Privately, she didn't imagine she would ever be able to bring herself to think of him as anything but 'Mr Laurence'.

'Well then, Sadie, there is something special I wanted to say today. I have to go back to the States. Quite soon.' He paused to watch the effect upon her, and to his pleasure saw disappointment in her face as she said slowly, 'Oh. I'm sorry.'

'Shall you miss me?'

'I . . . believe so.' Her voice brightened. 'But we could still write, couldn't we?'

'If you wanted, we could do better than that.'

'Whatever do you mean?'

She had paused to look at him and he slipped his hand beneath her elbow. 'We're blocking the pavement.'

They moved on, and when they reached the narrow passageway connecting King Street and St Ann's Square he drew her into it. In the semi-darkness he said urgently, 'Come with me. Come with me to Chicago.'

She looked blank. 'For goodness' sake. I couldn't. Ma would never allow it. And what would I do there? I don't know anyone.'

'You know me.'

46

'But how would I make a life there?'

'You wouldn't have to. I'd make it for you.'

Sadie was genuinely bewildered. 'I don't understand.'

'Sadie, I'm asking you to become my wife.'

She thought she must have reeled in surprise, but in fact she stood very still. '*What* are you saying?'

'Do you want it more formally?' He glanced round. 'I can't go down on one knee here, but I will later if you want. I am asking you, my dear Sadie, if you would do me the honour of marrying me.'

She whispered, 'I don't know what to say.'

'You *could* say yes.'

'No. Mr Laurence – Nathaniel – I couldn't. I can't marry you.'

Gently, he put a finger on her lips. 'Please think very carefully. Don't just refuse me without serious consideration.' Seeing her face, he hurried on. 'My family are very well placed, you know. I have excellent prospects – in a few years, I'll be a partner with the best architects in Chicago. I can look after you. I can give you a good life.' He took her hand. 'I love you, you know. And I believe you will come to love me.'

'It's not a question of love.'

He raised an eyebrow. 'Is it not? I had always supposed marriage to be very much concerned with love.'

She tried to pull herself together. Her thoughts were racing and muddled. She had not told him the truth when she said it was not a question of love. She did love him, she was sure of that now. She felt admiration for him, respect. She listened to what he said and believed what he told her. She enjoyed the very slight physical contacts they had – his arm under her elbow, the pressure of a hand, but she did not think she felt for Nathaniel Laurence what Miriam felt for Caspar.

Sadie's youth, her lack of experience, meant that she was unable to recognize the degree to which Nathaniel's

47

protective attitude, his almost paternal tenderness, appealed to her. It was this that made it possible for her to communicate easily with him on paper, removed, and yet remain inhibited in his presence. What she sought from him was to a large degree his undemanding, fatherly fondness. It was something of which she had only the faintest memory.

He broke in on her thoughts. 'Is it because I've been married already? Because I want you to know that I did love her. I would never pretend otherwise. But I was very young then, everything seemed so easy. I'm older now, little Sadie. I know how to cherish what is mine.'

She stared at him, brushing back her fringe, her mind in turmoil. She was conscious that the bells of St Ann's were striking the hour. Five o'clock.

When she said nothing, he asked suddenly, 'It's not Alice, is it? You don't mind about the child?'

Sadie found her tongue. 'No, how could you think that? Of course not. What difference could a little girl make? It's just that I can't marry you. Ma wouldn't have it, that's all. The family would go mad.'

'And you. What would you do? You tell me what your mother would do, and your family. But it's you I want, not them. It's your decision, not theirs. You are not a child any longer, you know. Surely the question I am asking you proves that? Are you going to accept forever their word on what is right and what is wrong?'

Flustered, she looked away from his intent eyes.

'I . . . hadn't thought of it like that. It's just that I've always known what would happen to me. And this isn't it.'

'Oh, and what have you always known?'

'That I'd marry someone like me and have a family. The way Miriam has.'

'And do you want Miriam's life?'

Defensively she said, 'It's a very nice life.'

'I'm sorry, I didn't mean to be rude. But Sadie, I can

48

offer you so much. You'll see the world, we'll have a wonderful time together. I want a family too, you must have seen that.'

She put her hand to her throat.

Insistently he went on. 'All those letters you wrote to me, all the things you said. Our park, you said. I miss you, you said. Didn't you mean all that? Did you lie to me?'

'No! No, I didn't.'

'Well, then, why is what I ask so impossible? I believed you when you wrote those things. I allowed myself to hope. And so here I am . . .' he paused, and his voice was hoarse, 'here I am, with my hopes. And you tell me that what you led me to believe might happen is impossible.'

'I feel so ashamed,' she whispered. 'I didn't think you would expect . . . I just wrote what I felt.'

'But if you feel it, for God's sake, why can you not accept me? I'm literally begging you to do so.'

'I can't accept you because you're not a Jew.'

He had been gripping her arm. Now, stunned, he released her and stood back. 'Are you seriously telling me that I am to be refused because of an accident of birth?'

Wretched, Sadie sought to avoid his eyes. Dumbly she nodded.

'So. I am dismissed out of hand because my religion is wrong. Not so wrong that you cannot write telling me that you miss me, that you think often about me. But sufficiently wrong so that my feelings are not considered.'

Just then a woman, passing them, turned to look curiously at him. He wiped his hand over his forehead, pulling himself together. 'Now it is I who must be sorry. I shouldn't have berated you like that. I did rather spring this upon you, and I ought to have known better. Let me get you a cab home. No.' He waved aside her protest. 'I'll pay for it. Don't worry, he can drop you away from your house. I'd like to know you were safely home.'

She felt exhausted. 'All right. Thank you.'

'But I'm staying in Manchester. I want you to think very carefully what you are doing. I hope you will change your mind. Please come and see me tomorrow.'

'I can't. I've got a wedding tomorrow.'

'The day after, then. I shall expect you at three. If you don't come, then I will return to Bristol.'

A cab was trotting slowly by. He hailed it, negotiated with the driver and helped Sadie inside.

'I shall hope to see you. Goodbye.' Trying not to cry, she nodded. 'Goodbye.'

Glancing back, she saw him walking away. Not at his usual brisk pace, but slowly, his shoulders slumped.

It was the first time in her life she had made anyone unhappy.

Sophie had been slightly surprised to receive an invitation from Mrs Chrystal to her daughter's wedding.

We invite you to the marriage of the virgin Bella, the invitation had read. The ceremony took place at the Cheetham Hill Synagogue and Sophie and the girls had felt slightly self-conscious among the highly Orthodox community, the men with their curling sideburns, the *payess*, their broad-brimmed hats and black silk coats. Afterwards, everyone gathered in the synagogue hall for the wedding party.

The celebrations were noisy and joyful. The guests sat at long tables, consuming more food than Sadie had ever seen before. She sat with her mother and Miriam on the bride's side of the room where all the women were unaccompanied. The groom's side was separated from them by a tall partition, covered in greenery. From behind it she could hear men's laughter and the stomp of feet; to the sweet, thin sound of violins they were dancing the *hora* on both sides of the partition. On the women's side a huge circle was growing, as they held hands, twisting and dipping to the deedle-deedle-dai-dai of the music.

'Come on, Sadie.'

Bella broke the circle open, and held out her hand. Sadie glanced at her mother, who pushed her to her feet. She caught the proffered hand, stumbling slightly in the dance, then the excitement and the rhythm caught her and she forgot her embarrassment at dancing with so many women. Opposite her a little girl clutched her grandmother's arm, and she realized that almost everyone in the room was on their feet. As she passed her mother she saw that Sophie was watching Bella, who glowed with happiness, and from her expression Sadie knew that she was wishing she could do all this for her own daughters. Beside her Flora beamed, unaware of the poignancy of her own situation. With her glasses and her slightly bent spine it seemed impossible that she would ever marry.

When the *hora* ended Bella disappeared, together with a crowd of her female relatives, all talking excitedly. When she reappeared thirty minutes later she stood demurely in the doorway.

'What's she done?' whispered Sadie to her mother. 'She looks different.'

'I know. It's the *sheitel*.'

'You mean that's a wig? They've cut her hair off already?'

Sophie swallowed the last of her little cinnamon cake and looked at her daughter with amusement. 'Of course. She's a married woman now. Her pretty hair mustn't be allowed to distract Morris from his studies.'

Her tone was ironic and Flora said nervously, 'Hush. They'll hear you.'

Sadie thought of Bella's warm brown curls and shuddered. Sophie gave a wry smile. 'You needn't worry. It's not going to happen to you, is it?'

'No. I suppose not. But I hadn't known they did it straight away. She's only just seventeen.'

Sophie was about to answer when the music started again. It grew louder, wilder, and now Sadie could see, over

51

the partition, the young bridegroom sitting on a chair hoisted high on the shoulders of the dancing men as they whirled dizzily about the room. The youth's eyes and beard were startlingly dark in his pale face, and his fine white hands grasped desperately at the chair arms for support. Sadie looked from him across to Bella, the smooth reddish bun of the *sheitel* showing beneath her wedding veil. And suddenly, for them both, she felt a remote and inexplicable pity.

Walking home afterwards, Flora chattered excitedly about the wedding. The other two said nothing. Sophie was brooding over her inability to make such an affair for her girls. Sadie was thinking of the stiff knot of the wig she had glimpsed beneath Bella's veil. Of Miriam and Caspar back in Bristol with the new baby. Of the joy and excitement at the wedding, the new life starting for the new couple.

When they got home she went into the kitchen to make a cup of tea. It was dark and smelt stuffy, the fire had fallen to cold grey ash. She shivered and opened the back door to fill the kettle. Next door she could hear quarrelling: the two Sieff boys were arguing again. Somewhere beyond the back yard a cat wailed and another answered.

And standing there in the darkness, kettle in hand, Sadie made her decision.

Nathaniel was pale and tense when she arrived at three the following afternoon. He looked as if he had not slept, and she was touched again by his affection for her. When she told him she had changed her mind, he said simply, 'Thank you,' and took her hand in his. 'I promise you, I will do everything I can to make you happy.'

'I know.'

'And I will always take care of you. My little girl.'

She looked up at him, tears standing in her eyes so that she could hardly see. And in the quiet corner of the lounge, beneath the lithograph of the Town Hall and another of the

Royal Exchange, he put his arm about her waist and pressed her head down upon his shoulder.

Before she left they arranged that Nathaniel would stay on for two days to meet Sophie.

'We must tell your mother immediately,' he insisted. 'It would be dishonourable of me to let you do this alone. And I must meet her now. You never know, she might quite like me.'

Sadie's imagination had taken her to the point of accepting Nathaniel, but she found it almost impossible to predict how Sophie and the family would react. She knew they would be violently against the marriage – but what, if anything, would they do about it? Would they try to prevent her?

'I'll tell Ma when I get home. And I'll say you're coming to the house tomorrow at four o'clock. That way, it'll be too late for her to refuse to see you.'

'This won't be easy. Are you sure it's what you want?'

She thought of Sophie, still walking each morning to the fish-market in the darkness, and of the gloomy factories in Strangeways where the seamstresses sewed for a pittance. She thought of Bella Rosenberg. She thought of Miriam. 'Yes,' she said.

When she arrived home, Sophie was waiting for her, a warning look in her eye. 'Well, miss, and what have you been up to?'

Very slowly, Sadie started to draw off her gloves.

'And before you answer, please don't tell me you went to Leonie's, because I've been there already. I want the truth. Where have you been that you couldn't tell me?'

'I've been into town.'

'Just that? You've been into town? You don't tell me any more where you're going?'

'To the Midland Hotel.'

'You went *where*?' Sophie's voice rose in amazement.

'To the Midland Hotel.'

'Don't say it again. I heard you the first time. What did you want to go there for? People like us don't go to hotels.'

'I just . . . had tea there.'

'By *yourself*?'

'No. With a friend.'

'Aha. Now we come to it. Which friend? Do I know her?'

'No. It's not anyone you know. He came from Bristol to see me.'

'Who's "he"?' Sophie's voice was dangerously quiet.

'Ma.' Sadie tried to keep her own voice calm. 'Ma, I've got something to tell you. I want to be married. He's coming here tomorrow for tea, to meet you.'

'Oh, my God.' Sophie stared at her daughter, disbelief mingling with excitement. 'You? Married? But to who? Who is he? Tell me!'

'His name's Nathaniel Laurence. I met him in Bristol. He's very nice. He's American – from Chicago. He wants us to be married quite quickly, and we'll go over there soon, just for a time. Then we'll probably settle in Bristol for a while so I'll be near Miriam.'

Sophie was hugging Sadie. 'I can't believe it – it's wonderful. What does Miriam think of him? Why didn't she tell me?'

'Miriam hasn't met him.'

Sophie was puzzled, her hands dropped from the girl's shoulders. 'But didn't she and Caspar – how did you meet him, then, if Miriam didn't arrange it?'

Sadie swallowed. 'I met him myself.'

Sophie asked, 'Where?'

'In a park.'

Sophie repeated incredulously, 'You met him in a *park*? You started talking to a *stranger*?' Sadie nodded. 'How could you behave like that after all I've taught you? How do we know who he is? Doesn't he have any family here?' Sadie shook her head. Watching her, Sophie said sharply, 'There's something else, isn't there? I know you – there's something you haven't told me. *What*?'

'It's – not important.'

'*Tell me.*'

'Nathaniel is – he's a widower. He has a little girl. She's nine.'

Sophie closed her eyes. Faintly she asked, 'How old is this man?'

'Thirty-one.'

Sophie's cheeks were scarlet. She opened the high collar of her dress and jumped to her feet. Walking up and down the confined kitchen she talked distractedly, half to herself. 'I can't believe it, I don't believe it. My seventeen-year-old daughter comes home and tells me she's going to marry a stranger, a man she met in a park. And that's not enough. That's not bad enough. Then she says he's a widower, thirty-one years old, with a child of his own. And this man wants *my* daughter?' Despairingly, she flung out her arms towards Sadie. 'Tell me you're making it up!'

'No, I'm not.' Sadie was trying not to cry. 'It's true. But it's not as bad as you're making it sound. He loves me, he's from a good family.'

'Do men from good families go around seducing young girls?' Sophie demanded of the kitchen ceiling.

'He hasn't seduced me. He loves me, I tell you.'

'Hasn't he? What have you been up to, then? Men don't ask girls to marry them just like that, you know. Not without the family to arrange things. What have you been doing with him?'

'Nothing, Ma, I promise you, nothing. We used to walk in the park, and once he asked me back to the house where he stayed . . .'

'Sadie, you didn't!' Sophie cried.

'But it was all right, his landlady was there, she was there all the time, she gave the children tea. It's not the way you think at all, really it's not.'

Slightly mollified, Sophie asked, 'Who is his landlady? Maybe Miriam knows her?'

Sadie could see that Sophie was trying to place Nathaniel

in a context she could visualize. She replied, carefully, 'I don't think Miriam does. Her name's Mrs Winter.'

Sophie looked surprised.

'He's not staying with a Jewish family? What kind of man is that?'

Sadie swallowed, hard.

'Ma, Nathaniel isn't a Jew.'

Sophie looked at her daughter, uncomprehending. 'What are you saying?'

'He's not Jewish.'

Very slowly, Sophie reached out, feeling blindly for the chairback, and sat down. She whispered in a hoarse voice quite unlike her own, 'You are not going to marry this man. I won't have it.'

Urgently, Sadie said, 'But Ma, I *must*. What else is there for me? You keep telling me no one will want me, you say we can't afford for me to be married. Well, Nathaniel wants me. He doesn't care about money, he's got enough of his own.'

Sophie shut her eyes. Flatly she said, 'You are not to do this thing. It will kill me.'

'No it won't. You'll like him, I know you will.' Sadie moved towards her mother. 'Talk to him tomorrow, just meet him. Please.'

Sophie wasn't listening. She was rocking herself forward and back, talking in a flat voice. 'You can do this to me, who's slaved for you all these years, your own mother, you can bring this shame on me. I haven't had enough *tsuris* in my life, you have to bring me more. Oh, my God, what am I going to do?'

'Don't be so upset, Ma, it's not the way you make it sound. It's not *like* that, it's not what you think.'

'It's *just* the way I think! That's *just* the way it is!'

Sophie rounded on the girl, furious now, on her feet. 'You little cheat. You liar. You're nothing but a street-girl.' She slapped Sadie hard across the face so that she half fell.

Sniffing back her tears, holding a hand to her smarting cheek, Sadie pleaded, 'Don't carry on like this, please, please, let me make you a cup of tea.'

'Don't you come smarming over me, you slut.' Sophie rushed from the room. Sadie heard her going upstairs, then the door of the bedroom slammed violently. Very slowly, she took the dishcloth, wrung it out in cold water, and held it to her face. Then she sat down in front of the range. She was shivering, her hands were like ice.

The kitchen door opened very softly. Without moving Sadie said, 'Flora?'

'Yes.'

She turned, and held out her arms. The elder girl ran to her, and they hugged.

'Oh, Flora, did you hear?'

'Everything. I was reading in the sitting room. Sadie, are you really getting married, are you really going away?'

Sadie stroked her sister's face gently. 'Now don't you start, or whatever shall I do? Yes, I am, but it'll be much better. You'll see. You can come and stay with me, can't you? We'll have a lovely time.'

'But you can't marry a man who isn't a Jew, can you? What will you do? What will you do on *Shabbes*, and on Friday night? What will you do by yourself?'

'I won't be by myself. I'll be with Nathaniel. And we've never been that fussy, have we, about observing holy days. And Flora, what else should I do? You've heard Ma going on about our not having dowries. After the wedding yesterday you saw how depressed she was. She thinks no one'll want us if we can't provide a house. Or at least the furniture. Do you know how much Bella's father provided for that Rosenberg boy? Everything, that's what. Every single thing they're going to need. Can you see Ma doing that?'

Miserably Flora shook her head.

'No, nor can I. But Flora, I don't want her to have to. If she had any money, I'd rather she kept it, or gave it to you. By marrying Nathaniel, I'm removing the need for the dowry. She ought to be grateful.'

'She's not, though.'

They looked at each other.

'Perhaps she'll come round,' Flora said, without much hope.

Sadie sighed. 'I'm going over to Leonie's. Will you be all right?'

'Yes. I'll take Ma up a drink in a minute.'

'Good girl.'

Sadie kissed her sister again.

'I'll look after you, too, you know.'

'You'll be going soon yourself.'

Flora gave her a strange look. 'Do you really think so?'

Sadie didn't, but the self-knowledge in Flora's eyes made her deny it. 'Of course you will. You just wait and see.'

Flora brightened perceptibly. 'Go on,' she said. 'You go out. I'll deal with things here.'

Sophie did not emerge from her room for the rest of the evening. Next morning she came down unexpectedly late. Looking haggard, she spoke in monosyllables to Flora, completely ignoring Sadie, who was already baking for tea. Her mother glanced at the preparations, but said nothing.

That afternoon Sadie, having already cleaned the house, laid tea in the living room. At three-thirty Sophie came downstairs in her best black. Surprised, Sadie said, 'Are you going out?'

'Would I feel like going out? Certainly not. I understand from you I have a visitor this afternoon.'

'But you said . . .'

'I'm not doing this to please you, my girl. But nobody is going to come to my house and not be properly received.'

'Ma, thank you.'

58

'Thank you nothing. I'll give him a piece of my mind.'

But when Nathaniel arrived, carrying a bunch of parchment-coloured roses which he presented to Sophie, she behaved with a chilly dignity. The flowers pleased her, Sadie knew. They were accepted with a small smile. For the first few minutes, she could not bring herself to look properly at Nathaniel. He, serious and concerned, made small talk with Flora while Sadie prepared the tea. He asked her about her books. When she discovered that he enjoyed Disraeli, Flora was won over completely.

'Ah,' he said to her, 'but if you haven't read *Huckleberry Finn* you've a great treat in store. I'll send you my copy.'

Sadie poured her mother's tea, then Nathaniel's. He watched her appreciatively as she cut the sponge cake.

'Is this your baking, Mrs Browne? It's delicious.'

'It is not,' Sophie answered coldly. 'Sadie made it this morning.'

He turned to her. 'You didn't tell me you made such superlative cake.'

'Sadie is an excellent housekeeper, Mr Laurence.' Sophie's voice was like ice. 'She was brought up to keep a proper Jewish home.'

Abashed, Nathaniel said nothing.

'However,' Sophie went on, 'apparently that is not to be.'

Sadie blushed for her mother, but Nathaniel said gravely, 'Mrs Browne, I know this must be a disappointment to you. But I too want the best for your daughter and I'm in a position to see that she has it. She shall want for nothing.'

Sophie inclined her head. 'I don't doubt your capacity to provide for her, Mr Laurence. But I am deeply distressed that you should both have gone behind my back to arrange this marriage. In my eyes it is highly unsuitable, and my family will feel the same way.'

In a low voice, Nathaniel said, 'Has Sadie told you this would not be my first marriage?'

'She has told me, yes. And I must confess that doesn't

59

make me any happier. But that is not the main thing.' She drew a deep breath. 'Mr Laurence, I have nothing against you personally, please understand that. But you are a Christian and Sadie a Jew. This is not a proper match for her.'

'Mrs Browne, I love her. And I believe she feels for me. I'm sorry you feel we conducted this matter incorrectly. It was just the way it happened: Sadie was away from home, and I was . . .' He paused, and gave a wry smile, 'most persistent in the face of her evident reluctance to have anything to do with me.'

Slightly mollified, Sophie glanced at Sadie.

'You know,' Nathaniel went on, 'you shouldn't have lovely daughters if you don't wish people to pursue them.'

Sophie closed her eyes for a moment. Then she said, 'I must tell you, Mr Laurence, that I do not give my consent to this marriage. Sadie is too young: barely seventeen. She doesn't know what she wants. You are a great deal older than she, and you will understand that I cannot let her ruin her life.'

'I don't believe,' Nathaniel sought to pacify her, 'that it would be ruined.'

'It would in my opinion,' Sophie replied sharply. 'I must therefore tell you both that I do not give my consent. I am Sadie's legal guardian until she reaches twenty-one. She told me yesterday that you intend to marry. If in four years you still wish to be man and wife, I will not stand in your way. And now,' she rose to her feet, 'if you will excuse me, I have business to attend to.'

When she had gone Nathaniel said, 'Sadie, she didn't give me a chance to explain anything.'

'I know. I was afraid it'd be like this.'

He shook his head. 'I don't know. Look, come back to the hotel with me and we'll talk there.'

She got her coat, kissed Flora goodbye, and they left immediately.

Before Nathaniel returned, despondent, to Bristol he and Sadie agreed that in two months, if things had not changed, he would travel to Manchester again to speak to Sophie.

'But what if Ma says no again?' Sadie was still young enough to be unable to contemplate total disobedience to Sophie.

'Then we'll see. But I have to go back to Chicago then for a time anyway. I do so want to take you with me.'

'It's funny, you know.' Sadie's scarf lay on her lap. She was pleating the thin silk into neat folds between her fingers, then unconsciously smoothing it with her palm, over and over again. 'It's funny. Two days ago I would never have thought anything like this could happen. And now all I want is for us to be married.'

He smoothed her hair.

'As long as I know that.'

For the first few days after Nathaniel's departure Sophie and Sadie barely spoke except at mealtimes, or when they passed in the passage. On the fifth day Grandpa Diamond arrived at the house, stooped and anxious, to speak to Sadie. He took her into the living room and placed himself opposite her on the high-backed wooden chair. Sadie sat stiffly, avoiding his eyes, staring at the picture on the wall. It was of Hope, the blindfold, youthful figure seated on the world, holding the single-stringed lyre. Sadie thought, I'll never forget this picture, never. For as she looked at it Grandpa Diamond told her what would happen if she did indeed marry Nathaniel Laurence. She listened in horror, and could find no answer. He told her that on the day of the marriage the family would consider that she was lost to them. They would gather together and mourn for her, they would sit *shivah* for seven nights as though she were indeed dead. When he told her this, Grandpa Diamond stopped speaking, rubbing a shaking hand over his lined cheeks to hide his emotion.

61

'He is not the man for you,' he pleaded with her. 'He is too old for you, *bubbe*. You need a young companion, not a man carrying his sorrow with him. This fellow, he has already known the best things of life: another woman gave him his firstborn child.'

Sadie said nothing, and he climbed unsteadily to his feet. 'Dear child,' he said, as he stood in the doorway. 'Dear child. Don't do this to us.'

Sadie sat and stared at the picture and thought, It can't go on for ever, it must change, all this will surely be different soon.

That evening, Sophie asked, abruptly, 'Well? Have you thought about what Grandpa said?'

'Yes.'

'Has it made you see sense?'

Sadie answered without thinking, but the moment the words were spoken, she knew she had found the only means of achieving what she wanted. 'If I'm to be dead to all of you, then you won't care what I do, will you? I shall just go to Nathaniel, and I'll marry him in Bristol where no one knows me.'

Sophie looked at her, and her mouth set in a determined line. 'All right,' she said finally. 'I don't want that, and you know it. I'll strike a bargain with you.'

The girl put down the cloth she had been using to dry the dishes.

'If you promise me you won't run off,' Sophie went on, 'I'll promise you that you can marry Nathaniel. But on one condition. I want you to go to London for a month or so. I want you to get away from here, to see a different way of life. If, after that, you still want Nathaniel, I won't stand in your way.'

'But where am I to go in London?'

'I've already written to Uncle Mark. He replied today. He and Zipporah want you to go to them.'

Chapter Five

Sophie, her back rigid with fatigue and nerves, stood stiffly in the pillared hall. They had been travelling for a whole day on what was only the second journey of her life. She had steeled herself to endure the racketing railway train, the shiny high seats and wooden backrests of third class. Then the ride across London in the motor had bewildered her further with unaccustomed noise and speed. Now all she wanted to do was collapse.

For Sadie the same experiences had produced nothing but carefully concealed delight. She stood quietly beside her mother, a sombre figure in her grey woollen coat. While the talk and the welcomes eddied around her she absorbed the warm opulence of her surroundings: marble floors half hidden by Persian rugs, dark oil-paintings in ornate frames. In one corner a stuffed black bear reared up, glass eyes gleaming red. Beside it, on a lacquered Chinese table, stood a deep bowl of orchids.

She found it difficult to think this was Uncle Mark's house. When he visited them in Manchester he seemed to be so at home in their hot little parlour. Here, as he ordered the manservant easily, he was a different person. Instead of the formal black travelling clothes in which she had always seen him, he wore a lavender grey suit and an opal gleamed on his silk tie.

Sadie watched him with adoration. He had been a hero for as long as she could remember. Twelve years younger than Sophie, he had seemed less like an uncle to his trio of small nieces than a mysterious voyager, who would arrive late at night loaded with gifts, and whose presence brought excitement and laughter. He was, she had recognized as she grew older, an opportunist – but that had increased rather

63

than diminished his attraction for her. During the years after her father's death, her mother would regularly receive letters from Mark containing sums of money. Sophie was loath to accept help from her brother, but as he always tactfully stated that it was to buy 'something for my girls,' she could never refuse. Sophie was well aware that, appearances to the contrary, Mark was not a wealthy man: he did not hold the purse strings. His looks and ready charm had won him a rich wife; his wits and deft tongue, combined with her money, made him a moderately successful diamond merchant. He believed, as he once told Sadie, that 'to sell a diamond you have and that a man wants – that isn't business. To sell one that you don't have and he doesn't want – now that's business.' She thought he had been trying to display his worldliness, but she was impressed by it nevertheless.

Now, taking their arms, Uncle Mark escorted Sophie and Sadie towards the saloon. A door slammed above, and with a rich sweep of moire silks a tall woman, her hair swept back from her face, came down the stairway to meet them. She paused at the bottom and held out her hands to Sophie.

'My dear, we're so happy to see you.''

The voice sounded sincere, but the appraising eyes took in Sophie's awkwardness and her unfashionable clothes. She kissed her sister-in-law quickly and turned to Sadie. Her look was more gentle.

'May we not see you, child?'

She lifted the little veil from Sadie's eyes and embraced her warmly. Sadie took an involuntary step back. She scarcely remembered Aunt Zipporah, who had appeared only fleetingly during her childhood. She was more familiar in the silver-framed photograph on the mantelshelf, encased to the throat in a cream lace wedding gown. This elegant woman left her unable to speak. Aunt Zipporah, however, appeared not to require an answer as she led them both upstairs to their rooms. As they passed the Chinese table,

Sadie saw her flick the orchids with irritable, jewel-laden fingers.

Sadie grew to know the house well in the next two days, for she spent most of her time wandering around it alone, while Sophie remained closeted with her brother in his study. The girl was well aware that they were discussing her future. She felt annoyance that they should do so without her, and certainty that in any event no decision of theirs would alter her determination to marry Nathaniel.

It was with relief that she learnt on the third day that her mother would return home next morning. Sophie, still preoccupied and worried, sat on the edge of Sadie's bed in the half-light that evening, and tried once more to understand what her daughter wanted. But although she thought she could recall how she herself had felt as a girl, time and experience had distorted the memory.

When she attempted to explain to Sadie, she was perplexed that her thoughts should find voice in such platitudes; where she wanted to justify and convince, she could produce only sentiment.

'I've been able to do so little for you,' she said, 'and I wanted to do so much. But you mustn't marry this man. I know you think you'll be happy, but there are things you don't understand. I can't let you throw away your life like this. And what will you do when you want us and we aren't there . . . ?' She held Sadie's hand to her cheek and it was wet with tears. 'I've lived much of my life without your father. And I've gone on, I've managed, at times I've even been happy. There's a moment when you feel that a man is not everything.'

Sadie, crying herself, hugged her mother. She knew what it had cost Sophie to bring them up: the endless work, the lack of sleep, constant worry about money. She had helped with the careful darning of clothes, the cutting and mending of sheets, the refashioning of hats with a new feather and a piece of ribbon. So when, finally, Sophie rose, Sadie felt nothing but guilt and remorse for the pain she was causing.

'Promise me just this,' begged Sophie. 'You'll stay for the three months we planned – Uncle Mark is happy to have you for that long. And then we'll see.'

Sadie would have promised anything at that moment. It was only the next morning, as she lay waiting for the house to waken round her, that she was able to put into words for herself how passionately she intended her own life to be different from her mother's. With seventeen-year-old arrogance, she believed she could do anything. Nathaniel represented a freedom she had never known. He was the future, Sophie the past.

At ten o'clock that morning, Sadie watched Uncle Mark leave with her mother for the station. As the sound of the engine faded from the tree-lined avenue, Sadie turned from the house and descended shallow stone steps into the Italian garden. Never before had she been parted from both her mother and her sisters; she was elated by the unaccustomed solitude.

It was with mixed feelings that she realized Aunt Zipporah was following her into the garden. Her aunt – who had risen at an unprecedentedly early hour to see Sophie off – had not previously shown any desire at all for her company. Now she linked the girl's arm into her own, and her voice was friendly.

'May I walk with you?'

They strolled beneath budding limes. A few yards away, in the sun, an old man in a green baize apron carefully trimmed a bush shaped like a peacock. Sadie watched him in silence. The next three months stretched limitless before her, an interruption, a stumbling block in her plans. Although she still could not clearly envisage just what marriage to Nathaniel would entail, she had assumed it would happen quickly and that she would go with him to Chicago to meet his family. They would live for a year or two in Bristol in the house he was planning to rent for them, and then return permanently to America, a prospect that filled her with pleasure. Yet for the moment she could do nothing but sit out the time here as she had promised. She sighed, and Aunt Zipporah stopped her pacing.

The older woman was the first to speak. She twisted a flower stem between her fingers, and her voice cracked slightly with what Sadie recognized in surprise as nervousness.

'Are you pleased to be staying with us, Sadie?'

After a moment's thought Sadie decided diplomacy was her best course.

'You are very kind to allow me to do so.'

'There's no need for such formality, you know.'

Sadie bent her head in recognition of the small rebuke.

'We do understand what's been going on,' Zipporah continued, 'and we're both sorry about all the trouble. But since you are here, we should like you to enjoy it. We want to take you out and show you London – that would give us great pleasure.'

Sadie was taken aback by the generosity of the offer. She had somehow expected that the three months were to be spent largely in seclusion, as a sort of penance; she had not for a moment imagined that she would be encouraged to take advantage of her stay. Then, even while she considered the possibility, she began to see it as a conspiracy between her elders.

The old gardener had now reached the peacock's fanned tail. He paused to consider his next move. So did she. Her voice, when she finally spoke, was sharper than Zipporah had yet heard her.

'You know that it won't make any difference to anything? I'm not going to change my mind.'

The flower stalk twirled again. The aunt waited, wondering what she could say that would convince Sadie that in her she had an ally, not a wardress. The previous day she had glanced quickly into the wardrobe in Sadie's room.

Only three dresses hung there, none of them, in Zipporah's eyes, more than barely prepossessing.

'I should love to get you some new clothes,' she said on impulse. 'Would you let me do that for you?'

Sadie hesitated. For all of her seventeen years she had been dressed in Miriam's outgrown garments, carefully altered. But now the thought of new, sophisticated London costumes was an almost unbearable temptation. Yet all too well she knew what her mother would have said. Despite the longing to accept, despite being genuinely touched by her aunt's kindness, she knew she had to make at least this small token gesture to Sophie.

'You're very generous, really. Only you're doing quite enough for me already. I really cannot let you clothe me as well.'

Aunt Zipporah started to speak again, then checked herself tactfully. The two walked on without speaking, and it was with some relief that she excused herself for her daily discussion with the housekeeper.

Neither of them referred to their conversation for the rest of the day, and it was the following afternoon before Aunt Zipporah tried again. She stopped Sadie, who was heading for her room to write to Nathaniel. She was going out visiting shortly – would Sadie care to accompany her? The girl's immediate reaction was to refuse, but before she had even framed the words Zipporah was reinforcing her invitation.

'Of course you must come. You cannot spend your days wandering around this house. Besides, I should like to show you off.'

Sadie raised her eyebrows and held out the skirts of her dark dress.

'I am not much to exhibit, I think.'

But the phrase, as Zipporah knew, had been well-chosen. Sadie had been so firmly told of the ordinariness of her appearance that the unlooked for compliment was doubly effective: a little vanity, for almost the first time in her life, was stirred. Then, too, she had to confess to herself that she would enjoy the chance to satisfy her curiosity about Aunt Zipporah's daily pursuits. She smiled.

'Very well. Thank you – I should like to.'

Uncle Mark, passing through the hallway to return to his office for the afternoon, wagged a joking finger at his wife.

'Now, my dear, don't start corrupting the girl already.'

Zipporah laughed. Sadie, though, found herself wondering why he should have chosen so dramatic a word for so innocuous an outing.

It was the beginning of a new pattern to Sadie's days. Aunt Zipporah increasingly took her niece on her social rounds. In the mornings, after the aunt had breakfasted in her room and conducted her elaborate toilette with the help of her maid, they went shopping. They visited haberdashers in Cork Street, where Aunt Zipporah unerringly selected the most expensive fabrics. Then to the dressmakers in Bruton Street, where a young woman with a mouthful of pins taken from the velvet pad bound to her wrist knelt for hours on the floor as she swatched and draped the material round Aunt Zipporah.

After luncheon, there were excursions to the houses of other wealthy women. And tea. There would be pâté sandwiches and scones, walnut and coffee cake – and gently malicious discussion about acquaintances not present. In the evenings there were dinner parties which Sadie, worried about some potential social gaffe, tried to avoid. Instead, she would go to her room and read her way voraciously through Uncle Mark's library.

Gradually, as the days became weeks, the older woman softened. She was less edgy and nervous, more comfortable when they were alone together. At first Sadie suspected her aunt was treating her as she might have done a daughter. It did not take long to discard that impression. Aunt

Zipporah had too little of the maternal in her. Even with children of her own, Sadie could not imagine her behaving towards them as Sophie did.

Her second calculation was that her aunt was acting in accordance with some plan she had devised with Sophie, to somehow turn her from marriage to Nathaniel. The more she thought of this, the more likely it seemed. Then, as the days went by and the subject of her unacceptable suitor was not raised, she began to think she must be wrong.

Finally, she came to what she thought was probably the truth. What her aunt really sought was a confidante. She was essentially a lonely woman, who lacked the gift of easy friendship even had her strong sense of superiority allowed it. She did not particularly like other women. 'They have nothing to say,' she would complain to Sadie, 'and are interested only in their children and what their husbands' money can buy for them.' But nor, it soon became apparent, did she like men much better. If women did not provide enough competition, men were too much: Zipporah needed to excel, to outshine everyone around her. Her aggression rejected men, but her vanity sought their attentions.

Late one afternoon Sadie began to see how Zipporah reconciled one with the other. They had been visiting a small antique gallery where Zipporah had purchased two miniature jade figures. She was triumphant, 'A find, my dear! He didn't know what he had in his hands,' and happier than Sadie had ever seen her. On an impulse she had lifted the speaking tube to the chauffeur.

'Lambert, I'd like to call in for a moment at Motcomb Street.'

The man touched his grey uniform cap and ten minutes later they were driving round the leafy sweep of Belgrave Square to stop outside a narrow terraced house. Zipporah, who had been busy writing on a calling card, handed Lambert the unaddressed envelope. He pulled the doorbell, which was answered by a maidservant in a frilled hat who greeted him, bobbed a curtsey towards the motor and withdrew. Within minutes she had returned and Lambert handed the proffered letter to Zipporah. As they moved off, Zipporah glanced up. Sadie, following her gaze, saw a young, fair-haired man watching them from behind the first floor curtains.

Zipporah drummed her fingers on the envelope lying in her lap.

'Do you,' she asked abruptly, 'write often to Nathaniel?'

Sadie was taken aback by the suddenness of the question, though she had been expecting it for so long. She had already decided in anticipation to tell the truth.

'About three times a week.'

'And his letters – what are they like?'

'He tells me about his work, and about the house. He speaks of things he's buying for us.'

'Does he ever,' Zipporah's voice was low, 'tell you of his love for you?'

Sadie, embarrassed, thought of Nathaniel's letters. She had to admit he rarely referred to his feelings. His letters were practical, warm, matter-of-fact. He talked of his plans for their future, and how he would take care of her. He told her of the china he had seen, and how he thought she would like the design of red and pink roses. He mentioned the cutlery he was about to buy, and the inlaid mahogany clock he had chosen for the dining room.

'I suppose,' she admitted reluctantly, 'that his writing is very . . . sensible. But he says often that he misses me.' And then, in a defensive rush, 'I'm sure he takes it for granted that I know how he feels.'

Zipporah fingered the envelope meditatively, preoccupied with her thoughts. Then she looked at Sadie carefully as though she had suddenly come to a decision.

'Why,' she asked slowly, 'do you imagine we just stopped at Motcomb Street?'

71

Sadie shook her head. 'I don't know.'

'What would you say—' Zipporah paused. 'What would you think if I told you I have a young – friend – living there?'

Sadie's puzzlement was obvious. 'You've got so many friends, I don't . . .' Then she noticed her aunt's small and secret smile, and in a burst of comprehension saw what Zipporah was saying to her. She found herself stammering.

'Do you – do you mean that you and Uncle Mark . . . ?' Her voice   'Do you – do you mean that you and Uncle Mark . . ?' Her voice trailed away.

Zipporah patted her hand.

'Oh my dear, I don't mean there is anything wrong between your uncle and myself. Far from it. Only surely you are aware that women – some women – have relationships outside their marriages?'

Sadie was completely disconcerted. Certainly she knew of such things. She and Leonie had often discussed the romantic sin of Lancelot and Guinevere. It was simply that she had never connected these passions with the people she knew. Aunt Zipporah was evidently delighted by the expression on her face, and her animation increased.

'Little flirtations, you know, add excitement to matrimony. It is not only men who are entitled to such pleasures.'

The idea of flirtation as a pleasure was new to Sadie, whose upbringing had been strict. Although Sophie had privately laughed at the more rigorous Orthodox practices which decreed that young couples were never alone before the wedding, and would never dance together, nor walk arm in arm along the street, she nonetheless approved of the moral ideas behind them: after all, she had three young daughters to marry off.

So now, anxiously, Sadie attempted to reprove her aunt. 'Surely it is wicked to deceive Uncle Mark?'

She received a chilly stare

'Deceive? There is no question of deception, I assure you.'

72

Sadie wanted to argue, but Zipporah's face set, and she fell silent, trying to order her thoughts. She knew she ought to defend her uncle against Zipporah's implied betrayals, but she was too uncertain of her ground to attempt it. Later that evening, when she and her uncle sat together in the library, she tried to tell him something of the afternoon's events. He appeared oblivious to her worried hints. It was only years later, looking back on that incident, that she knew he had not needed to be told. He relished his wife's hard glitter. It gave him confidence in himself, that he could hold such a woman.

Although Sadie was unaware of it, she was herself changing as these things became apparent to her. Her innocence was fast disappearing as Zipporah described a way of life that she found at first incomprehensible, then disturbing. And, finally, exciting.

On the last evening in July they went to the Opera. Sadie, ecstatic, dressed carefully two hours sooner than necessary. She was passing the door of her aunt's room when she was called in. Zipporah, in a loose robe, was putting the finishing touches to a careful coiffure. Her hair was entwined with diamonds and Sadie watched fascinated as the maid deftly pinned in yet more.

Watching her niece in the glass, Zipporah smiled.

'Have you heard from your Nathaniel? I saw you had a letter today.''

Sadie nodded.

'You didn't look especially pleased.'

'It was only a letter, Aunt Zipporah.'

'*Only* a letter? You surprise me. I expected you to rush to your room, and you simply sat there calmly and put it in your pocket. I should not have been so . . . contained.'

Sadie remembered her aunt clutching that letter on the ride home from Belgrave Square, and it occurred to her for the first time that, although she felt love for him, she was not thrilled by the thought of Nathaniel. It was, she had to admit, a temperate relationship. On his part it was the measured love of an orderly man. He made no demands on her which she could not, at seventeen, meet. He treated her as she wished with a steady, fatherly affection. She had not questioned her own emotions. Until now. She had played a passive role: Nathaniel had pursued, she had accepted. She still found it easier to talk to him through her letters than she did when she saw him. Their love was shaped on paper. Struck by a thought, she spoke it aloud.

'Do you know, I've only spent a few hours with him.'

'And has he – I don't want to offend you – has he ever kissed you?'

Sadie flushed.

'Once.'

'And was that after you had agreed to marry him?'

She nodded.

'Did you enjoy it?'

'I thought . . . I remember thinking, his beard felt very soft.'

Zipporah burst out laughing and turned back to the glass.

'My dear, you are delicious! And is this memory of passion to sustain you for the next few months? Looking at you, I would think not.'

From an elaborate flask she began to apply a colourless liquid to her skin. She noted Sadie's curiosity.

'Rose and glycerine water,' she explained. Then, though she already knew the answer, she added, 'Would you like to try some?'

Sadie shook her head, and watched while the other woman continued smoothing her skin. Since the previous day her head had been pounding with questions she longed to ask. She hesitated, partly out of pride – she felt they would make her look ridiculously naïve – and partly from fear of alienating her aunt. But watching her tend her beauty Sadie felt this woman was as anxious to talk as she was to listen. When the maid left the room, Sadie said:

'There is one thing – you said nothing was wrong between you and Uncle Mark. But how do you manage? I mean, where do you go?'

Zipporah brushed her eyebrows upwards with a tiny comb, and smoothed them with a licked finger.

'My dear, ways and means can always be found. I might call upon a woman friend and leave an hour earlier than anticipated. Or I might take longer to choose the fabric for new curtains than I had expected. One must be discreet about these things. As to . . . there are some friends who are most accommodating, as I am to them when necessary.'

Sadie absorbed this information. Then, tentatively, she asked:

'How do you meet them?'

'There are many presentable young men in London. One has only to go about, to be seen. It's not hard to acquire willing – companions.'

'But don't they mind that you are already married?'

'To be a married woman is a positive asset in such matters. My respectability . . .' Zipporah laughed 'is never in doubt, my reputation is untarnished.'

She pulled open a small envelope labelled *riz de poudre* and with a little swan's-down puff applied it to her face and throat. Until now Sadie had assumed only actresses used such things, and she still found herself disturbed by Zipporah's laconic skill. She had to admit though, that her aunt looked more dramatic than ever.

When, later, Uncle Mark shepherded them into their box at Covent Garden, she noted how everyone's eyes went to Aunt Zipporah, who treated their scrutiny with complete disregard. But Uncle Mark was watching his niece carefully as she gazed around her absorbing the lavish splendours of the great auditorium, the dark velvet curtains and the massed tiers of seats rising to the painted roof. She was far too absorbed to notice the door of the box open and admit a man, sliding quietly into the seat behind Aunt Zipporah as the lights dimmed. Only Mark acknowledged the newcomer's presence.

Sadie's attention was riveted on the stage, and not until the end of the act did she turn back to the box, when the art nouveau lights, carried aloft by naked bronze figures, were beginning to brighten. The stranger rose to his feet and as he did so his hand slid down Aunt Zipporah's shoulder briefly cupping her breast. Suddenly breathless, Sadie glanced at her uncle. He was putting his opera glasses carefully into their case.

She refused an invitation to leave the box during the interval, thinking only that she wanted to be by herself, to subdue the strange emotions aroused by that secretive caress. Fascinated though she had been by Zipporah's revelations, she had half thought them to be fantasy. Even the incident in Motcomb Street had not totally convinced her. Now, for the first time, she sensed the physical reality behind Zipporah's words. She sat alone and watched the audience below her chattering and laughing, the women parading their dresses and jewels, the men exquisite in evening finery. In her high-necked dress, her hair in its customary heavy loops, she felt awkward and childish, and hoped that in the half-shadow she would be invisible to them. In reality, she looked vivid and odd. And she was noticed.

She did not observe, in the stalls, a slender man looking towards their box through his opera glasses. When she did, it took her a few moments to become aware that she herself was his object. She thought again of that possessive hand upon Aunt Zipporah's body and in a flush of embarrassment moved her chair sideways behind a pillar and out of his sight. A little later when she glanced back with careful nonchalance he was gone.

When her uncle and aunt returned, they were accompanied by a young man. Sadie felt almost certain he was the watcher from the stalls. Flustered, she scarcely heard the words of introduction: 'Mr Raphael, Sadie . . . father and I are old business acquaintances. Asher, this is my favourite niece.'

The man bent over her hand, murmured politely and took the seat beside her. Sadie wondered wildly whether he could be yet another of her aunt's lovers. But the older woman was paying him no further attention and now chatted to a small group of people at the door of the box. Sadie composed herself to be polite. The young man spoke first.

'Are you enjoying the performance, Miss Browne? Melba is in fine voice tonight.'

'Oh, yes, it's splendid. Only I find it hard to follow.'

'That is the idea. The greater the confusion, the more successful the production, and the more people flock to hear it. One must never, ever, understand an opera. Comprehension entirely spoils the music.'

Uncertain how to reply, Sadie looked at him to see if this were a joke. He met her eyes gravely. The low voice and laconic self-assurance intimidated her.

The house lights softened again, and the audience rustled into silence. This time, however, she was scarcely conscious of the stage. She found herself aware of his presence beside her: the signet ring on his little finger set with a heavily carved turquoise, the frilled and tucked white shirt, the faint smell of Euchrisma. Once, she slid her eyes sideways to see him and found with a slight shock that he was watching her.

It was almost with disappointment that she found the act had ended. He excused himself, explaining that his mother would be waiting. He bowed over Aunt Zipporah's hand, patted Uncle Mark on the shoulder. He turned to Sadie.

77

She felt her colour deepen as he spoke.

'I hope we meet again soon, Miss Browne. Perhaps you will be in Hyde Park one afternoon if this weather holds?'

Even as she searched for the correct reply, Zipporah interrupted.

'We are planning to visit the roses on Tuesday, aren't we, Sadie? I've been promising for a week now that we should go.'

He continued as though he had not heard.

'My favourite ride is round the Serpentine. Do you know that? Perhaps you and your aunt would accompany me?'

Ignorant of the protocol of receiving such an invitation, Sadie contented herself with a smile. He gave her a slight bow and left the box. She waited as the door closed behind him to see how the others would react. Uncle Mark was lighting one of his narrow black cheroots and puffing in concentration. Zipporah could scarcely contain her elation.

'My dear, he's the most acceptable fellow. His father is the biggest art-dealer in London – Moritz Raphael, you know – and his sister Lena is one of the best-known society hostesses. We must encourage him.'

Sadie felt a sudden anger towards her aunt. The slight incident she had witnessed earlier had shocked, even while it had not surprised her. She felt that in encouraging her to accept the attentions of this unknown man, Aunt Zipporah was trying to make her behave as she did herself. She, Sadie, would remain loyal to Nathaniel.

Nevertheless, it was with an emotion she could not precisely define that she saw Asher Raphael again. They were in the porticoed foyer, waiting for the de Dion to collect them. He was helping an elderly woman into a sleek black tandem. As he seated himself he turned and saw Sadie, and raised his hand to his top hat in formal salutation. He did not smile. Then he tapped on the glass pane and the red-buttonholed driver flicked a whip. The polished hooves of the horses beat staccato on the cobbles as the carriage drew away.

Chapter Six

Early the following week Zipporah announced she was going to take the waters at Leamington Spa.

'Just for a day or two, my dear. I would take you with me, only I fear you'd be bored. I do nothing there all day, I assure you, but rest. And the water itself tastes horrible – if it were not doing me good I couldn't stand it.'

Sadie regarded her with some surprise. In the days following their evening at Covent Garden the events had blurred and softened in her mind. Her instinctive recoil at Zipporah's behaviour now seemed childish and immature: a woman of the world, she told herself, would not have been shocked. All the same, she wondered whether Zipporah would be entirely unaccompanied. Uncle Mark seemed unperturbed. Watching Zipporah prepare for her journey he had leant negligently in the doorway of his study as his wife instructed Sadie on how she should spend her time.

'Try not to be bored,' she had concluded. 'And don't write too many letters.'

'Sadie and I,' interrupted Mark, 'will console ourselves in your absence as best we may.'

Zipporah glanced at him sharply as she speared her velvet travelling hat with a pin on which perched a bird of paradise in spun glass. She held out her arms as Mark swathed her in a voluminous dustcoat, and kissed them both a formal goodbye.

For two days Sadie had been left to her own devices. The housekeeper, Mrs Marriott, had clearly been told to keep a close eye on her. A subdued woman for whom the girl felt a good deal of sympathy, an unspoken conspiracy developed between them in the absence of the exacting mistress of the house. Mrs Marriott brought her hot chocolate in the mornings, an unheard of treat since Zipporah considered it a proletarian drink. When Sadie went for a drive the housekeeper accompanied her and on the second afternoon they walked together to admire the graceful architecture of the white town houses on the river at Little Venice. On the third day Sadie was surprised to see the de Dion turning in at the house in the late morning. The chauffeur brought in a note: Uncle Mark suggested she might like to dine out with him that evening. Mrs Marriott, when told they would not be in for dinner, looked at her charge consideringly.

'May I ask, Miss, what you're going to wear?'

'I hadn't thought, Mrs Marriott. I haven't actually got much choice, you know.'

'If I might make a suggestion. I don't believe the Madam would mind if I were to get out one of her old dresses. We've got time to alter it to fit you.'

When Sadie hesitated she added persuasively, 'You must do Mr Mark justice, Miss. You want him to be proud of you.'

'No. Thank you.' Sadie refused with an effort.

When Mark came down that evening she was already waiting in the library. He offered her his arm with exaggerated courtesy.

'My dear young lady, you look as though you are in need of some *divertissement*. I am entirely at your disposal.'

She beamed at him. 'Why, how kind of you, sir. I should be delighted to accompany you.'

Just as the manservant was holding out her grey woollen coat Mrs Marriott hurried into the hallway. Over her arm was a black velvet cape heavily embroidered in silver thread. Despite Sadie's protests she placed it round her shoulders and stood back to admire the result.

'Now don't you argue with me, Miss. It was a present from the Madam and if I want to lend it to you then it will please me to do so.'

Sadie, seeing herself in the glass, demurely knotted hair gleaming against the blackness, had no further wish to refuse. Impulsively she hugged the housekeeper.

'Oh, how lovely of you. I'll take great care of it.'

Settled in the motor under the plaid travelling rug she asked eagerly, 'Where are we going?'

'I am not, regrettably, at liberty to divulge so important a secret. You must just wait and see.' Mark smiled to himself at her excitement. They drove quickly round the outer perimeter of Regents Park and across the Marylebone Road to the great sweep of Portland Place. Past All Soul's in Langham Place and they crossed into Regent Street, driving more slowly because of the pressure of crowds swarming across the pavements. They reached Piccadilly and finally drew up outside an entrance canopied in red. Uncle Mark jumped out and held out his hand to her.

'Welcome to the Café Royal,' he said.

They passed through the brilliantly lit foyer and followed the sound of laughter and raised voices from behind mahogany doors. Uncle Mark pushed his way in and on a blast of sound Sadie found herself in a huge room, packed to the walls with little marble-topped tables. Conversations bubbled around her, animated men and women moved from table to table, everyone seemed to know everyone else. Cigarette smoke wreathed up to the heavily gilded and painted ceiling, and the whole scene was repeated endlessly in curved mirrors which multiplied the curtains of crimson velvet, the carved and panelled walls. A waiter in a long white apron hurried forward and led them to a table by a wall. Behind Sadie, as the chair was pulled out for her, she noticed the white statue of a woman whose head supported one of the moulded arches. Without looking at a menu Uncle Mark ordered, then sat back and regarded his niece with some satisfaction.

'This, my dear, is the most exciting place in London. It's

called' – he nodded in explanation towards the next table where two men were bent in concentration – 'the Domino Room.' As he spoke Sadie became aware of the sharp click of the dominoes in other parts of the room and saw that on many tables, among the wine bottles and used glasses, people were moving the oblong shapes.

'Who are they all?' Sadie was fascinated by the faces around her. They were totally different from the group she had previously met through Mark and Zipporah: the slightly sharp, expensively dressed women, the fleshy, clever-faced men. Here, clothes were eccentric and often untidy. Men wore bright waistcoats and many had removed their jackets.

'They're almost all in the arts, one way or another. There are dozens of painters, writers, journalists. Actors come in later, when the plays are over. You can see poets reciting their new work to each other – I met Yeats here once. And the others' – he gestured widely – 'everyone you can think of. Frenchmen and Russians, Poles and Hungarians, students and their professors, bank clerks . . . the world and their women.'

Sadie gazed avidly about her. 'I can't believe I'm here with you. I've never been anywhere like this in my life.' She sighed with pleasure. 'Everything's changing, isn't it? At home I always knew what would happen. Everything was – expected. But now I feel I've only to reach out a hand and anything could become possible.' She sat back as the waiter deftly wove his way to their table, tray balanced at shoulder height, and set before them bowls of thick soup, sticks of bread and a carafe of white wine.

When she peered apprehensively into the soup Uncle Mark laughed at her.

'*Moules*,' he said, 'with garlic. Mussels to you.'

She gasped.

'We can't eat that. It's not kosher.'

'It may not be kosher but it's the most delicious food

you'll ever taste. And I won't be telling, will I?'

'It's not a question of *telling*.' She pursed her lips primly.
'I couldn't possibly.'

Her uncle grinned and gently mocked her tone.

'Not possibly, my dear? I thought tonight you were really
living, reaching out, changing . . .'

She hesitated. It really was too silly, she reflected, and it
did smell wonderful. Tentatively she lifted her spoon to her
lips, while Mark watched her reaction with amusement. She
tasted cautiously, then giggled.

'You're right. It's delicious.'

Mark patted her hand.

'There you are, another hurdle over. We'll liberate you
yet from the shackles of your childhood.'

'I'm not sure I want to be liberated, thank you.'

'You're not very consistent, are you? You plan to marry a
man who is not a Jew and yet you worry about dietary
laws.'

Sadie stiffened. This was the first time in all these weeks
that Uncle Mark had ever referred to Nathaniel. Watching
her, Mark asked, curiously, 'Have you really thought out
what your marriage will mean, I wonder? Have you realized
that you will lose contact with all your friends and some of
your family? They will regard it as an act of cruelty on your
part, something calculated to hurt them.'

She thought of Grandpa Diamond pleading with tears in
his eyes and burst out, 'But *why* should they feel that? I
don't want to upset anyone. It's my choice, it's my
marriage.'

'That's just where you're wrong. Which of your friends
will marry men they choose themselves? Look at your own
sister – did Miriam even know that young man before they
were introduced as a prospective couple? No.' He leant
forward. 'Sadie. Do you honestly think happy marriages
are accidents? Or even unhappy ones, come to that?'

Struck by a sudden thought she asked nervously, 'How

did you meet Aunt Zipporah? That wasn't arranged, was it?'

'Well, in a way it was, yes. Her father thought it was time for her to marry and I was working for him as a junior. Most suitable. Keep it all in the family. The fact that I had no money was no obstacle, simply because they had so much. And so you see , my dear,' he gave a wry little smile, 'so you see, it was no romantic accident like you and Nathaniel. Zipporah would not, I think, have cared for love in a cottage.'

As Mark finished speaking a great gale of laughter from the other side of the room caught their attention and both turned to see who had caused it. A group of men had risen to their feet and were drinking a toast, glasses clinking. Sadie realized that a young man in a black velvet smoking jacket and ruffled shirt had turned and his glass was raised towards her. Mark, who had seen the same thing, lifted his own glass in return.

Sadie felt herself grow scarlet. The young man was Asher Raphael.

Five minutes later he extricated himself from the group and joined them, politely bowing to Sadie as he asked Mark whether he might sit down. By then she had recovered her composure and was able to listen calmly as he and Mark talked about a painting Mark wanted to buy.

'My father,' said Asher, turning to Sadie, 'is an art-dealer, and I am just going into partnership with him.'

'I know,' said Sadie, 'Aunt Zipporah told me.'

'I should have been happier if you had not been told but instead had asked.'

Recognizing the gentle flirtation, Sadie relaxed and gave him a wide smile.

'Either way,' she said, 'I have discovered your situation.'

'Do you know anything of paintings, Miss Browne?'

She shook her head. 'My parents had a painting over the fire at home in a copper frame and I used to spend hours making up stories about it. But I don't even know who the artist was.'

'Would you care to come and see the gallery one afternoon – I can promise pictures to ravish you.' She immediately agreed, and he went on eagerly, 'And if you would like, I can introduce you to the artists. In fact, many of them are here tonight.'

He nodded towards a group sitting in the opposite corner who had drawn several tables together in a large circle. Among the young men were several women. They wore clothes which looked to Sadie most exotic. One was swathed in a brilliant shawl, egret feathers in her hair.

'That's the Regent Street end,' Asher went on, 'and those are the painters from Chelsea and Camden Town. Look, that short man is Sickert, and next to him there's Stanley Spencer.'

'Are those pretty girls painters too?'

'No,' Asher said and pointed to a strange figure, a man bundled up in a greatcoat with a yachting cap on his head. 'That's Steer. He always dresses like that because he's terrified of catching cold. We've just got a new painting from him. I'll show it to you.'

She noticed two men in particular. One was slight, with quick, nervous movements. His eyes were green and he wore a golden beard. Next to him was a man who literally dwarfed the table with his presence. His head was massive, it seemed carved in wide, sweeping lines and his hair grew strongly like a horse's mane. She could see his powerful hands round his glass, the wide, square-nailed thumbs.

Asher, following her gaze, said, 'The fair man is Swinburne. And the one who looks like a carving, that's Rodin. Do you see that young man opposite, the broad-shouldered fellow? That's Jacob Epstein. He's a sculptor too, from New York. His parents didn't want him to be an artist, so Papa has been helping him: he's been approached to do some huge figures for the British Medical Council's new building at Charing Cross.'

Fascinated, Sadie gazed at the intent group.

'I'd never imagined artists to be so young. I thought they would be old men with paint in their beards and greasy berets.'

Asher laughed, then composed his face and said gravely to Mark, 'I can see we must take in hand your niece's artistic education if she is to be a credit to you. Why don't you both come tomorrow to pick up the Nash and I'll take you round then.'

'We'd be delighted,' Mark answered for both of them.

As they rose to leave, Asher settled the black velvet cape round Sadie's shoulders. This time, it was he who watched her depart as Mark guided her from the restaurant.

The Raphael Gallery had its premises in one of the fashionable streets between Bond Street and Berkeley Square. Uncle Mark and Sadie arrived late next morning and were ushered in by the uniformed doorman.

'You are just in time for a glass of Madeira,' Asher greeted them. 'And, Miss Browne, I want you to meet my father.'

Moritz Raphael rose from a leather chair as they entered the small room behind the gallery. A rotund man with thick white hair and an immaculate morning suit, he grasped Sadie's hand between his own and gave her an appreciative smile. Then he turned to Uncle Mark.

'My dear Diamond, it is always a pleasure to see you. We have the picture ready, but I'd like to show you something we've just acquired.' He gestured towards the walls of the rooms which were covered with pictures. More canvasses, unframed, were propped against chairs or lying on tables. He picked up a small country scene.

'Look what Rothenstein's just sent me from Sussex. Have you ever seen anything to touch it? It positively glows.'

Mark laughed and flung out a protesting hand.

'For heaven's sake, tempt me no further or you'll be the ruin of me!'

Discreetly Asher said at Sadie's back, 'Let's leave them to it, shall we? They go on like this for hours. Come and see the rest of our things.'

Out of earshot he laughed. 'My father was born to be a confectioner like his own father in Vienna. He sells pictures as though they were delicacies and he the cook pressing his patrons to have one more morsel. He can't bear to be refused: he takes it as an affront if they don't like them as much as he does.'

They walked around the grey-carpeted rooms together. Heavy cream curtains screened off the morning and the room was in semi-shadow except for brilliantly lit paintings. As they paused before them, Asher explained them to Sadie and talked about the artists. Her eyes swam with colour as he led her from one to the other.

'Here's the Steer I told you about. This lovely girl, her hair is the same red as yours. And this is a Tonks – d'you like it? And you must see this one, it's by Charles Conder; isn't it superb?'

Sadie stopped in front of the painting of a dancer, her dress opalescent, her face dreamy.

'Degas,' said Asher. 'You're clearly a romantic. You should see the Cézanne my father has at home. Better still,' his face lit up, 'I'll show you the paintings of the pre-Raphaelites. Have you ever seen a Rossetti?'

Sadie watched and listened, enraptured. She felt as though a window in her mind had been opened. When they had discussed practically everything in the gallery Asher asked if she would take tea with his mother. By the time Uncle Mark and Moritz Raphael had finished and the Nash was loaded into the de Dion, Sadie knew, for the first time in her adult life, what she really wanted.

She wanted Asher Raphael.

Chapter Seven

Asher Raphael was the last-born of Moritz and Rose, their only and longed-for boy. 'A *mitzvah*, a *mitzvah*, my son, a little son,' his father had crooned, ecstatic with joy, while Rose looked on in exhausted contentment. The girls were treasures, of course, but a son was fulfilment of a different kind: this was assurance that the line would go on, the name not die out. When he was born the couple were already in their early forties: any later, said Rose with relief, and it would have been too late.

She and Moritz had not had an easy time of it and if now they began to enjoy their security, they felt they had earned it. Moritz's father had indeed been a Viennese confectioner. His minuscule shop in the old district of Josefstadt near the Theater was famous for exquisitely decorated cakes; he worked far into the night preparing wonderful edifices to deck the tables of society ladies. He moulded miniatures of their pets; sculpted scrupulous likenesses of the women themselves, perfect even to details of their dresses; carved charming dolls-size tea tables laden with edible china. There were ten children to support and in their small apartment over the shop meals were served in relays.

When Moritz was old enough – fourteen to be exact – he was deemed ready to earn a living and sent to his father's brother, who had gone to London as cook to a diplomatic family. The boy was apprenticed in the kitchens of the Savoy, which he cordially hated. Within two years he had started training under a master printer. At twenty-one he was doing intricate engraving work for artists' blocks and soon was so much in demand that he set up a small business of his own in Cheapside, backed by the master printer. By now he had married.

Rose was the daughter of immigrant parents with almost no English but a desperate desire to improve themselves. When Moritz met her at his cousin's wedding she was nineteen and working in Liberty and Company in Regent Street, hand-embroidering their silks in the attic work-rooms. They married quickly, and with her help and eye Moritz decided he could afford to open a shop attached to the premises to sell the work of lesser known artists. Moritz was not only a superb craftsman but a shrewd businessman. He had an instinctive knowledge of how much a painting would fetch and who would buy it.

Eventually the Raphaels established their own gallery in Bruton Street and from a rented house in the wrong end of St John's Wood they moved to the splendid porticoes of Portland Place. They adapted easily to their changed circumstances. The two girls, Lena and Betty, had a fashionable governess. Asher was also educated at home but with a tutor, since his lessons were more academic. Later he went to the Haberdashers' Aske's School and spent three years at university in Switzerland perfecting his French.

The girls, naturally, married. Lena was the bride of a banker older than herself. Her bosom and hips rapidly broadened with matrimony and two children, but so did her wit. Harry Da Costa encouraged her and by the time she was thirty-five she was renowned for her salon, which attracted both her husband's business associates and her father's artists – a most beneficial arrangement for all concerned. Betty, the younger sister, who had been treated as a delicate child and worried about her health, was now an introspective woman just married to John Epstein, newly created director of a firm of publishers in Holborn. He was in the process of discovering that his fragile bride had a will of iron.

Asher was as adored by the two sisters as by his parents. A precociously intelligent child, he had become a young man who cloaked his emotions with amused reticence. He had the quiet self-assurance of those who had always had every whim gratified without having to ask twice and he cultivated a slightly diffident manner which alarmed and delighted his ebullient father. When he met Sadie Browne he was twenty-five years old. He was used to being overwhelmed by the women in his family, and Sadie's hesitant youth gave him an unaccustomed sense of power. The pleasure he found in showing her paintings and pointing out celebrities at the Café Royal was a new experience for him.

He acted quickly. The following day he wrote to Mark Diamond, inviting him and his niece to a private view of a new exhibition. After that, he saw to it that Mark asked him to dine privately with them at home. During the evening, Sadie mentioned that she and Mrs Marriott planned to visit the village of Hampstead the next day: by an extraordinary coincidence, declared Asher, he would be there himself, visiting one of his artists – perhaps he could show them the Heath? After that meeting, he called upon Sadie one afternoon, and Mrs Marriott served them ginger beer and kept a close eye on her charge as she walked demurely with her escort in the Italian garden.

On the Sunday afternoon, Asher Raphael arranged to take Sadie for a drive. The manservant did not need to announce him: she was already by the window when he drove up, sitting behind the groom in the gleaming black carriage. He jumped down as she appeared on the steps, sweeping a mock bow.

'Your conveyance awaits.'

Hesitantly she said, 'Uncle Mark wants Mrs Marriott to come with us. He promised Aunt Zipporah I'd be chaperoned.'

'Of course.' He handed them both in and sat facing the two women. As they neared Regents Park the number of carriages began to swell as other Sunday visitors arrived:

the steady stream of landaus and wagonettes, drags and Victorias filled the road between the great white villas and the green borders of the park. When they arrived at the wrought iron park gates Asher suggested they walk, and dismissed the carriage.

'Will you pick us up here at four, Greaves, please?'

The park was thronged with strollers; the first flowers of autumn, the dahlias and antirrhinums, vying in colour and brilliance with the artificial flowers on the women's hats. Children in velvet coats and gaiters played amongst the parading couples. Ornamental dogs strutted by, old ladies were wheeled in Bath chairs. As they neared the lake Sadie could see rowing boats on the water and hear the delighted shrieks of the occupants. In the hazy autumn afternoon the coppery trees gave off a slightly sweet scent, a hint of decay, and on the ground already a few brittle leaves crisped underfoot. They moved beneath the trees, out of the sun, and the chill struck suddenly. She shivered and Asher took her arm.

'Are you warm enough?' She nodded and buttoned up her grey coat to the throat. Mrs Marriott had fallen a few paces behind and they strolled on alone.

'Miss Browne. Sadie. I've got something I want to say to you and really I don't know how to begin.'

'Then don't.' She laughed, to take the sharpness out of her words. She knew a sudden apprehension at what he might say. They walked in silence until they reached a wooden bridge. Beyond it the lake narrowed and willows met and clung over the water. Asher gave Sadie his hand to negotiate the steep bank.

'Shall we sit her?' He indicated a low bench. Mrs Marriott, on the bridge, turned tactfully to survey the rowers on the wide stretch of water.

'Look, I know this is silly, because we've hardly known each other any time at all. But there's something I want to know.'

Sadie looked at him in silence, not allowing herself to believe the expression on his face.

'I know there's someone else . . . no . . .' as Sadie started to interrupt, 'let me finish. I know there's someone else, and I'm not asking you to tell me about him. What I *do* want to know is whether there is a chance for me?'

Sadie was bewildered by his intensity.

'What do you mean, a chance?'

He relaxed suddenly, amusement softening the frown lines between his eyes.

'It is evident that you're no schemer, or you'd have seen this coming.' He looked at her seriously, then took her hand, pulling as she resisted until it lay over his heart on the fine linen pleats of his shirt. She turned pink, but he held it tightly.

'Listen,' he said quietly, 'can't you feel my heart beating for you?'

Horrified she snatched her hand away.

'I thought you knew.' Her voice was choked. 'I thought Aunt Zipporah and Mark would have told you.'

'Told me what? What am I supposed to know?'

'It's not just that there's someone else.' Her voice was shaking. 'I'm actually engaged. I'm going to be married.'

In the silence that followed, Asher closed his eyes.

'No,' he said heavily. 'Your aunt didn't tell me. I'm sorry. I shouldn't have spoken. Please let us forget all about it.' He rose. 'Shall we move on? It's getting cold here.'

Sadie saw that he had spoken before he meant to and admitted more than he had intended. His anger now was directed not at her, but at himself. They moved off across the grass. She was in turmoil: she had given her word to Nathaniel but he seemed so remote she could scarcely recall how she felt about him. Perhaps – she found it difficult to admit this even to herself – perhaps she wanted Nathaniel because everyone else was against it? She only knew that the man beside her was more vital, more alive, more attractive to her than anyone she had ever met. On impulse she turned to him.

'It's my fault. I shouldn't be here like this, as if I were free like any other girl, when all the time I knew I was spoken for. I'm sorry.'

He made a visible effort and bowed slightly in acceptance of her apology.

'Please don't think me rude, but I should get you home. It's late and your uncle will be worried.'

Chastened, Sadie fell silent. Mrs Marriott rejoined them cheerfully talking of the band who were still playing on the white rostrum.

'*Annie Laurie*,' she said happily. 'My, but it takes me back.'

Asher and Sadie, both grateful for her voluble chatter, exchanged no word until they were again seated in the carriage. Asher looked strained and felt his head beginning to ache, but forced himself to answer Mrs Marriott's polite trivialities until they reached Maida Vale. Then he excused himself and drove off. Mrs Marriott bustled Sadie inside, still chattering. The girl suddenly felt so inert she could hardly move. Slowly she went upstairs, took off her dress and lay down on her bed.

Uncle Mark peered at her across the dinner table. 'What's the matter? You look terrible.'

'I don't think I can tell you. I'm not even sure myself what happened.'

He gave her a quizzical look.

'Don't tell me the elegant Asher forced his attentions on you.'

'In a way he did. I think he was about to propose marriage to me.'

The humour died on Mark's face.

'And what did you reply?'

'I stopped him. I told him I was engaged to marry someone else.'

Mark thought for a moment.

'What *would* you have said if you had made no promise to Nathaniel?'

Sadie tried to be honest with herself. She spoke almost in a whisper.

'I should have accepted.'

'Then,' Mark said, and his voice was cold, 'you're a damned fool.'

Shocked by the sudden cruelty of his words Sadie stared at him.

'You came here,' he went on, 'because your mother and I thought a change of scene might make you forget Nathaniel. You meet a man like Asher and by some miracle he is actually taken with you. You admit to me you want him – and yet stand by a promise you made to a man who is not suitable for you, who is unacceptable to your family and who, moreover, is years older than you.'

Sadie put a shaking hand to her face.

'But Uncle, I gave my word. I promised. Even Ma says she will let me marry Nathaniel when I leave here.'

Mark snorted in exasperation.

'You're not looking at this straight. If only you would let yourself see it, you made a mistake. You were swept up by this Nathaniel because you had never met anyone like him before and you're only a child still. But Asher is the one to make you happy. Asher is the man you must marry. Good God, girl, look at the life you could have with him!'

In the confusion of her emotions, Sadie understood her uncle was speaking the truth: she knew she was drawn to Asher, that he touched in her depths of feeling she had not known she possessed.

'How can I go to Nathaniel now and tell him no?'

She appealed to Mark, tears in her eyes, and his face softened.

'I know it seems an awful thing to do, but in the end it'll be for the best. He's asking you to give up a great deal, you know. To leave your family, and your religion – and your mother tells me you're planning to live in Chicago, so he's asking you to leave even your country.' He leant forward and took her hand.

'Look, Sadie, I'll help. We'll write a letter between us to Nathaniel, to explain. He won't be so surprised, he's a man of the world. And he knows your family are unhappy at this match.' Seeing the doubt in her eyes he added persuasively, 'He won't be too hurt. We'll be very tactful about it.'

Sadie stared at him. It had all been so precipitate. She loved Nathaniel. Of that she was sure. But the attraction she felt for Asher Raphael was too powerful to be denied. Wretchedly she twisted her napkin. 'I don't know . . . I can't tell.'

Uncle Mark patted her arm. 'I know it's a big step. Look, think about it overnight. We'll talk in the morning.'

Not since that sad night in Miriam's house, when she had tried to peer into an uncertain future, had she slept so badly. She tossed restlessly, trying to make sense of her muddled emotions. Although she could hardly bring herself to admit it, she felt now that she had indeed acted unwisely in agreeing to marry Nathaniel Laurence. Here in London, removed from the cramped Salford house which she loved and wanted to escape, she thought that perhaps Uncle Mark was right, that she had been swept along by Nathaniel's plans. It certainly made her feel better to think so. And, she comforted herself, her uncle knew what to say so that Nathaniel need not be too upset. And then – her mind ran ahead – the unofficial engagement ended, she would be free to listen to Asher.

In the morning, she went downstairs to where Uncle Mark was eating kedgeree, *The Times* propped open before him. She stood looking out of the window, and told him what she had decided.

95

'Splendid,' said her uncle, 'I'll get young Raphael over to the club and tell him there.'

'No!' Sadie's vehemence surprised them both. 'Not until Nathaniel knows. That would be a despicable thing to do.'

'You're right, of course. I was being too hasty.'

He wiped his moustache with the linen napkin and pushed back his chair.

'Come on. Let's write those letters.'

Chapter Eight

Sophie answered the letter immediately. Thank God, she wrote, and her immense relief was more than evident, thank God Sadie had seen sense at last. It was wonderful news, but – she knew this was stupid, but she did so hope Nathaniel would take it well. Having opposed the match fiercely she now hated to hurt this man she scarcely knew, but who also had loved her daughter. To Mark – who had written to her himself, a letter in which he hinted at the possibility of another, more suitable match – she wrote separately, full of thanks and gratitude.

And there was a letter for Sadie from Nathaniel. It was the last time, he said, that he would write to her, and he wanted her to know that she was again completely free.

> I would not, even if I could, ask anything more of you. I love you very much, but perhaps I was wrong to think there would ever be a future for us together, perhaps we are from two different worlds. Thank you for saying you are sorry. You have, I must confess, hurt me, but I will not die of it. I am sure that, as you say, I will find someone else. Only I think it will take me a long time. I wish you happiness.

Sadie cried over that letter, and kept it for many years.

Zipporah returned home sleeker than ever and smiled her approval when Mark told her the engagement was over. That night, in the privacy of Zipporah's room, he added that it looked as though young Asher was going to propose to Sadie. She nodded thoughtfully, dabbing a new perfume on her wrist, and said she would set about getting the girl decently dressed.

She was as good as her word. Next morning, completely

overriding her half-hearted protests, she swept Sadie off to the dress-makers.

'Do you, or do you not, want to look as pretty as possible now?' she asked. 'After all,' she added, pointedly, finally, 'you must make the most of what you have.'

'Because,' Sadie finished for her, in rueful agreement, 'because I haven't got much.'

For the ten days it took for the two dresses – all Sadie would accept – to arrive, she did not hear from Asher Raphael, nor did she attempt to contact him. Mark had promised her he would not say anything. She was living in a state of deliberately induced anxiety as a punishment to herself. She still hated what she had done to Nathaniel, and it seemed only right that she should be miserable.

At the end of two weeks Zipporah returned from a soirée with a note of triumph in her voice. She had been to Lena Da Costa's, and her brother Asher had dropped in.

'Did you say anything?' Sadie hated to ask, but desperately wanted to know; she carefully looked away, out of the window, as she waited for the reply.

'Naturally I mentioned that you were somewhat unhappy at the moment. And when he asked why . . . I told him you had broken off your engagement.'

Sadie waited, but Zipporah was laying out a hand of patience with apparent unconcern. Then she glanced at the girl, and relented.

'I have also invited him to dine with us tomorrow. Mark will take us all to the Savoy. And from then on, my dear, it's up to you.'

They did go to the Savoy, driving there along the Embankment in heavy rain. At the hotel Asher, among the heavy draperies and rich scents of many meals, was quieter than she had seen him, and she could not know that he was surprised to find himself unnerved by her. For the first time she looked like the other women he knew: in a slender cream dress, her fringe brushed back, she had a sophistication he had not anticipated. But she wore no jewels, her throat and arms were bare.

He could not prevent his eyes from resting on her with longing and Mark and Zipporah were well aware of what was going on. While Asher was dutifully dancing with Zipporah, Mark and Sadie sat at their table. Mark reached into his pocket and held out a soft chamois leather purse. He swung it from his fingers.

'This is for you.'

'Uncle Mark, what is it?'

He pulled open the strings of the purse, tipped it up and said, 'Hold out your hands.' Into her spread palms he poured a small glittering stream of blue-white diamonds. When she gasped out her pleasure he closed her hands over them.

'They're for your engagement ring, my dear. I'll have them mounted for you whenever you want.'

'But Uncle, I'm not engaged.'

He grinned at her. 'No. It won't take long, though, will it?'

She beamed back at him.

'I do hope not."

That evening, after they had returned to Maida Vale to sit in the saloon and talk and drink brandy and Tokay, Asher asked Sadie to go for a drive with him next day. Zipporah decreed that Mrs Marriott need not be in attendance and she even offered them the use of the de Dion. Asher took her to Regents Park again, to the rose garden with its tall latticed walls and sheltered walks. This time, he did not take her hand. He stood with her looking at a fading bush of Queen Ena roses, their almost black petals curling and dropping.

'You know what it is I want to ask you,' he said quietly.

'Yes. I know.'

'And may I now do so?'

99

'Yes,' she said. 'Oh, yes. Please.'

He laughed at the please, and turned her proffered hands over and kissed her palms.

She looked at his bent head, the silky black hair and the nape of his neck, and the surge of physical joy that swept over her was like nothing she had experienced before.

'And now,' he said, his voice muffled against her hands, 'and now will you marry me, Sadie Browne?'

The wedding was planned for Sadie's eighteenth birthday in November. It was to take place in Manchester, at her mother's express wish, so that she could start her married life as Sophie had done at the Great Synagogue in Cheetham Hill Road. Sadie had left London only days after she agreed to marry Asher. His parents were travelling abroad, and he had telegraphed them for their approval. They were to be away for a month while his father bought paintings, but they would be back for the wedding. Asher took Sadie to meet his sisters. Lena enveloped her in a cloud of perfume and pressed her to a satin bosom. 'My dear, we couldn't be more happy.' Betty touched Sadie's cheek formally with her own, and quietly told her she was welcome in the family. Then, because Asher was anxious for everything to take place as quickly as possible, Mark took Sadie up to Manchester and promised to give her away in a month's time.

The weeks were eaten up by the frantic preparations. The dress must be made. Zipporah wanted her dressmaker to do it, but Sophie declared that she would make it herself. Creamy slipper satin, the skirt caught up in a myriad tiny gathers each held with a silk rosebud, it was the dress of dreams, Sadie cried, hugging Sophie. Sadie and Flora both helped with the sewing. Poor Flora: Sadie had bequeathed her the small trousseau that had been amassing for her over the years. The linen sheets, the table cloths of Nottingham lace, the hand-sewn underwear and blouses with tucked fronts she had made herself, she gave them all to her sister. Zipporah and Mark had asked if they could give Sadie a trousseau for her wedding present.

'It would be more in keeping with your new life,' said Zipporah firmly. 'I'll order and you can approve it when you are back in London. And it'll make up for all those clothes you never let me buy you . . .'

Sophie was planning a party afterwards in the synagogue with sweet raisin wine and cakes made by the family. The Raphaels had taken care of everything else, and a room had been booked for the young couple at the Midland Hotel. On learning this, Sadie felt momentary unhappiness for Nathaniel and their meetings there; she intended to suggest that they stay elsewhere, but in the excitement of the wedding preparations she forgot. It was, in any case, only for one night: the next day they were to set off on a tour of Europe.

It was this last detail which enthralled the neighbours. Unimpressed by a young man of whom they had never heard, this display of ostentatious wealth was something outside their experience: little Sadie, contrary to all their expectations, had finally made a real *shiddach*.

Sophie was less impressed.

'Honeymoon, for a month, trouble for life,' she had muttered darkly as she slapped the flat-iron about on the sheets.

Sadie had argued strenuously with her mother over the ritual bath, the *mikvah*, she was supposed to take before the wedding.

'It's so undignified,' she had wailed at Sophie. 'It's as if I wasn't clean enough already.'

'It's not a question of dignity,' Sophie had snapped. 'You're marrying in *schul*, you must do it properly. Everyone goes to the *mikvah*, it's part of the ritual. I did it. Your sister did it. And you'll do it.'

'But Asher and I aren't going to live our lives under that

kind of code: he's not going to expect me to sleep in a separate bed once a month! The whole thing is too old-fashioned.'

'Old-fashioned or not, my girl, you're going to the *mikvah*.'

Finally, Sadie had capitulated. It had seemed little enough to do: in a week or two she would be forever out of her mother's jurisdiction.

Sophie planned to take her the evening before the wedding.

'We'll go about five o'clock,' she said. 'It must be after dark, you have to be very delicate about these things.'

Waiting for Sophie to come home that afternoon, Sadie remarked reflectively to Leonie Samson, 'Do you know, I'm really very pleased I'm doing this. It feels like making a brand new start.'

'Well, you wouldn't be doing it if it had been Nathaniel you were marrying tomorrow.'

'I still feel I treated him terribly. Mother keeps saying better a broken engagement than a broken marriage, and of course she's right. But he was such a nice man, and he was so happy getting things ready for us. I didn't ever think I would hurt him the way I did.'

Leonie was standing before the mirror, re-coiling her hair.

'Well,' she said with an air of practicality as she shoved in a pin, 'you didn't have much choice. From everything you've told me, Asher isn't a man to be missed. Do you have any *idea* how lucky you are? I'm four years older than you, and who's asked for me? Simon Kindler, who comes up to my shoulder and works in a cap factory, and Harry David from down the market, and I've known him ever since school.'

'But you don't want to get married. You always said you wanted to work on the stage. You can't give that up for someone like Harry.'

'The problem is finding people who aren't like Harry. With the hours I work, I'm too exhausted even to visit friends in the evenings. During the day when I'm at home everyone else is working and . . .' she gave Sadie a mock-glare, 'I forbid you to suggest I use a *shadchen* and end up with a rabbinical student who will hardly talk to me until we're married and is only allowed to dance with other men.'

Sadie burst out laughing.

'You fool, what would a rabbinical student want with you?'

Leonie gave her a demure sidelong look.

'Now that would be telling, little Sadie. However, the question will not arise because by the end of next month I shall have saved the fare to New York.' At Sadie's gasp she twirled round triumphantly. 'I'm off to see Florenz Ziegfeld, and if he doesn't hire me on the spot for the Follies I shall sit on his doorstep until he does.'

Just then they heard Sophie's key in the door, and Leonie said hurriedly, 'Don't say anything, please. I'm not telling my parents until just before I go. I don't think they'd want to stop me, but I'm taking no chances.'

Sophie called, 'Sadie. Hurry up, get the towels, we'll be late.' Leonie kissed her friend warmly. 'See you in *schul*,' she said. 'Don't lose your nerve.'

Ten minutes later mother and daughter were on the tram to the Hadassah Synagogue. The *mikvah* was situated in a small house kept for the purpose nearby. It looked dark, and Sadie waited nervously as Sophie pressed the doorbell. The elderly Jewish woman attendant who answered showed them into a small room containing a tub and a washbasin. Sophie took Sadie's clothes and waited outside while she washed, using the soap they had brought with them. Then she cut her nails while Sophie combed the tangles out of her hair.

'Right,' said Sophie when she was satisfied, and she gestured Sadie to go through a second door. Beyond was a room containing a deep rectangular pool, very small. Under her mother's eye, Sadie went down the half-dozen tiled steps. The water rose from her knees to her waist, and she found that within the pool itself a further step deepened the water still further. It was quite warm, and greenish in colour.

'It feels funny,' she said, shivering, 'very soft.'

'It's rainwater,' Sophie explained. 'It's collected on the roof and comes into the bathhouse through a big pipe. It's stored in a special tank, and then heated. Only rainwater is really kosher. Now, do you remember the *broche* you have to make?'

'Mmm.' Silently, Sadie said to herself the Hebrew words. 'Blessing be to God and his holy commandment,' then she held her breath and ducked down beneath the water, immersing herself entirely. As she came up gasping for air Sophie said approvingly, 'Good. Now again.'

Sadie obeyed, but not until the third immersion did Sophie pronounce herself satisfied.

Shivering, Sadie climbed out, wringing water from her hair. The attendant brought heated towels, and Sophie helped rub her dry.

'You can count yourself lucky,' she said, towelling briskly, 'that you didn't have to do that seven times. And plenty of women consider nine times necessary.'

'I can't imagine doing this every month.'

'Well, if we were really strictly Orthodox you'd do it. I used to, when I was first married.' She paused. 'It used to be very sweet, being together after the *mikvah*, after keeping apart for nearly two weeks. Like a reunion.' She wiped her cheek with the back of a hand.

'Oh, well, let's get you dry.'

Tying on her headscarf over damp hair, Sadie watched her mother with a sudden rush of tenderness for her tired face and roughened hands. As they stepped out into the dark street she slipped her arm through her mother's, and the two women fell into step.

On the morning of the wedding Sadie awoke to ice-flowers on the inside of her window. She luxuriated for a while in the warmth of the bed, thinking that this was the last time that she would do so as a single girl. Would she and Asher, she wondered, share a bed as her parents had done? Or would they have their own rooms like Mark and Zipporah? It seemed odd that they had not had time to discuss such things, but there was no hurry. Asher said his father would arrange a house for them when he returned, and until then they were to live in Portland Place with his parents. But before that, she would see Europe. And with Asher beside her . . .

The happiness she felt was beyond words. She had never thought her life would hold anything to touch the future she now saw. She had love, security, she would travel, live in a beautiful home – everything was like a child's storybook. She wanted to sing out loud, but the sleeping presence of Flora in the bed beside hers restrained her. And at that thought she grew suddenly sober, for she loved her sister and Flora had nothing. Still – she cheered herself quickly – she would be able to help her, have her to stay. Then she saw that Flora was not asleep and that her eyes were red and swollen from her silent weeping.

Four hours later Sadie was sitting in the front room in her creamy wedding dress, her hair coiled in mahogany coloured loops around her head beneath the veil. She sat on a chair covered with a white sheet, her feet on a white pillow. 'It's a sign of purity,' Sophie had said, arranging the train and giving her a sharp look. The neighbourhood women clustered in to wish her luck, her former school-friends kissed her and pushed gifts into her hands.

Uncle Mark had driven down so that the de Dion could take her and Sophie to the synagogue. They were late arriving, and the motor seemed to take forever negotiating the landscape of her childhood, the meagre streets, the stunted trees. Finally they reached the Cheetham Hill Road, thronged with factory girls in their lunch-hour, who gazed with undisguised envy at the luxurious vehicle and its romantic passenger.

When they drew up outside the Great Synagogue all the guests had already entered. The three of them hurried up the flight of steps between the polished stone pillars of the ornate, Italianate building, so incongruous in its drab surroundings.

Inside, Sadie was surrounded by a small crowd of women: her sisters – Miriam had come specially from Bristol – aunts, cousins who smiled and chattered softly at her, as hands pulled her dress straight and smoothed her train and veil. Then they all went through the double doors into the synagogue. The usher gestured towards Sophie, who nodded. She kissed Sadie, twitched the train straight, and then took her place with Uncle Mark behind the girl. Uncle Mark adjusted his top hat, pulled his prayer-shawl more firmly around his shoulders and said under his breath, 'We who are about to die salute you.'

So that when the doors were opened for them to enter Sadie stood there with a wide smile on her face. The synagogue was almost silent as they entered, except for the soft, resonant buzz of men quietly praying, and their footsteps were muffled on dark Persian carpets. The centre of the room was dominated by a dais five steps high, flanked by two pedestals bearing bronze candelabra. And in their light gleamed the dark Spanish mahogany of the Ark, the square and sacred centre of the synagogue, holder of the parchment scrolls of the Law. Below it waited the rabbi in his long dark garments and four cornered hat, the white and black fringe of his prayer shawl, the *talis*, reaching his feet.

Sadie glanced up: Miriam and Flora were at the front of the Ladies' Gallery with Miriam's children, and around

106

them were many faces from her childhood. Leonie was there too, dramatic in a black hat. Who else, Sadie asked herself in amusement, would wear black to a wedding?

Mark's hand under her elbow brought her back to the present. They had almost reached the white silk marriage canopy, the *chuppa*, which swayed slightly, its long fringes shivering, as the four young men supporting its wooden poles took the weight.

Beneath it waited Asher.

He turned, a mysterious figure in the *tallis* she had given him as her wedding gift, to see her face. They had not seen each other for nearly two weeks and for a moment she faltered: he seemed suddenly a near stranger to whom she must go. Then she was beside him and they regarded each other for an endless moment. He took her hand in his own. It was shaking, she felt with relief, and its warmth reassured her. The rabbi beckoned Sophie forward under the *chuppa*. She took Sadie's hand and led her three times around Asher, in three repetitions of a single phrase, 'And I will betroth thee unto me. And I will betroth thee unto me. And I will betroth thee unto me.'

The rabbi began to read the *Ketubah*, the marriage contract, in Hebrew. Sadie and Asher knew that it spelled out their obligations to each other, and that it would become Sadie's property, her surety – she smiled at the thought – against Asher's violation of her rights. When they had both signed it, the rabbi gestured to Asher. Very carefully he took her veil, and brought it down to cover her face, in symbolic recognition that now she was his alone, and would never again be gazed upon by any man other than himself. As it fell over her eyes she shivered.

Then the rabbi took a chased silver goblet and made a blessing. He sipped and then handed the goblet to Sophie, who lifted Sadie's veil and held the wine to her lips. It was sweet and syrupy, not like wine at all, she thought, but some strange magic cordial. She glanced at Asher, who was

107

concentrating with such intensity that he did not see her movement: she watched with tenderness as he shakily lifted the goblet to his lips.

Sadie and Asher moved forward, and Asher took the proffered ring. He made his vows to her in a firm voice, following the rabbi's Hebrew. Sadie was silent, as custom demanded. She plighted her troth only with her eyes and her heart. Asher slid the ring gently on to her first finger, and then on to the fourth.

'Thou art consecrated to me,' he intoned, 'according to the law of Moses and Israel.'

There were more sips of wine. The climax of the wedding was approaching, and Sadie could feel the rustle of anticipation amongst the guests. A wine glass was placed at Asher's feet, wrapped in a white napkin, and the rabbi nodded. Asher stamped hard, and smashed the glass into fragments. A burst of joy went up from the synagogue: '*Mazel Tov! Mazel Tov!*'

They were married.

Tentatively, Asher placed his cool lips on her own. They tasted of the wine. All she could hear was the rich voice of the cantor filling the synagogue with the longing words of his elegaic chant: 'If I forget thee, O Jerusalem, let my right hand forget her cunning. Let my tongue cleave to the roof of my mouth if I remember thee not. If I set not Jerusalem above my chiefest joy . . .'

And now, she thought exultantly, as she moved forward on Asher's arm, *and now everything can begin*.

Chapter Nine

The night of the wedding was spent in one of the vast bedrooms of the Midland Hotel, Manchester. But, as Sadie told Leonie afterwards, her wedding night really took place in Compartment No 5, Voiture 7, of the Orient Express.

The new Mr and Mrs Raphael had left Cheetham Hill in a shower of rice thrown by the wedding guests.

'If that doesn't ensure your fertility,' Uncle Mark had drily observed to Sadie, brushing the remaining particles from her shoulders, 'then nothing will.'

She had been cried over, she thought, by everyone she had ever known, and she felt, as she told Asher, 'as though Ma had put me through the mangle.'

In the haven of their hotel room they had been debating what to order when a discreet knock at the door had brought a waiter with chicken sandwiches and champagne, 'with the compliments of Mr and Mrs Raphael, sir.'

'Having one's parents in the same hotel,' Asher had mused, pouring the last of the champagne, 'does make one feel somewhat inhibited in . . . certain matters.'

'And having one's uncle and aunt here as well,' Sadie teased, 'makes one feel even more so.'

'Well, I suppose it could be worse. According to ancient Chasidic custom,' Asher took out one of his little black cigars and lit it carefully, raising his eyebrows to her for permission, 'according to *that*, we would have to be visited by our relatives in the morning to prove that, um, to prove that we have actually . . .'

'Asher, you're embarrassing me, and I'm sure you're making it up.' Sadie was pink and laughing.

'It's all right. I'm embarrassing myself, too. Look, I'll go for a short walk and finish this cigar, and you get into bed.'

When he returned fifteen minutes later she was almost asleep from the accumulated excitement of the day and the unaccustomed champagne. When he got into bed beside her, beneath the thick eiderdown, he took her hand and whispered, 'Sleep well.'

She gave him a grateful smile and slept.

Next day they left for London and went straight to Victoria.

Their luggage, already packed and – in Sadie's case, largely bought for her by Zipporah – was brought by the Raphaels' driver. They were in excellent time for the boat-train, Moritz Raphael remarked with satisfaction, consulting his gold fob watch on the platform. Rose, who had disappeared, returned with *Punch* for Asher, an *Illustrated London News* and the *Tatler* for Sadie.

'And this is for you, my dear,' she added, and pinned on Sadie's shoulder a bunch of tiny bronze orchids.

'Have a wonderful journey,' Mark shouted, and Zipporah put her handkerchief to her eyes in the first really emotional gesture Sadie had ever seen her make.

After successfully negotiating the Dover–Calais crossing ('If you can do this in November, my love, without being seasick, I shall be able to take you anywhere,' Asher had said with proprietorial pride), they had made the train journey to Paris. A demonic hansom cab had raced them to the Gare de l'Est with only minutes to spare, and Asher's waving handful of francs had brought porters rushing up. He and Sadie hurried along in their wake to the main platform, where the royal blue coaches of the Orient Express were marked in gold along the full length of the coaches 'Compagnie Internationale des Wagons-Lits et des Grands Express Européens'. Most of the coaches were already in semi-darkness, but the lights gleamed out invitingly from the pink and gold furnished dining-car.

A porter consulted their tickets and stopped to open a door. He piled in their cabin-baggage – the big trunks were in the luggage van – and the Chef du Train, gloved and immaculate in a blue uniform, led them to their wagon-lit. He smiled at Sadie.

'It is just seven o'clock, Madame. One minute only to go.'

A stentorian voice on the platform called, *'En voiture, s'il vous plait!'*

Doors banged, there were shouts, a child cried and the Orient Express gathered momentum as it pulled out into the Paris suburbs.

Sadie sank back against the red velvet seat and leant her head on an antimacassar of Brussels lace.

'How on earth did you organize all this?' There was undisguised admiration in her voice. 'It must have taken days of planning – it really feels like an expedition.'

'Merely one of my many talents.' Asher's self-deprecating smile broadened. 'I simply used my superb brain and brought it to bear upon *Bradshaw's Continental Railway Steam Travel and General Guide.* I then consulted the majordomo at the Ritz, who is infallible, and here we are.'

'Well, I think you're wonderful.'

'Now that, my love, is just what a husband needs to hear. But isn't it all splendid?' He gestured round at the red-lacquered walls, the thick blue rugs covering the narrow berths, and the lush damask curtains at the windows. Hand-cut glass separated their sleeping compartment from the outside aisle, and all the fittings were of solid oak and mahogany. Sadie sighed in contentment.

'It's like a furnished nest. I'd like to live in here for ever.'

Asher moved forward to embrace her. Just at that moment, the Wagons-Lits attendant passed their door.

'Messieurs les voyageurs, dîner est servi.'

They looked at each other and Asher made a resigned face.

'Now I'm afraid this is the only acceptable interruption. You are about to sample one of life's pleasures – to dine on

111

the Orient Express is a gastronomic delight not to be foregone.'

He drew his hand lightly over her hair.

'We'll have to leave your nest, though. But I promise to bring you back before midnight, in case you decide to vanish like a fairy.'

'I don't think,' she answered softly, her face against his chest, 'I don't think I'm going to vanish just yet.'

They walked through the heavily carpeted corridors to the dining-car. Seated at the softly lit table, the napery and silver gleaming, Sadie found it hard to think they were moving: the water in the carafe was barely tilted by the motion of the train. The meal was superb and as they finished their *gigot mouton bretanne* the chef, a black-bearded Burgundian in a vast white hat, came out of his hot kitchen to drink a glass of brandy with two men at an adjoining table.

Asher and Sadie lingered over their meal, their coffee and liqueurs, prolonging the time spent in the company of the others, deliberately postponing the moment when they would be alone. They looked at each other with longing, separated by the narrow table, and touched each other's fingertips on the snowy cloth.

When finally they rose to leave Sadie found she had drunk enough wine to make her step uncertain: Asher had to propel her out into the corridor. She was so tipsy, he told her affectionately, that she needed some fresh air. They went on to the open platform at the end of the wagon-lit. She gasped as the cold air hit her, and Asher hugged her to him. After a moment they turned and went back to their compartment.

Asher undid his watch and hung it carefully on the brass hook provided for it beside his berth. He removed first his shoes, then his cuff-links, and stretched out on the bed.

'Getting married,' he observed, his arm over his eyes, 'is undoubtedly the most exhausting occupation ever invented.'

112

'Be grateful, then, that you don't need to do it again tomorrow.'

'Tomorrow,' he replied, and now he was looking at her, 'is a long way off.'

She was standing before the glass, taking off her hat and watching his reflection. Hurriedly she said, 'I'll be back in a moment.'

She grabbed her toilet case and escaped into the corridor. On her way back she stopped, looking out of the window at the flat French fields rimed with silver from the cold and the sudden glow from the door of a small country station as they steamed past. Her breath frosted against the glass and she relished the pleasure of being warm inside the snug shell of the train. As she returned to her compartment she passed the conductor seated at his desk at the end of the coach. A stove burned at his feet, and above his head a mirror reflected the doors of the compartments in his charge.

'*Bon soir*, Madame. Sleep well.'

Asher had taken off his shirt and wore a thin silk dressing-gown. He watched as she moved round the confined space, tidying her clothes, putting her jacket on a quilted hanger. When she began to fumble in her valise he sat up and held out his hand.

'Haven't you done enough housekeeping for one evening?'

His voice mocked her, but his eyes did not. She stopped uncertain what to do, and he reached out and took the jar she was holding and put it in a drawer

'Now,' he said, 'what shall we talk about?'

'We could discuss our travel itinerary?'

'So we could,' he replied, and his breath now was warm against her neck. 'So we could. But perhaps after all we've talked enough.'

They kissed properly for the first time, moving closer and closer until they were pressed against each other and Sadie could feel the length of his body against hers in an embrace which emptied her mind of all thought. She knew only that he must not stop. He leant away a little, and she heard his breathing as very gently he concentrated on undoing the tiny mother-of-pearl buttons at the top of her blouse. She shut her eyes as his fingers moved down fumbling carefully with the little corded loops of the buttonholes, until he reached her breasts. Her breath caught and rasped in her throat as he pushed aside the lace of her petticoat and smoothed his hand over her skin, over and over, in a trance of desire. His arm around her, he moved back a pace until he was sitting on the narrow berth holding her to him. A sudden lurch as the carriage ran over a point caught her off balance so that she half-fell against him, and his face was pressed against her breast. 'You smell like green flowers,' he said softly, 'so young and clean and tender. Sadie, Sadie, hold me now . . .'

She freed her arms and pulled the blouse off her shoulders and dropped it on the floor. She slid the straps of her petticoat down and unbuttoned her skirt.

'Wait,' she said, 'wait just one moment more.' She started to undo the many little hooks of her corsets until Asher pushed aside her hands and did it for her, very slowly, so that she shivered with anticipation. 'It's like undoing a delicious present,' he whispered, and as he finished the garment parted and fell open. 'Oh, my God, Sadie, my love . . .'

She leant down to him and pulled open the sash of his dressing-gown and he shrugged it off. She slipped down beside him on the berth, and as he turned and half-rose to pull her beneath him, she reached out with her free hand and slid shut the bolt on the cabin door.

The next few days became, for Sadie and Asher, like the telling of a fairy-tale. The excitement of the journey, the cities through which they passed – Strasbourg, Munich, Linz – the countryside they saw through their windows as

114

the train swallowed the miles of Alsace, Wurtemberg, passed over the narrow Danube – everything paled against the over-riding delight they found in each other.

Sadie went to Asher for the first time in an innocence so total that she had no words with which to describe the parts of her body. He, equally innocent in practice, had taken chorus girls out to dinner – always with a group of friends – and the only naked women he had ever seen had been in paintings. His rapture over her was complete. At night their daytime roles were reversed, and his gentle, slightly paternal teasing gave way to dependence he had not known before. Their initial mutual incompetence did not matter to either of them: rather, it increased their ardour for each other.

'We'll get even better at this soon,' Asher murmured into her ear, as she pillowed his head on her breast in an embrace they had discovered pleased them both.

'I know. Won't it be lovely?' she sleepily replied.

And she held him to her in the sudden fierce joy of possession.

They left the train at Vienna, to visit Asher's family.

'We'll spend a couple of weeks at the Sacher Hotel,' Asher told Sadie as they drove towards the Opera, 'and meet hundreds of relatives, most of them speak some sort of English, and we'll go to Lobmeyr and buy ourselves some crystal.'

For two weeks they relished the ornate and opulent city. Asher took her to Josefstädterstrasse and they walked along the narrow pavements, peering into the enticing windows of the minute and bustling shops, until just beyond the Piaristengasse they came to the confectioner's shop started by his grandfather, and which the Raphaels still owned. And when they went in Uncle Heinrich in his tall white hat squeezed himself out from behind the counter to embrace them both, and press upon Sadie a box of *Mehlspeise*.

'Sweet pastries,' whispered Asher. 'His are the best in the city.'

They went to Gerngross, the magnificent new department store on Mariahilferstrasse and Sadie marvelled at its size and bought a pair of silk stockings. They journeyed to the north of the city on the far side of the Danube Canal and wandered up the Taborstrasse, visiting the workshops where they watched women painting the delicate Augarten porcelain. They spent an evening at the Theater an der Wien, where busts of the composers stared down upon the gold-leafed galleries, and heard the *Merry Widow*, then stood in the cold at the *Würstelstand* and ate hot sausages.

The old Raphaels exclaimed in delight over the young couple, praising Sadie's eyes and Asher's English suits in German which she could not understand and Yiddish where she did very little better. The couple were toasted in neat Schnapps and cigars were stuffed into Asher's top pocket. One afternoon the cousins, rotund men with comfortably creased faces, swept Asher off with them 'zum Weihburggasse,' they said, with knowing winks. Meanwhile the women took Sadie to a coffee house full of brass and glass and polished cabinets and taught her how to order the many varieties: she ended up with *Einspanner*, a tall glass filled with hot mocha coffee and whipped cream. 'And now,' they said firmly, 'the cakes. *Marillenknödel* or *Milchrahmstrudel*? *Palatsshinken* or *Topfenknödel* with *Zwetschkenröster*?'

Sadie capitulated and promised herself to do up her corsets less tightly. 'I feel like a stuffed goose,' she confided to Asher, when finally they were recovering in one of the Sacher's reception rooms, among the paintings and statues. Asher, pink-faced and laughing, was telling her about his enforced visit to Kaiserbründl. 'So then,' he was saying, 'you patter over freezing marble floors to the hot air baths, from which you're only released to sit in a freezing hip-bath. And have an obligatory swim in this great green

116

rectangular pool – and then they started wondering what they'd be having for dinner!'

Just then a short man in a heavily embroidered waistcoat paused on the staircase, and stared hard at Asher. He hurried over. 'My dear Mr Raphael, isn't it? It's been a very long time . . . and I hear you have married . . . *Enchanté*, Madame.' He bent over Sadie's hand. Asher, who looked a shade anxious, chatted briefly, and the man left. Next evening, after they had dined, Asher excused himself for a short walk. When finally he returned to their room Sadie had given up waiting for him and started to get ready for bed.

'I was worried,' she objected, cross and concerned.

'I'm sorry, it was rude of me. But I bumped into Clements again, and we had a brandy, and he suggested a game of cards. I thought it'd only take twenty minutes,' he yawned, 'but it went on longer than that.'

'I didn't know you played cards.' Sadie was vigorously brushing her teeth. She dipped her brush in the little pot of cherry tooth powder and looked at him in the mirror.

'Mmmm. Well, yes, sometimes, you know, a little flutter. A fellow needs a bit of relaxation, don't you think?'

She turned to survey him, collapsed in a pink velvet armchair.

'Any more relaxation, my love,' she observed, 'and you'd be unconscious.'

'Now don't be hard on me, Sadie,' he mock-pleaded with her. 'You know the duties of a husband are beginning to weigh very heavily upon me . . . don't!' He ducked as she pretended that his silver topped cane was a sword, and feigned a thrust at him.

'I surrender! I am your slave! Do with me what you will.'

'Undo my boots,' she ordered.

'Willingly.'

He dropped to his knees and she gave him the little buttonhook. Starting at the top he painstakingly undid each of the round buttons on her glace kid boots. When he reached the ankle, he pulled the first boot off, and threw it behind him. He did the same with the other, and then started to rub her feet in their cashmere stockings. His hands pressed upwards, moulding and caressing under her petticoat, until her trembling legs would no longer support her and they collapsed together on to the carpet.

'Dear Mrs Raphael,' he breathed into her hair. 'I do believe I'm going to pleasure you on the floor of this illustrious hotel.'

'Wouldn't we be more comfortable in their equally illustrious bed?'

'Maybe so, but I don't think,' he struggled with his own buttons, 'I don't think I've time to get you there.'

She helped him undo his trousers, and pushed his braces off his shoulders. He took her hand and guided it down and held it to the front of his body. She gasped as he hardened and grew under her smoothing fingers, and he groaned voluptuously as she caressed him.

'Quick,' he breathed, 'be quick. I can't wait.' He rolled over so that he was heavy above her, his weight pressing her shoulders painfully against the floor. He pushed the skirt of her petticoat out of his way, and she guided his body to her own.

'Is it all right, is this all right?' he whispered.

'Yes, yes, come on, come in,' she replied softly, and he pressed gently and then more strongly against her, and she opened so that he sank into her. She melted for him and no longer felt her shoulders against the floor as he moved above her. There was nothing but the dark and secret voyaging of him inside her, so that she was pinioned and transfixed by his ever-deepening thrusts. She wrapped her arms around his head, twined her legs about his back, pressing him deeper into herself. Her feelings gathered with such intensity that she thought they must be visible: great circles spiralling inward to a peak. And then suddenly fragmenting, eddying away, leaving her undulating, lost in sensation, shivering with receding pleasure. Asher felt her inward involuntary movements like soft reverberations of a distant sea, exquisite hidden touches on his body that irresistibly impelled him to his own climax. They gathered each other more closely, and lay in an accomplished silence.

Sadie was the first to move: she covered his face with a flurry of grateful kisses.

'Now,' she murmured, 'really, we would be more comfortable in bed.'

'It's all very well for you,' he grumbled, his face buried in the curve of her arm. 'We've taken your boots off. Mine, I'll have you know, are still on. The *zimmer mädchen* will definitely not be amused by boot polish on the bedsheets.'

'Very well then.' She reached up and pulled the fluffy quilt off the bed. She tucked it round Asher's shoulders, and resumed their embrace. 'We'll just stay here.'

He opened one eye and looked at her sleepily.

'That's the trouble with you Mancunians,' he said, 'always thinking of your creature comforts.'

After Vienna they made their way in leisurely fashion to Italy, to Lake Garda and the Victoria Hotel. Asher showed her the palace on Isola Bella, and the white peacocks. They idled their way around the still winter lakes and Sadie, muffled to the ears in fur, gazed as though she could never see enough.

Then they went to Brussels, for Asher announced that they were to buy furniture there. By the time it reached England, they would be ready to put it in a house. This was the first Sadie had heard of furniture.

'But can we afford it?' she asked nervously. 'You know I haven't any money?'

'Of course I know, you goose. But Papa has plenty, and to what better use could he put it? Besides, it's his idea: he insists on Brussels, because that's where he and Mama bought the furniture when they moved to Regents Park: he says it's the best in the world.'

And so they travelled to Brussels, and wandered around the shops gleaming in the grey streets. They bought objects both desirable and expensive: Sadie shuddered at the cost, but Asher appeared not to notice. They went to Gustave Polspoel, and chose a magnificent Louis XVI *buffet de salon*. They visited Van de Broeck *fils* and Asher insisted on purchasing four gilded looking glasses.

'So you can see how pretty you are.'

For curtain materials they went to Elise Louis et Soeurs, a decorous salon where three urbane sisters helped them choose heavily embossed material: when measurements were available, details would be sent to the sisters and the curtains would be made up for them.

When they arrived back in London they went to stay at Portland Place. Sadie felt a pang of trepidation as she walked up the steps. The house, even after the buildings she had just seen in Europe, still managed to awe her: the Louis XV furniture and the Coromandel screens, the great Italian woodcuts in the hallway, the prints and drawings which covered the walls from top to bottom of the staircases. The dining room was dominated by Walter Crane and Legros, the drawing rooms by Turner and Blake.

In the midst of all this pictorial magnificence, almost anyone but the Raphaels might have paled into insignificance. Moritz loved his pictures, venerating the skill he so admired but did not possess. But he remained a pragmatist about them, and paintings would disappear from his walls to be replaced from the gallery whenever he made what he called a 'social sale'. Rose, on the other hand, was totally unimpressed by their merits, seeing them more in terms of security than art. 'So if things get bad,' she was fond of saying, 'we can always realize them.' Things never had got bad, and there seemed little likelihood that they would. Rather, they became progressively better. But the anxious girl from Spital Square in the East End still lingered somewhere behind the trim and confident exterior, the glossy bun of discreetly greying hair, the well-upholstered figure in its heavy dark silks: Rose could not quite believe her good fortune.

She and Moritz welcomed the travellers effusively.

'Come in, come in, it's chilly,' Rose said, in total defiance of the great fire in the hallway. 'Keep your wrap on till you warm up.'

She kissed them both, and linked her arm with Asher's. 'And how's my boy?' she asked fondly. Asher, who was used to this, smiled and made some non-committal reply; when his mother led them into the drawing room, he gave Sadie a reassuring wink.

For the next two hours, Rose and Moritz questioned them about the honeymoon, exclaiming delightedly over the stories about the Viennese cousins. Moritz seized on the little marzipan cakes they had brought back until admonished by Rose.

'Your dinner, you'll ruin yourself!'

Finally Rose took Sadie upstairs.

'Now I know this won't suit you for long,' she said, plumping up cushions as she showed Sadie their room. 'You need a home of your own now. But we'll do our best to see that you're comfortable, and we'll start finding you a house tomorrow.'

She was a woman of her word. By the end of the week they had a shortlist, and finally settled on a narrow town house in St John's Wood with many-paned Georgian windows set in a white façade. Asher and Sadie took Moritz to see it, and he declared himself delighted and clapped Asher on the back.

'Now, my boy, you really have responsibilities. I think it's high time I upped your salary to meet your new position.'

'Thank you very much, but you don't have to. You're

doing enough as it is buying us the house.'

'Nonsense. You'll have to work harder for it, that's all.'

Sadie spent much of the next few months in her empty house, watching decorators working, and worrying about minute details, which she would recount meticulously to Asher in the evenings.

He praised and laughed at her, and promised that all would be well if only she would stop taking it all so seriously and enjoy it.

'No, I can't,' she replied, crossly. 'I can't not worry. I'm making a home for you, it's a serious business.'

She found to her pleasure that they needed few carpets. The floors would polish and a few rugs suffice. For the main rooms they chose elaborately flowered wallpapers designed by William Morris, which sent Sadie into raptures of delight. The little morning room, which was to be hers, they painted in a deep soft red, the same colour as the pleated silk fronts of the two cabinets which were Lena's wedding present. The drawing room with its antique Turkey carpet – a gift from Mark and Zipporah – looked out on to a small verandah which they had glassed in to hold several *jardinières* of plants. Before the carved wood of the fireplace stood two great Chinese urns, also full of plants, and Sadie covered the two sofas with lace cushions. The lampshades she painted herself, copying watercolour sketches Asher had encouraged her to make of the Italian Lakes.

Sadie was aghast at the amount still to do when she thought everything finished. Asher suddenly decided they had to have a patent shower bath, and insisted that they get roller blinds for every window in the house. There were riding lamps for the front door. An ironing board was purchased – it cost five shillings, to Sadie's horror – and a collection of flat-irons. They needed tea pots and jugs, blankets and sheets. And when all was surely complete, they added a case of firelighters, half a dozen bottles each

122

of port and sherry. When he had purchased three dozen locks to protect all their acquisitions, and the firm of F. J. Thelwell had been engaged for the yearly winding of clocks at a cost of £1/10 shillings, Asher declared himself satisfied and they moved in.

Sadie spent hours rearranging the furniture, shoving chairs around, posing and reposing occasional tables. 'I can just see you playing with your doll's house,' teased Asher. 'Would you like me to sit so,' he draped himself across the sofa, one leg dangling, 'or so,' and he sprang up to prop an elbow on the mantelshelf.

'Either way, just so long as you don't move until you've been kissed.' Sadie, listening to his heart as she leant against him, thought, *Time could stand still.*

This, she was sure, was perfection.

Chapter Ten

Their lives on Ordnance Hill soon assumed a pleasant pattern. If they were not rich, they lived as though they were. They employed a cook, and a tweeny for the rough. They now had a motor of their own, a Riley, a dashing vehicle which Asher insisted on driving at forty miles an hour. The gardener had painstakingly learnt to drive it, for Sadie's use.

Rose had offered to let them have one of her domestic staff, but Sadie decided to arrange things herself. She duly went to the Employment Exchange, and during the following week five women arrived for interview. The first four were too near her own age, she felt, to know much more about house management than she did. The fifth, a widow, was Lancashire born, which immediately endeared her to Sadie. She was a broad, stocky woman wearing a sensible black flat hat. She sat, her wide hands folded on her capacious handbag, and answered Sadie's uncertain questions. Yes, she had been in service for the last ten years, since her husband died. They had kept a grocery shop for which she had done all the cooking: they specialized in selling savoury pies. Yes, she liked to do her own shopping, insisted upon it. Her sister worked nearby, she knew the area and would be happy to live in. Sadie took her upstairs and showed her the bedroom that had been prepared for the cook, with its cotton curtains and counterpane, the plain table and wooden towel-horse. Mrs Evans nodded with satisfaction.

'This would do me very well, Madam. Would it be agreeable to you if I brought my own things?'

'Of course. There isn't much here. Whatever you like.'

'There's not a great deal. Just a couple of easy chairs and

124

my bits of ornaments.'

'Well, Mrs Evans, and I forgot to ask, is the money agreeable to you?'

'Oh yes, thank you. Twelve shillings a week, they said at the Exchange.'

'That's right.'

'Well, Madam,' Mrs Evans gave Sadie a cheerful smile. 'I hope then that I will suit?'

'Yes, Mrs Evans, I think we'll suit very well.'

Within two months, Annie Evans had become indispensable. She was used to looking after large families, and relished the evenings when Sadie and Asher entertained and she could provide sirloin of beef and boiled salmon, great racks of lamb garnished with paper frills and elaborate trifles. Gradually, she took over the role of housekeeper. Without making Sadie feel inexperienced, she tactfully suggested changes and innovations to improve the running of the house. She boiled the washing in the copper with her own bluebags and found a superior butcher. She bullied the shopkeepers into sending only their best by firmly returning inferior items. When the knife grinder came, she watched him with an eagle eye, and the step girl who whitened the stone steps once a week for sixpence worked harder for Annie than for anyone else in the road.

Sadie, who by now had very little to do, was seized upon by Zipporah and coerced – without too much trouble – into resuming the round of shopping and teas, private views and gossip, that she had started before her marriage. Only now Sadie would go home and recount to Asher the things she had seen and heard. Encouraged by his laughter she began to develop a small gift for mimicry: without being cruel, she found she could be genuinely funny about idiosyncrasies of looks and conversation. Asher also urged her to buy items which appealed to her. He found she had an eye for the unusual; on one occasion she brought home a picture made from carved ivory on black velvet that Moritz eyed covetously whenever he visited.

Sadie was by nature a hoarder and a magpie, and soon every available surface was cluttered with the harvest of hours spent poking around in shabby shops in Camden and Holloway: an intricately carved and beaded set of bobbins for lace making, a family of minuscule dolls, a vase of red and white barley sugar glass, a Georgian travelling clock which seemed irreparable until she found a watch mender in Clerkenwell who restored even its silvery chime.

She seemed to have everything. When she stopped to consider – which she rarely did – it almost frightened her that the fates could be so generous. From day to day she was living with a zest and enjoyment that she had not displayed before. Everything delighted her, she responded to everyone with vivacity. The most boring conversationalist found he sparkled when he talked to her, and the young Raphaels' soirées attracted more and more people.

Sadie matured during these first four years of her marriage. She acquired a distinctive style of her own, brought about by her increasing self-confidence. By the time she was twenty her youthful gaucheness had been superseded by a new found physical grace, as though love informed her every movement.

As Sadie's style developed, so did her allure. Asher, watching her with satisfaction, thought that it had nothing to do with classic good looks, which hers certainly were not. Her features were too big, too irregular for beauty. It was a combination of her now intriguing appearance, her developing personality, and an odd charm that was entirely her own. She held the eye, she caught the imagination. It was an elusive, pervasive quality. It clung around her like a faint scent.

When Sadie was twenty-one, Asher took her to Paris for a week.

'This isn't just for pleasure,' he warned her. 'We're going to transform you.'

126

'What do you mean?' She put a defensive hand up to her hair. 'What's wrong with me?'

'Nothing. But I've always had a fancy to gild a lily, and you know I like choosing clothes for you.'

The following day they drove to the Faubourg Saint-Honoré, and turned into the Avenue d'Atin. They stopped at a great wrought iron gate, screening a house in spacious gardens.

'We're going to see the Sultan,' Asher explained, helping her down. Sadie said, 'I'm not going another step until you explain. It sounds far too dangerous.'

Asher put his hand on his heart. 'Don't you trust me yet?'

'No.'

'Come on, it's your birthday surprise.'

Inside, the house was decorated in Directoire style, except that it was a brilliant blue-pink throughout – walls, chair coverings, even the carpet. An elegant black-clad woman conducted them to a door. As she knocked and pushed it open a loud voice reached them: a man was shouting in French, gesticulating wildly. 'That's not it, you fool. That's not it at all. *This* is what I wanted,' and he seized an iris from a bowl on a table, scattering blossoms on the polished wood. 'Look, cretin, *this* is the colour.' He prodded the deep blue flower at the chest of the man he was addressing. The man, clutching it, nodding bemused, headed for the door, not seeing Sadie and Asher until he bumped into them.

'And don't come back till you've got it,' roared his tormentor. As soon as the door had closed behind him, the loud-voiced man hurried towards them, transformed into a genial, sophisticated figure.

'Sadie, this is Monsieur Paul Poiret, arguably the greatest couturier in France.'

'Forgive me, Madame, Monsieur, my bad temper is legendary but,' he shrugged, 'when one is surrounded by idiots, then what is to be done?'

127

He looked at Sadie with interest. Equally interested, she took in a shortish, plump man, with protuberant eyes and a luxurious full beard. His skin was swarthy, and to offset his almost Eastern appearance he wore a brilliantly coloured brocade jacket.

'So, Madame, you would like me to dress you, yes?'

Taken aback, Sadie, stammered, 'I don't know . . .'

Swiftly Asher said, 'Yes, please, Maestro.'

'You understand then that I am to have a free rein to choose for you, Madame?' He raised an eyebrow at her. Completely intimidated, she nodded silently, glancing at Asher for confirmation.

'Very well. Very well.' The couturier walked round her meditatively, arms folded, head sunk in thought, suddenly recollected himself, and offered them both a seat. Then he picked up a large pad and sketched rapidly upon it, humming to himself. Once he stopped to ask, 'It is to be an evening dress, that is right?'

Asher nodded.

'And I have in mind,' Monsieur Poiret went on, 'something to make you look extraordinary. This,' he gestured dismissively at the costume she was wearing, 'this does nothing for you. It is very, very boring.'

Sadie, who was wearing her best outfit of lavender blue gaberdine, said with some asperity, 'It is very pretty.'

'Yes, Madame.' He shrugged. 'It is, as you say, pretty. But I do not think you want to look *pretty*.' He invested the word with deep scorn.

'Women today put themselves into drab, dreary colours. Insipid blues, that terrible mauve – so difficult to wear – and that horrible colour of the field, what do you call it, maize? And I cannot tell you how much I loathe *eau-de-nil*.'

Sadie, who possessed garments in all of these colours, opened her mouth to protest when he stopped her with a gesture.

'*Eau de-nil*, Madame, is a colour best left to the Nile itself. Now for you,' he reached into a drawer of the table, and took out a handful of fabrics, 'for you, we will find something different.'

He held them out to her; and she took them with some apprehension. They were scarlet and green and orange. There was the brilliant blue-pink of the walls, and deep royal blue – vibrant colours it had never occurred to her to wear.

'Now this would, I think, be perfect.'

He fished out a piece of velvet in glowing violet and folded it against her skin.

'Yes, I think so. This will make you look, Madame, like a bird of paradise.' He glanced at her questioningly.

'It *is* beautiful.'

'As to design,' he continued, 'I will create something like this.'

He held out his pad, with a dress roughly outlined upon it. She and Asher could see that it had a high waist and a deep square neckline.

'If you will return in two days I will have a *toile* ready for fitting.'

On their arrival, Sadie was hurried off to a fitting room where three young women pinned gauzy material around her. When they had finished Poiret arrived and shook his head, and muttered beneath his breath, replacing the pins, tightening here, gathering there. Eventually he stood back.

'For this dress, Madame, it is necessary for you to stand differently.'

Sadie looked puzzled. 'I don't think I understand you.'

'Women, Madame, are conditioned by their corsets. They stand so, with the *poitrine* forward, and the *derrière* back.' He pouted his chest and stuck out his bottom, like a pigeon, and Sadie started to laugh.

'Yes, yes it is, I just hadn't thought of it quite like that.'

'But this dress, Madame, is a romantic garment, and you must hold yourself so,' he put his hands on her waist, tilting her torso slightly backwards, so that her shoulders went back.

'And the stomach forward, like this, like the medieval ladies. Do you see?'

In the mirror, Sadie saw what he meant. 'But won't I look peculiar?'

He shrugged. 'You will look, Madame, like the avant-garde. In a year or two, everyone will be doing the same.'

'Now Madame, before you dress I have a garment I should like you to try. It was designed not for you, but for a lady I have dressed for many years. She decided it was not for her – no, I decided it was not. I thought perhaps it might appeal to you.' He snapped his fingers, and a fitter brought in a dress on a hanger.

'It looks very – naked,' Sadie said nervously.

'Ah yes, it is not a garment of concealment, I think. But then, it was not designed with concealment in mind.' He smiled, teeth very white against his beard. 'I must confess to you, Madame Raphael, that the lady is a – shall we say, a professional beauty? Of perfect taste, you understand, but no longer as young as she was.' He sighed.

'Do you know Nice, Madame?'

Surprised by the question, Sadie shook her head.

'You must go there. When you do, go to the Carlton Hotel. There are twin cupolas on the roof, perfectly shaped. They were modelled on the lady's breasts.'

While he talked, he was adjusting the dress, shortening the shoulder straps, pinning up the hem. 'So.'

Sadie looked at herself silently, and a stranger watched her from the glass.

The dress was matt black, a material she did not know, heavy and silky, hanging in sculptured folds. The skirt was plain, the bodice cut wide and low, supported only on the narrow jewelled bands.

Poiret said, 'Perhaps you should show your husband?'

'I think I'd better!'

Sadie moved out of the fitting room to where Asher was reading *France-Soir*. He lowered the paper, and gazed at her over the top.

'You look – amazing.'

'I feel amazing. I couldn't possibly wear it, though, could I?'

'Of course you could. Is it for you?'

'M Poiret says it was for a "professional beauty", in his own words.'

'Well, I must confess it does seem the sort of thing a *poule de luxe* might wear.'

'And what is a *poule de luxe*?'

'A *poule de luxe* is something you are definitely not, my dear. A courtesan. A kept woman.'

'Oh, I see. Well, I think that's what I look like.'

'You certainly look spectacular. You are completely different. Have it.'

'Asher, I *can't*. I couldn't ever wear such a dress.'

'Nonsense, it's only because you're not used to it.' He nodded at the couturier. 'Yes, please, it's a stunner.'

Sadie looked at herself again. She had never worn black since the pinafore dresses of school, and she was surprised to find it so flattering. Over her shoulder, Asher beamed at her.

'You can wear it to Papa's birthday dinner. It'll knock 'em sideways.'

She put up her hand and stroked his cheek.

'You are wonderful to me. What a birthday surprise this was.'

He touched the back of her neck. 'Come on, get dressed. We're going to look at some pictures.'

The sixtieth birthday party Rose gave for Moritz was a memorable one. The house was ablaze with lights and flowers, there was to be dancing until the early hours. Before the majority of the guests arrived Rose had planned a dinner for twenty people. Dressing for this, Sadie confided to Asher that she was more nervous than usual of going to Portland Place.

'But why? My parents adore you, you know that. They approve because you are well brought up and they consider you to be demure, not having the benefit of my experience of you . . .'

He laughed as she pulled a face at him in the glass.

'It's not your parents this time, actually. It's this dress.'

Asher had asked her to wear the black Poiret: she had complied but was ill-at-ease.

'Darling, I know you like it but I do feel a trifle theatrical. Do you see me in one of the divine Sarah's roles?'

'No.' His voice dropped. 'But I know where I do see you.'

'Not *now*,' she protested in mock-alarm. 'Have you no sense of the fitness of things?'

He sighed heavily.

'It's that dress, there's not a doubt of it. It does its job all too well. I can't keep my hands off you. The Sultan knows what he's about.'

Anxiously, Sadie glanced at herself in the glass.

Amused, Asher said, 'Don't worry, I'll hover at your side in case you arouse the violent passions of any male guest.'

'You fool, you.'

Seated at Raphaels' vast dining table she felt more comfortable. Her neighbours were familiar to her as the husbands of Rose's friends and she enjoyed the avuncular gossip to which they treated her. Across the expanse of white linen and silver she looked around the table. Moritz was bubbling with pleasure at entertaining his friends and family, Rose observed him with proprietorial pride as he paused for effect before the punchline of one of his best anecdotes. Sadie watched the candles flickering in the glass

132

holder at the centre of the table, with its myriad flower petals linked to the central glass pillar by crystal ropes.

Her gaze moved beyond the freesias and candles to the face of a man seated opposite. He was watching, assessing her from beneath bushy black brows. Embarrassed, conscious of the cut of the dress she wore, she glanced away. He was, she supposed, in his late forties, a burly figure in a high winged collar, hair brushed flat, his heavy moustache lending his face a sardonic quality. He did not talk a great deal but sat, head inclined, listening politely to his neighbours who were clearly at pains to amuse him. Often, during the course of the meal, she was aware of his eyes upon her.

Precisely at nine Rose led the women from the room, and half-an-hour later the men swallowed the last of the port and joined them in the red drawing room. The party guests were beginning to arrive, and the orchestra was already playing Franz Lehar, and the waltzes of Strauss.

Moritz led Rose on to the floor to begin the evening.

'*Just* like the royal couple,' remarked Asher quietly to Sadie.

'You mustn't laugh. It's a big evening for them.'

'I'm not laughing at them – I love them too much for that. But you must recognize the absurdity of all this pomp and circumstance.'

'I think it's perfectly splendid.'

'Yes. Well. Just don't ever let me do the same thing, will you?'

'On the contrary, I shall positively encourage it. When you're sixty I hope I shall be able to give an even larger party for you, because you'll deserve it.'

They looked at each other tenderly.

Just then, Moritz danced Rose to a stop beside them.

'Mama, may I have this dance?' Asher and Rose moved off. Moritz turned to Sadie.

'And I, my dear, may I claim you for this?'

Warmly, she smiled at him.

'Of course you may.'

More and more couples now were moving on to the floor.

After a while, the music was almost drowned by the excited voices. Sadie passed from partner to partner. After the set was over, she looked around for Asher. He must be in the salon, she thought, and set off to look for him. On the way, she paused at the door of the morning room. It looked cool and quiet, and she went in to sit down for a moment and collect herself. She started unbuttoning her long white gloves to rearrange her hair, and nearly jumped out of her skin when a man's voice said,

'You look as though you have been enjoying the night's festivities.'

It was the watching man from the dinner table. He sat in a chair half-turned from her, hidden by the high winged back.

'I'm sorry,' Sadie murmured. 'I didn't realize anyone was in here.' She started for the door.

He rose to his feet.

'Would you join me?'

'Oh, no, I don't want to intrude.'

'It would be no intrusion, but a pleasure.' His voice was cordial, calm, the accent unusual.

She hesitated. 'Just for a moment, then.'

He drew a chair forward.

'Won't you sit here, Mrs Raphael?'

She accepted gratefully, then, 'You have the advantage of me, for I don't believe we have been introduced.'

'You're quite right. But you see, only the most elementary detection was required to place you.'

She raised her eyebrows.

'Oh?'

'Well, you must be either a close friend or family to be at

134

the dinner. You're too young for a close friend so, evidently, you are family. I know Lena well, and Betty too, but as you say, you and I haven't met. I've been out of London a great deal the last three years; my mother has been unwell, but I knew that Asher had married. I had heard,' he inclined his head towards her, 'I had heard that the new Mrs Raphael was an attractive woman. 'So . . .' he let the sentence drift.

Sadie gazed at him.

'It sounds convoluted. You could just have asked.'

'Ah, no. That would have been tedious.'

'Well, I shall have to resort to asking, or my husband will be able to accuse me of talking to perfect strangers.'

He bent forward and bowed.

'John Singer Sargent, Madam, your servant.'

Sadie exclaimed in exasperation.

'Of course, do forgive me. I should have known who you were. I've heard enough about you, heaven knows, from Asher and Moritz. But I didn't know you were going to be here tonight.'

'I didn't know myself. I just got back from Boston two days ago, and bumped into Moritz by chance. He extended an invitation, and I naturally accepted it.'

They looked at each other for a moment, both with considerable interest.

Sadie observed, 'I saw your portrait of Philip Sassoon the other day. I can't imagine you want praise from me, you have it from so many better sources, but I do like it: you make him look like a Spanish nobleman.'

Sargent inclined his head.

'Thank you. I am quite pleased myself. But you need never fear praising any artist, Mrs Raphael. It is balm to the soul, I assure you.'

Incredulous, she asked, '*Is* it? For you?'

'Most assuredly for me.'

'But, Mr Sargent, you can't mean that. After your last

Royal Academy exhibition, *The Times* described you as a daring innovator. My father-in-law says your work is a marvel of constructive skill.'

'Moritz is very kind. And of course,' he permitted himself a smile, 'one is tempted to believe him. But I am well aware of how other artists generally think of me. Whistler and Degas, for instance, consider that I am a brilliant executant rather than an artist of high rank. Oh, yes,' he held up his hand as Sadie started to interrupt, 'I know that everyone acknowledges what they call my "artistic accomplishments". It saddens me nonetheless, not least because I am a great admirer of Whistler's work.' He paused. 'Do forgive me, I don't know why I'm telling you all this.'

He fingered his collar self-consciously. Sadie, remembering how he had listened but not talked at the dinner table, saw that he was by nature a reticent man. Perhaps he'd had a little too much to drink. She hoped he was not regretting the sudden surprising candour of their conversation. Hurriedly she said, 'We went to Roger Fry's exhibition at the Grafton Galleries in November. Did you see it?'

'No, I was on the Continent, but I was sorry to miss it. What did you think of it? Do you like the post-Impressionists?'

'Very much.' She laughed. 'They're just so pretty, aren't they? Those gorgeous colours. Moritz thinks I'm the right generation for them – he says if you're like him, and connected with the generation from which it's a transition, then you don't like it. But if you're a factor in the reaction it represents, then you do.'

Sargent looked comically puzzled.

'I *believe* I follow you, Mrs Raphael. No, seriously, he's right, of course. For myself, I think Monet is superb. Superb. Now there is an innovator for you. And do you know, I believe I envy him?'

Sadie looked at him in disbelief.

'Yes, I do. He has a freedom that I do not possess.'

136

'Mr Sargent, you can't mean that. You are *the* portrait painter of the day. You're a gigantic figure in the art world, Asher says. You can do whatever you like.'

'Mrs Raphael, I only wish that were true. But at times I feel I should dearly like to escape the slavery of the model stand.'

'What would you do instead?'

'Simple. I want to devote myself to my experiments in landscape and mural art.'

'Mural art?'

'Yes. I'm doing some for the library in Boston which gives me immense pleasure. So to make more time, I'm declining most commissions for portraits now.'

'But people still want to be painted by you. You're the greatest portraitist of the age – you can't just stop.'

'Well, in a very few cases I am badgered into changing my rule. Mostly, I find I can offer an alternative – I suggest I do a charcoal drawing of them instead. It doesn't take as long and it costs less.'

Sadie sighed. 'It seems a shame to me. You paint such fascinating people.'

'Indeed I do. Or rather,' he gave a wry smile, 'they become fascinating when I've finished with them.'

'Why do them if you don't care to?'

'I am not, as you may observe, a young man. I have achieved worldly success and I wish it to continue. I like comfort – luxury – and I am too old a campaigner to starve in a garret.'

'You couldn't paint people the way you do,' Sadie countered, 'if you didn't like them.'

Sargent's face relaxed, and he smiled broadly at her.

'No, I couldn't. How very perceptive of you, Mrs Raphael. I suspect the truth is that I do, as you say, like my portraits. But the aesthete in me objects to the easy life. I relish my work, and yet am puritanical enough to feel I should be paying for the pleasure, not sitting in the lap of luxury.'

He stopped, and lit a long cigar. Puffing carefully to get it alight, he watched her for a moment or two in silence. Then, 'Mrs Raphael, would you care to sit for me?'

'But you said . . .'

'I was talking about commissions. Commissions are a burden. This is something I should like to do for myself.'

Flattered at the implied compliment, Sadie nevertheless asked, incredulous, 'Are you serious?'

'Mrs Raphael, I am not an impetuous man. I would not ask if I wasn't serious.'

'It's just that for all of my childhood, my mother used to tell me I was no oil painting. It's rather hard to overcome my years of conditioning.'

'Will your mother take my word for it that you are an oil painting, do you suppose?'

They were both laughing now, and Sadie said, helplessly, 'She'd probably insist on verifying the signature first.'

'We'll do better than that. We'll get her to the exhibition.'

Sadie looked alarmed. 'What exhibition?'

'Next year's Royal Academy. That's what I want to paint you for.'

She caught her breath.

'I think I'd better talk to Asher, if you don't mind.'

'By all means. But you do want to sit for me?'

She gave him a sudden, wide smile.

'It would be thrilling.'

'There is just one condition, if I may. Will you wear that dress?'

She glanced down at herself. 'I'm a trifle uncertain about this. I feel it is rather too daring for me.'

He said, consideringly, 'Yes, it's certainly dramatic. But the line is perfect. It's a Poiret, isn't it?'

Surprised, she nodded.

'Don't look so impressed. I paint society women all the time, you know. Cultivated cosmopolitans like myself,' he gave a mock shrug, 'know a couture garment when we see one.'

At the beginning of February Sadie started a series of sittings for John Singer Sargent.

She was nervous the first time she arrived at his Tite Street studio. It was a bright, frosty morning and she dismissed the motor early and walked up from the Embankment carrying the black dress in a valise. She knew the street well now: she and Asher had dined several times with the Rothensteins at Number 26, and the week before Sadie had been asking Alice Rothenstein how on earth she should behave. Alice had looked at her and replied simply, 'Be yourself.'

Sadie was repeating this injunction beneath her breath as she rang the doorbell of Number 31. A maid opened the door and led her to a dressing room where she could change. There was a strong smell of turpentine and from behind the closed door she could hear someone playing Chopin on the piano. The door opened and Sargent was there, guiding her into his studio with the correct and formal manners she remembered. It was a light, busy room. At one side a fire burned in a white marble fireplace, flanked by candelabra. Above it a gilded looking glass reflected the windows. The wooden floor was partly hidden by a darkly patterned carpet and pieces of furniture round the walls were covered with objects: vases, an ornate fan. Several portraits hung on the walls. Sadie recognized one of them as a great friend of Rose and Moritz. Adèle Meyer, the banker's wife, had been painted in satin and from behind the Louis XV sofa on which she sat, her two children looked shyly out.

Sargent conducted Sadie to a silk covered chair with a low back and rounded arms which stood beside his easel and chair. He asked her to sit, and arranged the fold of her dress around her feet, then he walked around the room and stood looking at her from different angles, rubbing his beard thoughtfully.

Finally he spoke.

'I don't know, I don't know at all. This is what I had envisaged, but it doesn't seem right. Are you at ease?'

'I think so.'

'Move around a bit. Cross your knees, perhaps?'

Sadie obeyed, but he still seemed dissatisfied.

'Would you mind standing for me? Over here, against this table?'

Sadie stood self-consciously against the mahogany table he indicated, looking towards him.

'No. Still not right. Would you turn slightly away from me, please. Just your head – leave the shoulders as they are. Yes, yes. Much better. Now, the hands. Are you able to stand like that?'

When Sadie nodded, he moved his easel so that it was next to her.

'I want to see both you and the painting in the same light.'

He was sketching rapidly in charcoal, working in a silence, hissing through his teeth. He suddenly said, 'Talk to me, if you would.'

Sadie, who had been carefully maintaining her expression, said stiffly, 'About what?'

'Don't worry, you aren't having your photograph taken, you know. You don't need to sit absolutely still for three minutes while I get my exposure right. Just relax and talk, I like conversation while I paint.'

She looked around the crowded room, searching for inspiration. Across one corner, a huge Cashmere shawl was draped over a brass rod. Relieved, she asked what it was for.

'I've some paintings in mind. I'm fascinated by these shawls. Look at the folds, the subtle textures, the sombre colours – marvellous, isn't it? I'm planning to use Reine, my youngest niece, as model for a series of figures.'

He worked in silence for a while, then he stopped, put down his charcoal and flexed his fingers.

'Let's have a little music, shall we?'

He strode over to the piano and seated himself.

'Let me see. What would suit you? Fauré? No, not quite.'

He started playing a lilting, melancholy tune she did not know. 'Do you like this?'

'Mmm. What is it?'

'I was in the Middle East a few years ago and heard this. Played on a lute, late at night in the Old City, while I was eating halvah and drinking coffee like thick syrup. But that's all I know, I'm afraid. I always play bits of things, the ends and middles mostly. It's a habit I've had from a boy.'

When he asked her to take up her pose again, she said, 'She's exquisite, isn't she?'

Sargent glanced over at the portrait standing on an easel, half draped with a white cloth.

'Lovely bone structure. Good eyes.'

'She looks very aristocratic.'

'Blood of the very bluest. See that string of pearls? They look like pigeons' eggs in the painting, but I played them down, if you can believe it, so they should not appear too vulgar.'

'I wish I looked like that.'

He turned back to her, and said firmly, 'That, if you'll forgive me saying so, Mrs Raphael, is a misguided desire. She's delightful, I admit. Only a little anaemic, don't you think? A trifle insipid. At their best your English aristocrats have a nervous elegance, an hauteur, that is splendid. But sometimes I find them somewhat dull.'

'I haven't your experience of English society,' Sadie said, 'but I imagine they enjoy sitting for you.'

'I am an amusing American oddity,' he said, wrinkling his eyes at the canvas. 'But for pleasure, for myself, I prefer my Jewish clients. And that's not simply because they are the most reliable patrons – although they are – but I thoroughly relish painting them.'

'Why is that?'

'They have interesting faces – energetic, vivacious. They have a drama I enjoy committing to canvas.' He paused, wrinkling up his eyes again as he looked at her. 'You have it yourself.'

She felt herself blushing. But he was hard at work again, and seemed not to notice.

'Yes,' he went on, thoughtfully, 'I recommend my artist friends to go to the East End and paint what they see there – the intimate side of their lives, the interior of tailors' shops, the barrows of Petticoat Lane. Only I have to confess,' he smiled wryly, 'that I have little time myself to do so. Will Rothenstein got a room in Spitalfields, he's painting the old men from the synagogue there, and he keeps inviting me, but I just seem too busy. Mind you, he had a terrible time with them. They come mostly from the ghettoes of Russia and Galicia, they're superstitious old men, terrified that poor Will is a missionary from the Society to convert the Jews. They've taken months to be convinced he just wants to paint them.'

Sadie, growing tired, started to sway, and put her hand behind her to steady herself, holding on to the edge of the table. Sargent, glancing up, exclaimed, 'Don't move! That's it, that's what I wanted.'

He tore off the sheet he was using out of the easel, and flung it on the floor.

'We'll start again, this is so much better. Don't you feel it to be so?'

He was swiftly indicating the new outline with charcoal lines, working with a speed and excitement he had not shown before.

'Now,' he said, 'I believe I can get it right. I feel I know you.''

Sadie sat for Sargent more than a dozen times, each

sitting lasting about two hours. Early on he had said, jokingly, 'I am painting you chlorate-of-potash-lozenge colour all over. If you find the colour pleasant in itself, I shall be more than gratified.'

She found those hours enthralling. He would work with his brush heavily loaded with colour.

'The thicker you paint,' he once explained when she commented on this, 'the more your colour flows.'

Sometimes he would stand back to view his handiwork, then charge towards the canvas, brush in hand, uttering what Sadie reported to Asher as 'incomprehensible noises'. He would then retire to consider the result. One day, when the light was particularly good, he begged her to hold her pose for another hour.

'There is nothing to match the effect of natural light,' he told her. As a result, he was still working when his next client arrived. Sir Frank Swettenham bowed to Sadie when they were introduced.

'Mr Sargent has been kinder to you than to me,' he commented, after looking at the canvas.

Sadie raised her eyebrows.

'Yes,' he continued. 'You have only a fan and a table to share the canvas with you. For myself, Mr Sargent thinks to draw attention from my visage by filling the spaces not occupied by my person with threatening accessories. I am a mere foil to a leopard skin rug, Malaysian brocades, unrolled documents, ivory batons, topis – you name it, we have it.'

Sargent looked at him from under his brows.

'My very dear sir, I have made you an heroic figure, the epitome of the proconsul. You cannot doubt your dominance over a French *bergère* and a hunk of fur?' Sadie, flexing her stiff right arm before going to change, laughed, and Sargent turned to her in appeal.

'What, Mrs Raphael, am I to do with this incorrigible statesman? He is the centre of one of my grandest designs, and yet does nothing but mock me!'

Sadie said, over her shoulder as she headed for the dressing room, 'As one sitter to another, I think you have a distinct advantage over me. Mr Sargent has made me look entirely lavender in hue. People will think I am on my last legs, whereas with you, they will be in no doubt that you are still breathing.'

When it was exhibited at the Royal Academy later that year Sargent's portrait of Sadie caused a sensation. The critics were aghast at the impropriety of her *décolletage* and the curious lavender of her skin. They had expected Sargent's subtle treatment of sumptuous fabrics, and the stark simplicity of the black-clad figure, the unadorned dark wood table, failed to impress them.

Moritz and Rose were bemused: they too had anticipated the accomplished flattery with which they were familiar, not this attenuated, dramatized figure. Sophie was brought up to London to see it and hated it immediately. Looking at the challenging, knowing beauty in the picture, flaunting her body like some exotic bird, she actually wrung her hands together in her distress.

'You look so *brazen*,' she said distractedly, 'whatever will people think of you? And that dress – why did you wear that? It's indecent to present yourself this way.'

Asher took her arm comfortingly.

'But Ma, we think it's superb. Sargent meant her to look striking, and you must see that she does.'

'It's no good, I can't get used to it. She's half-naked!'

'Look,' Asher guided her across the room to where the new Alma-Tadema hung.

'That's naked. Those girls haven't got a stitch on.'

Sophie peered at the picture. 'No better than they ought to be,' she sniffed.

'You must admit they look charming.'

'That's not the point, my boy. To my mind, you shouldn't want people to see your wife like this.'

Sadie and Asher exchanged glances over her head and Asher tactfully led her away to the tea room.

Sadie remained in front of the picture. Then she walked slowly round the room, examining once again the other works; the Whistler, the Rothenstein, the new Augustus John. She stopped again in front of her own likeness, standing well back in case anyone should notice and recognize her. It aroused in her the most extraordinary emotions.

Sadie acknowledged that despite the sophisticated life she now led with Asher, she was still basically uncertain, easily awed by the personalities she met. She contrived carefully to hide her shyness, but for her to do so remained an effort. She knew, looking at this woman who was herself, that Sargent had in his painting revealed something of her that he sensed, rather than observed. There was a quality of strength, a definition in the face, as though he had seen her as she would be in ten years' time. Seeing herself critically, Sadie felt that never before had she liked the way she looked. Yet in the painting she could appreciate the odd, striking quality of her face; the too-big features, the too-heavy eyelids, the arched nose, the sensuous curves of her mouth.

Alone in their room that evening, she looked thoughtfully at her reflection in the mirror. She felt that already, in a curious way, she had begun to develop along the lines foreshadowed by the painting.

She had begun to look more like herself.

Chapter Eleven

One evening, after a dinner they had all attended, Asher suggested that Woolf Lander, one of his oldest friends, might care to join them in a visit to some gaming rooms he knew. Woolf Lander – who looked, as Sadie had privately remarked to Asher – the perfect bachelor solicitor, with his slight stoop and gold-rimmed spectacles, assented amiably. He had nothing better to do, and enjoyed the Raphaels' company.

The gaming rooms were in a tall, seedy building off the Tottenham Court Road in Goodge Street.

The heavily built doorman tipped his hat to Asher and Woolf as they arrived.

'Evening, Mr Raphael. Evening, Sir.' As an afterthought he added, 'Madam.'

'Have you been here before, then?' Sadie was faintly surprised.

Asher had told her he played cards with his friends. He had never mentioned visiting establishments like this.

'Oh, a couple of times. Ages ago. Fellow must have a marvellous memory.'

Inside they found themselves in the first of a series of small rooms. An arched doorway with heavy curtains led into the next room. Beyond, Sadie could see a similar opening into further rooms. In each, groups of people sat intently round tables. There was a steady murmur of conversation. Asher led them through three such rooms until he found a plump, middle-aged man with dark hair and soft white hands. After a short conversation, both men came back to Woolf and Sadie.

'Mr de Vries is the manager here, and he has a private *chemin de fer* game going on in the last room. He says I can take you in for a few minutes to watch.'

The manager held open a heavy door. The room beyond was larger than the others and the atmosphere was very different. The intent silence was broken only by the occasional comment from the croupier who sat in the concavity of a vast, kidney shaped table. Its green baize surface was padded and divided into numbered sections and with a long, thin paddle he pushed cards and little heaps of money around the table to the twelve players. These were all men, heads bent in conversation under the single dark-shaded light above them. Slightly beyond the circle of light, behind their shoulders, stood equally absorbed watchers.

Most of these were women. Sadie noticed that one or two had their hands on the shoulders of their seated companions. One, a rounded girl with blonde hair, was kissing the ear of her escort: irritated, he shrugged her off as the croupier announced, 'One more hand, please.' Then he slid towards the man an open-topped mahogany box ('That's the shoe,' whispered Asher to Sadie). The man placed on the table what seemed to Sadie an enormous pile of notes, and one by one the other players followed his example.

'I've never seen anything like it,' muttered Woolf. 'There must be twenty thousand pounds on the table.'

As the game continued, Sadie realized that the players were betting against each other. There were two other croupiers, sitting opposite the first, who also used the long handled palettes to move cards and money around the large table. Then she saw that a fourth man sat a little way out of the light on a high stand. Asher followed her glance.

'That's the lookout,' he whispered. 'Just to make sure there's no cheating.'

One of the players turned up his cards, and put them face down on the table. '*La petite*!' he called.

The first man turned up his two cards. There was a rustle of excitement amongst the watchers, and someone laughed

147

nervously. The croupier's palette shot out, scooping all the piles of notes and pushing them towards the first player. 'He's the banker,' Asher said quietly, 'and he had the higher cards. So he's won the lot.'

Sadie was horrified. It seemed appalling to her that in a moment one man could earn more money than she had ever seen in her life for doing nothing. She tugged at Asher's arm, and they left the room.

A tall, greying man with an aquiline nose came towards them. His discreetly cut jacket revealed a gleam of brocaded waistcoat as he grasped Asher's hand.

'My dear fellow, just the man I've been looking for.'

Asher smiled and introduced him to Sadie.

'This is Henry Dereham. We've been promising each other a game of bezique for months. Would you mind if we played now?'

'No. I'd love to watch.'

The men seated themselves at a small table. Sadie took a wall-seat nearby, where she could watch the game.

'Two-handed bezique,' explained Asher.

Dereham raised his eyebrows. Asher nodded. The man flexed his fingers and ruffled the cards in a neat arc.

'Shall we say two thousand points?' he spoke enquiringly.

'I agree.'

'Right. And each brisque taken in a trick counts for ten. Will you cut?'

Asher took a block of cards from the top of the deck and placed them on the table. 'Seven.'

Dereham took them, shuffled again, cut. 'King. My deal, I think.'

Deftly he dealt out three cards to Asher, and to himself. Then two to each, and again three. The next card he dealt face up on the table.

'Queen of hearts,' Woolf murmured at Sadie's back. 'The suit determines the trump for that hand.'

The rest of the cards were flicked rapidly between the two

piles. Asher fanned his out and laid face up the ten of diamonds. The older man played his first card: seven of hearts. Sadie noticed the odd way he held his hand of cards: palm below them, three fingers on the edge of the long side of the deck, the index finger at the outer, right corner. His thumb was on top.

A sudden move of Asher's made her glance back at him. Before him lay the king and queen of hearts.

'Trump marriage,' said Woolf quietly. 'That's forty points.'

Sadie looked at their faces. The older man's showed nothing, but Asher looked extremely pleased with himself. As the game continued, Sadie's interest waned and she clenched the muscles of her jaw to stifle a yawn.

'Bezique,' Woolf said from behind her. 'Another forty points.'

Asher had the queen of spades and jack of diamonds before him. Again, she saw the pleasure in his eyes, but his opponent's face remained bland. Ten minutes later Asher stiffened slightly. Dereham's eyes were on him. He glanced down at his hand, back at Asher – and played a ten of spades. 'His trick,' said Woolf, in explanation. And then, immediately, the man spread four cards on the table: two queens of spades and two jacks of diamonds.

'Double bezique,' Woolf told her. 'That's five hundred points.'

She looked at Asher, read the disappointment in his eyes. She turned to Woolf.

'Do you see how Mr Dereham holds his cards?'

'I know. It's the way you can tell someone who's a professional dealer: they do it so players can't see the bottom card.'

'Goodness, is Asher playing against a dealer?'

'Oh no. Dereham's what they call a semi-pro.'

'What's that?'

Woolf's voice was hard.

'A cheat.'

Horrified, Sadie stared at him. 'What do you mean? How can you tell?'

'Holding cards that way has lots of advantages. He can look at the top card without being seen. Or he can conceal a card when it comes from the bottom of the deck.'

'But how does he look at the top card? He couldn't do that without being seen.'

'Oh yes he could. He just presses on the top card with his thumb and pushes it against his fingers – it buckles a bit near the corner, and he can look in and see the number. It's easy. Then he softens the thumb pressure and it flattens again.'

'And what about dealing from the bottom?'

'That depends on speed. Holding the cards the way Dereham does, if he deals very smoothly and very fast, he can pull out the bottom card while his thumb is pulling out the top card – no one can catch him at it.'

Sadie was growing increasingly upset.

'But we must stop the game. We must tell Asher.'

'You know what he's like. Tell him not to do something and it's the one thing he does want to do. Besides, Dereham's a very pleasant fellow: Asher likes him.'

Woolf paused, then added, 'And there's something else. I think he does know that Dereham cheats. And he wants to show that he can deal with it. It's a kind of bravado. Like the way he insists on riding that new horse of his – what's it called? Roman? Even though it's really too much of a handful for a relatively inexperienced rider.'

Sadie nodded. She knew exactly what he meant. What she privately added to herself, though, was that she found it immensely attractive. It was the one thing about her calm controlled husband that was absurd and endearing, like a child playing a daring game.

She turned back to watch the game. Within minutes Woolf commented, 'Bezique again,' and Dereham made a note on a pad.

'Two thousand, I'm afraid,' he said.

Asher smiled and shrugged, rose to his feet.

'Is it finished?' Sadie was at a loss. Nothing seemed to have happened. The two men shook hands. Asher asked, an edge of nervousness apparent in his manner, 'Will tomorrow be satisfactory?'

The older man hesitated, then, 'Of course,' he replied.

As they walked towards the buffet Sadie asked, 'Satisfactory for what?'

'I beg your pardon?'

'What is it that tomorrow will be satisfactory for, Asher?'

'Oh I see. I'm sorry. Tomorrow will be satisfactory for, for . . .' His voice trailed away as a white gloved manservant proffered a tray of slender glasses.

'For?' Sadie prompted, as she sipped champagne.

'Oh, to arrange another game.' His tone was abstracted, he spoke without attention. He's lying, she thought. Then, shocked by the conclusion, she softened it to herself. He'd had a busy day, it was late. Yet whatever excuses she conjured up, something she did not understand disturbed her.

'Woolf says Mr Dereham is a professional card player.'

'So he is. Damned good, too.'

'Too lucky, though, wouldn't you say?' Woolf's voice was quiet.

'Can't be too lucky.'

'Oh, but you can. Impossibly so.'

'What're you saying?'

'That Dereham is a cheat. That he's just cheated you.'

'You're making accusations that you can't possibly substantiate.'

'Oh yes I can. Where are the cards you were playing with?'

'On the table. They weren't a new pack.'

'All the better for Dereham's purpose.'

Woolf put down his glass and hurried back into the gaming room. In a moment he returned with the pack in his hands.

'Look.'

He riffled through the cards, looked at them carefully, held out a few to Asher.

'They seem all right to me.'

'Of course they do. But look at their edges.'

Asher examined them more carefully. 'Nothing wrong so far as I can see.'

'Now look at the rest of the pack.'

Asher took them, compared the edges. Silently he handed the two sets of cards back to Woolf. Sadie looked at them.

'Well, what is it?'

Woolf held out both sets of cards so that she could see that the edges of most of the cards were slightly grimy from use. The few cards Woolf had selected had one immaculately white edge.

'Dereham had a small bandage on his thumb. Did you notice?'

She shook her head.

'Well, anyway, under it was concealed a piece of fine sandpaper. Through a slit in the bandage it was slightly exposed. All he had to do was pull the card's edge along the slit to make it immaculate. And then of course he could spot it again.'

Sadie was puzzled.

'Yes, but what good does that do him? It's only on . . .' she counted, 'seven cards.'

'A card sharp only needs to know the location of a few cards to take your money. A good cheat only needs to know the exact position of just one of fifty-two cards, and you might as well hand him your money straight away.'

Asher looked increasingly annoyed. 'Well, say what you like, but it seems to me you're being very presumptuous. Anyone would think you were in the Force.'

'You don't have to be looking hard to see that Dereham is up to something. Those tricks are as old as Methuselah.'

Asher smiled suddenly at his friend, his aggression melting.

'I expect you're right. Oh, well, I'll go and organize our departure, shall I?'

As he went off, Sadie said to Woolf, 'Thank you for telling him. But I do think really it's a bit of a fuss about nothing. After all, that was just a friendly game, wasn't it? They weren't playing for money, so I suppose it doesn't really matter.'

Woolf started to speak, then thought better of it and stopped. It was only later that night, when Asher had fallen asleep, that the events of the evening returned to drag at her memory. She felt anxious, but unable to pin down the cause of her perturbation. Drowsily she thought about Asher. She loved him so much yet felt she knew him so little. When he spoke to her of his love and his desire, he held nothing back; but there was within him something private, something she did not know. His very charm acted as a barrier, a façade no one – not even she – could penetrate.

For a while she worried intermittently about the untruth she thought he had told her after the game of bezique.

And then something happened to make her forget.

For some weeks she had been feeling strange: slightly giddy when she got out of bed, her skin sensitive to the slightest touch. 'I must be getting influenza,' she had told Zipporah the week before, but although she had rested she felt no better, and clearly she did not even have a cold. Then Zipporah had said to her in some exasperation,

'Sadie, I don't want to pry, but have you checked your dates?'

'Oh, good Lord. I can't remember . . .' she scrabbled in her wallet for a diary, and feverishly counted back the days.

'It's been about eleven weeks now. Do you think . . ?'

Her aunt smiled. 'I do think.'

'But it can't be. I can't be.'

'Why ever not? It happens very easily, you know, in the best regulated households. And unless you've been taking very good care it doesn't . . .'

Sadie blushed. 'No, of course we haven't.'

'Well then, I think, from my necessarily limited experience, that impending maternity probably accounts for your little malaise.'

As the days went by, suspicion deepened into certainty. Sadie was filled with elation and relief. It was the fifth year of her marriage and she would soon be twenty-three. She and Asher wanted children, and it had begun to concern her during the past year that the months were going by and still she had not, as Leonie used to say, fallen for a baby. She knew the family watched her with more than interest: Rose and Moritz made no secret of their longing for more grandchildren, and even Sophie had begun to ask in her letters if there was any sewing she might do.

Two weeks after the conversation with Zipporah, Asher took Sadie to his parents' house in Surrey. They ate an inordinate amount, walked in the grounds, stayed late in bed. On the second morning, stretching out for a glass of Malvern water, she found beside her bed a white oblong box the size of a small hatbox, held shut with a narrow black cord secured by a glass bead. She waited until Asher came back, blue-chinned and rumpled, yawning in his Afghan dressing-gown and clutching the *Morning Post*. She poured him China tea, gave him a Marie biscuit and clambered back into bed.

'Is this for me? Can I open it now?'

He feigned puzzlement.

'What? Where? When?'

She reached for the box, pulled the cord. Twisted up inside was a skein of material, the deep soft red of claret.

'What is it? What *is* it?' She pulled it out of the box and unfolded it between her hands, fine pleats of gauzy silk rippling out over the bed, opaque and fluid. She gasped and held it up. It was a dress, with short, wide sleeves and a straight cut neckline. The bodice was held with a narrow cord into a high waist and the pleats flowed into a widening pool at the hem. Bodice and hem were decorated with a faint dark geometric design, in a pattern she did not know.

'Oh, my love, it's ravishing.'

She got out of bed, went over to the pier glass and held the dress in front of her. She had never owned anything of such a colour. It heightened the red of her hair, it made her seem mysterious and foreign even to herself.

'Where on earth did you get it?'

'It's made by a man called Fortuny. Mariano Fortuny.' He laughed at her obvious delight. 'I'm so pleased you like it, my darling. I got it through the gallery, really. He's a designer who's only just beginning to be known in this country, but the Pre-Raphaelites have taken him up. So when our Italian agent was in, I asked him to send me one from Venice.'

'But how did he know what I'd like?'

'He didn't. But Mariano Fortuny did. I described you, and the agent wrote it all down – how tall you are, and your colouring,' he paused and kissed her hand, 'and your strange grey eyes. And this one was picked out for you. And you see, size doesn't matter. You just pull it to where you want it.'

Sadie said, 'I've never seen anything to touch it. But how do I wear it – what do I put on underneath?'

Asher laughed. 'Well, not your famous corsets, that's for sure. I think perhaps they're worn mainly for entertaining at home. So perhaps – nothing?'

She felt her colour deepen. 'Perhaps. I don't think I'd dare, though.'

'Not even for me?'

'Maybe just for you.'

'Put it on now, then.'

When she came out of the dressing room, her hair on her

155

shoulders, Asher told her she looked like a Greek statue.

'Only warmer,' she said, hugging him.

'Much, much, much warmer. Warm enough, really, to take it off again?'

Against his shoulder she whispered her assent.

They kissed gently. Asher found her breasts, and rolled her nipples between his fingers under the fine silk. Desire flowered under his hands and she fell back across the bed, pulling him down to her. He pushed the fabric slowly up her thighs, and her breathing changed to match his.

Later, after the demands and then the sating, they lay under the ribboned swan's-down coverlet. Sadie stretched so that every muscle felt used.

'We should get up.'

Asher said, 'Sadie. Have you got something to tell me?'

'What sort of thing do you mean?'

'You were different just now. Very cautious. Very,' he hesitated, 'very protective. Of yourself, I mean, not of me. I have a distinct feeling there's something I should know.'

'I was about to tell you anyway.'

He sat up, excitement spreading across his face.

'Am I right? Is it a baby?'

'Yes. At least, I think it is. I haven't done it before, you know.'

Asher wrapped his arms round her.

'A baby. I can't believe it. A baby. Oh, my God, it's the most wonderful news anyone's ever given me. Are you pleased? Do you feel all right? Do you want anything? Sadie . . .' Sadie hugged him back.

'I'm fine, don't worry. And it's not for ages, yet. Not for six months.'

'We must tell my parents. We must tell your mother . . .'

Sadie put her hand over his lips. 'Oh no we mustn't. Nobody but us needs to know for ages, not till it starts to show. Let's keep it just for ourselves, just for a while.'

'Whatever you want. But I can't wait too long, you

know. I'm so proud, I want to yell it at the top of my voice.' He put a protective hand over her stomach. 'When will it begin to show? Is it all right in there?' He paused. 'Will it be a boy or a girl? I'd like a daughter, I think.'

'I'll do my best to oblige, sir. I'd like a daughter, too. But I can't imagine how it'll feel to be a parent. Will we know what to do with her?'

Asher said, 'I don't know what you're worrying about. You managed Miriam's brood very well, you're marvellous with them.'

'Yes, but they're not mine, are they? I could go away and not have to bother about them.'

'We'll talk to Lena. She has a wonderful nanny, we'll ask her. We'll take care of everything.'

She subsided against him. 'You're right. I'm being silly.'

'Of course you are. It's the most enormous step – I feel like a different person already, and you've only just told me about it. Look,' he sat up, suddenly concerned, 'have you been to a doctor yet? What is the procedure?'

'Oh, I think I tell Dr Newman and then we sort out the date and he recommends a midwife. And then we just see him on the day, I suppose. Oh, yes. And we have to get some things.'

'What do babies need?'

'Do you want me to answer that now?'

He looked puzzled. 'Of course I do.'

'Well. They need diapers and muslin diapers and shawls. They need dozens of dresses and nightdresses and little mittens. They need bonnets and bootees and bibs. You have to have a cradle upstairs, and another downstairs, and a bassinette for walks. And blankets and more blankets and mounds and mounds of cotton wool. Then you have to get . . .'

'Stop!' Asher laughed and shook his head. 'Are you sure we want to go ahead with this? The house won't hold all that amount, we'll have to move. And I'll have to ask for a rise. *Two* rises, and a bank loan.'

'No you won't. We'll manage.'

'I know we will, I'm only teasing.' He pulled her down deeper into the bed.

'Do you think, Mrs Raphael, if we were very careful, it would be all right if we just celebrated this piece of news in a suitable manner?'

'If by suitable you mean what I *think* you mean, I don't see why not.'

She twisted over so that she lay above him, and smoothed his eyebrows with her finger. Suddenly grave, Asher said, 'You know, my love, I do take this very seriously. It is a responsibility, and I will look after you.'

'I know you will,' she said. 'Now please stop talking. After all, I've never made love to a responsible man with a bank loan before.'

It was only after Dr Newman confirmed the pregnancy that Asher told his parents. They were beside themselves; Lena's daughters were still their adored only grandchildren, and it looked as if Betty would not bear children: she had already had three miscarriages. Rose rushed to see Sadie almost immediately, bringing her maid with her, carrying a great tureen of chicken soup with *matzoh* balls, carefully balanced on her knees and covered with a white damask napkin. This was immediately whisked off to the kitchen to be heated up.

'But it's only eleven o'clock,' Sadie wailed, in vain. Rose had already pushed her into a chair and placed her feet upon a stool.

'It's not for *you*,' her mother-in-law said with acerbity. 'It's for that little one in there. And just you remember you owe it to that child to give it the best.'

'For heaven's sake, it's only three months old.'

'Three months, three minutes – what's the difference? That's my grandchild you've got there, and you see you

158

take care of it. No riding in the motor for you, my girl, until after the birth.'

'But Greaves is a most careful driver – he never goes over fifteen miles-an-hour and at the mere thought of approaching twenty he goes apoplectic.'

'That's as may be. It's not the speed I object to, it's the shaking about.'

Sadie sighed and subsided. There was no arguing with Rose in this mood – or indeed, as she ruefully reflected, in any other. Her own mother's approach was, by contrast, mercifully matter-of-fact. Sadie had already written to give her and Flora the news. By return of post came the reply: Promise me you'll keep warm, and don't do up your corsets too tight. Get that nice dressmaker to run up a couple of loose smocks for the mornings. Tell Asher you're to have no more late nights, and ask him to get some milk stout. It tastes terrible but it does you good. I will travel to London well before the birth, unless you need me earlier. If you do, write immediately or telegraph if necessary. I shall bring with me two dozen white nightdresses for the baby, the sort that Miriam had. Grandma Diamond is making them now, and Flora is sewing the delicate bits and doing the embroidery. Do *not* eat too much, whatever Rose says. You may be eating for two, but one of you is too small to need a great deal.

Chapter Twelve

One afternoon in late December, early in the fifth month of Sadie's pregnancy, Asher rode his horse home to show her. She came out on to the verandah and watched with admiring apprehension as Roman stamped and clattered restlessly on the gravel.

'He looks fearsome,' she observed, as the grey shook his curb chain and arched his neck, anxious to be moving.

'He's all gas and gaiters.' Asher slapped the muscular shoulder with a proprietorial hand, and the creature's skin trembled slightly in response to his touch.

'He's not really been exercised for a couple of days after all this rain, and he needs to go all out. I'm taking him over towards the Heath – will you come part of the way with me?' Mischievously he added, 'You could have a ride.'

She pretended to shudder.

'Not for all the tea in China, thank you. But I could do with a walk. Wait while I get my shawl.'

She was glad she had come out. The gardens all smelt richly of wet and rotting leaves, and as she passed the hydrangea bushes in front of the house she touched the faded flower heads. A slight mistiness rose from the ground, rooks cawed disconsolately from the leafless elms. As they walked, Asher holding in Roman to keep pace with Sadie's steps, he told her of the new exhibition Moritz had just opened. 'Papa is thrilled with it; he says will you be able to get in this week?'

Just as she was about to reply, she paused, hearing the shrill voices of children on the far side of a high garden wall. The next instant, a white dog, a bull-terrier, had hurled itself, yapping wildly, from the dark driveway to pounce on her trailing skirts. She drew back in alarm, and a child's voice yelled, 'Rollo. Rollo! Come here, you bad dog!'

The animal took no notice, and now it was nipping at her ankles and growling low in its throat. She looked up at Asher in alarm and he, seeing her distress, gathered up the reins in his left hand as he prepared to dismount. Alerted by his movement, the dog suddenly turned towards the horse and darted between its hind legs, snapping at its fetlocks and snarling. Roman showed the whites of his eyes in panic. Asher shouted to the dog, 'Get down, down!' and hauled on the reins as Roman started to rear up to get away from the menacing white blur beneath him. But his right foot was already out of the stirrup in preparation for dismounting, and as he struggled to bring Roman under control his unevenly distributed weight started to drag the saddle sideways. Asher began to slip. He called something to Sadie but over the dog's barking she could not catch the words.

Roman's eyes were bulging with strain as he towered above her, huge and horrifying, his front legs flailing the air. She heard the breath whistle out of his nostrils as he toppled over backwards on top of his rider. Somewhere next to her a woman's voice was shrieking, but the only person she could see was the baker with his cart further down the road: the man had already started to run towards them, he was about fifty yards away.

Beneath the great grey body of the writhing horse Asher was pinioned; she could see one of his black boots caught in the stirrup. Ignoring the barking dog she ran round to the other side of the struggling Roman. Asher was half under the animal, only his head and shoulders free. His eyes were open but he was silent. Desperately, ineffectually, she leant over him, pushing with all her strength at the horse's hard, hairy belly, trying to move it off Asher. Suddenly the animal was rolling over, hauling itself to its feet, grunting with the effort. It was up on its forelegs, and now she could see that Asher's foot was still in the stirrup. As the horse

161

scrabbled furiously, trying to gain a foot-hold, the heavy hooves were digging into his body. She tried to grab the reins, gathered in Asher's hand, but the great teeth snapped out at her and terrified she drew back. She ran round behind it to try to pull Asher's foot from the trapped boot, but as she struggled the horse was up and starting to move, pulling away from her grasping hands. In utter horror she saw Asher being hauled beneath the horse, the back hooves kicking into his flesh, crushing down on to his hand as he was dragged along the road, his unprotected head bumping on the gritty surface. The baker was still running towards her, his mouth open. Frantic now, she stumbled beside the horse, not knowing what to do. Her mind was empty, she could see only Asher's open eyes.

Somewhere, the woman was shrieking again.

They thought at first that she would lose the child. For an hour, they told her afterwards, she had sobbed and screamed like a madwoman. After the baker had caught the quivering Roman and released Asher's foot, Sadie lay down on the damp ground beside him pillowing his head on her arm. When the neighbours reached them she was whispering to him, over and over, 'Tell me where it hurts, my little love, tell me where it hurts.'

When they saw how it was, and tried to make her get up so they could attend to him, she buried her face in his bloodied hair and crooned tunelessly to him. Then they pulled her to her feet and two of them carried her, struggling, into a house and held her down on a sofa until she collapsed into great convulsive sobs which shook her whole body. After an endless time a doctor arrived. He took her pulse and talked to Annie – where had Annie come from? – and gave her something to drink. After a while she fell, whirling, into darkness.

Sadie woke in her own bed and wondered why her throat should hurt so much. Then she knew, and her limbs quivered with the memory. She was quite calm, though, quite sensible. Annie brought her some tea with a lot of sugar and she drank it. Then Annie said, 'There's a gentleman to see you, Madam, and says I'm to bring him to your room. It's Rabbi Salaman.'

The bearded, reticent rabbi came in, and took her hand, and held it, and told her what she already knew. But to hear it was so impossible, so unbearable, that she started to scream to shut out the quiet, inexorable voice, so that she wouldn't have to hear, so that it would not be true. And then she could not stop screaming and the room reeled around her. Cold compresses were pressed against her forehead, and she beat them away. Phials were held under her nose but she knocked them aside. Then she stopped for a moment to draw breath and heard Moritz's voice, and he was crying too.

'Oh, my God, the baby, she'll lose the baby if she goes on like this!'

She had forgotten about the baby.

Shocked into sanity, she wrapped her arms protectively around her stomach and subsided into tears. There was a dragging cramp in her back, low down. She sat up to ease it but it would not go away. Then she got really frightened, and managed to tell Lena – goodness, was Lena here too – how she felt. The doctor arrived again, and looked at her very carefully, and told her she must stay in bed and everything would be fine.

She felt quieter then, but time seemed to be moving in a strange way.

The house was full of people, she could hear their voices, and doors opening and closing. Lena and her husband were in the sitting room – Betty was with her mother in Portland Place. Rabbi Salaman had spent an hour with Sadie. He spoke to her in his soft, oddly-accented English. 'You must try to be very quiet in yourself,' he told her. 'Do everything with slowness. There is no hurry, it will all be done. Just do be quiet.' He pressed her hand between his own. 'God is closest to those with broken hearts.'

Into the silence he said, meditatively, 'I have done this many times. Many times. But not often quite like this.' He looked at her with compassion. 'You will have to be very brave, Mrs Raphael. This is going to be hard for you. Harder than you know. You must call whenever you need me. I will come at once, have no fear.'

Sadie heard Annie's voice in the hallway, then she knocked at the door. 'It's a Mr Steinberg, Madam, for the rabbi.'

The old man rose to his feet. 'Thank you. I am coming.'

'Who is it?' Sadie asked.

'Mr Steinberg has come to take care of your husband, Mrs Raphael.'

'I will come with you.' She started to push aside the covers.

'No. I think not. It is better for you to stay here.'

'But I want to be with him. *Please.*'

The rabbi said, 'No, Mrs Raphael, let me get your sister-in-law. This is not for you to do. But you will see him – afterwards.'

He nodded to Annie, who hurried to call Lena. The two women returned together and Lena said, 'Lie down, Sadie, do. You look terrible.'

For an hour she lay on her bed and Lena sat beside her. She was rigid, trying to imagine what Mr Steinberg was doing. Her eyes were dry and burning: she dare not let them close, for behind her lids she saw again the writhing body of the horse crushing Asher's ribs, and his trailing hand on the road. And she could hear again her own shrieks.

Sadie thought she must have slept soon after, because next time she looked at Lena, her sister-in-law was asleep, slumped forward against a rosewood table, her head in her arms. A single lamp lit the room and the house seemed to be silent. The pain in her back had gone. Slowly she moved herself towards the edge of the bed, swung her legs carefully to the floor. Keeping one hand on the wall she felt her way to the door.

Coming back from the bathroom she paused at the door of Asher's dressing room. Without giving herself time to think she turned the handle. A lamp was lit, someone was asleep in the narrow bed. Joy flooded through her: oh God, she had imagined it all. He was here, sound asleep. She moved forward until she could see the sleeper and put out her hand to move back the blanket.

It was Betty's husband, John Epstein.

The black weight slid back on her heart.

The family must all be staying here for the night. Sadie went from the room, walking very carefully in case she started the nagging pain again. In the silence, she heard Moritz's voice, low and even. She wanted badly to talk to him, and turned towards the small upper study they used for dealing with household accounts. She opened the door a crack, not wishing to disturb the conversation.

Only Moritz seemed to be alone. He was just inside the door, turned away from her, leaning against an upright chair. He wore a black velvet skull-cap and his *tallis* was round his shoulders. Bound around his forehead and his upper arm were the soft leather thongs of his phylacteries. He was rocking gently, and chanting to himself in Hebrew. She could make out most of the words:

The Lord, he is God, the Lord he is God,
The Lord : the Lord hath reigned:
The Lord shall reign for ever and ever.
I have waited for thy salvation, O Lord.

His voice fell away into mumbles, then silence. Then he seemed to recollect himself, and went on in English, 'What can we say before thee? What can we say? O that it would

165

not sin against thy word: thy will be done. In thy love deal graciously with this, our dear one . . .'

Moritz's head sank lower and he was quiet. Noiselessly Sadie moved forward and pushed the door wider so that she could see into the room.

She stood quite still.

The desk had been pushed into the window and a narrow bed placed in the centre of the room. Two candles, one at either end of the bed, burned with a steady soft gleam.

In their light, Sadie saw Asher.

He lay on the bed, his feet pointing towards the door, wrapped around and around in a white sheet. His head was raised slightly, his eyes were now closed. His skin was waxy pale and in the candlelight he looked smooth and young. Over the sheet, across his shoulders, was the creamy *tallis* she had given him the day they were married, with its bands of soft blue embroidery. She saw that the long floating fringes were twisted round his thumbs, and one of the fringes had been torn.

Sadie leaned back against the door jamb and laced her arms protectively over her stomach, so that the baby should not see. She stood there for a long time. She wanted to kiss him just once more, but could not bring herself to do it. She could not bear to find his mouth cold under her own. She thought, He'll understand if I don't kiss him, he's not really here. There was a movement behind her and she spun round in panic. Thank God, it was only Lena, looking for her. The two women stood together in the doorway, then Lena took Sadie's arm and softly closed the door.

The two women stayed awake for the rest of the night. In the morning, Sophie arrived. The Raphaels had sent the motor for her, and Greaves had gone too, to share the driving. They had returned immediately and driven all night so that Sophie would be in time for the funeral. Even through her misery, Sadie was shocked by her mother's appearance. Haggard with sorrow, she had suddenly aged, her shoulders were stooped with the weight of unhappiness in a way she had never been through her own misfortunes. She stood at the door of Sadie's room, clutching her big black handbag and trying to smile. They hugged each other wordlessly.

'Oh,' Sadie exclaimed on a great breath of relief. 'I wanted you here so much.'

'Only I didn't think it would be like this.' In the emotion of seeing her daughter, Sophie was shedding tears for the first time since she heard of Asher's death. 'I thought I'd be coming for the baby,' she sobbed. 'We'd been making such plans, me and Flora, how we were going to surprise you with all the sewing . . . and now . . .'

'Oh, Ma, it was terrible. I didn't know what to do. I couldn't do anything for him.' Sadie's voice was hoarse, she could hardly speak above a whisper. Through her tears Sophie looked at her anxiously.

'Are you all right, is everything still safe?' Sadie gave a small smile. 'Oh yes, but I'm to stay in bed.'

'It'll be the best place for you for a while.' Sophie was recovering herself, mopping her eyes on Sadie's counterpane.

'Ma, we must get you some breakfast.' Sadie was about to ring for Annie, but a knock on the door forestalled her. Annie had already arrived, her eyes bruised from weeping, with a tray of tea and muffins.

'I've prepared a room for you, Madam,' she told Sophie. 'And I've taken the liberty of unpacking your case to save trouble. Will there be anything else?'

'No, thank you, Annie,' Sadie replied.

Halfway through a muffin, Sadie suddenly pushed away her plate. 'I can't eat any more.'

'When did you last have something?'

'I can't remember. Yesterday, I think.' She tried to recall the sequence of yesterday's events. 'I think I had lunch.'

'Well, you should certainly eat your breakfast. You must be starving.'

'I *am* hungry,' Sadie admitted. 'But it feels wrong to be eating.'

'Yes, I know. When your father died it was days before I ate a meal. But with you it's different.' Sophie spoke sternly. 'If you don't eat you really will make yourself ill.'

Obediently, under her mother's eyes, Sadie finished eating. She felt six years old again: the knowledge that someone was looking after her made her feel much better. It lasted only briefly. By the end of the day she was beyond caring whether she lived or died.

By ten o'clock that morning, the house was again full of family. Betty and her husband had arrived, bringing with them a heavily veiled Rose, who sat wordlessly by Sadie's bed for ten minutes and was then led away by her daughters. At eleven a motor drew up outside and Sadie heard men's voices. After a short pause the men came into the house and orders were given; they negotiated the stairs and went into the upstairs study. After a long interval they emerged. The three women sat round Sadie's bed listening and yet trying not to hear, all of them unable to speak. The men moved slowly now, treading heavily, and one of them said, 'Careful there on the corner!' The listeners could hear them breathing as they concentrated on carrying their burden down the staircase.

Sadie, anguish in her voice, asked Lena, 'Where is he?'

'In the dining room. We took all the furniture out.'

'Now what happens?'

'Rabbi Salaman will be here soon. Then there are prayers and then . . .' Lena stopped helplessly.

'Can I go down for the prayers?'

Lena and Sophie exchanged a look.

'Better not,' her mother said. 'But if you want, we could ask the rabbi to stand at the door of the dining room. You'd be able to hear.'

'Yes, please.'

Later, she and Sophie listened as the slow voice spoke the Hebrew words. Quietly, Sophie translated, 'Most merciful God, in thine inscrutable wisdom thou hast ordained that the shadow of a great sorrow should fall upon this house. Give us strength to bear our grief.'

She glanced at her daughter. Sadie sat bolt upright, her eyes open, hands so tightly clenched that the veins showed blue.

'Do you want me to go on?' Sophie whispered.

Sadie nodded.

'May his good name abide long in loving hearts,' Sophie continued. 'May we be grateful for the years during which he was spared to us and for the blessings and the comfort that he brought into our lives . . .' She stopped, shaking her head. Her daughter reached out and took her hand. The service continued, then there was a low 'Amen'. Sadie could hear people moving through the hallway and out on to the drive.

'What's happening now?'

Her mother went to the window. 'Everyone's waiting.'

'Where is he?'

'Oh, Sadie,' her voice broke again. 'Sadie, they're bringing him now.'

'I want to see.' She started to get up.

'No!' Sophie hurried over, her hand out. 'Don't look. Don't watch him.'

'I *must*!' She struggled with the covers. 'I must see him.'

Below her window, drawn up along the road, were five or six motors, a handful of carriages. Just before the front door a hearse stood, with drawn blinds. She could see movement among the onlookers, and then through the front door came a group of people. She found herself looking down at the coffin, draped in black. It was carried by four young men. She recognized them all, friends of Asher's. Slowly they negotiated the long front path, and

169

stopped. Carefully they lowered the coffin from their shoulders and placed it on the ground. They raised it again, fixed it on to poles, and slid it into the waiting hearse. Moritz, moving very slowly, was helped into the front seat beside the driver. Followed by the motors and carriages the gleaming black vehicle pulled out into the road.

Sadie stared in disbelief after the hearse as it moved away. She felt nothing but numbed amazement. This could not be happening. It was too monstrous to be true.

Asher was leaving her for the last time.

Chapter Thirteen

The family closed around Sadie.

Oyster-like, they tried to cushion the intrusion of tragedy. With love and concern they sought to soften the bleak landscape of her misery. She could see they meant well, but she could not manage to respond.

Through the horror of those first seven days, while the mourners sat *shivah* and the full realization of her loss grew slowly upon her, she felt there would never be anything for her again. She never wanted to die: the child in her body was now enough of a presence for her to realize she had to look after it. But she could not imagine a future for herself. There seemed no possibility of anything but this enveloping grief. Only her mother brought her comfort. She and Sadie sat for hours, talking endlessly about Asher, about the wedding and the honeymoon, about their life together.

'Cry, cry,' Sophie advised, her arms round her daughter. 'Don't worry, let it out, let it all go. You'll feel better soon. Soon be better now, love. Soon be better now.'

Sadie felt as though the gentle litany of her mother's words was the only reality.

Everything else happened without her agreement. She moved through crowded rooms and talked to people she scarcely knew and performed the actions required of her by her new and hideous circumstances. And all the time she felt totally remote, as though she were behind glass, so that nothing was said or done which directly involved her. Even when people were looking at her with kindness and anxiety and sadness, taking her hands and speaking words which she knew were meant to help, she found herself almost unable to reply.

'Yes,' she would say, 'yes. Thank you. Thank you.'

Sometimes the glass was frosted and opaque and she couldn't see through it properly. After a while she recognized that when it became this way she was crying. She did not know that she was, but would find that her face was wet with tears and her nose was running. Then people would get up and hurry over to her, and the words would begin again.

Sometimes her mother, or Miriam, or Lena, would suggest that she should try and rest. One of them would go with her, and help her take off her dress and put on a wrapper. They would draw the curtains for her, insist that she have a hot drink, and wait till she fell asleep. She always did so almost immediately. She slept not from exhaustion but to escape. In her own bed in the hospitable room with the apricot velvet curtains the glass walls retreated and she felt almost happy. She would lie on her side, her legs drawn up, her arm protectively over her stomach, and think about the baby. She would fall asleep quite serenely. But always, in an hour or two, she would wake out of a panic-stricken dream and find that her pillow was soaked with tears. The dream was always the same. She was looking out of a window at a steep and distant hill. An unseen person was telling her urgently that she must not go near this hill, or something terrible would happen, and the sick apprehension would rise and block her throat so she could not breathe. And always, when she hauled herself out of the nightmare, she would be unsure if she really was awake, and not still enmeshed in sleep.

As the days went by, some semblance of normality returned to her life. Sophie had to go back to Manchester and Sadie accompanied her, only to find herself a stranger now in the streets of her childhood. She was reluctant to see anyone, and after only a week she could no longer bear to share her old room again with her sister: she yearned for her own home. More than anything, she wanted to be where she could still see Asher clearly. His books and papers, his suits and shirts and shaving things: all the possessions which at first she felt she could never bear to see again, now she longed to have around her. When she got home, the first thing she did was to go to bed wearing one of his shirts for solace.

Sadie learnt that she could make her days bearable by filling them with small activities. She concocted errands for herself: she would visit Lena or Rose, go and see Moritz in the gallery, where she would linger for hours, helping to enter new works in his catalogue. There were things she needed for the baby, and she managed to spread out her purchases over weeks, buying one tiny item at a time and going to different shops. The Riley had gone now. She went by omnibus, and walked a good deal.

The worst part, though, was not the days. The days she could fill, if with an effort. It was the nights which defeated her. The endless empty acres of darkness bore down on her so that she came to dread the fading of the day. For hour after hour she would lie awake even though exhausted by the demands the coming child made upon her body. She remembered her grandmother telling her 'the stars in heaven weep with him who weeps at night' and the memory made her tears flow the more. The only way she could get to sleep, and then only after many hours, was to pull a pillow down the bed and mound it again to her back, so that it felt as though Asher were in bed beside her, and if she half-woke its solidity mitigated the loneliness. But she felt ashamed of this childishness and when Annie knocked each morning would drag it out of the covers before she answered.

As the pregnancy advanced, as her belly became hard and swollen with the coming child, the loneliness increased. She took to spending much of her time at Portland Place. She would go there even if the Raphaels were both out, and wander round the rooms: in fact, she preferred their absence. It was not their company she sought, but the

173

knowledge that soon, before the end of the day, someone would come home.

It was Moritz who now seemed the most affected by the loss of his son. His ebullience, his gaiety, were extinguished overnight. A short man, he had always held himself so erect that his lack of height was scarcely noticeable. Now he spent hours slumped dejectedly among his pictures. For the first time Sadie saw that her father-in-law was a shrivelled old man. For him, it was a double loss. Not only was his adored son gone, but he had built up a business for Asher to carry on, and without him there was no interest in the future at all.

Rose reacted differently. Her immediate response was an outpouring of grief. She pressed the heels of her hands against her temples as though her head was bursting with the comprehension of her loss, and rocked herself and wept, calling upon a pitiless God to bring back her child.

'Oh my Asher,' she sobbed and Lena, holding her, cried as much to hear the torment in her voice as she did out of her own unhappiness. 'Oh my Asher, my lovely boy, why have you left me? I can't live without you, I can't, I can't. I don't want to live, not any more.'

When she had calmed down, after the first few days, she began to speak of Asher when he was a small child, a baby. She talked obsessively of him; how he had smiled, when he first sat up, the look on Moritz's face when he rocked his new-born son in the cradle. She talked disjointedly and tirelessly, and her daughters listened. And then, after the thirty days of mourning, the *sheloshim*, Rose revived. It was as though she had plunged so deeply into her sorrow that she had worked through it, as Moritz could not. She had put it so clearly into words that she saw the worst there was to be feared. Rose knew herself. It was her great strength, and it did not fail her now, She had always been the pivot for them all, although her husband's vitality had hidden her role. It had looked as though it was Moritz, with his bustle and talk, who held the family together. Now, like a tree with the foliage stripped away, the form of her power was made plain.

One of the reasons for Rose's recovery was her passionate interest in the coming child. Her concern for Sadie was overwhelming; she worried about her daughter-in-law, did her best to console her. There was no doubt, though, that it was chiefly on account of the child that she did so.

'Try not to cry too much,' she begged Sadie, wiping her eyes and patting her hands, 'think of the baby. You mustn't upset him, you should keep calm, it won't be good for him, all this. You have to be so careful now, you can't worry about yourself.'

'I will try,' Sadie sobbed. 'I'm doing my best. It's all my fault, I know it is. I should never have let Asher ride that dreadful horse, I knew he couldn't manage it.' She blew her nose and drew a deep breath. 'I feel such a failure. Because I didn't take enough care, my baby has no father. No *father*. No one to hold him and be proud of him and look after us both . . .' She looked imploringly at Rose. 'What in God's name am I going to do? What can I do?'

Rose said firmly, 'You mustn't get so upset. I've told you, it's no good for that child. And it won't help. Look,' her voice softened and she knelt down and put her arms round the girl's waist. 'We'll all look after you. There's me and Moritz and Lena and Betty, we're all here. We'll love this baby, and he won't notice he doesn't have a father. We'll take care of you both.'

Sadie said, 'I know you will. But that doesn't solve all the problems. The house is so empty without him, so quiet. It'll be lonely for a child with just me.'

'Nonsense. The baby'll make enough noise for ten people. And anyway, I've been thinking. Moritz and I were saying last night, why don't you sell this house? You can always buy another later, if you want, something smaller.

175

Sell this one and come and live with us. We'll move around, and you can have a suite of your own. There's plenty of room, and we should like it so much.' She stopped, and watched the effect of her words, then added, persuasively, 'Please say you will. You know, it'd make all the difference to Moritz to have a child in the house again.'

Sadie said slowly, 'I think you may be right. I hate being by myself.'

'You don't have to decide anything right away. Only don't take too long. I think you should be with us well before the child arrives. As soon as possible, in fact.' Rose's voice was eager. 'And Moritz could handle the sale for you – he needs something to do, he's lost a lot of interest in the gallery. I'm sure once the baby's here and something positive has happened, he'll be so much better. It'll give us both something to live for.'

Sadie gave a small smile. 'Me, too.'

'Of course, my dear, of course.' She got off her knees, wincing. 'I'm getting too old for these acrobatics. But I can still play ball with the best of them. I was tidying . . .' she stopped, her voice faltering, then went on, 'I was tidying the baby things the other day, with Mabel, and we found Asher's rocking-horse, and skittles. They'll be lovely for the baby when he's a bit bigger. I was going to bring them over to you, but perhaps I'll keep them at Portland Place, shall I, now you're coming to us?'

Sadie nodded. It all seemed to be agreed between them. She felt mainly relief. It would, after all, be the best solution for the time being.

'That will be done, then,' continued Rose. 'I'm having the horse re-painted, and we'll stand it in the baby's room, ready. I thought we'd do the nursery in a nice soft blue, then we can use those velvet curtains I put away in the spring. I saw that patchwork cushion you're working on, dear. Why don't you start one in blues to match?'

Caught up in her enthusiasm, Sadie agreed. Not until

several days later, sorting out material for cushions, did she find herself thinking that this proposed move was not the sudden idea her mother-in-law had implied.

This plan hadn't occurred to Rose overnight, Sadie was sure. It was too neat, too convenient. Rose must have been scheming to think of a way to get her to come to them, and the plea that it would help Moritz was a masterstroke to make her feel she was helping them, rather than the other way around. She didn't mind, though, she was too grateful at the respite it offered from her loneliness.

When, later, she told Rose she would come to Portland Place until the baby was born, the older woman dismissed her time limit with a wave of the hand. 'But of course, my dear, you'll stay on as long as you want. We want to see our little grandson growing up, our little Asher . . .'

'*What*?' Sadie was horror-struck by Rose's slip. 'What did you say?'

Rose faced her calmly. 'I said, "our little Asher". What's wrong with that? Of course you'll name him after his father. It's the custom, you must.'

Sadie said, her throat closing with emotion, 'I can't. I won't. I don't even know if it will be a boy, but even so I couldn't bear to call him Asher. Don't ask me to. It would be awful to call Asher's name and not see the right person. Please don't ask me to.'

She leant forward over the table and buried her face in her folded arms. Rose was all concern.

'Whatever you want, my dear, whatever you say. You'll feel differently when the baby arrives, you see if you don't.'

She smoothed Sadie's hair, and pushed the fringe out of her eyes. 'I had a word with Norah yesterday, I forgot to tell you.'

Sadie sniffed and sat up. 'Who's Norah?'

'She's the children's old nanny. Asher must have told you about her. She was with us for years, and then she went to live with her sister in Richmond. I visit her every year on her birthday. We were talking about the baby,' Rose shot her a look, 'and about looking after him, of course. Norah's niece will be wanting a place in a month or two. She's just spent two years in Staffordshire, with a family who had a fourth baby, as an under-nurse, and Norah thinks she's ready to be promoted. So I said we'd send her fare and get her to come and talk to us – what do you think?'

Sadie nodded. 'Yes, I'd like to see her.'

'The best thing would be to get her to come to Portland Place,' Rose went on, busy straightening the Meissen ornaments on the mantelshelf. 'Then if you're not feeling up to it, I can deal with her.'

It was only afterwards, as she recovered her composure, that Sadie began to feel terrible misgivings. She could not yet put it into words, it was no more than the first stirrings of comprehension. But the more she thought, the more obvious it became. And then, finally, when there was no longer any room for doubt, she admitted to herself what she should have known all along.

Rose wanted this child for herself.

She had been a fool. How could she not have seen this coming? God knows it'd been obvious enough. *It'll give us both something to live for. We want to see our grandson growing up, our little Asher . . .*

Now Rose was even planning to engage a nanny herself. Sadie knew she could never stand up to her mother-in-law's determination. She retreated to her bedroom and sat on the low armless chair Asher had bought her for nursing the baby and tried to imagine what would happen if she moved in with the Raphaels. All too clearly she could see that decisions were already being taken for her, and she was accepting because it was the easy thing to do. Rose had even decided how to decorate the baby's room. And how could Sadie gainsay her? It was Rose's house, after all, and she could do what she liked in it.

A sudden decision pushed her to her feet and she hurried down the hall.

178

'I'm going to Portland Place,' she told Annie. 'I'll get a taximeter cab in the High Street.'

An hour later, face to face with Rose, she had to work to keep up her indignation.

'I don't think I can accept your invitation to come here. It was very kind of you, I'm very grateful, but I don't think it will do.'

'I don't understand.' Rose looked hurt. 'Why won't it do? You were so pleased with the idea.'

'Yes, I know, but I must look after my baby in my own way. I want to be the one who decides what colour the nursery's going to be, and who's going to be the nanny.'

Rose smiled.

'My dear Sadie, you're getting over-excited for nothing. Of course you can decide such things if you feel so strongly about it. Surely you know I only wanted to help? I thought I was making things easier for you.'

'You were making them too easy. I need to have something to think about or I'll go mad.'

Rose looked at her thoughtfully. 'So what will you do instead?'

Sadie paused. In her rush to disclaim Rose's assistance, she had not even considered her alternatives.

'I think I'll stay where I am for the moment. Then I'll decide later what to do.'

Rose poured more China tea and carefully set down the silver tea-pot shaped like a ripe melon.

'Will that be possible?' Her voice was quiet.

'What do you mean?'

'Will you be able to afford to maintain the house?'

Sadie found her hands were shaking so much she could not hold the tea-cup.

'I've managed up till now.' But she knew what was coming.

'Yes, my dear. Moritz has been continuing to pay Asher's salary. But of course . . .' She rose to her feet and went to

179

the window. 'Of course, that cannot continue indefinitely.'

The despair that swept through Sadie was so physical that she thought she was going to faint.

Rose slowly turned to face her, and the two women looked at each other in silence. Sadie knew what Rose was refraining from saying: that as she had brought nothing to the marriage but her trousseau, everything they did for her now was out of kindness. Until now she had deliberately avoided thinking about how she would live: she had grown out of the habit of worrying over money in the five comfortable years of her affluent marriage.

'The house is mine, though,' she said firmly. 'I shall sell and buy something small and the difference in price will keep me going for quite a long time.'

'Yes, my dear, that is possible.' Rose smoothed a fold of the heavy curtains. 'But there is just one problem. It has come to our notice that Asher owed certain – monies – which must be paid.'

'Well, of course there are bills. I will pay them.'

'I don't think you will be able to do that. They are for very considerable sums of money.'

Sadie said slowly, 'I didn't know Asher had other bills. We'd finished the house, and we hadn't had any big expenses except the baby, and those haven't come yet. And anyway,' she felt something was wrong, 'anyway, why did the bills go to you, not to me?'

'These are not bills,' Rose said carefully. 'They are debts.'

Sadie said nothing.

'And they came to us because they were – privately presented.'

'I still don't understand.'

Rose gestured to someone behind Sadie and turning, the girl saw Moritz entering the room. He came over to take her hand and kiss her forehead.

'My dear, a pleasure to see you.' He squeezed her fingers.

'I was just talking to Sadie about . . .'

'I know, I heard.' Moritz continued to hold Sadie's hand. 'Sadie, I don't like to tell you this. But they were gambling debts. Asher hadn't paid them for months, and they've mounted up.'

She looked at him with horror.

'I can't believe what you're saying. I know he gambled, but I thought he always paid promptly. And I didn't know it was for big amounts. He promised me he'd stopped playing for so much. He *promised* me.'

Moritz sighed and put his arm round her shoulders.

'I don't know what to say to you. He signed promissory notes. We've seen them, there's no question about it. He owed a lot of money.'

'How much?'

There was a short silence, then, 'Over one thousand pounds,' said Moritz heavily. Sadie slumped back in her chair.

'Oh no, that's impossible – how could he have lost so much?'

'He wasn't a very good card player.' Moritz gave a wry smile. 'And he played out of his class.'

Sadie remembered Henry Dereham.

'Yes, I know he did. He played against professionals. Woolf said he was cheated.'

'That's as may be. The result is still the same. Just because a man picks unscrupulous opponents, he's not absolved from his debts.'

'But surely I don't have to pay if the money was won from him dishonestly? I couldn't find that much even if I sold the house and moved into rented accommodation.'

'No, no, my dear,' Moritz put his hand on her shoulder. 'We know, and you don't have to pay anything. We'll do it.' Rose started to speak, and he turned to her. 'Will you give us a moment, Rose?' She left the room in silence.

Moritz pulled a chair over to Sadie and sat down.

'Now look, my dear, the way I see it, you'll have to compromise. You're an intelligent girl, you know what sort of a position you're in. We'll look after you, we'll take care of everything. But in return, Rose wants to be able to help you with the baby.'

'She doesn't just want to *help*,' Sadie broke in, 'she wants to take over, she wants it to be *her* baby. Rose has even decided what it's to be called, she's so sure it's going to be a boy. And that's not right. I'm having this child, not her.' Her voice rose in panic. 'Rose has had her family, and this baby is all I've got. All I've got left.'

'There, there.' Moritz made clucking noises, trying ineffectually to soothe her. 'I know, I know.' He sighed. 'Rose is a difficult woman, Sadie, and she's very unhappy. I see how you feel, but are we asking so much? Would it be so terrible if we look after our own grandchild?'

'I just feel I'm being pushed aside, that you're only putting up with me because of the child.' She brushed back her fringe and tried to breathe slowly. 'I have to bring up the baby the way Asher wanted. We talked and talked about it and it's all I can do for him now.'

Moritz tried again. 'Sadie, be reasonable. We're asking only that you move in with us. We're not trying to run your life for you. You'll be able to do what you want, we'll see to it that you have no worries, no responsibilities.'

Sadie stopped listening. There was no point: Moritz was unable to see that was just what she wished to avoid. He thought they were doing her a kindness.

The Raphaels, finally acknowledging that they could not overcome Sadie's incomprehensible refusal to accept their assistance, enlisted the help of their daughters.

Lena called on Sadie, hurrying in clutching an armful of tissue-wrapped parcels.

'I've sorted some of my baby things for you,' she said, impetuously embracing her sister-in-law. Lena was very much her father's daughter. Confident and competent as

182

she was in the glittering world in which she moved, sought after as a hostess, courted as a guest, she nonetheless drew her strength from the knowledge that behind her stood the solid buttress of the family. She was bewildered by Sadie's obstinacy, it made no sense to her to seek isolation: she was sure she could persuade her sister-in-law to see reason.

But it was Betty, finally, who drove Sadie irrevocably to cut herself off from the Raphaels.

The two had never found each other sympathetic. Betty Epstein was slender and dark, with pale skin and a finely etched mouth. At first, Sadie had thought her reserved. Later, she decided Betty was remote because she felt herself to be superior. Impeccably groomed and gowned, in perfect control of herself and every situation, she would watch Asher's nervous bride in the early days of her marriage with a faint amusement which she did not trouble to hide. Betty totally lacked Lena's wit. Nothing she ever said was light, she was incapable of tossing aside any remark. When she was twenty-one she had married John Epstein, a solemn, stolid, clever man who was bullied by his fragile wife. He wanted a family but three miscarriages had frightened them both. Sadie's pregnancy was causing Betty the first pangs of jealousy she had ever felt. So when Lena told her of the problem her parents were having with Sadie, she at first refused to have anything to do with the discussions.

'What has this to do with me?' she asked John when he got home. 'I don't care what Sadie does.'

John, who did not lack perception, said, 'Your parents would appreciate it.'

'It's just meddling, in my opinion. Why should I try to make her change her mind, if she's made it up?' John, who knew better than to oppose her, agreed that she was right. But Betty was enough her mother's daughter to want to be involved, despite her protestations. At eleven next morning she arrived at Ordnance Hill just after her sister.

It was Lena who broached the subject, with her customary lack of reticence.

'You know what we're going to say, don't you?' Sadie, who had asked Annie to bring in Madeira and almond biscuits, said nothing. Unabashed, Lena hurried on, until Sadie said, 'I wish you wouldn't, Lena. I had all this yesterday from your mother and father, and I won't change my mind now.'

'It's all very well being dignified. But what are you going to live on?'

'I'll do what I told them. I'll sell the house and pay some of Asher's debts. I can't meet them all, but I'll do my best. That's all I can do. And then I'll rent something small and have the baby.'

'You're being selfish. Why should the baby suffer because of your pride?'

'The baby won't suffer. It'll be perfectly happy, why shouldn't it be?'

Lena shook her head impatiently. 'I know what I'm talking about. Children need their family around them, they need security. And so do you.'

'Well, I'm going to have to do without, aren't I? I don't have much choice. But at least I can do things in my own way.'

Betty asked curiously, 'Did you really not know about Asher's gambling debts?'

'Do you mean did I know he gambled, or did I know he owed? The answer is yes to the first and no to the second. Though I don't see what business it is of yours.'

'It affects all of us if the debts aren't paid.'

'I said I'll do my best. I can't do more than that.'

'Yes you can. Mother and Father will settle everything if you'll only move in with them. You haven't any right to refuse in your situation. It's wonderful of them to want to help. Under the circumstances.'

Sadie stared at her.

'What do you mean?' she asked, and her voice was low. 'What do you mean, *under the circumstances*?'

Betty gave her a hard look. 'Well, you must admit you had something to do with those debts.'

Sadie felt completely breathless. 'How can you suggest that? I didn't want him to gamble – I hated it. I thought it was a waste of time. But for a long time I never even knew it was for money.' She turned to Lena, appealing to her. 'You must believe me, I had no idea he played for money. There was never any sign of it, I never saw any change hands. I didn't have any idea what was going on until a few months before . . . the accident. And then he promised me it would stop.'

Lena looked sympathetic but Betty said, 'I don't mean you encouraged him to play. I mean that it was because of you he had to.'

'Had to? How?'

'You asked him for things. You wanted things, more than he could afford. So he had to get them somehow and . . .'

'That's not *true*,' Sadie burst out. 'That's not true at all. I didn't ask him for anything.' She thought frantically how she could prove it, and waved her hand round the room. 'I didn't choose all this, all the furniture and pictures. It wasn't me who wanted it. It was your parents' idea, they even paid for it. We lived very simply.'

'You are naïve, aren't you?' Betty spoke with real unkindness, belying the faint smile she had assumed. 'Did you think living simply included carriages and having Sargent paint your portrait, and dresses from Fortuny?'

'But I never asked for those things.' Sadie was bewildered.

'That's not the point. You accepted them all happily enough, didn't you? You let Asher indulge you. And how did you think he could do it? He was only twenty-five when you married.'

Sadie stammered, 'I didn't think, it was all just so lovely,

185

I just thought it was all right.'

Lena said briskly, 'You know, Betty, I don't believe we can assume that Asher's chief motivation was to give things to Sadie. I seem to remember,' she paused meaningfully, 'I seem to remember there'd been trouble in that direction before, don't you?'

The other woman shook her head.

'Oh now, I'm sure you do,' Lena went on. 'When Asher was in Berne working on his French, don't you remember that fuss when Papa had to arrange for all the extra money to be put into his bank account there? And how furious he was, stamping about all over the house and shouting at Mother that she'd spoilt Asher?'

'Yes, you're right, I'd forgotten.' Betty seemed reluctant to admit that Asher had ever been less than perfect.

Lena turned to Sadie and said gently, 'It was a bit silly of you, though, wasn't it, not to be more careful? He loved you very much, you know, and he wanted to make you happy and give you things. And I suppose gambling seemed an easy way to go on doing that. Only surely you had some idea what a dress from Fortuny would cost? After all, Eleanora Duse wears them. I believe they can be as much as twelve pounds.'

Sadie shook her head.

'Or how much Sargent's fee would be?'

'I didn't know there *was* a fee.'

Lena and Betty exchanged glances.

Betty said, 'Father mentioned that most of the debts seem to have been incurred in the last few months. Did he seem any different. Did you notice anything?'

'He used to stay out very late, but,' she slammed her hand into her palm, 'I feel such a fool. I thought it was because I was tired and he was bored with me.'

Betty made an impatient sound, but Lena said, 'We can't blame you for feeling tired at the moment, you poor thing. But don't you think it's yet another reason for going to

Portland Place? You could rest there, without any problems. Sadie, please be sensible. Having a baby is quite an undertaking, believe me. To be alone towards the end will be impossible, you must be looked after. And then, when the baby arrives, you won't want to be by yourself.'

Sadie folded her arms over her stomach, hugging the baby to herself. Her throat hurt so much she could hardly speak. 'I don't want to be by myself. Of course I don't – I want to be with Asher! But I never will again, never again.' She wanted to scream, her eyes were burning, but the anger that she felt was greater than tears.

'And now I know what you really think of me, all of you. You think I've been extravagant and wasteful.'

Lena watched her with compassion, Betty with hostility.

'Well, maybe I've been ignorant and stupid, but those aren't crimes, are they? Maybe I didn't see what was happening, but if I didn't, it was because I trusted my husband.' Her voice rose. I'm getting hysterical, she thought, calm down. She tried to draw a deep breath. In the short silence, Betty's cool voice commented, 'Lena and I both manage our own household affairs. We know what money is earned and where it is. I certainly wouldn't dream of letting John do anything I didn't know about.'

'It's different for you,' Sadie said, helplessly. 'Don't you see the difference? It's your money as well, your parents gave it to you, when you married. But I never felt I had the right to keep a check on Asher. And I didn't want to. I never dreamt of prying or asking him what he was doing.'

She got to her feet and held out a hand to Lena. The older woman took it.

'I don't want you to think I didn't concern myself with Asher's affairs. But I was only eighteen when we got married. Asher was always the one who arranged things. And then somehow it just went on like that.' She turned to Betty and her voice was shaking.

'I see it was foolish of me. I see that I was being childish and thoughtless. But to make me pay the price you're all asking is cruel.'

'We're not asking you to pay a price, Sadie, you're talking wildly,' Betty protested.

'We're all trying to help,' Lena said. 'Papa and Mother are going to pay all the debts.'

'Yes,' Sadie said bitterly. 'And keep me. I know. I'll be fed and clothed and housed for nothing. And all I've got to do . . .' her voice rose, 'all I've got to do in exchange is give up my home and let your parents make all my decisions. Your mother will paint *her* nursery for *my* baby. She's already telling me what the baby is to be called. And since she'll be paying, she will undoubtedly also choose the baby's clothes and tell me what the baby eats.'

She looked at the two women. Betty's face was expressionless, Lena was nodding in reluctant agreement. If I don't get out of here, Sadie thought, I'm going to cry again.

'I'm not saying they're not kind. But surely to God I can live where I want with my own things?' She moved to the door. 'Do I have to go and sit in two rooms in your parents' house like an old servant?'

The door slammed behind her.

Chapter Fourteen

One morning Sadie received a letter from Almond, Pearson and Rose. Asher's lawyers suggested that she might care to visit their offices next Tuesday morning at eleven. She had never been there, but knew they were situated near Blackfriars, just off Ludgate Hill – it would be a pleasant enough journey by omnibus. She wrote to confirm the appointment, but two days later, waking to a heavy wet mist outside her windows, she wished she need not go. Dressed and ready, she was more than grateful when Annie insisted on accompanying her. The omnibus travelled with painful slowness down through St John's Wood. The sudden stops and lurches were making Sadie queasy and she was relieved when the conductor announced that they could go no further: gesturing outside at the clammy grey cloud he advised them all to go home.

'How'll we get back?' Annie asked anxiously.

'I think I'd rather go on, if we can. It might not be so bad in the City and I've nothing else to do today anyway.'

Annie looked horrified. 'Oh, I don't think we should do that. The conductor's right, it looks terrible. We might be stuck for hours.'

'I know.' Delighted with the inspiration, Sadie said excitedly, 'We'll go on the tuppenny tube. Why didn't I think of it before? It shouldn't be affected nearly so much by the weather.'

'Oh no, Madam!' Annie was shocked. 'You couldn't travel on the tube, not in your condition. It's far too dangerous.'

'Of course I can. Come on, it won't take long to walk to Baker Street Station.'

'No!' Annie was adamant. 'I couldn't face it, not at my

189

time of life. I'm sorry.'

'Well, what will you do?'

'I'll walk over to my sister, if you don't mind. She's in service in Marylebone, and it wouldn't take more than half an hour to walk. It's my afternoon off anyway, and if it gets no better, I expect she could find a bed for me.'

Sadie hurried alone through the dank streets to the tube station, anxious not to be late. She paid her tuppence at the booking office, and received a small piece of pink card. She hesitated at the grubby stairs, which seemed to stretch down for ever. The air smelt heavy and sickly sweet.

Undecided, she paused at the top of the stairway until a crowd of hurrying passengers behind her forced her to move forward. She started down, gripping the handrail: long before she reached the bottom her legs were trembling from the effort. She looked with apprehension at low arched passages, dimly lit with electric lights in the ceiling. They branched off in several directions, but signs marked them all. She stopped to catch her breath and read them. They listed the direction the trains were going. She made for the City branch, passing through heavy iron gates at the end of the platform. It was crowded with people waiting in silence in the half-light. As she moved forward a warm draught rushed against her face, bringing with it that overpowering smell of stale air. Sickened, she thought, I must sit down.

There was a bench near her, but it was crammed with people. She moved along the platform, looking for another. A new crush of passengers behind hurried her along, the crowd now packed so tightly that to get through she had to move towards the edge of the platform. A bell rang loudly, and a hoarse voice shouted, 'Train coming! Stand back. Stand back there, please!' A uniformed figure was waving a red flag and pushing people away from the rails.

Sadie stepped back obediently, and a bulky woman behind her cursed volubly as she stood on her foot. She could feel rather than hear a distant rumbling as though the earth beneath her was opening. From the tunnel where the track disappeared, dark and menacing as the lair of some prehistoric predator, the hot wind blew more fiercely. Her sense of smell was sharpened by pregnancy and the odour of human sweat and bad breath it brought with it, made her want to retch. Her ears began to ring, and her hands were cold and damp. Surely she was not going to be ill in such surroundings. She wished to God she'd listened to Annie.

Somewhere behind her metal clanged harshly on metal: they must be closing the platform gates. She would be trapped down here. Panic closed her throat. She must get out. She turned her back to the rails and started to push her way through the packed figures. Despite the shouted injunctions of the guards, 'Back there, no pushing!' they were beginning to surge forward, forcing her towards the drop. Wildly she tried to claw her way through, tearing at one man's shoulders, trying to squeeze under another's arm. Her ears were full of thunder, she saw the blazing eyes of the train rushing towards her through the tunnel. Panting, trying to steady herself, she clutched and shoved.

Using the last of her strength she found she had reached the back of the platform and the heavy iron gates. On the far side she could see the uniformed figure. She shouted at him to let her out but in the din he could not make out her meaning, merely shaking his head and pointing towards the train. Wearily she clung to the metal grille while behind her she heard the noise abate as the doors were closed on the passengers. After a pause the train clanged into life again and drew away from the platform. She felt the rush of wind as it departed and then, as the echoes of its passing died away, the welcome silence. The guard opened the grille, concerned now that he saw her state.

'All right, are you? It gets a bit 'ot if you're not used to it.'
She nodded.
'Sit down, I would, before tackling them stairs again,' he advised.

191

She saw that he was right, but could not bear to stay down there any longer than necessary. Slowly, holding on to the handrail, she climbed up the stairs, welcoming the damply curling fingers of fog. Outside the tube station she leaned against the wall to get her breath. It was too far to walk home and there was no sign of a taximeter cab. Desperately she wondered where she could go until she had a chance to recover. Looking up the road it suddenly occurred to her that Woolf Lander had a house just two roads away, towards the cricket ground.

'What on earth were you doing down there in the first place? I decided to work at home rather than brave the elements.' Woolf handed her a glass. She tasted it and winced.

'Go on, drink it,' he ordered. 'It's got plenty of water in it and you look as if you need a brandy.'

Obediently she drank some, then leaned her head against the high leather chair back. 'I was going to Asher's solicitors. The fog stopped the omnibus and so I thought I'd try the tube train. It seemed such a good idea at the time.'

He said curiously, 'Have you ever been on it before?'

'No.'

'I thought not. If you suffer from claustrophobia it was perhaps a mistake to have attempted such a journey.'

'I don't think I do. I've never felt like that before. It must be the baby.'

Seeing the puzzlement on his face she gave a half smile. 'I'm going to have a child. Didn't you know?'

He shook his head.

'Woolf, I'm sorry. I thought somehow you would have heard. Didn't Asher . . .' she faltered as she always did when she spoke his name, then went on, 'didn't Asher tell you?'

'I've been working in Birmingham for three months. I didn't even hear about the accident until a fortnight after it happened. Surely you received my letter?'

She blushed. 'Of course. My mind isn't working properly. When did you get back?'

'Four days ago. I was planning to write to you this evening, to see if I could call.'

She looked round the tall room. Woolf lived in half a house, and his mother had a separate apartment below him. The sitting room was unlike any she had been in. It seemed at first almost spartan in its simplicity. She was to think later, when she had more cause to do so, and when the word had entered her vocabulary, that it was almost monkish. The walls were pale, where they were visible, for they were covered with bookshelves containing sets of encyclopaedias, volumes of poetry, books on astronomy. She noticed with some surprise that he had all Jane Austen's novels. Seeing her glance he said, in explanation, 'I like her polished turns of phrase.'

The uncurtained windows looked out on to a secluded, slightly unkempt garden, and would normally, she imagined, let in the sun. Today they allowed the grey mist to intrude its chill into the room. The floor was well-polished wood with a few worn Persian rugs. The few chairs were hard-backed, of dark oak. Only the one in which Sadie sat could be used for relaxation. The single table was covered with papers: an open *Times*, with an article on a new song cycle, 'Pierrot Lunaire', by Schönberg, heavily ringed in black pencil, and a copy of the *Observer* headlined 'Woodrow Wilson, Democrat, wins American Presidential election.'

Woolf observed her taking in her surroundings and said defensively, 'I'm afraid I'm unused to entertaining ladies at home. A bachelor failing.'

'I wasn't being critical. I like it.'

'Are you warmer now? Can I take your coat?'

She rose and he helped her take off her voluminous cape.

Without its folds he saw just how advanced her pregnancy was. Never a man to make unpremeditated comments, he found himself saying: 'I'm so sorry.'

Sadie looked at him steadily. 'About Asher? Thank you.'

'And about the child. How terrible that he will never see his child.' His voice shook and he bent his head. Sadie was moved. She had known Woolf since early in her marriage and the three of them had been on cordial, though not intimate, terms. In all that time she had never seen his urbane calm disturbed. He recovered himself quickly, and they talked of his books and pictures. He collected mainly nineteenth-century English works and showed her his latest acquisition, a small country scene. Later, he took her home in a cab.

The next afternoon he called to see if she had recovered. She was lying on a sofa, stitching patchwork. Woolf had always seen Sadie at public gatherings: at gallery openings, at parties, at the gambling club. She had always seemed to him an elegant, self-possessed young woman. Yet here she was in a cotton smock with her hair pinned up on top of her head. She looked domesticated and defenceless, and he felt flattered that she had not made him wait while she dressed up for him.

While they talked – he was telling her about his cases in Birmingham – she continued to stitch away. He was fascinated by the care she was taking over the minute squares of flowered material. He didn't think he had ever seen anyone sewing. His mother had never done any, had employed a woman who came in one day a week to darn sheets and socks. He cleared his throat, adjusted his gold-rimmed glasses, and asked what she was making. Sadie said it was to be a nursery cushion, and then to her amazement, for she had not meant to tell him, the story of her rift with the Raphaels poured out.

When she had finished, she apologized, anxiously. 'I'm

not going around trying to justify myself. Only I felt I was going to lose all control over my own life.'

'Yes, I do see that. But I'm really worried now. What on earth are you going to do about money? You must get some advice.'

Sadie sighed. 'I know. But I don't like to go to anyone. It'd mean having to talk about Asher's gambling debts. It's one thing telling you – you've known all along, you tried to stop him. But how am I to tell a bank manager my husband gambled wildly? I just couldn't.'

Woolf got to his feet. He went to the window and stood looking at the narrow garden. His hands were clasped behind his back, shoulders hunched in thought.

'Apart from the house, have you anything to sell?'

Sadie sighed. 'Look around you. Most of the good things have gone already. And there'll be terrible rows when the Raphaels find out. They paid for all the furniture bought in Belgium. It was mine to sell, it was part of the marriage settlement, but they'll not like it. There really isn't anything else I can think of. The Riley has gone, I've hardly any jewellery, and next I'll start on my clothes.'

'Don't do that.'

She raised her eyebrows at him. 'No?'

'No. Wait a minute.'

He went out of the room, returned a moment later smiling with satisfaction. 'You've forgotten one thing, Sadie. Probably the most valuable item you've got.' Astonished she waited for him to go on.

Triumphantly he continued, 'Sargent's portrait of you.'

Slowly, Sadie said, 'I hadn't thought of that.'

'Well, I should think it's worth a small fortune to you now.'

She hesitated. 'I suppose it is. But I'd be sorry to part with it – I'll never have anything like that again. It's me. It's mine.'

Woolf looked at her for a long moment. Then he

smoothed his thinning brown hair carefully, and cleared his throat.

'There *is* a way round that.'

She brightened. 'What?'

'I'll buy it.'

Sadie was dumbfounded. 'It's not your sort of thing at all – Sargent's much too ostentatious for you. He's everything you dislike in a painter: he's fashionable and he's alive.'

Woolf looked shy. 'I know, I know. You've left out one other thing – it's a picture of a woman.'

'You're right,' Sadie said, slowly. 'Now I come to think of it, all the paintings you showed me yesterday were either of landscapes or buildings.' Struck by this curious thought, she asked, 'Why is that?'

Woolf shrugged, 'Who knows? Maybe I wouldn't feel at ease being watched from the walls. It's not a conscious thing. I don't go out and think, Aha, another landscape. But that's what I arrive home with.'

'Well then, why do you want me watching you from the walls?'

'That would be different.' He gave her a sudden, sweet smile. 'I know you.'

His sincerity was irresistible. Sadie said, 'I'd like you to have it. At least I'd know where I was.' She laughed. 'But I've no idea what it's worth.'

'Neither have I. But I'll find out. I should think around eight hundred guineas.'

Sadie gasped in surprise. 'Not really!'

'I'll pay the market price. The alternative is to sell it by auction. You'd probably get more that way.'

'Yes, but I couldn't ever see it again. And besides, think of the problems with Moritz. I don't want to upset the Raphaels, whatever I feel about them just now.'

Woolf Lander bought the painting of Sadie, and the money paid the majority of Asher's debts.

They went back together to his flat to hang it, and finally he put it on the wall dividing the two long windows. That evening, alone, he decided to move it, and hung it above the fireplace in his bedroom. He lay in bed contemplating his acquisition.

Woolf Lander was thirty-four years old and had never loved a woman. The only child of German-born parents, he was educated at Malvern College in Worcestershire, one of the first Jews to be admitted there. With his long face and fine-drawn features he scarcely looked Semitic and was spared much of the bullying he expected. He read law at Oxford and was accepted as a pupil by solicitors in Manchester Square who specialized in commercial law. The friends he made at university were drawn to him because he was an excellent listener, the perfect recipient of their problems and tribulations. He himself did not seem to have any: enough money to fulfil his wants, enough charm to smooth his path, enough talent to satisfy his tutors. When his contemporaries were making emotional forays he contented himself with reading books, and started, in a small way, to collect English landscape paintings. His university friends cherished him as a budding eccentric and invited him to their homes, when they married, for dinner-parties: he sometimes marvelled at the number of unmarried sisters and sister-in-laws to whom, over the years, he had been introduced. Occasionally he would make up a small group to visit a theatre or the ballet and afterwards dine: on these occasions there was always a presentable young woman available to accompany him, but she was rarely invited twice. Woolf Lander got on comfortably with everyone, offending none. He did well in his practice and was beginning to command considerable fees.

His father had recently died and he and his mother had purchased their present house together. The arrangement suited them both, for they were fond of each other. He treated his mother with courtly deference, she behaved

197

towards him with an odd mixture of adoration and flirtatiousness, almost as though he were a young husband. Her presence fended off his friends' anxieties about his loneliness, and the pair of them had settled into a routine which gave them both the exact amount of company they required. There were almost no emotional demands made upon Woolf Lander, and he liked it that way.

Until now.

He was not a self-aware man. He had made for himself a pleasant existence. His work was important to him and he knew a great many people. He acknowledged that he was not greatly interested in sexual matters but did not attach much importance to worrying about this. His mother would try to encourage him towards matrimony but he blandly deflected these attempts. Towards eligible women he had, over the years, perfected an air of charming preoccupation. Most of his friends assumed he had a long-established mistress and he did nothing to dissuade them. He had always been entirely satisfied with his arrangements. Nevertheless, he was vaguely aware that time was no longer quite so much on his side. He did not relish the prospect of ageing alone and he had recently begun to wonder whether he ought not to take steps to do something about this. However, he told himself, this was not the time to worry about such things; he had a great deal of work to get through the next day.

He got out of bed and opened his window exactly four inches, then laid his dressing gown neatly over a chair. He arranged himself in the middle of the bed on his back, and pulled the covers just as he liked them. He straightened his book, placed his glassed on their wooden stand, switched off his bedside light and was asleep within three minutes.

Old Mrs Lander did not often concern herself with the sorrows of others. A self-centred woman, age had not changed her, and she was incapable of putting herself in another's place. Woolf was therefore surprised at the interest she evinced when he spoke about Sadie Raphael. He did not mention the rift with the family, but told his mother about the expected child. Mrs Lander took it upon herself to call on Sadie, 'to see if there is anything I can do, my dear,' as she put it, but really just to see.

Towards the end of the half-hour they spent together Sadie said how grateful she was to Woolf for buying the Sargent.

Old Mrs Lander looked interested. 'I didn't notice he'd bought another picture.'

'Oh yes. We hung it between the windows.'

'Well, my dear, it isn't there now. I was upstairs only two days ago, for a little sherry, and nothing was said of a painting.'

Taken aback, Sadie said, 'Perhaps he didn't like it after all,' and turned the conversation away.

Afterwards she began to worry. She had been right: Woolf had bought the picture just to help her, not because he wanted it. Now he'd either sold it or hidden it in a cupboard. Either way she felt badly about letting him invest so much money in something he did not want. Without pausing to consider the action, she wrote telling him that she would return his money if he did not wish to keep the painting.

The next evening, Woolf Lander called again to see her. He was clearly perturbed. 'Why on earth should you think I don't want the Sargent? You know how much I like it.'

'I thought I did. I'm not trying to pry into your arrangements, honestly. But your mother very kindly came to see me, and we were chatting, and she said you did not have the painting.'

'Of course I have it. Oh, I see, you mean she hadn't seen it.' He looked slightly shamefaced. 'The truth is, it's not in the sitting room any more. I moved it. It's in the other room, that's all. It looks better there.'

Relieved, Sadie went on to tell him of her visit to the solicitors – a visit she had finally made. Woolf gave her some advice and shortly left. It was only when she was alone that Sadie realized something she had overlooked. Woolf's flat had only two rooms besides the bathroom: the living room and the bedroom. So her picture must be hanging in his bedroom. It took her some time to work out the significance of this.

She sat in her conservatory, unconsciously pleating the lace table cover between her fingers, then smoothing it out upon her knee with the flat of her hand, absorbed in her thoughts. The child stirred and stretched in her womb, and she felt the quickening with pleasure and a sense of panic.

She knew she must make some sensible plan for her child's future. She was nearing the end of her seventh month, and very soon she would be tied as never before, not only physically but emotionally. She must force herself to think clearly, for both their sakes.

Her greatest worry was financial. The Raphaels had continued her allowance, but she was conscious that if she did not relent and go to Portland Place this might stop at any moment, or at best be drastically reduced. There would shortly be the expenses of the child's birth: the doctor's fee alone would be around twelve guineas. Almond, Pearson and Rose had not helped matters greatly. Although Mr Rose had spoken of her best interests and produced numerous papers, Asher had left very little, and the gambling debts had eaten up anything due to her. Her mother had been wonderful, but Sadie was determined that whatever happened she would not return to Manchester.

Uncle Mark had already told her that he and Zipporah were waiting for her to go to them for as long as she wanted. This she saw as a last resort. They had done so much for her already, and she could imagine the expression on Zipporah's face if a bawling baby disturbed the stately routine of Maida Vale. No, she would have to think of something else.

Sadie pleated the lace again between her fingers. Absently she watched herself doing it: ordered precise movements while she reviewed her ravaged life.

She could make no deliberate attempts to overcome her sorrow: she had loved Asher too much to deny grieving for him. Yet she was twenty-three years old, and carrying her future within her. Despite herself, she was just starting to revive. She could think about him now, recount to herself things they said to each other. She would cry, but the wild hysteria had gone. What she could not do was accustom herself to the loneliness. Nothing in her life had prepared her for this: to commence each day by herself, to make plans and come to decisions independently, to eat meals alone and go out unaccompanied.

She thought now that she might one day recover from Asher's death. From his death, but not from the loss of him.

Woolf fell into the habit of calling upon Sadie in the evenings, during the course of his regular constitutional stroll. He always told himself he would only stay five minutes, and was regularly surprised as yet again he failed to notice than an hour had gone by.

One afternoon while Sadie was resting, Annie brought in Dora Lander's card.

'Don't get up, my dear,' her visitor called, seeing Sadie start to sit up as she entered the little red sitting room. 'It's an informal call – I hope you don't mind?'

Sadie shook her head. She had been crying again, her face must be blotched and scarlet, and the last thing she wanted from Woolf's mother was her sympathy. However, it soon became apparent from the brisk way in which the old lady smoothed the dark grosgrain of her skirt that she was intent upon some ploy of her own. She dispensed rapidly with the polite formalities about Sadie's health.

'I think I can speak directly to you, my dear,' she began. Sadie, alerted by the unlooked-for endearment, gave a guarded assent. 'Then I'll be frank with you. It's always been in my mind, you know, that you might be – how can I put it – something of an adventuress.' She nodded at the look of shocked anger on Sadie's face. 'Oh yes. I'm not a fool, and I'd heard there was talk of another man before your husband. And I know, too, that the wedding was all arranged very quickly. There wasn't money on your family's side, was there? So you made a good match for yourself.'

She leaned across and patted Sadie's hand. The younger woman stiffened perceptibly. 'I know I shouldn't say all this,' Dora Lander went on. 'It's not tactful, not at all discreet. But that has never been my way, and I'm too old to change now. For what I want to say to you, there must be honesty between us.'

'I don't understand.' Sadie, still not properly awake, was now cross and miserable, upset that anyone should have described her as an adventuress. If she hadn't felt so weak she would have asked the old lady to leave.

'Don't be so annoyed,' her visitor continued. 'I think now that I was wrong. You're not a fool, but you're not so calculating as that. I see why they wanted you, Asher and the other one. Even in your condition,' she averted her eyes carefully from Sadie's rounded stomach, 'even in your condition, you're a charming girl. Quite charming.'

Sadie closed her eyes. The wretched woman was rambling. 'Now,' she was saying, 'Woolf has told me something of the predicament you find yourself in. And I want to help if I can.' Sadie opened her eyes and kept quiet. 'Now I know this isn't the right time, with you still in mourning, but the way I see it, you need to sort out your future. Am I right?' She waited for Sadie's nod, then folded her hands together. 'Very well. You need a secure home, someone to look after you, and a father for the coming child.'

Sadie said, her voice flat, 'If wishes were horses.' To herself she thought, I just want Asher back, that's all. I want it to be the way it was before.

Dora Lander, who was not without compassion, nodded her understanding. 'I know it's hard to discuss, but we have to be practical now. So we know what you need. Now we come to what I need.' she sighed. 'My problem is that I have a son who has money, a good position – and no one to look after him but me. I can't last for ever, and what will happen to him when I'm gone?'

Puzzled, Sadie stared at her. Dora Lander gestured impatiently. 'Woolf has kept bachelor hall for quite long enough to my mind. I want you to take him on for me.'

'Take him on?' Sadie gasped.

'I want you and Woolf to marry. You'll get what you want, someone to look after you – and so will he. He needs a wife, my Woolf, but he doesn't know it. He doesn't see what's good for him. He thinks his work is all that matters, his work and music and those paintings of his. He's let his youth go by, he's got set in his ways, and soon it'll be too late. When he finds out what he wants, he'll be too old to get it.' She stopped, and gave the young woman a shrewd glance. 'So what do you think? It's a good plan. Will you do it?'

Sadie lay back, her mouth half open in amazement. She forced herself to say, 'But what if he doesn't want to?'

Woolf's mother sat a little straighter. 'Leave that to me. All I need to know is that you're willing. I'll handle everything.' She smiled at Sadie, suddenly conspiratorial, youthful, enjoying the plotting. 'Give me till next week. Then I want you to invite him here, serve him a nice meal, dress yourself up.' She held out a hand, cajoling, anxious now. 'To tell you the truth, it would be a *mitzvah* for me. You'd be doing me a kindness. I worry about him. It's not natural, to be alone, it's not good for him. And I've always been afraid he'd fall for the wrong sort, choose some silly little blonde *shiksa* with no brains. I'd rather he had you. I'd be happy to see him at your side.'

Sadie levered herself off the sofa and crossed the room to stare unseeing across the rain-soaked garden. She was bemused by the way the old lady had seemed at first to attack, only to proffer this incredible plan. In all her panic-stricken imaginings, the idea of re-marriage had never crossed her mind. Without looking at the other woman, she asked,

'Surely Woolf wouldn't want to marry me in my present state?'

Old Mrs Lander's response was brisk. 'Why not? Do him good. A man of his age needs responsibilities.'

Sadie continued to watch the rain. Certainly she liked Woolf. She had turned to him for help and he had given it. And he was far from averse to her: the incident of the painting had shown her that. So – what better solution would there be for her? And for him, too. If his mother was right, if he really had never taken the trouble to find a wife, then perhaps she could make him happy, take care of him. She glanced down at the roll-top desk. A letter had arrived by the afternoon post. *Mrs Asher Raphael.* Her identity for five years, and one that she would lose if she took another husband. Yet surely she would be the same person, whatever she was called. Asher would always be a part of her, whether or not she carried his name. She was silent for so long that Dora Lander twisted round in her chair to see, and watched with unaccustomed pity as the younger woman gathered the material of her dress into little folds, and smoothed them against her thigh, obsessively, over and over.

Annie was perturbed by the fuss. The house had been quiet for weeks, then suddenly there was this unaccustomed flurry of activity. Mrs Raphael had asked her to get the step

204

girl in, and the front steps had been whitened for an hour. She herself had polished the brass and was now – she groaned to herself – cleaning the silver, what there was left of it. She breathed on the candlestick she held, and rubbed the duster over it again before she was satisfied. Friday night too, just when she'd been hoping for a bit of a rest. Ah well, she'd better start on the dinner. She heaved herself to her feet and opened the door of the range fire with a poker. They were running low on coal again. And the Lord knew how she was supposed to provide a decent meal on the money they were spending now. And when she thought of how things used to be – she sighed again and shut the range door with a vicious slam. And the poor girl having a baby, too, and left all alone. Annie shook the flour sifter over the board and her hands, and started on the strudel paste.

Woolf had been mildly surprised by Sadie's invitation to dine on Friday night. 'It will not be a social occasion,' she had written. 'There will be no other guests, as I am not yet entertaining. But if you do not mind the lack of conversation, it would be so pleasant to see you.'

He had accepted without demur. Sadie was one of the rare women he found he liked to talk to. Perhaps it was because he had come to know her well during the years of her marriage. Then, as the wife of a close friend, she had expected nothing more of him than he had wished to give. He had been free to fulfil his favourite role as an amusing, uncommitted companion. Now, standing opposite her across the white napery of the Sabbath table, he waited for her to finish blessing the candles. She stood with her eyes closed, passing her hands palm down over the flames towards her.

'*Baruch attah adonai elohanu . . .*' She lifted a heavily embroidered cloth. Beneath it were two newly baked *challeh*, their shiny braided tops sprinkled with poppy seeds.

'Will you do it for me?'

Surprised, Woolf said, 'I haven't done this for years, you know.'

'Please.'

He cut a slice of the crust, broke it in two, sprinkled it with salt. Then he lifted the silver goblet into which Sadie had poured a measure of wine. He was surprised to find he remembered the blessing.

He finished, and sipped, and passed the goblet across to Sadie. Then he lifted the plate with the prepared *challeh*, and recited the blessing for bread, took his piece, and offered the plate. The small ritual filled him with unexpected pleasure, and he smiled appreciatively at Sadie.

She was exhausted this evening, but determined not to let it show. Usually she went to bed at nine, unable to hold herself upright any longer, but tonight she had made a special effort. She had dressed her hair high on her head and routed through her wardrobe to find something pretty. All her clothes by now were stretched tightly across her broadening figure. In the end she had made do with a long cream delaine dress that fell from a yoke. It was too summery for the early spring, and she shivered under its thin folds. But it was either that or one of her cotton smocks.

She thought unhappily as she dressed that Asher would have been cross with her for wearing something so cool in this weather. Well, she had no choice.

To Woolf, who knew nothing of women's clothes, she looked again like a milkmaid. He talked easily through dinner, greedily enjoying thick steaks of halibut. Sadie said little, but he scarcely noticed, and she relaxed and listened with interest. When they had finished and were each drinking a small glass of port Woolf tilted his chair back and looked up at the ceiling.

'I don't believe I've spent so pleasant an evening in months. Thank you.'

206

'I'm pleased you're here. I hate *Shabbes* alone. Usually I go to Lena, but I think it's a night to spend in your own home.' Hesitantly she added, 'Perhaps you would bring your mother next time?'

He agreed with alacrity and then lapsed into a thoughtful silence. He found himself in a situation he had not previously encountered. For years he had so carefully protected himself against women that the question of marriage had simply never arisen. He had become fond of Sadie almost without knowing it: as the wife of a friend she had presented him with no threat. But now the situation was very different. He had mentioned casually to his mother that he would be dining with Sadie Raphael, and for the first time that he could recall had been given unsought advice. He tapped his fingers against the glass and reflected that she had virtually issued an order, so determined was her manner. He had deflected her as he always could, but she had made him aware of possibilities that had not occurred to him. He continued to tap his glass, assessing advantages and disadvantages as if he were preparing a case.

Sadie was intelligent and prudent – he remembered how she hated seeing the gambling that evening when Asher was cheated at cards. He could certainly appreciate her value as an asset to him professionally. And a family would make him a more solid figure. But then, to set against that – he lifted his small gold spectacles and rubbed the bridge of his nose before replacing them – to set against that, what would she want of him? He did not care for close relationships, had never felt the need for a woman's company. He had put all his energies into his work, and had achieved considerable success. He sipped his port. Perhaps his mother had been right the other day when she said time was passing him by. He remembered that night not so long ago when he had lain awake and wondered what the future held, experiencing a presage of loneliness that had chilled him. He glanced up at his hostess, noting the curve of her neck as she sat sewing another of those little cushions of hers. It could be that he was too set in his ways, after all, too rigid. Maybe he should at least make the attempt, before it was too late.

He cleared his throat, not knowing what he was going to say, and as she looked up at him he saw that her eyes were blurred with tears. When he said, 'Now then, whatever is it?' his voice more brusque than he had intended, clumsy in the face of emotions to which he was a stranger, the look on her face was so desolate, so vulnerable, that for the first time in his life he experienced a desire to protect. He got up, the chair falling unheeded behind him, and put his arm about her shoulders. He whispered, 'There, there,' and she turned, clinging suddenly to him as no woman had clung before, desperate, despairing.

He sat, then, holding her to him, tentative and tense, oddly happy, hearing her breathing grow calmer. When he had lent her his immaculate handkerchief and she had composed herself he continued to watch her, holding her hand. She looked at him with gratitude and he found himself wondering what colour her eyes were: shadowed, smokey, serious, they made him feel that only he could help her. And in those moments he decided his mother was right after all.

'I have spent a good deal of time thinking about your problem,' he told her, suddenly resolute, 'and I believe I may have a possible solution, if you wish to hear it.' She nodded and he continued, defensive as ever in personal matters, 'Sadie, I do not believe I am the marrying kind. In thirty-four years I have never seriously thought of it.'

She watched him, very still now, as he told her that he was, indeed, fond of her, that he valued her friendship more than that of any woman he knew. He had, he said, been wondering whether he should not change his style of life, make some provision for the future. He had always lived carefully, he did not rush into anything, and temperament-ally found it hard to change that.

'But on this occasion,' he finished, 'I think a speedy decision might alleviate a good deal of unhappiness and I believe you would find it a not unsatisfactory outcome to all your difficulties. So I wondered if you would care to marry me?'

Sadie got to her feet, turning away to pull the velvet curtains into symmetrical folds and hide her expression. This was what she had already acceded to, after all. But now that she heard the words, now that her imaginings had become reality, it did not seem so straightforward. She had always liked Woolf, and his new tenderness towards her intensified this, but his aloof, slightly amused air intimidated her. If she was unable to picture him even in an informal situation, it was impossible to imagine him in an intimate one: how would they behave at breakfast, how pass an entire evening together? He seemed so settled, so orderly, that she could not place him in the frame of what she knew of married life. She found herself asking, 'But Woolf, why do you want to marry me? I don't understand.'

He frowned in puzzlement. 'I thought I'd explained. It seems to me to improve both our situations.'

'I know it would help me. But you – your life seems so well regulated, so neat. Are you sure you aren't doing this for Asher, really, not for me?'

Now it was Woolf's turn to pause. Thoughtfully he rubbed the side of his nose.

'I suppose you may be right. I was most fond of Asher. Most fond.' He could not say, I used to feel envy at your happiness, I would like to be a part of the closeness I saw between you, because he was not aware that this was true. Unused to sexual emotions, he simply failed to recognize them.

Very low, Sadie answered, 'I don't want you ever to think I would forget Asher. I could never do that.' She turned round to see him, waiting for his reaction.

'I would not want you to.'

She went on, 'And then there's the baby. What would you feel about bringing up Asher's child?'

Woolf folded his hands together. 'I've considered that, of course. It is very difficult for me, since I can hardly imagine what it means, having no experience of children. I am quite sure that any child of yours will be delightful, of course. Though,' he paused nervously, 'they cry a great deal, don't they?'

'Only at first.'

'Would you want me to adopt the baby?'

Surprised by the question she said, 'I don't know. It would be up to you. I wouldn't force anything on you.'

They hesitated uncertainly. Both knew they were in an artificial situation, acting out parts in a scenario already written for them by Dora Lander, and yet anxious to pretend that it was not so. Finally Woolf asked cautiously, 'Would you like perhaps to discuss the sort of life we might have together, before you make your decision?' When she assented he went on, 'I had thought that we should make a point of pursuing our own interest. Be, as it were, self-sufficient.' She nodded slowly, thinking how she and Asher had done almost everything together.

'However,' Woolf continued, 'I had hoped we might entertain a little, later on, when you feel up to it. And go out occasionally, of course. Do you care for opera?'

'I know very little about music.'

'Then perhaps I could teach you? If you would permit me, I am sure it would give you pleasure.'

At the eagerness he displayed she softened. 'It sounds – very nice.'

'Then, do you accept? Or do you want more time to consider?'

'I don't think so.' After all, she thought, what alternative do I have? I must take this, make it into something good.

But if only he would say he loves me, just a little, so that I could pretend to myself. Pretend what? her practical mind asked. Pretend that it's Asher again? Pretend it is romantic love, when you know it is a matter of mutual convenience? You'll have to make him love you, if that is what you want. Aloud she said, speaking with an odd formality,

'Thank you, Woolf. I do accept, gladly. I will be your wife. And I'll try to be a good one. I'll make a home for you, and look after you as well as I can. I'm sure we will be happy.'

With a look of real pleasure on his face he got up and moved across to the window.

'I'm so very pleased.' He took her hand and then softly, experimentally, kissed her cheek. She waited, in case he wanted to take her into his arms. When he did not she said into the slightly self-conscious silence, 'We must celebrate. What should we do?'

'A splendid idea. But tomorrow, I think, if that suits you. We'll go out to dinner, somewhere quiet.'

Taken aback she found herself agreeing.

'That's settled then. And now, my dear . . .' his manner became brisk. 'I'll take my leave, if you'll excuse me. I've a busy day tomorrow and you and I will have a lot to discuss at dinner.' He pressed her hand between both his own and hurried from the room.

Sadie sat down heavily. She felt no elation. It was an odd way to finish an evening during which two people had agreed to spend the rest of their lives together. She tried to stem the bleak sadness that was rising in her. A phrase kept going through her mind.

A marriage had been arranged.

Chapter Fifteen

It was not until they came to settling the date of the wedding that Sadie felt her first misgivings. She and Woolf had decided they would have a small ceremony. She had not yet told the Raphaels, but thought it unlikely that anyone but Lena would want to attend.

'And I don't want them to,' she said to Woolf. 'I think it would be very hard for them to accept but I'd hate to hurt their feelings. I'll write to Asher's parents and tell them what we're doing, and say that though we'd like them to come, we will understand if they don't.'

Sadie went alone to visit Rabbi Salaman. 'I think you'll need to come too,' she had said with some anxiety to Woolf.

'You sort everything out, and I'll go along with whatever you decide,' he had replied.

The rabbi had welcomed her with his usual courteous formality, assuming she was in need of comfort. He had a cup of tea brought for her, and then settled behind his desk.

'Now, my dear Mrs Raphael, how is everything with you? How can I be of assistance?'

'Thank you, I'm much better.' She paused. She had planned to broach the subject delicately, but her shyness with the tranquil old man made her blurt out, 'I'm planning to marry again.'

The rabbi, despite his appearance, was a worldly man, to whom the vagaries of human behaviour rarely caused any surprise. But his face was a comical mixture of emotions. 'Mrs Raphael, I don't know what to say. I congratulate you, of course, but in your condition . . . are you convinced this is the right decision?'

Fervently, Sadie said, 'I hope so. It seems to be the only

thing for me, to tell you the truth.'

'You have not told me who it is you are marrying.'

'Oh, no, I'm sorry. Not one of your congregation – his name is Woolf Lander.'

'And this Mr Lander – have you known each other long?'

Sadie found herself being questioned in a way she had not anticipated. She told the rabbi all about Woolf – his job, his mother, his collection of pictures.

At the end, the rabbi pressed his fingertips together and looked at her carefully. 'Are you sure you have considered this move sufficiently well? From what you tell me, this man is very different from your late husband. You could find things will be . . .' he hesitated, choosing his words carefully, 'more difficult than you anticipate.'

'He is different, certainly. But I think I know what I'm doing.'

Rabbi Salaman still looked worried. 'You know, Mrs Raphael, you have told me of your husband-to-be, you have described the sort of man he is, you have said you will make a home for him and look after him. Yet you have not told me of your feelings for him. Now this I find a matter of concern.'

Sadie blushed.

'Nor,' the rabbi added, 'of his for you. Now you and I are not unaware of the way these things can be brought about. A *shadchen* arranges a match, the couple barely knows each other, but they are young, they have no troubles, and there are things in common. Their family backgrounds, their interests perhaps, they are more or less compatible in the eyes of a third party. They will grow to love each other.' He sighed. 'But Mrs Raphael, you are in a different situation, no? You know what it is to be happily married. Will you be able to make do with something that is less than that?'

'I shall have to try. Woolf knows that I do not forget Asher, he understands.'

The rabbi nodded. 'Of course. I am not suggesting that you do not think of your late husband. Yet if we could not forget, we would never be free from grief.' He smiled at her. 'Then if you have thought carefully of all this, I can only wish you joy. You must bring Mr Lander to see me, if you will, and we can discuss everything in detail. Now tell me, when do you wish the ceremony to be held?'

'I thought – as soon as possible.'

Rabbi Salaman put down his pen, and shook his head. 'That will not be feasible, I'm afraid.'

Sadie felt her colour deepen. 'Why not?'

'Your husband died only a very short time ago, Mrs Raphael. Rabbinical law decrees that a widow may not remarry until three months have elapsed.'

'But that's . . . who says so?'

Rabbi Salaman spread out his hands, palms up. 'It is not my ruling. I'm quoting *Talmud*.'

Sadie said, 'I don't understand why that should be necessary.'

'It is a precaution,' said the rabbi carefully, 'so that we are certain of the paternity of any child conceived near the time of the husband's death. There must be no possible confusion.'

Bewildered, she pressed her stomach. 'But you all know this child is Asher's. There's no question in my case.' Rabbi Salaman made no response and she added urgently, 'Woolf wants to take care of me now, when I need it. Please!'

The rabbi sighed. 'I do sympathize, but there is nothing I can do. And besides, we are discussing a week or two only. Surely it would be best to just wait quietly and then I will be happy to perform the ceremony.'

'You don't understand! The baby's due in May and it'll be too late.'

'Too late, Mrs Raphael? I don't follow.'

'I'm afraid . . .' she started to say, trying to explain the irrational terror she had that Rose Raphael would somehow take over the child if she had no protector. Then, seeing the polite anxiety with which he strove to understand her she realized it was impossible to communicate. She shook her head.

Woolf couldn't understand her fury. 'But Sadie, what does it matter? So we'll marry after the baby's born. It will make no difference that I can see.'

'But I want it to be now. Woolf, this really is important to me. Don't let's wait, please.' She was beside herself with anxiety. 'I'm so afraid what might happen if the baby is born while I'm still on my own, even if I know we're going to marry. I'm scared Rose will convince me I ought to go to them. I realize it's ridiculous, but I feel she might – take control of me. She nearly did before.'

'Don't worry, she can't do anything that you don't want.'

'Rationally I know that. And now I feel strong enough to make my own decisions. Only,' she held out her hands towards him, 'only I'm scared that the nearer I get to the baby's birth, the more vulnerable I'll become. I'm already behaving like an idiot.' She tried to smile at herself, 'What'll I be like later?'

Woolf patted her hand briefly and disengaged himself. Sadie looked at him despairingly. She saw, as he did not, that this worry hid the deeper anxiety she felt. There was no way she could tell Woolf what she feared: that he had been manipulated towards this marriage because of her need and her loneliness. She was no fool. She could see well enough that he was for the moment captivated by her. But she was beginning to know Woolf. He had acted totally out of character in agreeing to this marriage. If she waited too long they would have time to grow into a relationship with each other deeper than mere friendship but less committed than marriage. If the wedding did not take place until Rabbi Salaman suggested, she realized instinctively that Woolf would begin to shy away. He had brought himself to this point once. He would not be able to do so again. If their momentum was lost, so was she.

Misinterpreting her despair, gratified by her eagerness, Woolf could not resist her pleas. 'All right, we'll marry now, if it means so much to you.' He smiled at her, and she reached out towards him. He drew back, so slightly she thought she must have imagined the movement.

'But,' he continued, 'it'll have to be a civil ceremony. Where would you like it to be?'

'What about Marylebone Town Hall? There's a registry office there, and it's near home. We can come back here afterwards.'

They agreed to celebrate as quietly as possible: a glass of champagne, said Woolf firmly, would do very well under the circumstances.

The older Raphaels declined the invitation. Conveniently, they would be travelling: they wished Sadie and Woolf every happiness, and a handsome cut-glass punchbowl arrived from Liberty's. Sadie, who knew her taste, saw that Lena had sent it on their behalf. She was grateful nonetheless for this smoothing-over. She had no wish to open the rift with them any further. She knew what she was doing, but she remained fond of them – especially Moritz – not only for Asher but for the sake of the coming baby. The child should not also be totally without its paternal grandparents.

Aside from a few mutual friends and old Mrs Lander, both her sisters-in-law and their husbands were coming to the wedding, though Lena had already told her Betty would only attend the small reception. Mark and Zipporah would be there, of course. Zipporah was preoccupied at the moment, and travelling alone a great deal; she had just returned from a visit to the hot baths at Baden. Mark, looking much older with his now rapidly greying hair, had teased her in the old way, 'This time, my dear, I fancy I shall not be called upon to give you away!' Then, becoming abruptly serious, he had asked whether she would like a stone for a ring.

Impulsively, she leant over and kissed him. 'No more engagements, Uncle Mark. No more diamonds.' She twisted the glittering hoop on her finger and said quietly, 'This looks as brilliant to me now as it did five years ago. And it means as much. Woolf and I are going to exchange wedding rings. That's all.'

He sighed. 'I hope you're doing the right thing. It all seems so sudden.' He got to his feet, and stared gloomily out on to the garden. 'I feel so damned responsible. I urged you to marry Asher, and look where you are now.'

'It's not your fault, Uncle Mark. How can you even think that? I've been very happy, and I'm sure I will be again.'

He swung round to see her. 'I believe you will,' he said slowly. 'You've changed, you know, Sadie. I used to think you were a soft little thing. But not any more.'

She said, soberly, 'I'm in no position to be soft. There will be a child to look after.' Suddenly anxious, she said, 'You do like Woolf, don't you? You do think he will love the child?'

Mark spoke slowly. 'He seems a very pleasant fellow, Sadie. I don't think it is in him to be to you what Asher was. He's a very different figure. But you must know that. And as for loving the baby,' he looked at her gravely, and she saw the sudden sadness, 'which of us would not love a baby?'

Sophie and Flora arrived a few days before the wedding. Sadie was on the station to meet them: Woolf standing a tactful pace behind her. Sophie's behaviour towards him was cordial but guarded – she found it hard to believe that Sadie was going ahead with this marriage.

Later, as she served the two women with chicken soup and *matzoh* balls in the morning room, Sadie thought how they had both changed. Sophie was now ageing. A little hump, 'my widow's hump,' she said, with resignation, altered her erect carriage, her hands were mottled with the brown spots of age. Flora had settled into maturity without ever having been a girl. Her skin was dry, her hair wispy, her body innocent of curves beneath her severe dress. She was, thought Sadie, without appeal. She suddenly remembered Aunt Zipporah. 'That *soufflé* will never rise,' she had observed, and Sadie, who had then thought her cruel, now saw that she was right. Such reflections did not, however, mar her delight at seeing them both. She even took it with good grace when Sophie started to question her about Woolf.

'I've been through all this with Rabbi Salaman,' she protested.

'But I wasn't there to hear the answers,' retorted her mother. 'And I'm still not sure about this marriage, not sure at all.'

'What else can I do?' Sadie was exasperated. 'If I have to sit alone I'll go mad. And Woolf is a friend, he's a good man.'

'He seems pleasant enough. But not like your Asher.'

'No one's ever going to be like him.'

'That marriage was arranged in heaven. *This* one,' she looked sharply at Sadie, 'was quite clearly arranged by people. And, I ask myself, which people?'

'What on earth d'you mean?'

'I mean, whose idea was it? Not Woolf's, I'll be bound. "More than a man desires to marry, woman desires to be married."'

'Ma, are you quoting *Talmud* at me again? All right, it was his mother. She asked if I'd be agreeable to the idea. She said it would be suitable for both of us.' At this she caught sight of Sophie nodding sagely and added, her voice rising in protestation, 'But *he* proposed to *me*. I didn't have to beat him about the head to do it.'

'I'm sure you didn't. How could he refuse you?'

'Quite easily, I should have thought, if he'd wanted to.

As you've said yourself often enough, I'm no oil painting.' They both laughed as they thought of the Sargent. 'Well, perhaps a bit more of one than I was. But honestly, Ma, he is really fond of me. And we'll do very well together, I'll make sure of that.'

'I wish I could think so.' Sophie sighed. 'I have a feeling that he's dazzled by you, whatever you say. Can't you see how flattering it must have been to him? He didn't have to lift a finger and there you were.'

'I don't think he's the sort of man to be dazzled.' Sadie felt uncertain. Sophie, she knew, saw the situation as it was. Forced into defiance she asked, 'And if he is, does it matter?'

Sophie looked at her daughter. 'I don't know. Something worries me. A man his age, he should have married years ago. Why didn't he? What's wrong with him?'

'He just remained single, that's all. Why should there have to be anything wrong with him? Not everyone rushes into marriage, you know.'

'Most normal people do. He's nice-looking, he can afford a wife, so what stopped him? Sadie, I have a feeling there's something we don't know.'

'Ma, don't go on.' Flora spoke for almost the first time. 'Sadie's going ahead anyway, so why make trouble for no reason?'

'You're right.' Sophie shrugged and subsided. 'I'm an old fool.'

Sadie Raphael married Woolf Lander at Marylebone Registry Office on 21 April, 1913. She was twenty-three years old and almost eight months pregnant. Flora helped her to dress in a loose frock of Monte Carlo zephyr, white striped on brown, cut high in the front to hide her condition. 'I don't want funny looks in the registry office,' she told her sister. 'Or outside it.' She removed her wedding and engagement rings to leave the fourth finger of her left hand bare for the service, and laid them carefully in her now almost empty jewel box. On an impulse, she hurried downstairs and unlocked the tantalus in the drawing room. She poured herself a large brandy. She thought of the baby and put some back: then she drank the rest at a gulp, gagging on the fumes. After that she felt much better, although slightly detached.

Just before leaving the house she slipped her rings on to her right hand. 'Asher's coming with me to the wedding,' she told Flora, tears in her eyes.

By the time they reached Marylebone she had recovered herself, and, as she stood beside Woolf in the green-carpeted registrar's office, thanked God that it was a civil ceremony. Now that she was actually hearing the wedding service she knew she could not have gone through another synagogue wedding without breaking down. There was a pause. They must be waiting for her response. Nervously, she looked at the Registrar, who prompted her. She followed the words in a low voice, telling herself that she did mean this, that she would cherish Woolf. And learn to love him. Please God, she thought, he will learn to love me.

'And now,' the Registrar was saying, 'I pronounce you man and wife. You may kiss the bride.'

They turned to one another. It was the first time Woolf had really looked at her since the service began. He kissed her quickly on the cheek. The ceremony was over. It was done.

This time, there was to be no honeymoon. Sadie was in no condition to travel and Woolf was anyway immersed in his work: he had a particularly important case coming up, and a great deal of reading to do.

When the last of the few guests had gone, and Sadie had seen off her mother and Flora – going tactfully to stay with Mark and Zipporah for a week before returning to Manchester – she came back into the drawing room moving slowly from exhaustion. Annie was busily removing glasses and plates, straightening chairs. Woolf and his mother were standing together in the window.

'I'll just see Mother home,' he said.

'You look tired, my dear,' Dora Lander commented, kissing Sadie goodbye and patting her arm. 'Don't let that son of mine keep you up too late.'

Sadie answered, grateful for the cue, 'I think I'll go straight to my – straight to bed, if you don't mind. Should we ask Annie to bring us up a sandwich and some tea? I could do with it.'

She saw Woolf shoot his mother a nervous glance as he answered, 'Why, yes, do. I won't be long.' Dora Lander maintained her smile. Sadie waited politely until they left the house, then mounted the stairs. It must be hard for the old lady, she reflected. All these years Woolf had been hers, and now . . . God knows she was aware how it felt to be alone, but until this moment she had not considered what the marriage would mean to Woolf's mother. Still, he wasn't exactly deserting her. He and Sadie had come to an arrangement which Sophie, on learning of it, had described with a grim expression about her mouth as 'quaint'.

Woolf was not moving out of his half of the house he shared with Mrs Lander. 'It's only a couple of rooms, really,' he had said, 'and they're jammed with books. I think Mother would feel better if I just left things there. Then I can pop back if I need somewhere quiet to work, and keep an eye on her at the same time.'

Sadie had not protested. After all, she was keeping her house. They had decided not to move immediately although she felt they should do so quite soon. 'Choosing a house together is an important part of being married,' she had observed. Woolf, to whom the idea had not occurred, agreed pleasantly.

In the meantime, Woolf was to settle himself into the big guest room. When, slightly worried, Sadie had broached

221

the subject, Woolf had commented that he thought for the moment separate rooms were a good idea. Sadie was relieved – the baby, after all, was due very soon – but felt Woolf might sense a rejection. 'You're sure you don't mind?' she had asked anxiously. 'Just till the baby's born?' He lifted his hand to silence her, in a school-masterish gesture. 'Not at all, not at all. I understand perfectly. It will suit me very well, my dear. Now think no more about it. But if we could just change the wallpaper . . .' he gestured at the dark flowered pattern Sadie had chosen so carefully, 'make it something lighter.'

He had moved in a few possessions, filled a couple of bookcases, brought his own bedside cabinet and shaving stand. There was an eighteenth-century bachelor's table of which he was fond. Proudly he showed Sadie how the top opened out to become a card table. 'I couldn't be without it,' he told her. 'It's the first thing I ever bought myself.' Sadie helped him position it, hoping that he did not intend to spend too many evenings playing solitary card games at it.

Now, tiredly climbing into bed, she looked at the new gold ring on her finger, and let her hand drop on the sheet. She laid her right hand on her distended stomach and felt the hard mound of the waiting child. It moved less now; she felt only the occasional stirrings, and she had been told this was a sign of its size: it had little room in which to turn. 'Are you all right in there, baby?' she asked softly. 'You've had quite a day. There aren't too many people your age who go to their mothers' weddings.'

After half-an-hour she heard Woolf come in, and then Annie brought in the tray. 'Mr Lander will be up directly,' she told Sadie. The two women looked at each other, both thinking the same thing.

'Don't cry, there's a love,' said Annie. 'There's no use living in the past, not for you. You've got to make yourself a future.'

222

'I know.'

'And you'd best be getting your rest,' Annie continued, plumping up her pillows and looking at her meaningfully.

'It's all right, don't worry. Mr Lander understands.' At least, she thought to herself, I hope he does. There was a hesitant knock on the door and Woolf entered. He crossed over to the bed and looked at her for a moment, clearly uncertain what to do.

'Pull up a chair,' she said, 'and we'll make ourselves cosy.' Gratefully, he seated himself, and accepted a cup.

'Why don't you take off your jacket?' she suggested. 'Although I must say you look very nice in it – I like that pale grey – it's quite warm in here.'

'No, no, thank you, I won't, if you don't mind.'

After a pause, Sadie asked, 'Well, did you enjoy your wedding?'

'I believe I did, rather. Though I must confess I still can't quite take it all in.'

Sadie rummaged in her bedside table and drew out a small parcel. She held it out to Woolf.

'What's this?'

'I bought you a wedding present.' He was astonished. 'Oh, you didn't . . . what is it?' He pulled off the wrapping paper, and discovered the silver cufflinks she had chosen so carefully for him in Asprey's. She had first decided on a finely decorated pair, set with a discreet amethyst. Then with a small shock she realized she was buying for Asher and finally settled on a pair which were narrow oblongs, plain except for the delicate scroll pattern. Woolf seemed delighted with them. 'How very kind of you,' he said formally. 'They're most acceptable.' He felt a little embarrassed: he was unused to either giving or receiving gifts. He put them carefully back in the box.

Sadie said, 'Put one on so we can see how it looks.'

'I shall wear them tomorrow,' he promised her.

Sadie lay back, suddenly filled with misery, and tried to

stifle the thought that Asher would have fitted them immediately into his shirt.

Her husband gave her a thoughtful look, and swallowed the last of his tea. 'I believe I'll go to bed myself. It's been a tiring day, and I've a lot to get through tomorrow. Is there anything I can get you?'

'No thank you. I'll ring for Annie when I've finished. What time do you leave the house?'

'About nine, I think.'

'May I join you for breakfast?'

'Oh no, my dear, no need for that. I prefer to start the day on my own. Force of habit.'

She nodded without speaking, and he got to his feet. 'I'll say goodnight then.' He leant down and gently kissed the top of her head. 'Sleep well.'

As she watched him close the door, a longing for Asher rose in her, a dark tide she did not try to fight down. Rabbi Salaman had been right. It was too soon, she should have waited.

Woolf methodically prepared for the night in his wife's guest room. He opened the window precisely four inches, laid his dressing gown neatly over a chair-back and got into bed. He reached for his book.

Due in part to Woolf's personality, in part to the imminent arrival of the child, Sadie perceived with apprehension that this new marriage was settling so quickly into a mould she had not anticipated. In a matter of days, it seemed to her, they were establishing a relationship which under more ordinary circumstances might have taken many months to emerge.

She and Woolf behaved towards each other with elaborate courtesy. Each tried so hard to understand the feelings of the other that they lost all spontaneity. Sadie, who was used to speaking and behaving impulsively, now

224

took great care not to encroach upon Woolf in any way.

He had always been solitary, from a child, and had no habits of sharing his life. He enjoyed his own company and did not feel the necessity of asking Sadie's advice or opinions about his work or his clothes, as Asher had done.

He was totally unprepared for the realities of married life: the closeness, the continuing dialogue, the lack of solitude. As the days went by he found these things harder, not easier, to maintain. Sadie in her distress had appealed to him and he had allowed himself to respond to an unprecedented degree. For the first time in his adult life he had acted impulsively. His feelings for her were sincere – affection, admiration, liking, respect – and because she also appealed to his sense of beauty he had assumed these emotions would sustain them both. He, who had never been in love, genuinely thought that what he felt was enough. He was not a man of strong desires, was unaccustomed to the simplest bodily contacts. Where Sadie drew strength and reassurance from the touch of others, Woolf did not even greatly care to shake hands with acquaintances, and he did not think to kiss Sadie when he left the house or on arriving home.

Each respected and liked the other: both thought that love would come. But their bodies did not speak the same language. So Sadie did not demand the affection that was imperative to her, for fear of presuming upon him. And he did not proffer it, for it did not occur to him to do so.

It was to be the pattern of their marriage.

Chapter Sixteen

One morning Sadie woke to find she had been crying again in the night: her hair was matted with tears and her eyes were sore. She lay in her warm bed and tried to reason with herself: it was absurd to feel such misery when she had so much. Her life had begun again. Woolf had lifted all her immediate worries from her, they seemed to be making a pattern for themselves. It was a very formal relationship, very civilized and courteous. She tried not to think of how it had been with Asher; of the way she had been enveloped by his presence. She had known Woolf was very different, she had surely accepted that. Only she never said goodnight to him, never received that slightly remote embrace, without a pang of remembrance.

And the child would be here in less than a month. Already she knew this baby. She felt its movements, the tiny foot that kicked under her ribs, the spasmodic stretching of the curled body. She was aware when it woke and when it slept. But she realized that what she knew was the fantasy child, the illusion, the little creature that had grown from her love of her beautiful Asher. It was the focus of all her hopes, the invisible axis of her world. Lying there, she thought that the baby's real existence was soon approaching. It would be a person, a living being, itself. She felt as though there were two babies. The dream, the womb-child and the other, the baby she would bring to birth and hold in her arms. She was drifting away from the enchanted image and moving inexorably towards the child that was to be. She laid her hand flat on her belly, and thought that if she kept very still, she would surely feel the beating of its heart.

With an effort she swung her legs to the floor and heaved

herself out of bed. She was carrying the baby high. Dressed in the loose gowns she now wore she scarcely looked pregnant, but she felt cumbersome and awkward. Towards the end of the day her ankles became swollen and she found it impossible to eat even normal sized meals without feeling sick. As she started towards the stairs, she suddenly felt giddy. She leant against the wall and tried to still the trembling of her legs. Below her, she could hear Annie talking to a tradesman at the front door. The housekeeper shut the door and turned.

'Good morning. It's a beautiful day, you ought to . . .' Seeing Sadie's face she stopped and hurried to the stairs. 'You look a bit queer.'

'I just feel very giddy. I must have got out of bed too quickly.'

'Let's get you downstairs for a breath of fresh air and a cup of tea.'

The fresh air helped. She sat in the conservatory and ate a piece of dry toast. The tea, though, made her feel worse. By mid-morning, she had a dull backache as well, and when she told Annie, was firmly ordered back to bed.

'I'm sorry to be such a nuisance,' Sadie apologized as they went slowly upstairs. 'But I feel so miserable today.' Annie looked sharply at her, but said nothing. When Sadie was in bed she tucked the blanket firmly in. 'There you are, love, and I'll be back in ten minutes to make sure you're asleep.'

'Annie, you are good to me. This is just what I needed.'

'I know.'

Sadie looked at her with affection. 'I've often wanted to ask – why didn't you have any babies of your own? You surely wanted them?'

'Oh, I did. I did want them.' Annie's face darkened at the memory, and she folded her hands in her apron.

Contrite, Sadie said, 'I'm sorry. I shouldn't have asked. I didn't mean to pry.'

'You're not prying. It's a natural question.' She sat down heavily. 'I just wasn't one of the lucky ones, you see. Things went wrong. God wasn't willing. It wasn't for us.' She attempted a smile. 'Perhaps it was for the best, with my Harry going young. Things would've been hard for me, bringing them up myself. But of course, I wouldn't have been so lonely as I have been.'

'What happened?'

'Now, if you'll excuse me, I don't think this is the kind of talk for someone in your condition.'

'But I'd like to know. Really I would.'

Annie sighed. 'There would have been three of them. We were two years trying for him, and then little Henry came. I had him just for the year . . .' she stopped and wiped her eyes on the hem of her apron. 'Just a year. He got bronchitis, little thing, after an influenza cold. I thought it was just an ordinary cold, you see, but feverish. I gave him a jacket poultice of linseed with a little mustard in it, then I put on a hot cotton wool jacket. Then in the night he quietened down, and I stopped worrying so much. Just a little muffled cough. I thought he was getting better.' She sighed. 'I was only young, I didn't know much.'

'How terrible it must have been.'

Soberly, Annie turned to her. 'Terrible. I hope you'll never know, love, what that's like. So then I thought, I can't have any more, I couldn't bear that again. But I fell, like you do. I had a little girl. Harry and me, we were so pleased. But then she had jaundice. Poor little thing. She died while I was still lying-in.'

'Annie. Whatever did you do?' Tears stood in Sadie's eyes.

'I was in an awful state, I can tell you. The milk had come in and no baby. So I was very low. Then it was like an act of God. A woman nearby, who'd had a baby at the same time, she died. And they brought the baby to me to rear. I had her for two years and I was saving her, just like she was saving me. She still keeps in touch, my Suke. So you see, I haven't been without children entirely, have I?'

'You said there would have been three. What happened to the other baby?'

'I couldn't bring it to birth. I was older then, and I got tired after three days. They had to bring in a doctor, that time.'

'What did they do?'

Annie's voice was abrupt. 'I can't speak about it. But I couldn't have any more, after.'

Sadie spoke slowly, 'I hadn't thought about things going wrong.'

Annie recovered herself and stood up. Briskly she smoothed the covers. 'No more you should. Your mother had hers easy and that means you will too: it's always like that. You've no call to worry.'

'I'd like her here now.'

'Do you feel your time's near, then?'

'I don't know. I just can't seem to settle. I can't concentrate on anything.'

'You'd best write to her when you get up. Or you could send her a wire.'

'I won't do that, it'd give her such a fright. She'd think something was wrong. But I will write today, and she'll have the letter tomorrow. The baby isn't supposed to be here for a week or so yet.'

Annie posted the letter that evening. Next day Sophie sent a wire: Arriving Thursday Euston 4 P.M.

Stimulated by the thought of her visitor, Sadie rearranged all the carefully ordered baby clothes and decided to re-hang the nursery curtains. She was perched on a chair unhooking them when Annie came in and scolded her for her foolishness.

'You come down right this minute and let me up. I don't know what you're thinking of, you daft girl. Begging your pardon, Ma'am.'

Shamefaced, Sadie clambered down, and Annie patted her arm.

'Nesting, that's what you're doing. It takes a lot of women that way. A day or two before the baby's due, they start their spring cleaning. We'll have to keep an eye on you.'

They were making the bed together on Thursday morning when Sadie suddenly said, 'Oh!'

'What's the matter?'

She put her hand to her back. 'I don't know. Just a funny twinge. I must have pulled the sheet too hard.'

'Sit down for a minute and I'll finish this.'

'No need. I'm fine, really, it's gone now.'

When Annie had gone downstairs, she dusted round the room and arranged some honeysuckle in a vase of lime green vaseline glass. As she stretched up to place it on the mantelpiece it came again, the sudden dull ache that lasted a moment and was gone. I must have eaten breakfast too quickly, she thought. She walked through to her own room and the next twinge caught her as she reached the door, so that she held on to the handle for support. Sadie tried to collect her thoughts. It was far too soon for the baby to be arriving, and anyway she knew what to expect. First labour pains were perhaps an hour apart, not a few minutes. And these sensations were not pains at all; more like faint rumours of unease. She was making her way to her low chair when the third one stopped her, as though a band were tightening round her abdomen. Dyspepsia, the midwife had said, but she had never known dyspepsia to feel like this. Oh God, if only she could tell Asher about it.

When the band loosened she mixed a glass of saccharated lime water and thought she would lie down. She got on to the bed, and when nothing more happened fell asleep thinking, there you are, it was dyspepsia after all.

An hour later she knew she was wrong.

She emerged from sleep to find herself gripped by the band again but stronger now, a fierce, compelling pressure that gradually faded, leaving her dazed and apprehensive. She got out of bed and walked to the window, leaning her face against the cool glass. For nearly ten minutes she remained there, gradually convincing herself it had been cramp, and then it came again, this peculiar flow and ebb of discomfort. She opened the bedroom door and called Annie. In a moment the older woman hurried into the room.

'The baby . . . ?'

'I think so. It hurts.'

'I'll send for the midwife. I won't be a moment.'

When she returned she carried a bowl of warm water. 'We'll get you undressed and you have a wash. Mrs Moran will be here soon. You are in a hurry, aren't you?'

Sadie nodded, unable to answer as she felt her body slowly tightening again.

'Here,' said Annie, authoritatively. 'Let me feel.' She laid her hand on Sadie's abdomen. 'That's very strong. How many pains have you felt?'

'I don't know. About six, I think.'

'All as strong as this?'

'No. At first I just thought it was indigestion.'

Annie hurried away, and returned after a moment with a large bottle and a spoon.

'What's this?'

'You just drink it, please. It's castor oil.'

'Whatever for?'

'Well, I don't think you're going to need it, but there's no harm in making sure. It helps give you an easy birth.'

Obediently she swallowed it, then as the next spasm of sensation began to pass over her body she said, helplessly, 'I'm going to be sick.'

'Never mind, never you mind, it doesn't matter.' Annie put her hand on the girl's forehead as the next contraction lengthened, strengthened, died away. At its height, the pain and the nausea made Sadie sob harshly, and she felt herself begin to slip out of control. In the grateful calm that followed she realized that the baby depended on her for its survival. If she was lost, so was the child. She had to do this herself, for them both. She was filled, then, with a surge of power so strong her fingers tingled with it. Firmly she said, 'I feel wonderful.'

Annie looked up at her in surprise, then gave her a quick hug. 'Good girl.'

She struck a match and lit a taper, holding it to the fire laid in the grate. The room filled with the sharp smell of cordite as the firelighters caught. She waited until the fire was alight, then piled extra pillows behind Sadie's back. Moving to the window she said crossly, 'I wish that Mrs Moran would get her boots on. She always says the first one takes hours to arrive but I don't know.' She shook her head. 'With you I think it's going to be quick.'

Sadie found it impossible to answer. The feeling that her abdomen was contracting was changing. Each sensation was longer, less gripping. She was mesmerized by the rhythm imposed on her body and although she knew the pain was considerable, she felt completely calm. Each contraction now came like a huge wave, starting gently, then rising to a crest before subsiding, rolling her down into the next.

Beside her, she was half-aware of Annie covering the table with a white towel, laying out cotton wool and a pile of muslin napkins. She had changed into a fresh white apron and Sadie saw that she had brought in the cradle and on it were heaped a pile of babyclothes and the white wool shawl Zipporah had given her. It would be here soon, then, the shadow-child she carried under her heart for Asher. She found that, although she felt elated, tears were streaming down her face. Clucking, Annie wiped her eyes for her, and held a wet flannel to her lips.

In the brief interval between the now increasingly strong

pains, Sadie asked, 'Time is it?'

'Nearly twelve. You've only been here half-an-hour.'

'Mrs Moran?'

'Never mind Mrs Moran. We're managing very well without her.'

Sadie said, faintly, 'I'm so hot.'

Annie loosened the collar of her nightdress, and sponged her face and throat gently. 'I know. But I daren't let the room get cold, we must keep the baby warm when it arrives.'

As the next wave started to roll over her Sadie groaned deeply and caught Annie's hand. She squeezed it so hard that her nails made indentations in the other woman's flesh. When she loosened her grip Annie said, 'I'll need my hands to myself, love, if I'm to help you.' While she spoke, she wound a towel into a thick plait and looped it to the foot of the brass bed, putting the end into Sadie's hands. 'Here, you grab this when you want to hold on. Now I'm just going to boil some water. It would be Peg's day off, wouldn't you know it?'

She hurried out of the room, and in the brief cessation of discomfort Sadie wondered about Woolf. He was meeting her mother at Euston and they would be home by five. She thought, it'd be a surprise if the baby was here first. Then Annie was back in the room, and another inexorable wave began to well within her, and the look on the older woman's face told her that the baby would indeed arrive before them.

'What's happening now?' she gasped.

'You're doing very nicely, love. Let me have a little look, will you? I shouldn't think it's going to be very long now, not if you're lucky.'

She put her hand on Sadie's abdomen and felt it begin to tighten again. 'There's another one coming now,' she said quietly. 'Get ready to push.'

Sadie obeyed, tensing herself to meet the fierce pressure

over which she could exert no possible control. When the effort was over she sank back, her face white and her eyes dark with strain. She was trembling violently.

'I wish we had some chloroform for you. Drat that woman. Wait a minute, though.' Annie dashed up to her own room. She returned after a moment with a small bottle. 'It's only laudanum but it'll help a bit. Breathe it deeply.'

Sadie did as she was told and the sickly sweet scent made her head swim. The next contraction was so severe she cried out. Another followed immediately; the pain was tangible, heavy, a great blunt ache that was pressing her down into the bed. Just at the moment when she felt she could not bear any more, something within her seemed to give, as though a cycle had been completed, and the great wave that had been building up to a crest broke over her. The change was an immense relief and, 'It's coming,' she cried, in a voice she did not recognize as her own. 'It's coming now.'

'Come on love, push, push!' Annie exhorted. 'I can see the head, the baby's head, just push a bit harder!'

'I *am*. I *am*.' Sadie held her breath and strained every muscle, holding on to the towelling rope with all her might. It was impossible, it could not be done. There was another sensation now, she experienced a fierce burning and Annie exclaimed half-laughing, half-crying, 'Look down, love, look down!' She opened her eyes and tried to focus and saw, lying on the sheet between her spread thighs, the baby's head, face like a little white clay mask, dark hair matted and sticking to the skull.

'Come on, another push, you haven't finished yet.'

Sadie pushed again, using every fibre of her being. And then it really was over. With a slithering rush the baby swam out of her body and she saw it all at once. She shouted and broke into a tearless, joyful crying, still trembling, but now with pleasure. She saw the glistening, bluish limbs, the starfish fingers plucking at the air, the long arched feet. She held her breath and then, after an eternity, heard the paper-thin, powerful cry. As it yelled, the bluish colour faded and the child turned pink in Annie's hands.

'Is it all right?' Sadie asked faintly, amazed and slightly horrified at the unexpectedly raw appearance of the wriggling, greasy little body.

It's a girl, a wonderful little girl,' Annie said, wiping round the face with cotton wool. 'I'm leaving the cord for Mrs Moran. It won't hurt. You can hold her if you sit up.' She quickly wrapped the little body in a towel and handed her to Sadie. 'Look, she'll hold your finger.'

Very carefully Sadie inserted her little finger into the fragile palm. The minute fingers grasped it immediately with astonishing strength, clinging to her in the instinctive, primeval lust for survival. At that moment the bedroom door opened and a woman's voice said crossly, 'I've been ringing and ringing that doorbell and in the end I got in round the back. Couldn't anyone answer?'

'We've been a bit on the busy side, Mrs Moran,' answered Annie, and moved so that the midwife could see Sadie.

'Lord bless us,' the woman said, 'give us a minute to wash.' In a moment she returned, wiping her hands, and looked carefully at the baby. 'Everything all right?' she asked Annie.

'Perfect. Just perfect.'

Satisfied, the midwife turned her attention to Sadie. 'We'll just sort you out, Mrs Raphael, if you please. Then I think I need a cup of tea. I've never had such a shock – I came straight away, you know. You should have given me a bit more warning.'

'I didn't have much myself.'

When the midwife had properly examined the baby she

235

washed her carefully and wrapped her tightly in a blanket. Then she gave her to Sadie. 'Put her to the breast, dear, see if she'll suck.'

Nervously, Sadie tried to obey. 'I'm sorry,' she said apologetically, 'I don't seem to know what to do.'

'Here, like this,' the midwife deftly held the child's head, and after a moment the tiny jaws clamped round Sadie's nipple.

'Oh,' Sadie exclaimed in tired delight, 'she's drinking.'

'Just give her a minute and then we'll let you both rest. Have you a name for her?'

'Oh, yes. She's my Esther, my little star.'

When the midwife had gone and the baby was asleep in the crib, Annie made them both more tea and they sat together in the quiet room. Sadie was experiencing freedom and lightness, energy and joy such as she had never known.

Annie said, 'Esther's a lovely name. Why did you decide on that?'

'It's for Asher. He chose it, right at the beginning. He so wanted a girl.'

She felt such total elation that even this did not spoil her mood. She remembered Rabbi Salaman teling her in his soft voice that 'The Lord gives and the Lord takes. Now, He has taken. But soon, Mrs Raphael, He will give.' Well, He had. Asher's child had come.

She scarcely noticed as Annie took the cup from her hands and went quietly from the room.

Chapter Seventeen

Sadie passed over the bridge of birth and confronted her baby with astonishment and alarm. She looked into the bright, wise, unfocused eyes. She touched the mysterious and yet already known face. And she fell in love. For two days she was buoyed up on a flood of ecstasy at her achievement.

Then on the third day she sank into a desolation worse than any she had known. Everything was lost. Nothing mattered. She was forsaken, forgotten. She could not cry, could barely speak. Even the baby failed to move her. Mechanically she put her to the breast, then silently handed her to the nurse. The child meant nothing; she would never care for anyone again. it was as though she had not mourned Asher through the long dark months, as though his death was again raw within her.

Sophie watched her anxiously. Thrilled as she had been by the baby's arrival, she was immediately worried by Sadie's wild exhilaration and had tried fruitlessly to calm her down, to stop her excited chattering. She knew that Sadie had barely emerged from the bleak despair that followed Asher's death. Her daughter's apparent calm in this new marriage had not deceived her. It was to her eyes a precarious balancing act of emotions. And now, she feared, the birth had tipped Sadie too far, she could not recover herself.

Sophie did everything she could think of to arouse her daughter from this lonely lethargy. She sat by the bed for hours at a time, sewing or talking, gossiping about the family. In return, she received blank stares.

Finally, in exasperation, she tried to reason with her. 'Look, you're not the only woman to feel this, you know.

It's natural, hundreds of women get the miseries just after giving birth. It's not peculiar to you.'

Sadie did not reply, merely shook her head slowly.

'I know,' Sophie went on, 'I know what you're going through. I've been through it myself, remember. But you can't let it get on top of you like this, you're not yourself at all.'

Sadie refused to respond, and Sophie was reduced to making her beef tea and insisting she drank a bottle of milk stout every day.

After a week of this, she and Annie decided Woolf must be involved.

'I don't like to raise it myself,' Sophie confided, anxiously. 'I'll just look like an interfering old busybody, he'll think I'm pointing out that *he* should have seen this. But I can't bring in the doctor without consulting Woolf first.'

Finally they decided to call back the midwife, and it was she, eventually, who spoke to Woolf. 'I'm sorry, Mr Lander, but she doesn't look right to me. I've been told what happened, and women often feel low at this time, it's only natural. But I don't like this. I'd get the doctor in if I were you.'

Woolf was all concern. 'Then of course we must. Immediately, I'll send for him now. I'd no idea, no idea . . .' He shook his head, frowning in consternation, hands clenched tight behind his back, shoulders hunched forward.

When Mrs Moran had left he sought out Sophie in the garden, to which she had discreetly retired. 'This is most upsetting, most upsetting.'

Shrewdly, Sophie looked at him. 'Didn't you think yourself she seemed rather odd?

He lifted his spectacles and rubbed the bridge of his nose where the thin gold frames pinched. 'Why yes, I suppose she has been a little low. But I thought, after an experience like childbirth, women always . . .' His voice trailed away, he stared at his mother-in-law helplessly.

'What can I do?'

'We'll just get the doctor in quickly,' she said consolingly. 'He'll know best.'

'Yes, yes of course,' Woolf muttered as he hurried away.

As an afterthought, Sophie called after him, 'Oh, Woolf, one thing.'

He turned, enquiringly. 'Perhaps if you brought her in a bunch of flowers, that might brighten her up a bit?'

He beamed. 'A splendid notion. I'll see to it.'

Watching his angular departing back, Sophie sighed. What a business, what a business.

Sadie endured Dr Verity's examination in silence. When he asked a question she answered reluctantly, in monosyllables. She was unable to volunteer anything. When he asked her how she felt, she shook her head. He watched her hands lying listlessly in her lap, and pressed his fingertips together. He looked at her coolly and scribbled his notes. After ten minutes he gathered himself together and bade her good day.

'I will call again later in the week, Mrs Lander. In the meantime I shall leave my instructions. Try to get plenty of rest.'

With a great effort Sadie said flatly, 'Thank you.' Sophie met him in the hallway, and Sadie could hear the lowered voices beyond the door.

'My dear lady,' Doctor Verity was saying in his precise tones, 'reproductive insanity, I assure you, is most common. Most common, particularly after a precipitate delivery. It is often of the depressed, melancholic type.'

'Is it, indeed?' Sophie's voice was dangerously controlled.

'We will start,' the doctor continued, 'by treating the premonitory sleeplessness and headache with large doses of alcohol and by hypnotic drugs.'

'Alcohol?' Sophie's tone now was incredulous. 'Hypnotic drugs?'

239

'Certainly. The prognosis is excellent. Almost eighty per cent of patients recover.'

'Small thanks, I would imagine, to you.'

'I *beg* your pardon. We must take the greatest possible care that this disease does not fully manifest itself – a slight fever, and we could well find we have an acute outbreak of mania on our hands.'

'Stuff and nonsense.' Sophie's voice was so quiet Sadie could hardly hear her.

'Indeed it is not, Madam.' The imperturbable voice continued. 'Seven per cent of the cases revealed by recent statistics of the Lunacy Commissioners . . .'

'*Lunacy Commissioners*? It is not my daughter who is going out of her mind, Dr Verity, but you.' Sophie's voice was rising now, her anger making her lose her careful self-control. 'You talk of lunacy when a young woman has witnessed the death of her husband only months before? You talk of lunacy when she has borne a child to a dead man?' Sophie's scorn was total. There was no response from the doctor.

'My daughter is deeply unhappy. She is no more insane, Dr Verity, than I am. She is no more insane than the King of England. I have no more to say to you. Good day.'

She came into the bedroom and closed the door. She stood leaning against it, her face ashen with strain. Sadie opened her eyes, and the two women looked at each other.

'You heard.' It was more a statement than a question.

Sadie's eyes, drained of their colour, held more emotion than they had for days.

'Is it – true?'

'Don't be silly.' Her mother's tone was fierce. 'I've never heard such claptrap in my life. The man's been reading too many books. Doctors. *Men*.' She invested the last words with massive scorn.

'How did you come to this–' she searched for a suitable

240

offensive word – 'this person, anyway? I thought you had old Dr Newman.'

'He said,' Sadie's voice was so low Sophie could hardly hear, 'Woolf said Dr Newman was more or less retired now. He recommended Dr Verity. He treats people round here.'

'More fool them. I'd not have him over the doorstep again.' She sighed. 'Lot of good that's done us. On the other hand,' she smiled wryly at Sadie, 'it's raised two words out of you, my girl, and that's more than you've said in a week.'

She moved across to the bed, and took Sadie's hand between her own. 'Now look. You've got to pull yourself together, or see what you're going to get. This is what these modern doctors think. You'll have to snap out of this, or there's no telling where it'll lead.'

Reluctantly, Sadie turned her head. 'Ma, I can't. I can't.'

Finally, Sophie lost all patience. She had brought in some sewing for the baby, and when she returned an hour later, the half-finished garment lay untouched on the bed. Sophie was furious. 'Couldn't you just hem it, for heaven's sake?'

Sadie gave her a blank look.

'Answer me, can't you?'

'I . . . was going to.'

'Were you? Wonderful. Only some other time, I suppose.' Sadie stared at her mother, hearing something in her voice she had not heard for many years. Welling up in Sophie was the memory of her own anguish over Saul's death, of the three fatherless little girls and the endless, exhausting, mind-emptying struggle to keep going from week to week. Now she just said, very quietly,

'I know what it's like. I know what you're going through. Only I ask you, don't make it so hard for me to watch you, please. I haven't the reserves any more to cope with your unhappiness. You have a very great deal on your side.

241

There is a man ready to take care of you, there is Annie and a nurse for the child. You haven't been left as I was left. There are people you can look to for help. For God's sake, Sadie, Esther won't be a baby for long. Don't waste these lovely days.'

There was silence. Then Sadie took up the small white dress and threaded a needle. 'Don't worry, Ma,' she said. 'I'll be all right."

It took a long time to regain her equanimity. Dr Verity's words had shocked her into realizing that she was losing her grip on herself, and the willpower she had discovered over the last few months came to her aid again. She now genuinely wanted to get back to normal. But determination was not enough. The demands made on her since Asher's death had been more than she could take. She had experienced despair and misery at a time when, for fear of injuring the child, she could not fully act out her grief. She had done her best, she had heeded the well-meaning exhortations that she must pull herself together for the sake of the coming child. She had even married and gained a measure of equanimity. But in doing so it was as though she had bent her nature further than it would go.

Very gradually, as her body recovered from childbirth, she regained her composure. For a long time afterwards – for nearly a year – there were many days when everything lost its colour, when she did not care what clothes she put on, what food she ate, what the child needed. Fortunately, she was hedged about with support. When these days came Annie laid out her clothes for her and did not ask what meals were to be prepared that day. And the nurse looked after little Esther with love and efficiency.

It was Woolf, oddly enough, who helped her most. When he had arrived home with Sophie to find the birth had taken place he had been pleased and uncertain how to behave. Sophie had rushed up to see them both. He had beamed and later, prompted by Mark, brought up a bottle of champagne from the cellar. They had all gone up and toasted the baby. It was the first time he had seen Sadie that day – he had not wanted to tire her – and he preferred to have others present, in case he was not sure what to say. The baby was a queer little creature, with its odd snuffled and bleating cries. Mystified, he had watched Sadie gazing enraptured into the crib.

Now, seeing her enveloped in misery, he had no idea how to help. He was totally unable to comprehend the storm of feeling through which Sadie was passing. He was afraid of overpowering passions in others as much as in himself. He had been brought up to mask his feelings, and in time the mask had become the reality. He had never been exposed to either great happiness or great misery and as a result he rather doubted that they could exist. To be tranquil, to be ordered, to remain in control, these were virtues. He had known when he first agreed to marry Sadie how she suffered from Asher's loss. He had imagined, though, that she would calm down, as in fact she had. It had simply never occurred to him that the arrival of the baby would bring anything but pleasure and relief. Bewildered by the strong emotional currents around him, his impulse was to run.

He started to spend a great deal of time in the rooms he kept at his mother's house. He took his evening meal there and frequently spent the night. To Sadie he said that his mother was not well, which was not less than the truth. Old Mrs Lander, presented with the baby and Sadie's despair, could no more face the situation than her son, and conveniently developed a malaise which incommoded her. Sophie, whose health had always been robust, heard of this with a slight curl of the nostrils. As it turned out, old Dora Lander fooled her. Since Woolf had gone, she had neglected herself. She would not bother to eat regular meals, preferring to sit for hours over cups of rich coffee and sweet cakes from Maison Sagne in Marylebone High Street. As a result she developed diabetes, and her headaches and giddy spells were only eventually diagnosed.

Woolf's desertion was effective in a way he could not have foreseen. Sadie, far from feeling he had walked out on her, saw it as her own fault. She felt guilty that she had ever exposed him to this situation and his discomfiture upset her.

One day, about six weeks after the birth, she went into his room. She saw without surprise that he had not been home the previous night. The sun, streaming in at the window, showed a down of dust on the wooden surfaces and the room smelt pleasant but unoccupied. Woolf used an old-fashioned shaving stand with a round, tilting mirror on a mahogany post. Below it three circular shelves held his toilet articles. There were two silver backed hairbrushes that had belonged to his father, the heavy china bowl and mug he used for his shaving cream and beside them, on its brass hook, the badger hair shaving brush. Two bottles stood on the third shelf. One was bay rum, the other a bottle of Floris elderflower water. She saw it with a start of recognition: Asher had used the same aftershave in the summer. Reluctantly she stretched out her hand and picked it up. In the act of unscrewing the bottle she stopped, and put it back on the shelf. Pandora's box, she thought to herself. Don't risk it. Nothing but memory would flood out. Instead, she opened the bottle of bay rum that Woolf used on his hair. She spent her days now breathing in baby smells; the milky sweetness of Esther's soft little face, oatmeal soap used in her bath, the faint scent of Woolley's rose powder and the astringent sharpness of the hazeline cream Nurse used when she changed Esther's nappies. The dry, masculine odour of the bay rum was unexpectedly pungent. She sniffed it again, poured a drop on to her wrist and rubbed it in, so that she would carry it with her out of the room. As she turned away to the door, she recognized

the sensation it had produced in her.
She felt comforted.

Chapter Eighteen

When Esther was three months old Annie started bullying Sadie to go out.

'It's been weeks since you went anywhere. You're slim enough now to get into your clothes. Put them on, there's a love, and go visiting.'

'Whatever for? I'm perfectly contented here.'

'It'd do you good to see people, that's what for. You've not stirred from here since before the birth, and that's not like you. I'll take care of Esther well enough and glad to have her to myself.'

There was a pause. 'I expect you're right,' Sadie said slowly. 'Tomorrow. I'll go out somewhere then.'

Dressing the next day, though, she found there was nowhere she wished to go. Zipporah visited her regularly. The Raphaels had dutifully called to see the baby. Since the marriage Rose Raphael had not sought out Sadie. When they returned from Europe they had paid a courtesy visit and Sadie and Woolf had received a formal invitation to dine. They had accepted, but Sadie had been feeling too ill to go when the appointed day came. She thought privately that it was probably fortuitous: she hated the thought of spending an evening there, albeit with others present, in the company of any man other than Asher. Rose and Moritz, she felt sure, shared her feelings.

Throughout her pregnancy Sadie had continued to see Moritz. The affection they shared for Asher had always drawn them to each other, and their mutual loss was a bond too strong to be broken even by temporary estrangement. Sadie frequently visited the gallery; they spent long afternoons talking together and working in a desultory way in his snug office.

After the birth of Esther, Rose seemed finally to relinquish her attempted hold over the grandchild. She was extremely pleased – on her first visit, she had embraced Sadie with immense affection – but in this child she had sought the reincarnation of her lost son. Little Esther could not fulfil that role for her. Sadie had not foreseen this, but it afforded her considerable relief. Then, too, Betty Epstein was pregnant, had at last managed to carry a child to the fifth month. The Raphaels were holding their breath. Rose transferred her longings to Betty and left Sadie to herself.

Sadie thought briefly of calling on Moritz, then decided against it. Nor was there any need for her to start again upon a social round yet. No one would expect it for another month or two. She looked at the clock, and had a sudden inspiration. At four on Thursdays Woolf left the office early and went to his fencing lesson at Angelo's. She had been surprised when she learned of this activity of his. Up till then she had assumed that walking was the only exercise he took. He was not very good at fencing, he had admitted, his timing was less than perfect. 'My instructor says my style's not bad, but I lack the necessary aggression.'

Sadie decided to go and meet him. Then immediately she wondered whether he would mind her doing so unannounced. But if he did, she could always pretend she was on her way somewhere else. She would go. She got a taxi in the High Street. It took longer than she had expected to get to St James's and by the time she arrived at the entrance she realized his lesson would have begun. Paying the driver, standing undecided in the doorway, she summoned up her courage and went in.

The hallway was a place of unadorned chilliness: marble floors and walls lit by a high chandelier. A doorman looked at her in surprise: women were not often to be found here. She asked for Mr Lander and was told he would not be expected out for another hour.

'But there's a viewing gallery in the *salle d'armes*,

Madam, if you'd care to go up.'

'Thank you, I will.'

'Who shall I say is here, Madam?'

'Mrs Lander.'

She mounted the stairs at his direction, and opening the door found herself in a narrow gallery overlooking a many-windowed room. One side was covered with ceiling-high mirrors. Several men dressed in white tunics with roll collars, white knee breeches and soft-soled white shoes were practising before them, foils in hand, advancing and retiring, making practice lunges, carefully studying their reflections as they did so.

An authoritative voice spoke. 'Take your places on the *piste*, gentlemen, please.' Two of the men, their faces hidden by the fine-meshed masks they wore, stepped forward. They faced each other behind the painted lines which marked the long, narrow field of play.

'On guard.'

The adversaries assumed a formalized stance, feet at right angles, knees bent. The left arm was raised and bent behind the head, the sword arm holding the foil was breast high. Sadie continued to watch, absorbed, as the two began to lunge towards each other and then, smoothly, to retreat. One man flicked his blade over his opponent's, and the other man parried by carrying his sword rapidly from right to left.

She gradually realized that attack was met by defence and then riposte, as the attacker was in turn attacked. It was like a conversation between blades: an argument was presented and refuted, then a counter-argument offered and in turn repulsed. It took some time for Sadie to recognize Woolf beneath the disguising visors, but gradually she knew which was he. Something in his movements even through the formal, exaggerated poses of the sport, revealed the man. It was as though he had no feeling for his opponent's intentions, lacked any anticipatory knowledge of what the other man would do. He could not read his adversary's actions correctly and so nothing prepared him in advance: he was continually taken by surprise. Woolf, she thought sadly to herself, approached fencing as he did everything else. With his intellect, not his instincts.

The door opened behind her, and she heard someone move into the gallery and sit down behind her.

A man's voice asked enquiringly, 'Mrs Lander?'

Sadie turned round, to encounter a young man visibly surprised by her.

'What's the matter?' she asked. She put a nervous hand up to her face – was she covered in soot, that he should be looking at her like this?

The young man, dressed for fencing, holding his mask in his hand, said apologetically, 'I just didn't expect – I thought you were going to be Woolf's mother.'

'Well, I'm not.'

'I can see that. But the doorman said Mrs Lander was here.'

'So she is.'

Realization at last began to come into his eyes. 'I'm so sorry, I didn't know Woolf had a brother.'

'A *brother*?

'Yes. Aren't you his sister-in-law?'

'This conversation is losing me, I'm afraid. I'm Woolf's wife.'

The man said, 'Good Lord. Good Lord. I'd no idea, I do apologize. Woolf never mentioned he was married.'

'Did he not? Well, we've only been married a few months.'

The young man settled down beside her, and started chatting.

'We were talking the other day, and do you know, he is a dark horse! He never said a thing about you. I'd never have thought it of him, though. Woolf married!'

The bout below them was becoming more complex. The

249

fencers had moved nearer each other and the foils clashed as they met and parried. Suddenly there was an indrawn gasp from the spectators: half-turning to take a hit on his sword-arm, Woolf stumbled and struggled to regain his balance. His opponent moved swiftly and jabbed the foil at Woolf's chest, exposed by his drooping right arm.

'*Tierce*,' murmured the young man behind her. 'Neat.'

'Six minutes,' called the authoritative voice below, and the two adversaries bowed to each other and moved away.

Sadie got up. 'If you'll excuse me, I believe I'll go down and see if I can find my husband.'

The young man continued to look at her with interest as he clambered to his feet. Sadie swept past him to the door.

As she descended the stairs, Woolf was coming up. He greeted her cheerfully. 'Mostyn told me you were here. This is a very pleasant surprise, my dear.'

'I was just passing, and I thought I'd drop in.'

'Did you see me fence?' he asked diffidently.

'I thought you were splendid. I was most impressed. It must be very difficult.'

He beamed at her. 'Did you think so? That's capital. It was one of my good days, I think. Now, I usually walk round to Fortnum's for tea. Will you wait while I change?'

As they walked up St James's, Sadie said, 'I met a strange young man upstairs.'

'The doorman said Chatham had gone up. He's a good enough sort.'

'He thought I was your mother until I turned round.' Woolf looked puzzled.

'The doorman said Mrs Lander had arrived. Apparently he didn't know there was a young one. He seemed quite amazed to discover you were married.'

Woolf walked on in silence, twirling his umbrella.

Sadie continued, 'Have you never mentioned our marriage?'

'Well, I suppose I don't gossip much.'

'It's not exactly gossip. Do they know at the office.?'

'Oh, of course they do. It's just that I don't generally discuss my private life.'

Sadie, conscious that she was looking for difficulties, nonetheless could not stop herself from asking, 'Surely this is the sort of thing you might mention?'

Casually, glancing at the traffic before crossing the road, Woolf replied, 'It just didn't seem important to tell people.'

Sadie walked on in silence. Then she said, 'Goodness, I completely forgot. I was supposed to collect something in Bond Street, and it's nearly closing time. I'd better hurry. Will you excuse me?'

'Of course. Shall I wait for you?'

'No, I might be some time. I'll see you at home.'

She smiled brightly and hurried across the road towards Bond Street. When she had turned the corner, she walked more slowly. Tears were pouring down her cheeks. You silly idiot, she told herself, you're just feeling emotional. It's the baby, Ma told you everyone was like this. He didn't say anything unpleasant, that's just the sort of man he is.

She stood, wiping her eyes and peering blindly at the amber necklaces in Sac Frères. On a sudden impulse she blew her nose, stuffed her handkerchief in her handbag and walked quickly along the street to find a cab.

Zipporah was at home. 'You're lucky to find me in, I've an awful headache.'

'Would you prefer I didn't stay?'

'No, of course not, sit down. We'll have some tea and you'll do me good.'

'I was hoping you'd do *me* good.'

Zipporah shot her a sharp glance. 'That doesn't sound like the happy bride of five months.'

'Oh God, Zipporah, don't laugh at me. I'm in an awful state. I'm such a fool, I've been so stupid.'

She told Zipporah everything: about the afternoon, and Woolf's pleasant indifference. About their lives together,

251

and the kind and disinterested way in which Woolf treated her.

'I've really tried,' she finished, pleating her damp handkerchief on her knee and smoothing the fabric with the heel of her palm. 'I've done everything I can think of. I've even asked him outright.'

'What did he say?'

She sniffed miserably. 'He told me I was sweet and he'd had a very full day.'

Zipporah carefully fitted a cigarette into a tortoise-shell holder. 'Scarcely the voice of passion.'

'Don't be flippant. It's getting into a pattern I can't break. This marriage hasn't even been consummated yet.'

Zipporah's eyebrows rose. 'What a revelation. Do you want me to get Mark to speak to him?'

'Heavens no. I've got to do this myself. But what? What am I to do?'

Zipporah smoothed her heavy bun of hair, slightly self-conscious. 'You'll just have to be more – forward.'

'Aunt Zipporah, I've been forward, and it hasn't worked. If anything I feel I'm driving him away. I'm afraid he just doesn't want me.'

'It makes no sense. He married you, didn't he? What's the matter with the man?'

Sadie gave a rueful grimace. 'He was rather pushed into it, you know.' Zipporah looked startled. 'His mother suggested it,' Sadie explained. 'She came to me and asked if I'd agree, and then I think she manoeuvred him towards me.'

'And you connived at this? I wouldn't have thought it of you.'

'I suppose I did. And as I made my bed, I must lie on it.' She gave a sudden giggle. 'I just didn't expect to have to do so entirely alone.'

Zipporah regarded her thoughtfully for a moment. 'If you want my advice – and I assume you do, or you wouldn't have told me all this – I think you must just forget everything you've heard about how a lady behaves. Forget how things were before. Just act as though you weren't his wife and a respectable married woman. From the sound of it, half the trouble is that he thinks of you rather as he does his mother – someone who shares his meals and chats gently to him, and lets him lead his own life. You'll have to change that.'

'But how?'

Zipporah exhaled a puff of smoke. Her voice was hard. 'You'll have to play Salome for him.'

When they finished dinner that night and Annie was clearing away, Sadie suggested they take some port. Woolf, who was abstemious about his drinking, if not his eating, looked surprised. 'I hadn't thought of it. But now you mention it, that might be rather nice. Will you join me?'

'Please.'

She moved into the drawing room, where they usually drank their coffee. As he was pouring the port into two small glasses she switched off the main lights and just left two lamps burning. She sat on the settee, and piled the cushions behind her back. He wandered in after a moment, carrying the two glasses carefully hooked in the fingers of one hand, his book in the other. She accepted her glass, then as he settled himself she asked, 'What are you reading?'

'Just finishing *The New Machiavelli*. Wells is superb.'

'Can I borrow it from you?'

'Of course. I'll leave it on your bureau in the morning.'

He adjusted his spectacles and switched on the lamp at his side. When he had read for fifteen minutes Sadie asked, 'Did you have an interesting day?'

'What's that?' He looked up at her. His finger, she noticed, marked his place on the page. Clearly he did not intend to talk for long.

'I said, did you have an interesting day?'

'Not particularly, my dear.' He looked more closely. 'Aren't you sewing tonight?'

'I don't feel like it.'

Woolf went back to his book, and Sadie thought grimly to herself, it's going to become interesting though. At ten o'clock she said she was going up. She went over to kiss him, and he took her hand and patted it. 'Sleep well, my dear.'

Sadie took a long time bathing. She got out her nightdress and put it on, and brushed out her hair. She opened her wardrobe and took out the bottle of perfume Zipporah had given her, *Shem-el-Nezzim*. It was extremely potent. She dabbed it on heavily on her wrists and behind her ears, then rubbed it between her breasts. When she had finished she went quietly next door to check that Esther was sleeping. The child breathed so lightly she could hear nothing, and put her face close to the baby to smell the sweet, milky warmth of her body. She heard Woolf go to his room, and then to the bathroom. She waited for another half-hour, then knocked softly on his door. There was no reply. She turned the handle and went in.

The room was, as always, immaculate. His clothes were ranged neatly upon the gentleman's valet, his shoes treed beneath them. The window was slightly open, and he lay precisely in the middle of the bed. She opened the curtains to let in some light.

'Who's that?' His voice was sleepy.

'It's me.'

He propped himself up on one elbow. 'Is something wrong?'

'Nothing at all. I just wanted to see you.'

'What's happened. What do you want to talk about?'

Sadie drew a deep breath. 'I don't want to talk at all.' She moved over to the bed, and lay down beside him on

254

top of the covers. She put her hand on his shoulder. Beneath the thin flannel of his sleeping suit she felt his skin flinch slightly. I'm lovely, she thought, Asher said I was lovely, I can make him want me. She tightened her hold on his shoulder, and pressed him down so that their heads were together on the pillow. He lay rigid, and she pulled his arm and put his hand on her hip.

'Woolf, hold me, I need you to hold me.'

He patted her hip. 'Now then, my dear, it's late.'

'Not too late.'

She brushed her lips over his, and let her hair swing against his skin. The smell of the perfume she had put on was heavy about her, and it gave her confidence.

She started to unbutton the top of his suit and he held her hand and stopped her.

'What are you doing?'

'Don't you know?' she asked quietly. I sound like a cheap novelette, she thought, and almost giggled. She checked herself as his hand tightened on her hip.

'You've hardly any clothes on,' he said. 'You'll catch cold. Better get back to bed.'

In answer she moved the covers from under her and got beneath them. As she did so the little mother of pearl buttons on her nightdress pulled open, and she took his hand and held it to her breast. For a moment he resisted and she thought, he's going to push me away. Then his hand closed around her breast and he groaned. 'Sadie, what are you doing to me?'

What I should have done weeks ago, she thought, but whispered, 'Woolf, I want you. I want you.'

Almost to her surprise, she found that she did. Her nipples stiffened at his touch, and she started again to open his jacket so she could feel his skin against her own. This time he did not resist, even when she loosened the cord at his waist. She sat up and pulled the nightdress over her head and dropped it on the floor. He looked at her, and at

255

last she saw the excitement in his eyes. He did not smile at her. Very carefully he put his arms round her and pulled her to him, then he buried his head between her breasts and hugged her tightly.

They lay like that for a long time, until she thought he had gone to sleep. 'Woolf?'

'Mmm.'

She moved and cupped him between her hands. He was soft, quiescent beneath her fingers.

'Come on,' she whispered, caressing him, 'come on.' She wriggled down and fitted her body against his. She was still coaxing with her fingers, and she opened her thighs and moved him softly against her. His arms were still around her, his face now in her hair, and he continued to lie still. She took the lobe of his ear between her lips, then kissed his jaw and put her mouth against his. He began, finally, to kiss her back, and she relaxed against him.

'Is this what you want?' he muttered, as his body started to push into hers.

Almost inaudibly she replied, 'Yes. Yes.' She held her breath as he inserted himself, fearful that after childbirth it would hurt but he moved most carefully for her, waiting for her assent before continuing. She felt inordinate gratitude for his consideration, and on the rush of affection he inspired she spoke softly, intimately. Immediately he hesitated, uncertain how to respond, and she saw that he desired only her silent compliance.

He was a touching lover. She learnt that night what she had previously hesitated to ask: he had obviously never before had a continuing physical relationship with a woman. He was more sensuous than she had imagined, but oddly innocent: he's in his mid-thirties, she thought, and yet in bed he's like an adolescent boy.

She had grown used to the man who cloaked his emotions beneath an imperturbable exterior. To her surprise he dropped all restraint. He was unselfconsciously eager and only when she responded with too much ardour did he falter. In their lovemaking it was Woolf who lost himself. Sadie, while she exulted that it was happening at last, derived satisfaction more from his pleasure than her own. Even as she waited for the unmistakeable inner rhythm to emerge from their movements, it was over.

Woolf, solicitous, tucked the covers around her and asked, 'Are you all right?'

In response, she touched his hand with her lips. 'Yes. Certainly I am.' And then, in a lower tone, 'Thank you.'

'Thank *you*.'

They smiled at each other in the darkness, and both, almost immediately, fell asleep.

Once during the night Esther's murmurs of hunger woke Sadie. She fed the child in the nursery, then settled her again and returned to Woolf. He did not stir as she got in beside him and put her arm across his back, and as she grew drowsy she realized that this was the first time in many long months that she had gone to sleep without fear of her dreams.

When she awoke she knew it was early because the baby still slept. Woolf was not in the room: his clothes had gone. She hurriedly put on a robe and splashed her face with cold water. She combed her hair and went downstairs. It was seven-fifteen, and Annie was setting the breakfast table.

'Mr Lander said to tell you he was breakfasting out today. Had a lot of extra work to get through, he said. Very cheerful, he was.'

'He must have forgotten to tell me last night. Never mind, now I'm up, I'll have breakfast early too. Oh, before I forget— could we have a special dinner tonight? One of your lovely poussins perhaps? I thought we'd have a little celebration.'

The day passed in a blur of contentment; she had forgotten how it felt to wait eagerly for a man to come home to her. She took the baby in the perambulator for a long walk, relishing the warmth of the sun on her shoulders. In a park she took Esther out and looked lovingly at the puzzled frown she bestowed upon the moving leaves above them. She held the baby in the hollow of her neck and hummed to her a wordless lullaby of love. Life was going on, it would be all right. She and Woolf would make a life for each other.

She dressed carefully, as she always did before Woolf returned, and made sure Esther was safely asleep. Then she went to the piano and started playing, slowly, *Für Elise*.

Woolf arrived carrying an extra document case. 'Good evening, dear. Had a pleasant day?'

'Woolf, hallo.' She rose to embrace him, but he had already moved away.

'I must go up and change, I think, the day's been stifling in town.'

At the table he said enthusiastically, 'Delicious. Annie's done marvels this evening.'

'I told her we are celebrating.'

'Ah, that's why the excellent hock? But you didn't tell me – is it your birthday?'

Sadie looked at him in confusion. 'Why, no.'

'Then what are we celebrating?'

'I just thought – last night?' I've done the wrong thing, she thought. I shouldn't have mentioned it.

Woolf, a slight frown on his face, was watching her, his raised fork halfway to his mouth.

'I'm sorry.' She spoke anxiously. 'I just felt so – happy.'

'Not at all. I just hadn't expected it.' He lifted his glass. 'Well, my dear, here's to us.' They drank and he added, 'But I mustn't linger too long over dinner, I'm afraid. I've had to bring those Pendlebury papers home tonight. The case isn't going at all as I expected, and I need to spend a couple of hours on them.'

She nodded silently, and later she sat in the morning room

while he worked at the desk. Finally at ten o'clock she said, 'I think I'll go up. Will you be long?'

'I'm not quite through yet.' His voice was remote, he did not look up. 'I think I'll be about another hour.' He put down his pen and turned to her. 'Don't you wait for me. I'll be up shortly.'

Sadie asked, with an effort, 'Will you – would you sleep in my room tonight?'

He patted her upper arm. 'No, I think not, if you don't mind. I don't want to disturb you, and anyway I've a busy day tomorrow.'

To hide her face Sadie bent to fiddle with two perfectly healthy leaves of the aspidistra. 'I'll say goodnight then.'

She waited as he got to his feet and kissed her lightly on the top of her head. 'Sleep well.'

When she had gone Woolf exhaled slowly. Then he took off his jacket and settled back to work. But he found it hard to concentrate. He sat slumped over the roll-top desk, head in hands. He had seen her face when he refused her, and knew the pain it had caused. But what could he do? She had her rights, of course, she was his wife. But he expected her to behave like a lady, with decorum. To be so indiscreet, to want to mention, let alone celebrate, that act which rightly belonged to the night – it simply would not do. It wasn't proper. It wasn't decent. He sighed again. Well, she was young. She would settle down soon. He took up his pen.

Chapter Nineteen

During the autumn and winter of 1913 Sadie, for the first time in her life, read the newspapers with passionate concern. She pored over Woolf's *Times* in the evening while he worked. She had cared little for politics and less for foreign politics, but even she was aware of the tumult beyond Europe. China and Japan, Bulgaria and Turkey, invaded and retreated, signed treaties and broke them. In Europe, the French imposed military service. The Germans held military conversations with the Turks, and in Alsace Lorraine one November day a German officer soured diplomatic relations with France by insulting Alsatian recruits at Zabern. The following month, Britain and France opposed the German–Turkish military convention. At home, Ireland seethed with bitter and bloody opposition to the Liberal call for Home Rule and by December Parliament forbade the sending of arms there.

Woolf began to read a new magazine, the *New Statesman*, and Zipporah arrived one afternoon to teach Sadie the foxtrot.

'For this, my dear, you'll have to shorten your skirts, or you'll never manage.'

Sadie, who foresaw no possibility of actually dancing in the immediate future, laughingly agreed, but a couple of weeks later she decided, after consulting the *Ladies Journal*, that Zipporah was right, and that if she failed to take immediate steps she would become a dowdy frump. She had a little money of her own left from the sale of the Sargent and she decided to spend it on clothes. So far she and Woolf had not discussed an allowance for her. He paid the household bills cheerfully, but it had not occurred to him that she might have any needs beyond the purely domestic. She did not feel yet that she could raise the subject, despite the fact that the house cost him nothing but its upkeep. She'd wait till things were more settled between them. In the meantime she spent two days shopping. She bought herself a costume at Peter Robinson with a sailor collar and a three-flounced skirt, and felt more cheerful than she had for weeks.

When Woolf arrived home she was still changing for dinner. She heard him passing her door and called 'Woolf, hallo. Come in.'

He opened the door and peered in. 'Good evening, my dear. Ah, forgive me . . .' and made to close it again.

Sadie, who was wearing a loose robe over her corset, glanced down at herself. 'I'm sorry. I wasn't thinking.' Then she laughed. 'For heaven's sake, it's all right. I'm your wife! You can see me in my nothings, you know.'

Nervously, he advanced, trying to keep his eyes averted. Sadie did not know whether to be amused or exasperated by his discomfiture. She was, as it happened, so stoutly bound into her 'Bandel corset' that she could hardly breathe. She'd been sent up to Addley Bourne in Sloane Street by Lena, and there had spent £1 3s on a specially designed garment which promised to be successful for restoring the figure to a graceful form, having the new arrangement of adjustable webbing straps. These crossed firmly over her stomach, holding it flat, and were tightly buckled. Staggered by the sheer size of the garment, she had weakly purchased one in black with blue broche.

Now she held open her robe and said to Woolf, 'See what I look like in this iron maiden? I don't imagine you've seen its like before.'

'Er, no. No, I think you may be right.' He was not, however, looking at her but towards the window.

She shrugged and turned back to finish putting up her hair. 'I'm sorry,' she said, her mouth full of hairpins, 'I wasn't trying to lure you in here with evil intent, you know.'

Startled by the sarcasm in her voice he glanced round. She

went on with her hair. 'Only, Woolf, we do seem to be getting very staid.'

'Staid?'

'Middle-aged. Settled. Boring. Predictable.'

His face was blank. She went on, trying not to make the words cruel, seeking to explain. 'We agreed when we first discussed this marriage that we would each go our own way much of the time, and we do. But I never imagined that we should have so little private life together.'

Woolf was genuinely amazed. 'But we have. We spend our evenings together. We had a dinner party only last week. You may be right, we should talk more, but my dear, I think you're exaggerating slightly.'

Slowly Sadie said, 'I don't believe so. I'm not thinking of our meals, Woolf, or even of our conversations, though I agree with you there. I'm referring to the marriage rite.'

He had turned back to the window and now he stood very still, looking out. She watched his hunched shoulders, hands gripping each other behind his back.

When he spoke it was in a low voice. 'Sadie. I'm sorry. I thought it would be a success. I hoped it would – I have tried. I just don't think I can be the man you need.'

Instinctively she moved forward, put her hands on his shoulders. 'But you can. I know you can, Woolf. It'll be all right, really it will, you'll see.'

'I think not.'

Even as he spoke she felt him flinch under her touch. Her arms dropped to her sides. Dully, she said, surprising herself by the admission, 'You're right. I'm asking too much of you, aren't I?'

Still turned away from her – he seemed to find it easier to speak when he could not see her face – he replied, with an effort, 'It's not your fault, I know that. It's me. I just don't seem to be able to sustain our relationship the way you would wish. This is hard for me to say, Sadie. I'm not a man who questions himself overmuch – but I think I'm happier alone.'

So it's come at last, she thought. Aloud, she said, 'What shall we do?'

'Do? Why, nothing, I imagine. We're in this now, for better or worse,' he gave a wry smile, 'and this isn't the time for worrying about one's personal difficulties. We shall just have to make the best of it.' He made her a stiff little bow. 'And now, if you'll excuse me, I'll get ready for dinner.'

Silently she stood as he walked to the door. Without turning, she spoke. 'I could have loved you, Woolf. I want you to know that.'

'Thank you. I don't blame you, I don't doubt for a minute that is the truth. But–' he searched for the words – 'how can I make you see that this is not a disaster? We tried, and I believe we have failed. But there are compensations, aren't there? We are pleasant companions, are we not? We are not averse to one another. We simply have to say that the – er – physical side of our marriage is not one to pursue.'

'But Woolf,' Sadie entreated, 'we can't live like that. It would be a sham.'

He raised his eyebrows. 'Would it, my dear?'

Exasperated she snapped, 'Of course it would. We're both young. We can't give up all hope of love for *ever*. It's unnatural.'

Mildly, he protested, 'Now that's putting it a little strongly, wouldn't you say?'

'I don't think so. I'm not asking for so much, am I? It's not for myself that I'm saying this, but for both of us. Woolf . . .' Sadie tried to keep her voice low, not to let Annie hear, not to embarrass him. 'Woolf, when we do . . .' she hesitated, seeking not to offend him, 'when we do make love, you seem to like it, and I don't . . .'

'Sadie. Please.' He interrupted her sharply. 'This conservation is becoming crude and sordid. Nor can I see why this causes you such concern. You have a child, after all. You have fulfilled yourself as a woman. What more can you want?'

263

Sadie regarded him with a mixture of so many conflicting emotions she hardly knew what to say. She was horrified at his lack of understanding, filled with despair by the bleak future which faced them. But most of all, she was overwhelmed with pity. For herself, and for him, this man who saw the act of love not as spontaneous delight, but as a crude lust which in no way touched or affected his other, his real life. She thought of the way in which, self-forgetful though he had been with her on those few rare occasions, next day he had never referred to the previous evening, as though the act had never taken place.

She tried to keep some measure of control as she said, 'I don't think I can live like that. I'm not a nun. I'm twenty-four years old – are you suggesting that for the rest of my life I forget the "physical side" of our marriage, as you delicately put it?'

He winced and said stiffly, 'I think, my dear, that celibacy is no real hardship for a woman.'

'I think that it will be a hardship for me. What do you suggest I do instead? Practise secret bad habits?'

He gave her a look of contempt and turned the handle of the door. She began to speak again and he held up his hand. 'No, I do not wish to continue this conversation any further. I shall not be dining at home tonight.'

Throughout the spring Sadie and Woolf struggled to maintain appearances for each other. Sadie's pride refused to allow her to admit defeat. She told herself that Woolf's growing aloofness, his sudden bursts of irritability, were the result of exhaustion. She knew too that he was increasingly disturbed by rumours of war. He was violently opposed to it, and certain it would come. He had explained to her, when they first heard that a student had assassinated the Archduke Ferdinand, that the fate of nations could be changed because of a single human act. Sadie cuddled Esther and listened with half an ear. She could not for a moment believe war would touch them. There had been wars before, after all – Afghanistan, the Boer War . . . There were always soldiers around in London, young men in uniform whose career was the regiment. This would be no different; it was a storm in a teacup.

By July the heat in London was almost unbearable. The grass in Hyde Park was scorched brown and people moved lethargically along the dusty streets. Geraniums withered in window boxes and shops were empty of customers. Even as far out as St John's Wood, where painted villas stood calmly back from the road, each cooled by its own green oasis of trees, it was impossible to keep out the heat. Blinds were drawn, water sprayed in shaded rooms. In the kitchens flyscreens covered all the windows, and every jar and jug had its own muslin cover weighted with beads. Food was served cold, but no one had appetite even for iced soup or boiled salmon.

The baby was fractious and sleepless in the heat and her teething made it worse. Sadie spent hours each night walking her up and down to soothe her, anxious that Woolf should not be disturbed. In fact, he rarely heard her crying and would not have minded if he had. The baby did not intrude upon him in any way, but for the sake of Asher – for whom he had felt more affection than any person outside his own family – Woolf would have been prepared to tolerate a great deal from his child. When Esther arrived his first emotion had been faint surprise at her ridiculously small size and inordinately loud voice. Knowing nothing of children and less of babies he had not anticipated what changes her presence might bring into the household. In the event, any there were did not appear to touch him. True, there was another woman, the nurse, but she kept herself very much to herself. The baby was always in bed before he returned in the evenings, and though Sadie complained of her broken nights

265

he couldn't see what the fuss was about: the child seemed easy enough to him. As she became older and more communicative he liked to make her chuckle, but when she was able to reach towards him and grab his glittering gold-rimmed spectacles, he shied away. After that he kept his distance and contented himself with letting her clutch his finger. Once, Sadie found him in the nursery dangling a toy for the crowing child, but he seemed embarrassed at having been discovered and the incident was not repeated.

On the first Saturday of August, the Bank Holiday weekend, Sadie was bathing Esther in the late afternoon. It was Nurse's day off, but this anyway was her prerogative each evening. She loved to be in the nursery, with its painted furniture and flowery chintz. She sat facing the sunny window, the child wrapped in a white towel in her lap. She popped the thermometer into the water to check the temperature – Nurse strongly disapproved of using the elbow – and wiped Esther's face and eyes carefully with absorbent wool. Then she gently patted her dry, removed the towel and washed her all over with a soapy hand. Esther lay quietly, watching her with intent, affectionate eyes, and Sadie sang to her in a soft, tuneless flow of sound the words of a song she remembered from her childhood, when they celebrated the Passover.

> One only kid, one only kid
> That my father bought
> For two *zuzim*
> One only kid . . .

While she sang she thought of nothing but the child she held; they were totally absorbed in each other. She turned Esther face down on her lap and dabbed her dry, then she put on her vest and flannel petticoat. She had just finished fastening the dress, and was doing up Esther's head flannel, when there was a gentle tapping at the door.

'Come in.'

To her delight it was Mark and swinging from his little finger was a small parcel. He kissed them both on the forehead, and put the parcel on Esther's chest.

'That's for you, Miss.'

'Uncle Mark, you're spoiling her disgracefully. You never come without something.'

'It's a pleasure I have no intention of forgoing, so you may save your breath. By the time she is twenty-one I shall see to it she is thoroughly vain, self-satisfied and generally as unbearable as any beauty should be. However, on this occasion you may open it for her.'

Inside was a bracelet of oval gold links, so fine and supple that Sadie said, 'Oh, it's not fair, I want it. You are kind, thank you so much.'

'It's a long time since I've enjoyed buying trinkets. Zipporah is interested only in the magnificent, and you won't have anything at all. This way, I can indulge myself.'

Sadie looked at him affectionately. 'You make it sound very convincing, but I think you know how much I appreciate it.'

Mark waggled the thumb Esther was clutching, and said suddenly, 'If I could go back and do it all again, I'd do it differently. When I was younger I thought I didn't want this. Now I'm too old I see what a fool I was. The only compensation for either of us is her sex. No soldiering for her, thank God.'

'Will there be for others?'

'Oh Lord, yes. I can't think how we've kept out of it so long. There's no hope now, you know, we're for it.'

'That's what Woolf says. But honestly I can't believe it. Surely someone will see sense and keep us out of it. It's not our concern.'

'Woolf's right. He saw it coming long before I did and I should have listened.' He grimaced. 'Do you know, my dear, what the result will be so far as I'm concerned? I've no one to lose, and am too old to go myself. So all that can happen is that I shall become richer.'

To Sadie's look of surprise, he shrugged. 'Name one of the very few commodities that retains its value – increases it – in time of war. Name an item that takes up almost no space, is viable currency in any country, keeps under any conditions . . .'

'Diamonds?'

'Diamonds. Ironic, isn't it, that this war might cost millions of lives but will make my fortune, quite unnecessarily.'

'Surely it's not really going to happen?' Sadie looked alarmed, and the baby burped gently into her ear.

'God knows. Did you read the manifesto in the *Manchester Guardian* this morning?'

'No. What did it say?'

'Oh, the usual pacifist things about how the British people can best serve the cause of right and justice, and the interests of civilization, by remaining the one Great Power in Europe that has not yielded to war madness. Signed by a whole string of eminent men.'

'There you are, then. Surely the politicians will take notice of that and stop it?'

'I wish I could think so.' He walked over to the window, and stood looking out. 'This incredible heat. You'd think all those old men would want peace, just so they could sit in their gardens and drink barley water. But now I must get home. Zipporah has a dinner party tonight, and it's getting late.'

When he had gone Sadie sat nursing Esther. She listened to the child's contented murmurs and the sounds of summer from the garden. It was safe and secure, so far from risk or danger.

The Bank Holiday Sunday was a quiet day for the Landers. Woolf lunched with his mother and afterwards he and Sadie wheeled Esther along the canal banks at Little Venice. In the late afternoon the streets were deserted, and the air was loud with the murmur of insects.

'All the idle rich,' Woolf observed drily, 'are doubtless pushing punts around at Richmond. And the rest are spending the weekend in Brighton.'

'I'd rather be here.' Sadie stopped to adjust the canopy over the bassinette to shield Esther's eyes from the slanting sunlight.

'I think we should be getting back, though. Johnson went up to the House this afternoon to hear Grey speak: I'm anxious to know what was said. I'll stop off on the way home, I think.'

When he joined Sadie in the early evening, his face was strained and drawn.

'Bad news?'

'Hard to tell. Grey was explaining that we *might* be drawn into what he calls the continental conflict. Nothing definite, though.'

The following day he arrived home from work unexpectedly early. Sadie was bathing Esther. He stood hunched in the doorway, watching them both. Sadie glanced round. 'Hallo. Come on in and shut the door – Esther'll catch cold.'

'In this heat? Hardly.' But he sat down in the window seat.

'What's the matter?'

'Have you heard the news today?'

'Zipporah called in, she told me German troops were in Belgium, marching through to France.'

'Asquith's given them an ultimatum. They're to withdraw from Belgium.'

'When will we know?'

'Eleven tonight.'

'What shall you do?'

'I think I'll go up to town. I want to hear for myself.'

Sadie gave the cradle a last rock, and waited until Esther had slotted herself safely into sleep.

She stood and held out her hand to Woolf. 'Let's go down. We'll eat early if you like.'

Later, waiting alone, she heard the clock in the hall chime eleven. Midnight in Berlin. An hour later, Woolf arrived home. He knocked on her door, and one look at his face told her. She said, 'We're in?'

'Up to our damned necks. I must get some sleep, I'm worn out. I'm meeting Counsel tomorrow afternoon. If you aren't busy come and join me at the Temple and we'll talk then. Goodnight, my dear.'

That day Sadie walked through London in a daze. The streets were thronged as people flowed through Piccadilly Circus down the expanse of Haymarket to Trafalgar Square. She was jostled and pushed by excited women clutching their children by the hand, by nervous young men in stiff collars. And everywhere were soldiers, moving with bravado and swagger. The uniforms were pressed and new, their puttees smooth, their faces unlined. The flood of khaki swept Sadie towards Nelson's Column. On its great base she saw one of the new recruiting posters had been pasted: 'Forward to Victory – Enlist Now.' Managing eventually to board a tramcar, she opened the *Daily Mail* she had bought. On the inside page the royal coat of arms was blazoned beneath the words 'Your King and Country Need You.'

She got off in Fleet Street, meaning to walk through the Inns of Court and meet Woolf as they had arranged. She turned off the busy street and sought the green and cloistered Temple, passing the old tobacconist on the corner and the shouting newsboy, hurrying with relief through the stone porch to the silence beyond. It was a different world here, untouched by the clatter and hurry of Fleet Street and Ludgate Circus. Dignified men, heads bent in conversation, moved slowly between their chambers. Sadie found the bench where she had occasionally before waited for Woolf.

She had only been there for two minutes when a stentorian voice broke the peace. 'Left march, keep it up there, call yourselves soldiers?' From the narrow road leading to the river emerged a company of young men, their faces nervous and intent as they formed a square on the trim lawns and proceeded to drill to the shouted instructions. It was only when they obeyed the command 'Present . . . *arms*!' that Sadie realized they were carrying walking sticks instead of rifles.

When Woolf joined her she gestured, laughing, towards the khaki figures. 'Look, isn't it absurd. What do they think they're doing with those walking sticks?'

'It's not absurd. It's pathetic. They have no equipment. There *is* no equipment. We have gone into this totally unprepared. The whole thing is madness, madness.' He sighed heavily and sat down beside her.

'Everyone I've seen seems so excited.'

'Of course they are. They see it as an opportunity, a change. Do you realize what's going to happen, though?'

She shook her head.

'Hundreds of thousands of men are going to leave their homes and families to fight for a better world, and what are they going to find, do you suppose? Danger and dirt and death. That's what war is all about. Not gallantry and courage. That's politicians' talk.'

Woolf adjusted his glasses and continued to watch the distant, matching figures in the late afternoon sunshine. 'They look like toy soldiers from here, don't they? And before too long, those boys will doubtless be lying maimed on some battlefield.'

Shocked, Sadie stared at him. 'For heaven's sake, how can you talk like that?'

'Too strong for you, is it my dear? I can talk like that because the truth is like that.' Then he asked, curiously, 'How do you envisage this war?'

'I don't know. I suppose I thought it would be somehow – heroic.'

Woolf gave an ironical smile. 'So Mr Lloyd George has made an impression on you too, I see.'

'Well, I read his speech in Parliament.'

'Ah yes,' Woolf's voice was mocking. 'We have been living in a sheltered valley for generations, comfortable, indulgent, selfish. We have forgotten the great pinnacle of sacrifice pointing like a rugged finger to heaven . . .'

Angrily, Sadie turned on him. 'What's wrong with that? I thought it was a wonderful speech.'

'As a speech it may be splendid. As an incitement to the nation to wage war with a good heart, it's perfect. But for God's sake, why? War is a barbarity, it's unthinkable!'

'What is the alternative?'

His shoulders slumped. He fingered his spectacles. 'There is no alternative. Not now. War has been declared, and war there will be. But it won't be the war Lloyd George promises us. What did he say, "The great peaks of honour we had forgotten, duty and patriotism, clad in glittering white." It will be violent death for thousands of young men, lives lost in the name of loyalty. Useless waste. Useless.' He sighed, and put his hand on Sadie's in a gesture rare for him. 'I'm sorry. I've been fearing this for so long, now it's here I just want to scream "I told you so, I told you so". It's as bad as I thought it'd be – and worse.'

Sadie returned the pressure of his hand. 'It won't be so awful, surely? There must be something we could do to help – I'll talk to Lena, she's on committees for everything, there'll be dozens of organizations rolling bandages and making blankets for the soldiers.' She paused under Woolf's caustic expression and said defensively, 'Well, it'd be useful, wouldn't it?'

'Oh yes, my dear. Very useful, if not exactly central to the issue.'

Stung, Sadie retorted, 'So what are you going to do?'

'I? Oh, I've already done my bit.'

'What do you mean?'

'I did it this morning. At ten o'clock I presented myself in the appropriate offices and took the King's sovereign.'

She stammered in disbelief. 'You did *what*?'

'I volunteered for the Army.'

That evening Woolf and Sadie walked in the darkening garden, redolent of night-scented stock and the green damp of the freshly watered lawn. Woolf attempted to explain his decision, and Sadie tried to come to terms with it.

When she said, not for the first time, 'I wish we'd talked about it first, I wish you'd told me before you did it,' he could only offer, in some bewilderment, the suddenness of his decision. 'I hadn't planned it – you know what I think of the whole damned business. It suddenly became the thing I had to do.'

'But you so despise the very idea of the war. I just don't understand.'

He sighed, hands clenched tightly behind his back. 'Neither do I. I think it must be my public school education.' He gave a brief smile. 'Or possibly a sense of duty? God knows. Mother says . . .'

'Your mother knows?'

'Why yes. I told her this morning.'

Sadie's voice was low. 'Before you told me?'

'I . . .' he dropped his eyes. 'Yes. Before I told you. I'm sorry, my dear. The habit of a lifetime is hard to break.'

Sadie stood for a long moment, absorbing the implication of his words. She knew that Woolf would not do anything deliberately to hurt her. It was simply that he continued to think and act exactly as he had all his adult life. However long they continued to be man and wife, Woolf Lander would always remain at heart unmarried.

She swallowed and said, keeping her voice steady, 'That's not the important thing. It doesn't matter now. What matters is that you've done something very brave. I'm proud of you.'

He looked at her with surprise and gratitude, and she

273

touched his cheek with her finger. 'You will be careful?'

'Have no doubt of that. I'm no hero.'

On impulse he put his arm around her shoulders.

'Sadie, I'm sorry if everything hasn't gone right between us. When I get back, we'll start again, shall we?'

'Yes. Of course.' Sadie tried to find words for a deep anxiety she had felt since Woolf told her of his decision. Hesitantly, she asked, 'You're sure you haven't done this – to get away from me?' He considered his answer so carefully that she could hardly bear to hear what he would say.

Finally, he spoke. 'I do not believe that was in my mind at all.' Then, seeing in her face the need for reassurance, he added, for he was a kind man, 'Of course I wouldn't go for such a reason. That would be foolish in the extreme. I tell you, much as I abhor the idea of war, this is just something I must do. Will you be able to manage here?'

'I won't be the only woman coping alone. And Woolf, I'll keep an eye on your mother.'

She had not heard him laugh like that for a long time. 'Knowing Mother as I do, I think she'll be keeping an eye on you.'

Two weeks later Woolf reported to an Officers' Training course in Northamptonshire. He came home on leave once, and immediately afterwards was sent to France. They said goodbye to each other, with an odd mixture of formality and affection, at home – Woolf insisted that he travel to the station alone. When Sadie clung for a moment he gently disengaged her. 'Now my dear, you must look after yourself. Try to keep everything under control, whatever happens.'

'I'll try. Woolf, you will write, won't you?'

He waved his cap at her as the cab pulled away. She called after him, in a sudden burst of emotion, 'Woolf, come home safe!'

Chapter Twenty

In the weeks following Woolf's departure Sadie read the papers avidly for progress of the war. It was over two months before any letters arrived from him, and then they were dated weeks before, for they had been held up by the censor. He told her little of his day-to-day existence, he did not mention the battlefront at all, and this she realized would not be allowed. Sometimes a sentence would be heavily scored through.

Mostly, he described events like the occasional good meal at a restaurant behind the lines, or a walk in a wood when he was relieved from duty. More than anything, he told her, he felt the lack of privacy. Knowing Woolf's nature she understood this. 'It reminds me horribly of schooldays,' he wrote. 'The regimentation and the lists, the rigid timekeeping and the monotonous diet. One is never, ever alone. Any kind of comfort is savoured voraciously: hot coffee, a lamp in one's room. Silence.'

Sadie found that her feelings for her husband grew stronger in his absence. Without the unconscious rebuffs he imposed, her naturally affectionate nature asserted itself. She wrote fond letters – not intimate, she knew he would hate that – and every other day she would post one to him, telling what she had done, now Esther had smiled, that his mother had called in. She described the garden, told him of reviews in the *New Statesman*. She read the new Henry James novel, *The Golden Bowl*, and Sargent invited her to look at his new portrait of the author, which she had missed at the Royal Academy. 'It's superb,' she wrote to Woolf. 'You would enjoy it. One of the critics says he looks like a businessman from the provinces, but I think he would look most at home presiding in a courtroom. Sadly it has proved impossible to hide the scars where that wretched suffragette slashed it at the Academy.'

Despite the gossip, Sadie was restless. She spent long hours with the baby, reluctant to lose a moment of her company. Woolf's decision fired her with an ambition to achieve something herself. All around her women were shouldering new tasks. The newspapers reported that they were working as chauffeurs, and Annie's sister had started work in the canteen of a munitions factory where, she reported, hundreds of young women worked.

It was only brought home to Sadie just what they were doing when instead of Tom Dutton arriving to give the chimneys their six monthly cleaning, his wife appeared, her hair bound up in a turban, her face grimy. Emboldened by this, Sadie got in touch with Lena. 'My sister-in-law has us all organized,' she wrote. 'Dozens of comfortable married ladies, all panting to help the brave boys at the front, roll bandages by the yard and the hour. Some of us knit balaclavas and bodybelts, but my fingers never would learn to knit. I have managed to sew some squares together to make blankets, and am absurdly proud of this achievement. It is very pleasant, in a boring way, to be thrust into so much feminine company. I wish there was more I could do to help you win this wretched war.'

But by the end of the second week Sadie had had enough of those bandages and the gossip. When the ladies interrupted the work yet again for cups of tea and sandwiches, carefully served on tiny plates by Lena's housekeeper, her annoyance wound her up like a spring. 'Can you not forget your own needs for two hours at a time?' Mrs Montefiore, beside her, would have flushed at the sharpness of her tone had her colour not already been so high. For the next fifteen minutes the silence was broken only by the occasional sigh as the ladies worked. Then Mrs Magdeburg forgot the slight and began to describe in minute detail the dress her eldest planned to wear at the party for young officers on leave from the Front.

The following morning Sadie dressed more plainly than usual and travelled across London. Every van she saw seemed to bear Kitchener's accusatory finger: it even appeared inside the tramcar which finally deposited her outside Guy's Hospital. St Thomas' Street was grey and drab; from the kitchen windows came the clatter of crockery and the smell of institution tea and cabbage water. She shuddered and hurried on. Matron, when she was finally free to see Sadie after a two-hour wait, was a harassed woman who explained that she was losing nurses rapidly to the Front.

'You won't be able to take their place, you know,' she told Sadie. 'If you imagine yourself taking temperatures and administering medicine, I'm afraid you're in for a disappointment.'

Sadie, who had imagined just that, said, 'I don't mind what I do. Really, I just want to do something practical.'

'Oh, you'll do that all right. Very well, Mrs Lander. If you think you can take it, I'm pleased to accept your application. Subject, of course, to making a brief check.'

She began to work at Guy's Hospital two weeks later. Her elation that first morning did not last long. She was hurried into a coarse linen uniform, buttoned too tightly at the throat, and set to work in the sluice, rubbing plaster into bandages for fractures. After two hours of this she tentatively stuck her head into the corridor and asked if she might have a chair. The hurrying sister, barely pausing, told her tersely that Matron permitted no such indulgence. Chastened, Sadie retreated into her cupboard.

For the next few months she was rarely allowed outside it. Occasionally she would be summoned to help in the ward, and after the first time she realized this was more of a horror than the hours on her feet cleaning medical utensils. The wards were high, and so tightly packed with iron beds that it was almost impossible to move between them. The sight and stench of so many invalids was overpowering. Everywhere she looked she saw people labouring for breath or groaning with pain. She held water while a trained nurse dressed an abscess on the back of an old man, and waited with a spittoon at the ready as a docker with foetid bronchitis coughed endlessly.

Sadie felt helpless and exhausted. At dusk she could barely keep awake on the omnibus, and when she got home would lie in a bath and go straight to bed. The baby would crawl in with her, and her gurgles and Annie's hot soup seemed to bring the only warmth in her day. After four months Sadie was drained of energy and interest. Annie, fearing a return of the deep depression that had burdened her after Esther's birth, saw this with anxiety. Finally she said briskly, as she was picking Esther up to take her to the nursery, 'It won't do, you know, love, it really won't. You're knocking yourself out doing this, and there's no need for you to work this hard.'

'I suppose not.' Sadie's voice was flat. 'What should I do?' she asked childishly.

'You'd best tell them the truth, hadn't you? Just say it's getting too much for you.'

'But that's . . . I can't just give up. Woolf can't just give up, none of them can. I don't want it to be easier for me.'

'Maybe not. But you've a responsibility to this child. She sees little enough of you as it is. What happens to her with Mr Lander away if you get into that awful state again?'

Sadie sighed. 'You'd be here.'

Sharply, Annie said, 'Don't bank on it. I'm not so young as I was, you know. I can't take on someone else's child.'

Shocked out of her self-pity, Sadie said contritely, 'You're right. I'm sorry. I'll talk to Matron tomorrow.'

It was easier said than done. Facing Matron, in the stark office with cream walls and dark brown panelling, Sadie gazed over her head at the painting of an eminent surgeon, his mouth set in a firm line, his high collar emphasizing the forceful chin. Below him Matron looked, she thought, much the same.

Weakly, Sadie stammered out her request to be moved. During her months there she had only rarely been called upon to speak in Matron's presence. Usually her role was to answer 'Yes, Ma'am' or 'No, Matron' to staccato questions. Now she said apologetically, 'I am sorry. I don't mean to be a nuisance. It's just that I am getting very tired, and I can't sleep properly. I don't have much chance to talk to anyone, and I'm feeling very lonely, I think.'

Matron stared at her, with an impenetrable expression. 'Very well. As a volunteer, you of course may stop work at any time you wish.'

'Oh, no, I don't want to stop. But if I could just do something else, part-time, please?'

'Very well, Mrs Lander.' Matron rose dismissively. 'Perhaps you would be good enough to finish the week for me. I will let you know my decision.'

Two days later, while Sadie was scrubbing away at a rack of test tubes, the door opened to admit a young woman in a severe grey suit, her hair in a neat bun. Sadie, used to seeing staff in uniform, started telling her that visitors were not allowed in the staff area. 'It's all right,' the young woman said. 'You're Mrs Lander, aren't you? I'm from Admin. And I just wondered whether you'd be interested in another job in the hospital. It's only part-time, I'm afraid.'

'I *want* to stay.' Sadie wiped her arm across her forehead, brushing away the wisps of fringe, and leant against the sink to stop her back aching. ' I just can't carry on doing this work.'

The young woman grimaced. 'You've been at it about three months longer than most, but I'd lay money Matron didn't tell you that.'

'Good heavens, no. She made me feel I was a rank deserter.'

'She would. I couldn't do this day after day either. But the

279

job I've got is quite different. It's not much – just clerical work, really. But it's not skilled, you don't need to be a typewriter girl. Much of it is keeping ledgers, things like that.'

'Will I be sitting down?'

'Endlessly.' The young woman laughed.

Fervently, Sadie said, 'Then yes please. I'd like it.'

'Well, don't decide straight away. Come in and see me on Monday, and we'll discuss it. I'm Janet Openshaw. I'll look forward to seeing you around ten.'

Sadie moved into the offices at the back of the hospital. The work was routine but undemanding and occasionally it really interested her. There was a great deal of noise and bustle, and she and Janet Openshaw would lunch together regularly in the canteen, or take sandwiches and walk towards the river. She was no longer exhausted, much to Annie's relief. She felt she was doing something useful, and yet still having a reasonable life. But it meant she did not have much time to think and this, she reasoned, was a boon. The last thing she needed at the moment was an encouragement to be introspective. More than anything else, she appreciated having more time to spend with Esther. Uncle Mark, who seemed to be working less himself, would arrive many afternoons to walk with them. Esther was toddling now and would potter along between them on plump legs, in her many-buttoned coat and gaiters, emitting squeaks of delight and dismay as she spied a bird or tried to catch a floating leaf. It was almost Christmas: Woolf had been away nearly eighteen months and was due for leave. But at the last moment it was cancelled.

As it turned out, Woolf came home only twice during his four years of service. Later, he admitted that he had deliberately engineered this, not wanting to exacerbate the situation between them. The first leave he did spend in St John's Wood, for three weeks, was remarkably pleasant.

Sadie remembered his words exactly, for he used them on a note of some surprise as Sadie saw him to the station before leaving herself for work. The second occasion, in the autumn of 1917, was made difficult by Woolf's exhaustion. He was clearly almost at the end of his tether and more remote than ever. On his previous visit he had carefully tried to make things appear as normal as possible. But this time his mind was welling over with his experiences.

He had seen men die in flooded bunkers, had heard them coughing away their lives from mustard gas. Sadie thought of the wards and the spitting, dying men and tried to comfort him, but Woolf was beyond the comfort of words and the other solace offered to him was not what he sought. He did try: they did their best for each other. But both, staring afterwards into the darkness, knew this was not the answer.

The day Woolf finally arrived home, Sadie vowed to herself that she would try to be the wife he wanted. If indeed, she added ruefully, he wanted one at all. She would be undemanding, unquestioning. She would ask nothing he could not easily give. And if it became unbearable, she would have to think again. Perhaps she would become like Zipporah. The thought was not so impossible to her now. In the four years of Woolf's absence she had come to see that perhaps he was right, that companionship was important. She had lived without any real emotional life for a long time, and she had managed well enough. All her longings had been satisfied by Esther. Perhaps, she thought, she would at least be able to have another child. Woolf could not deny her that, surely.

In the event, Woolf's presence sapped her good intentions. How, she wondered, as she watched him place his bookmark carefully in the page before answering her question, how could I have thought he would change? At first he did not speak of the war. It was as though he had been away on business, she thought. The only evidence of his experiences was a new irascibility she found quite terrifying. His patience had always charmed her, but now it seemed totally to have disappeared. He was annoyed by the slightest change she made in the house. To celebrate his homecoming she had his room repainted. Her first impulse had been to put some of his belongings into her room but caution had prevailed and held her back. Woolf's reaction to the redecorating – she had chosen a soft magnolia – was intense irritation. It seemed that some of his books had been incorrectly arranged, and why had she changed his pictures round? Sadie, who had not noticed they were not as they had been, could find no reply.

When he had been home for just two weeks he started talking one evening after dinner. He tried to explain to her just what the experience had been, and what it had done to him.

'I feel,' he finished sadly, 'as though I had nothing left inside. I seem to be standing outside myself, watching.'

Sadie pleated her napkin between her fingers and said carefully, 'But Woolf, you have always been a watcher, haven't you? There was a time when I thought you – rather prided yourself on that.'

He gave a rueful smile.' Possibly I did. But this is different. I feel now so detached from everything that I'm almost afraid for my sanity.' Woolf spoke quietly, but she could see the sweat beading his upper lip.

She put out a hand, stopped as she saw him draw back imperceptibly. 'Doesn't the fact that you can talk about it mean your sanity is not impaired?'

'If I were arguing this in court, I should say the accused was in complete control. Perhaps that's how it looks from outside. But I know . . .' he paused, dabbing at his forehead with his napkin, 'I know that it's as though I were on another planet.'

Consolingly, she said, 'I'm sure you'll feel better when your memories have faded a little.'

'Faded? Faded? Do you honestly think they'll fade?' His face working, he stared at her. 'Less than two months ago I saw a man lying face down in six inches of mud. Except that he wasn't a man. Just a trunk. His legs were blown off. And do you want to know the really horrible thing?'

He was speaking in a voice so low she could barely hear him. She whispered, 'What?'

'He lived. He's somewhere now, in a hospital, wondering why his legs still hurt him when they're no longer there. Wondering what his wife will do, what his little boy will say.'

Wordlessly, Sadie shook her head.

'And I'll tell you something else. For the last six months I'd been sharing my quarters with another Lieutenant, younger than me, a man with a fiancée back in Leicester and everything to look forward to. The day before this . . . this slaughter was declared finished, he was told he had tuberculosis. They'll get him fit, I expect. He'll have a life, of sorts. A few years, anyway. No real future, you understand. Nothing long term.'

Woolf stopped speaking, and let his hand drop on the table. Sadie thought, I wish he'd stop. But he started again in that low, monotonous tone. 'And I haven't told you about Captain Stanford, have I?'

'He was your superior officer, that's all I know.'

'A good man. I admired him. He was capable and sensible, and he liked Jane Austen, too.' Woolf essayed a smile. 'We got on well, and there weren't many people I could talk to there. But I won't talk to him again, because he went at Cambrai. He was being driven to an urgent meeting with the Chiefs of Staff and the staff car took a direct hit. It was ironic, really. It was absolutely freezing, the ground was like iron. We'd been cold for so long it was impossible to remember what warmth felt like. Stanford got warm though.'

He stopped and Sadie asked, fearfully, 'What happened?'

'They couldn't get him out. He burnt to death.'

The following day, Sadie found herself alone with Mrs Lander. Talking about Woolf, she suddenly found herself telling her mother-in-law about their conversation of the previous night. When she spoke about Captain Stanford, Mrs Lander clucked her tongue.

'I know my dear. He was only a young man, Woolf said.'

'Has he told you about it?' Sadie was genuinely surprised: Woolf had said almost nothing until yesterday about his experiences.

'Oh, yes, my dear.' Dora Lander looked slightly complacent. 'He told me days ago. Woolf's always talked to me, you know.'

Sadie shook her head. It was useless. Woolf, as he always had and always would, had confided in his mother first. Pride kept her from saying anything more. She was determined still to do her best. But secretly, from that moment, she doubted whether she would succeed.

Gradually, life assumed very much the pattern of their pre-war days, except that Sadie continued to work at Guy's Hospital part-time. After a few months she was asked if she would mind relinquishing her job in favour of an ex-soldier whose injuries meant he could no longer work, as he had previously done, as a porter. She agreed, of course, but she found that she now had long hours to fill. With Woolf back at his practice, and apparently in increasing demand, she once again spent much of her time with Esther. Now almost five, she would soon be going to school. And Sadie found herself longing to hold a baby again.

One Tuesday evening Woolf returned home to find her in the garden. She was usually changing for dinner when he arrived, and they had developed a small ritual of having a glass of sherry in the morning room before they ate. But this evening she was outside, wrapped in a wide woollen coat against the April chill, poking around among the flower beds. He watched her for a while from the morning room, then went out into the conservatory and opened the garden door.

'What are you up to so late?'

'I just wanted to see what was coming up.'

'You can't see much at all, I shouldn't think. It's getting too dark.'

Absently she agreed.

'Well, come in then.'

Reluctantly, she got up from where she had been crouching, looking at the hopeful spiking of the narcissi and met him at the door.

He took her coat, and poured her a drink. Curious, he asked again, 'What took you out at this hour?'

'I don't know. I just wanted to see.'

She was quiet all through the meal, crumbling her roll between her fingers, forgetting to make conversation. Afterwards they went into the drawing room and Woolf sat, as he always did, in the armchair beneath his reading lamp. Sadie was sewing a dress for Esther's doll, but her mind was busy elsewhere. Pulling the doll's pinafore straight she said, 'Could we talk, do you think?'

'Of course, my dear.' He laid his book upon his knee, his index finger marking the page he had reached, and waited.

'Woolf, I've been thinking. I don't seem to have enough to do at the moment. I've been used to doing a lot more than I am now, and this inactivity feels like wasting time.'

Mildly he said, 'I agree. Why don't you take some sort of training?'

She looked startled.

'Training? What in?'

'I don't know. You seemed to enjoy hospital work. Perhaps you ought to start thinking about becoming an almoner?'

'Oh, I don't think so. I've spent most of my time there for the past three years, you know. I think I've had enough.'

'Well, what then?'

She gathered herself together. 'Woolf. Why don't we have a baby?'

285

The moment she had said them she wanted to recall the words. They hung in the air, and she remembered something her grandfather used to say: The word you have not uttered is your slave. The word you have spoken is your master.

Woolf made no reply. He sat stiffly, a finger nervously stroking his cheek. She watched him for a moment, and then burst out, 'These years have been so awful. So many dead, so many gone. We could begin again, making something lovely happen.'

She paused, trying to see if her words had any effect on him. She thought of the cold garden and the hidden life there, and said urgently, 'Woolf, please let us try. I do so want another child, and I believe you would find . . .' she searched for the word she wanted, 'I believe you would find benefit too.'

He sighed, and placed his book on the table beside him. Then, before replying, he moved it meticulously so that the edge of the book was exactly in line with the edge of the table. 'Do you think that's sensible?'

'I don't know.' Sadie felt her temper rising. 'I haven't asked myself if it's sensible, I must confess.'

He would not look at her. Instead he said, 'I think we must consider such a question in the light of the situation, wouldn't you agree?'

With growing hostility, she watched him. He pressed his fingertips together.

Judiciously he said, 'It seems to me this is not the time for such a step. The war has scarcely finished. There is still turmoil. This is no world into which to bring a child. You must see that.'

She tried to keep her voice calm, but it shook slightly. 'I know about the world. But if there are no babies, Woolf, no children, then there's no future. If men had looked at the results of war and said what you are saying, civilization would have come to an end years ago. Living has to go on, whatever happens.'

286

Stubbornly he said, 'I still say I do not think a baby is a good idea. It is not wise.'

Sadie was horrified. 'It's not a question of *wisdom*. It's not a question of thinking.' Her words shrilled in her ears. Careful. She forced herself to sit back in her chair. 'Very well.' Now her voice was quiet. 'As you wish.'

Woolf looked at her for a moment, then nodded his head and resumed his reading. Sadie sewed for a while in silence, then excused herself. As she passed his chair, she laid her hand deliberately on his shoulder as she said goodnight. He patted it lightly, then dislodged it.

She waited for almost two weeks. When she had spoken to Woolf that night it had been out of a sudden surge of longing. She had not considered what she would say. Indeed, until it had burst out, she had not even planned to speak. She thought now she must be more subtle. Woolf was too rigid a man to change his given opinion. But there were other ways.

On the following Saturday they gave a small dinner-party. One of the guests was an up-and-coming politician, the other a fellow solicitor. The wives were amusing, the evening a success. Woolf talked more than usual, and for almost the first time since he got home he seemed relaxed and convivial. The brandy went round several times, and as they said goodbye to their guests, he laid his arm across her shoulders in an unusual display of affection.

She put her arm around his waist under his jacket, and as the door closed she turned quickly and clung to him. She had also drunk more than she normally did. When she closed her eyes, her head whirled. She closed them now.

'Woolf,' she said, her lips against his neck. He murmured her name in reply, and with his free hand locked the front door. Arms round each other, they went upstairs, and into Sadie's room. He had not been in since he returned from France, and as he inhaled the feminine scents of the perfumed sachets she kept among her clothes, the creams and powder on her dressing table, desire welled in him. He fumbled with his tie, but the studs in his shirt defeated his clumsy fingers. Smiling, Sadie did it for him, and he pulled his shirt over his head.

She undressed quickly so he should not have time to change his mind, and loosened her hair. He half-fell into bed, and she undid the buttons on his combinations and kissed his chest. She smoothed her hands down his back, stroking and pressing. With greater abandonment than she had ever known from him he nuzzled her throat and she arched her back, insinuating herself against him, circling her hips until she felt him swell and harden. Then she parted her legs and he quested softly, pressing until he was within her. He started to move slowly back and forth, then faster and faster. She wrapped herself around him, caught up in his increasing momentum, determined that nothing should be wasted. She would get a child from this night. Woolf's eyes were closed, he panted urgently above her, lost in sensation.

Sadie cupped his head in her hands, clutching him closer: it seemed a lifetime since she had experienced so much feeling. Words broke from her, disjointed, supplicating, entreating – she did not know what she said, did not check the sounds that came instinctively to her lips. But something – some word, some meaning – communicated itself to Woolf. He faltered, lost his rhythm and stopped moving. She felt him wither and shrink.

'What's the matter?' she whispered. 'Don't stop. I want you.'

Still lying above her, heavy now on her chest, he was suddenly cold sober.

'You don't want me. You want another child.'

Abruptly he rolled off her, and lay there, his arms across his eyes against the lamplight. Sadie lay beside him. She felt abandoned, empty, unsatisfied. Without the warmth of Woolf's weight on her, she shivered, and pulled the blanket high over her breasts.

'You can't – just *stop*.'

When he did not reply, she leant on one elbow so she could see him better. She said again, 'You can't do this. It's terrible. It's cruel.'

After a moment, his arm still across his eyes, he said, 'You took advantage of me, you know. I was too drunk to remember to use a sheath.' He dropped his arm, and looked at her. 'And can you tell me honestly you were going to *douche* afterwards?'

She shook her head. They lay in silence for a long time, then Woolf started to get out of bed. Sadie said, harshly, 'Stay where you are.'

'I *beg* your pardon?'

'Woolf, I want to discuss this now.' The sudden hardness in her voice had shocked him.

'Couldn't we choose a more opportune moment?'

'This *is* an opportune moment. I'm not prepared to wait for the time to be right, for the weather to be suitable, or the share index to be favourable.' She found that all trace of the wine had vanished from her head.

Woolf, unused to sarcasm from her, said a trifle petulantly, 'I don't think I care for your tone.'

'And I don't care whether you do or not. We've been married for nearly six years, Woolf. I know the war came in between, but it's still six years of our lives. I've tried not to be demanding. But I do demand this.' She stared up at the ceiling. Without looking at him, she added, 'I must have a baby. It's something I need to do. Don't refuse me this.' She could hear herself pleading and thought, what have I to lose? She added, persuasively, 'You need not concern yourself about bringing the child up. I will take care of everything. But let us at least make this one gesture to our marriage.' She sat up, and looked down at him. 'Woolf. Please.'

There was no reply, for a long moment. When he spoke, his voice was without expression. 'You don't know what I know, Sadie. You haven't seen what I've seen. When I say

289

the world is no place for children, I mean it. I do not want a child of mine to experience what I've been through, ever. I appreciate your feelings about wanting a baby. It's a very understandable emotion. But that's what it is: an emotion. There's no valid reason for taking such a step. It's not enough to talk about gestures. When we married, I must remind you, there was no mention of our having any children beyond the one you were expecting.'

Stunned, she stared up at the ceiling. 'I can't believe what you're saying. Of course I can't give valid reasons for wanting a child. Of course it's only an emotion. For God's sake, Woolf, I'm your wife. I want to have your child.'

When he did not speak, she went on, 'What did you think our marriage would mean? I wasn't planning clearly for the future then, but if I had, our children would have been in it.' She sat up, and leant over him holding back her hair. 'Just tell me one thing. Why don't you want a child? The real reason, not this nonsense about the world and moral situations.'

His face was strained, he looked wretched and unhappy. 'I know I'm not explaining myself well. But I tell you. I've seen men die. They are all somebody's children. And I just can't see that there's any point to it all.'

He got out of bed, and stood for a moment looking at her. Then he gathered his clothes together and went out of the room. Sadie continued to sit huddled against the pillows, long after he had gone, as the fire died down and the room grew cold. Finally, sadly, she switched off her bedside lamp and tried to sleep.

Chapter Twenty-One

During the following months Sadie was forced to acknowledge that she had, after all, failed. Woolf had proved stronger than she; she could neither move nor mould him to the man she wished him to be. The marriage had become untenable; they could no longer live together under any conditions.

Since their union, they had contrived to preserve a slightly formal but agreeable companionship. This appeared to suit Woolf, though for Sadie it merely masked the dissonance of their physical relationship. But since his return from France they talked very little. They had no interests in common. And Woolf had not wanted her. He had made not a single overture towards her and she, mindful of her intention not to ask too much, had been entirely passive. Until now.

Each, the night of that dinner-party, had so hurt the other that there was no possible retrieval. Woolf had seen her as a woman determined to get what she wanted regardless of his feelings, snatching what she needed against his wishes. And Sadie had been appalled by his icy self-control. When she was, against all her expectations, moved to desire; when she had abandoned herself utterly to him, helpless, lost – he had recoiled from her. She found herself remembering a phrase her mother had used when an Orthodox acquaintance had divorced his wife. After the civil divorce there had been a religious one, a *get*. 'He put her aside,' Sophie had said. Grieving, Sadie thought now, that's what Woolf has done. He has put me aside.

And the result was that where there had been a lack of physical harmony between them, now there was hatred. What had started as dissidence turned into repugnance. She had to force herself to sit opposite him at the table, to be with him in the same room. He froze in the face of her unspoken contempt and felt nothing for her at all.

It took almost a year for their relationship to deteriorate to this point, a year during which Sadie grew increasingly unhappy, Woolf increasingly detached. One night at dinner, as she watched him chewing in silence, she suddenly found herself saying,

'It's enough, Woolf. We can't go on like this.'

She half-expected him to react as he had done years before, when they had discussed their marriage and he had told her they must make the best of it. Instead, he looked at her briefly and then nodded.

'Very well. If that is what you want, I will make arrangements.' His tone was as formal as though he had agreed to sell some shares. Then she noticed that his fingers twitched convulsively on the white cloth.

When she told Uncle Mark that she and Woolf were planning to divorce, he shook his head. 'That's shocking. Shocking.'

'It's not,' Sadie protested, 'People do divorce nowadays, you know. They don't expect to go on living together if they're not suited.'

Irritated, he stared at her. 'No, no. You misunderstand me. I find the fact that you are treating Woolf this way shocking.'

As she started to answer, he said sternly, 'Please, let me speak. You've come here to exonerate yourself, to explain the circumstances. Well, you've no father to reprimand you and God knows you're too old to be told what to do. But don't you go telling me everyone is doing it, or that you're not suited to each other. You never were suited and you know it. I don't care what your marriage has been like and I don't want to hear: it's not my business. But I can't believe it's been so bad that it should have come to this. After what that man's been through, to treat him this way – it's shameful.'

Stunned by his outburst, Sadie had subsided into a chair. Mark was staring out of the window. Without turning he added, 'Divorcing Woolf is the worst thing you've ever done, Sadie.'

'Uncle Mark.' She was almost whispering. 'Please don't say this. I'm not doing it lightly. I've tried for years, I really have.'

As though he had not heard, Uncle Mark continued talking, half to himself. 'That man took you on, and the child, when he had no need to. He looked after you when you were unhappy, and I should have expected you to do the same for him.'

She could hardly answer him. 'I could have gone on with all of it. I was prepared to, but he wouldn't concede anything. Not anything.' She groped for a handkerchief and at that moment Zipporah came into the room. When Mark told her what was happening, her habitual poise deserted her. 'I don't believe it!'

'Neither did I.' Mark's tone was dry. 'Nevertheless it would appear to be true.'

Zipporah was for once at a loss for words. Mark moved towards the door. 'I think I've already said more than I should do on the subject. If you will both excuse me.'

When he had gone, Zipporah continued to stare at Sadie as though at an apparition. 'For heaven's sake,' Sadie protested, 'stop acting as though I'd suddenly gone mad.'

Zipporah found her voice at last. 'I think you must have done just that. Sadie, you can't be divorced. The scandal! What will people say?'

'I never thought you cared much for what people said,' she answered quietly.

Zipporah gave a tight smile. 'True enough. But my dear, I gave them cause for speculation, no more. No one could ever say anything with certainty, so what did it matter? But this. It will be known everywhere, details of your private life. In the newspapers . . .'

Sadie interrupted, 'I really doubt very much that the newspapers will be at all interested. We're hardly celebrities.'

'The newspapers always report on divorce cases now. It's what people want to read these days. My God, Sadie, it'll kill your mother.'

Sadie's anger at Zipporah disappeared. 'I know. I know what it'll do to her. But Zipporah, what else can I do? We can't go on as we have been, it's no marriage at all.'

Zipporah shrugged. 'You surely knew when you contracted it that it was at best an unlikely alliance. It didn't seem to worry you then.'

Soberly, Sadie said, 'If you remember my circumstances, I wasn't in a position to be over-critical.'

Zipporah sighed. 'No, you're quite right. I'm sorry.' Suddenly curious, she asked, 'But it's gone on for quite a long time. What suddenly sparked this off?'

'I said I wanted another baby. Woolf didn't.'

Zipporah nodded, but Sadie could see that this meant very little to her. Her mind was clearly elsewhere. 'The thing is, how are we to keep it quiet? How are we to deal with the publicity? Apart from anything else, we must make sure your character is still impeccable.'

Sadie sad, 'You don't need to worry. Woolf's going to fix everything so that nothing can be imputed to me. I will be unblemished.'

'I'll introduce you to David Zuckerman,' Zipporah continued pensively. 'He's just been widowed, a delightful man . . .'

'No, thank you!' Sadie gathered up her handbag and packages. 'One mistake is quite sufficient for the moment.'

On her way home, she reflected with some bitterness that Uncle Mark had worried about Woolf, and Aunt Zipporah about the scandal. Neither of them seemed to spare a thought for her feelings.

*　　*　　*

She was to find the same reactions among the rest of the family. To her consternation, they seemed without exception to feel she had been unduly harsh on Woolf, had in fact deliberately abandoned him when he needed her care. The only unlikely champion she found was Woolf's mother.

The old lady turned up unexpectedly one afternoon. Woolf had moved out of Ordnance Hill back to his flat, and Mrs Lander had, in deference to his feelings, waited for a fortnight before contacting Sadie. Now she was anxious to talk.

'My dear, I know how difficult Woolf can be, believe me. He's immovable, like his father. Once he gets an idea into his head, nothing will change it.' She gave Sadie an unexpectedly shrewd look. 'And I believe you're much the same, aren't you? Too determined for your own good. Woolf hasn't told me much, you know. D'you want to say anything, or are you being as close-mouthed as he is?'

'What is there to say? We hoped for different things, I suppose. I did want it to work, I'd like you to know that.'

Soberly Dora Lander replied, 'I know you did. It's just that I feel responsible. I talked you into it in the first place. I'm an old busy-body. My husband always said so, poor man. But I only acted for the best. At first I did fear I'd pushed you both too hard. Then gradually you seemed to be settling down together, and I thought it was all working.' She sighed. 'I was wrong. I should have left well alone.'

Sadie told her gently, 'I'll always be grateful to Woolf. I don't know how I would have got through those first years without him.'

'And you were beginning to change him, I thought at one time, and that would have been no bad thing. He was always too old for his age, even when he was a little boy.' Dora Lander sighed heavily. 'That horrible war. He's so bad-tempered now, so irritable. And what he's been through.'

The two women sat silent. They were in the conservatory and the air smelt damp and green. There always seemed to be

295

a faint rustling here, thought Sadie, as though things were always growing, crowding up on each other.

'You will let me see Esther, won't you? She's a lovely child, and I don't want to lose touch with her. Or you.'

Sadie glanced up and saw that the old lady was wiping tears from her cheeks. She gave an apologetic sniff. 'Don't mind me. I never used to like children much, you know. A nuisance. But I wish you and Woolf had had a baby. It would have made all the difference. And I should have liked a grandchild of my own.'

Sadie started to speak and then stopped. It would do no good now. It was too late.

In the months that followed, when she looked back on that conversation, Sadie would wonder whether her mother-in-law's reaction had been quite as simple as it had seemed at the time. It was easy for her to be sympathetic: she was regaining her son as a companion, he was back in her house. But when Sadie remembered how the conversation ended, she knew the old lady had been sincere.

Sadie received a note from Woolf two days later, asking her to take tea with him at Fortnum's after his fencing lesson. 'I would be grateful if you could manage this,' he wrote. 'I hope to see you at 4.15 P.M. If, however, you are otherwise engaged, perhaps we can make an alternative arrangement.'

The formality of the note showed her that he wished to discuss their affairs, and had chosen deliberately to do so in public. She thought she knew why. In private, he feared she might resort to tears, make a scene. In Fortnum's this would be avoided.

When he emerged from Angelo's, he looked pale and taut. He lifted his hat courteously, but made no move towards her. She had wondered whether to proffer her hand, but checked the movement. They stood awkwardly for a moment, before moving off up St James's. Woolf made what little conversation there was: he spoke of his work, mostly, and his mother's health. When they were seated at Fortnum's he ordered tea for them both.

'Would you care for a teacake? A slice of gâteau?'

She shook her head.

He stirred his tea thoughtfully and said, 'I hope you don't mind my asking you here?'

She raised her eyebrows. 'Why should I mind?'

'Only I thought it might be easier to talk in neutral surroundings. And I have something very important to say to you.'

'I gathered as much.'

He pressed his fingertips together, bowed his head over them. It stirred something in her memory: she thought of his austere living room in his mother's house, before they married, and the self-contained way in which he lived his life. Looking at his bent head, she thought that in another life he would have been happy as a monk.

He took a bite of his sandwich and wiped his lips carefully before speaking. 'I've been talking to one or two people about the divorce. Seeking advice.'

She nodded.

'And there is a problem. The only grounds are still adultery, despite the royal commission a few years ago.'

'Your adultery or mine?'

Her flippancy clearly annoyed him.

'Mine, naturally. It's easy enough to arrange – an overnight trip to Brighton, a chambermaid anxious to earn a little extra for a few hours playing cards in the room. Simple. But it will do me no good.'

'You mean professionally?'

'I don't want this business to ruin me, Sadie. I've just begun to establish myself. I've ambitions for the future.' He pushed aside his plate, looking suddenly hunted. 'I must confess, I don't know what to do.'

Sadie sat silent, watching her husband, experiencing a wave of pity for him. It was of her doing, all this. She had connived at the mésalliance they were now seeking to terminate. She should get him out of it.

'If we have to act out this lie, why can't it be my adultery? I don't care. Then you will be the innocent party, and surely no blame will attach to you then? People will forget.'

He gazed at her in shocked surprise. 'How can you even suggest such a thing? That's totally impossible, I forbid it. God knows it'd be bad enough for me, but it would finish you entirely: the judges are very harsh on the adulterous wife.'

'Perhaps,' she said very low, 'I would not care.'

'But I should. We are not, I hope, sworn enemies. I could not live with myself if I did not think you would have a reasonable life before you.'

Sadie looked round the room. Against the trellised wall-coverings, the soft green and yellow furnishings, numerous well-fed people sat talking in subdued tones. Occasionally, there was a burst of laughter, a turning of heads when some particularly well-dressed woman entered. They seemed to Sadie to be supremely unimportant. She turned back to Woolf.

'But I don't care! A reasonable life, you say. Among people like this? What are they to me, or I to them, that it matters what such people think? I don't give a ha'penny for them. I've got Esther, and that's the important thing.'

'There's no need for histrionics.' He spoke reprovingly and Sadie, admonished, poured them both more tea. 'No,' Woolf went on, 'I think I have an idea but I don't like it.'

'What is that?'

'We will not divorce.'

Into the frozen moment she whispered, 'What are you saying?'

Woolf smiled thinly at her reaction. 'Don't worry. I am not proposing to resume our marital life. But I do suggest that we merely make a formal separation. We avoid any possible scandal and yet each go our own way. It seems to me the only possible solution.'

'But we would still be – tied?'

'Man and wife? Yes.'

'And if either of us wished to marry again?'

Woolf selected another sandwich before replying.

'I do not think,' he commented drily, 'that I will enter again upon the state of matrimony.'

'But I might wish to.'

'Indeed. But surely, not just yet.'

She wanted to cry, wildly, why not? Instead she said, trying to keep her tone level, 'I am not so patient as you. Not so – resigned.'

She saw the hurt in his face at the taunt and chose to ignore it. 'You know what I want. I made it all too plain. I am almost thirty, Woolf. For a woman, that is no longer young. I want Esther to have a brother or sister. I cannot wait. There is no time.'

'I will not beg. But I tell you this – it is your freedom, or my future. Which will you choose?'

'Are there no other possible grounds for divorce?'

'There is talk of making cruelty and desertion possible grounds, but it will take twenty years before we see that. Whatever happens, unfortunate hints of criminality attach to a divorce suit, at least in this country. In America for instance, it merely guarantees one a brief notoriety. But here' – he sighed heavily – 'it cannot but bring me permanently into bad odour.' He shook his head and said dejectedly into his sandwich, 'I had so hoped you would agree to a separation.'

'I'll do better than that!'

The elation in her voice made him look up: she was fairly sparkling with excitement.

'I'll get us a divorce *and* keep your reputation untarnished. And I won't make myself a pariah in doing it.'

He swallowed. 'How?'

'I'll be the guilty party. But not here. I'll go to America

with Esther, and I won't come back. I'll provide you with exactly the sort of evidence you need – presumably there are specialists in these things everywhere? Only I'll play cards in a hotel room instead of you. Over there no one will know, and over here no one will notice. It's the perfect answer.'

Woolf, bemused, raised his cup to his lips and put it down again without tasting the contents. 'I believe you might have something. But where would you go? What would you do?'

'I've been thinking about it for ages. Leonie is always writing and asking me to go over there. She says I should make a new start, as she did. We'll stay with her in New York.' Delighted with her inspiration, her ability to be generous to him, Sadie gave Woolf a brilliant smile. He looked at her a trifle sadly, seeing again after so long the look she had worn when first he knew her, when Asher was alive.

'That would be – for me – a most acceptable way out. But are you sure? You know you have these sudden enthusiasms. Is this really something you wish to do?'

Serious now, she nodded.

'Very well,' he continued. 'I will do everything I can to facilitate matters here. And before you go, I will make an undertaking that though I am Esther's legal guardian, she is to remain with you.' When Sadie started to protest, he held up a hand. 'I assure you it is an advisable precaution. You will be the guilty party. A judge may well consider you an unsuitable person to have custody of the child.'

'I'd never even thought . . . that would be dreadful.'

'I give you my word it won't happen.'

She listened with gratitude. This was the Woolf she had thought to love, the man who showed care and concern, who had supported her when she was bereft. It was ironic that she should find him again only when they discussed their parting.

'It's not a ship. It's a small city!'

Sadie had laughed at Uncle Mark's exlamation as he

escorted her to the dock at Southampton. 'You're being very naïve,' she had teased. 'You've been on a boat or two in your time.'

'Nothing to touch this, though. Have we, my dear?' He had turned to Zipporah for corroboration.

'The last boat on which we ventured was a racy little number at Cowes. We were on it three minutes, as I recall, before your uncle declared he was about to see his breakfast again unless we rapidly disembarked.'

'You're telling tales out of court again, my dear. But seriously,' he turned back to Sadie, 'the last time I visited the United States was about ten years ago. The difference really is astonishing. You won't know where the sea is on this beauty.'

Sadie found he was right: it was hard to think they were afloat. The luxury of the *Aquitania*, its sheer size, seemed to render the sea docile. Sadie had at first been highly nervous about the idea of the voyage, but now the water seemed so far away, so unimportant, that she had ceased to think about it. The boat had been built before the war, and even the second class was lavishly decorated. She and Esther wandered around the staterooms, all panelled in fine English woods, and looked at the walnut furniture covered with tapestry. A battery of lifts carried them up and down between the Reynolds, the Gainsborough, the Holbein suites, each with the appropriate paintings. Even the Turkish bath was opulent, with its mosaic floor, blue-green tiled walls under a dark red ceiling, and carved teak doors. And at night, to the strains of one of the ship's orchestras playing Elgar, Sadie would make her way to the dining room, where she sat at a table with an elderly couple from Cheltenham going to visit their married daughter, and consumed meals of daunting proportions.

The luxury seemed, after the abstemious war years, almost sinful. And if theirs was luxurious enough – bouillabaises

301

and rare beef, salmon and sorbets – that of the first class was rumoured to be even more so. Sadie's table companions had heard that for the captain's dinner grilled antelope was served, surrounding Strasbourg *foie gras* surmounted by peacock feathers. Sadie shuddered for the antelope, and concentrated on her *boeuf en daube*.

She had planned to use the time to reflect on her next move, but for long hours she would sit on the deck wrapped in blankets, or read to Esther in their cabin, and consciously close her mind equally to the past and the future. The journey appeared like a blank page in her life, with nothing asked of her, no impetus required. She was held by a curious inertia, like someone recovering from a serious illness; every action seemed to require an immense effort, her limbs felt heavy, as though she were wading through water. It took a huge amount of will to satisfy Esther's demands on her time, which normally she welcomed. To be asked to take part in a game, to visit the swimming pool, was a massive undertaking. She told herself that the past few months had been emotionally exhausting. But she had been through worse than that before. What's the matter with you, woman? She smiled at the image she could so easily conjure up of Sophie remarking with brisk snappiness that nothing was so tiring as leisure. The smile faded. She and Esther had spent a fortnight in Manchester before leaving England and as always she was shocked by fresh evidence of Sophie's age. Sadie had not seen her sit like that before, on a hardbacked chair as usual, but not upright. This time she sat bent forward, bowed over her folded arms, legs planted firmly apart, rocking slightly when she thought she was not observed. She had been deeply upset at first by the news of the separation. Although she had never really come to terms with Woolf, who had remained for her an inadequate substitute for Asher, she had grown used to the idea of the marriage.

But whatever she felt about the break-up paled into

insignificance beside her reaction to Sadie's departure. America seemed to her the ends of the earth, a continent made up of mountains and deserts, peopled by savages. Vainly had Sadie and Flora protested. She remained adamant: if Sadie went, she had lost a daughter. Dry-eyed, she had mourned over Esther, touching her hair when the child passed, catching the hem of her dress as she played beside her.

On the night before Sadie and Esther were to leave for Southampton to take the *Aquitania* to New York, they had stayed up late, talking till the early hours over the fire in the sitting room, trying to plan a future where they would meet before too long. Sadie had promised to return as soon as she could afford to do so. Perhaps in a year or two, she had said. To her horror, Sophie had slipped from the chair on to the carpet, and clutched Sadie round the knees. 'Don't go. Don't go, I don't want you to go. I may not see you again.'

Tears had streamed down her face, her skin was blotched red with emotion. Sadie had tried unsuccessfully to comfort her, but her own uncertainty and fear of the unknown had rendered her assurances unconvincing. In the end, the two sisters had persuaded Sophie to go to bed, and had sat by themselves over a cup of tea. Flora had said, matter-of-factly, 'You won't come back here, you know.'

'Of course I will. Don't be silly.'

Flora replied, with more firmness than Sadie had ever heard from her before, 'No. You don't go back. You just move on. I'm the one who clings, who doesn't like change. For you, it's life.'

Sadie had not replied. It was not a thought that had occurred to her before, but once Flora had voiced it, she knew it to be the truth.

At her shoulder Esther said, 'Can I go and play deck-quoits?'

'Of course. I'll come and watch presently.'

She watched as the child walked sedately from the room.

Esther had changed imperceptibly from a rollicking baby into a self-possessed child who looked so like Asher that she made Sadie's heart turn over. She had all her father's formal charm, so that Sadie would remark with mock despair that there was no evidence at all in the child of any maternal inheritance. Certainly Esther's manner was not Sadie's. She was a child who observed, thoughtfully, all that went on around her. Where Sadie even at that age had been desperate to be part of whatever was going on, Esther preferred to stand slightly to one side. It took her a long time to accept new friends, to adapt to change.

Sadie's fingers unconsciously pleated and repleated the folds of her skirt as she thought. Not a child to haul off to a strange country. Not a child to be taken from the people she knew. The parting with Woolf had not seemed to affect Esther, though. She was fond of him but no more than that. There was no strong affection between them, although Sadie knew there could have been, had Woolf encouraged the friendship. But of course, the war years had been Esther's growing ones, with Woolf entirely absent. Esther had been tearful at leaving Grandma Browne, and only the prospect of a visit 'soon' had torn her away. Sadie had taken her to say goodbye to Rose and Moritz in Portland Place. They were upset at the whole business, Moritz said, shaking his head. Rose had dabbed her eyes and told Esther they would be in New York soon to see her. For them, the departure was distressing, Sadie could tell, for they saw the loss of Asher's family. But travel to them was so commonplace that they had none of Sophie's fears. Lena had been by far the most emotional over their going. She had remained closer to Sadie than her sister, for she was a woman whose affection, once given, was not withdrawn. She would be over inside twelve months she had promised, hugging the travellers as they left Ordnance Hill.

The house was to be sold later. Sadie had decided to keep it as security, in case she wished to return; Woolf would see to the sale when she felt settled in America. She had already decided which few items of furniture she wanted stored until she could send for them, and the rest would be sold with the house. Annie was to remain at Ordnance Hill until the sale, the proceeds of which were to be Sadie's entirely. Out of them, she planned to give Annie a lump sum. She had tried hard to persuade Annie to make the journey with her. Tempted, she had finally refused – she was too old to start a new life, in a year or two she would be ready to retire; her eyesight was not what it had been, her sister had been ill . . . Sadie, aware that Annie was being torn two ways, tactfully suggested that it would be of immense value if the older woman would organize the household affairs for her. But parting from Annie had been a wrench. They had been through a great deal together, and she had virtually brought Esther up while Sadie worked at the hospital. Esther had seemed to recover quickly from the idea of leaving Annie. Six year olds, the women had agreed between laughter and tears, had a capacity for rapid emotions. In fact, as Sadie was later to find, Esther felt the loss of Annie for a long time. Thinking this, Sadie found the energy to go and watch Esther on C-Deck, playing with three children of a diplomatic family on their way to Washington. The children were boisterous; Esther took her turn, then waited patiently for her next one. The father arrived, and with a smile at Sadie proceeded to join in the game. She saw him with a pang of remorse: Esther was fatherless again, she did not have what these children had.

For the first time since telling Woolf she was prepared to give him grounds for divorce, Sadie felt genuine concern. She had to pull her life around again. She wondered just how she was to do it.

Chapter Twenty-Two

Sadie's nervousness increased as the *Aquitania* drew into New York harbour. The endless shoreline, the bustle of boats, the air of excitement which grew among the watching passengers, all combined to make her feel totally inadequate. To combat the unwelcome sensation she went below and changed into her smartest costume and hat. Going down the gangway hand in hand with Esther into the customs shed, she was caught up in the jostling, preoccupied crowd. Esther, feeling her grip tighten apprehensively, glanced up at her and she tried to smile for the child, not to show the loneliness she felt. Then it was dispelled, suddenly, by a loud shout.

'Sadie! Over here, *Sadie*!'

She turned, in a blaze of relief and pleasure. 'Leonie! I was afraid you wouldn't get here.'

They hugged each other warmly, and Sadie said, 'May I introduce you formally to my daughter?'

Leonie bent down and proffered her hand to the little girl in the gesture of a woman unused to children.

Esther looked at her gravely. 'Are you to be my new auntie? Mama said you would like that.'

'I'd love it, you dear baby.'

Leonie took her hand, and with the other grasped Sadie's arm, shepherding her towards the exit. 'Let's go. I've got a cab waiting. Porter,' she made a gesture with a ringed hand, 'we're over here.'

Sadie smiled to herself. Leonie had taken charge, as usual.

Leonie took charge not only of Sadie's luggage but also her life. The younger woman found New York a devastating place. The cacophony of sound that burst around them as they drove uptown, the horns and the shouting drivers, the clanging of construction work on the towering skyscrapers, were like nothing she or Esther had ever experienced before. They gazed around them as Leonie nonchalantly pointed out shops and theatres, galleries and nickelodeons, restaurants and museums. Hemmed in by the press of Packards, Perlesses and Pierce Arrows, the cab made its way to Fifth Avenue. Number 506, between Forty-second and Forty-third Streets, was an impressive brownstone house. As Leonie paid off the driver and the doorman hurried to take their bags, Sadie suddenly noticed, standing there on the sidewalk, just how much Leonie had changed. From the exuberant, forthright girl who had so adored Sophie all those years ago, Leonie had become a formidable woman. In her discreet dark woollen suit, with the streaming silk scarf, her hair cut short and, Sadie could swear, redder than ever, she was elegantly impressive. So was her apartment.

She rented the entire third floor of the brownstone.

'You wouldn't believe what it was like when I moved in,' she confided, throwing open door after door, leading them into cool bedrooms and large reception rooms. 'It was like Bluebeard's cave in here, full of carved wooden whatsits and dusty velvet drapes.' Now everything Sadie could see was stylishly modern: she had never been in a home furnished with such immediate fashion. Walls, carpets, lamps were all off-white. Curtains the colour of clotted cream hung at the windows, slightly drawn to shade the room from the slanting afternoon sun. On a long coffee table of heavy glass stood a fruit bowl of pearly marble filled with black grapes, and on one wall hung a single painting, blocks of brilliant colour providing the focal point for the room.

The cool rooms were in total contrast to the bustle outside. Fifth Avenue seemed to Sadie a street so extraordinary she could not tell whether she liked it or not. A few years ago, explained Leonie, the houses above Forty-second Street had been gentlemen's clubs and the town houses of the fashionable rich. As commerce had marched uptown from

Madison Square, bringing gleaming shops fronts as far as Fifty-seventh Street, the wealthy had retreated. They had abandoned the sham Tudor mansions, the imitation Rhine castles and the false French chateaux. Swiss chalets and Georgian façades were left as their monuments and some still bore names that resounded their power – Gould and Carnegie, Astor and Vanderbilt. But among them now, new high buildings rose, and discreet lettering proclaimed Sherry's Restaurant and Delmonico's. Sadie, gazing from her window, marvelled at herself. New York made her feel like a provincial and after all, as she told Leonie, she had been used to a reasonably sophisticated life in London.

It was two weeks before she found the nerve to walk about the streets alone, and when she did she was bewildered by the rich variety of impressions that crowded in on her as she moved among the hustling crowds. Greeks and Romanians, Scandinavians and Poles, Negroes and Chinese – Esther would gaze at them all with open fascination until Sadie hauled her away, exclaiming that it was rude to stare.

Leonie worked long hours, Sadie discovered, and had little free time: she was mostly at home in the afternoons and then she rested in preparation for the work of the evening. So Sadie took pleasure in keeping house for her. The marketing was a revelation, for she found in the foodstores items she had never seen before. Pumpernickel bread and rye, cornbread and sourdough bread, exotic fruits and vegetables like watermelon and corn on the cob. There were dried vegetables she had never tasted, black-eyed peas and lima beans, and in the butchers' shops meats and cuts which she had no idea how to prepare. She enjoyed herself hugely, and occupied her time by making elaborate dishes for the three of them.

Gradually her days assumed a pattern. She would take Esther to school and by the time she had organized the apartment and the meals, it was almost four o'clock. With help from Leonie she had decided on a nearby private school where Esther seemed at first nervous as she had anticipated, but after a few weeks she settled down reasonably well. The children were well supervised, and once Esther became used to the accent her shyness began to disappear. Sadie rather wished that she, too, could go to school: her social contacts were limited to the shopkeepers and the mothers of Esther's classmates.

Gradually she began to know people, to smile in passing, but she found herself for the first time in her life hampered by embarrassment. To explain that she was waiting for a divorce was more than she could bring herself to do, for it seemed to cast a slur on her that she could not deal with. So, despite her inclinations to make friends easily, she began consciously to avoid doing so. In her isolation, she felt the inertia that had gripped her on the boat from England.

One afternoon Leonie took Sadie and Esther walking in Central Park. It was late October, they were scuffing through drifts of fallen leaves, watching the surprising skyline of the city around them. Esther ran ahead with her skipping rope and the two women watched her in companionable silence. Within a very short time they had fallen into the same pattern of relationship they had had as girls: Leonie knowing and maternal, Sadie admiring and dependent. It was a feeling the young women vastly enjoyed. Now Leonie asked, 'What are you going to do?'

Sadie, watching Esther, said absently, 'I thought we'd have waffles for tea and then I've made some *pot-au-feu* . . .'

'No, no, no. Not what are you going to do for supper, you goose. What are you going to do about yourself?'

Sadie bent to pick up a russet leaf and said, 'I don't think about it.'

'Evidently,' Leonie made the observation drily. 'I don't want you here as a housekeeper, you know, admirably though you are fulfilling the role.'

'To be honest, I'm rather enjoying it,' Sadie protested. 'With Annie about, I never did all this. It's pleasant.'

Leonie shook her head impatiently. 'It's piffling. I'm shocked at you, really I am. It's one thing to be enveloped in domesticity over a man you want, but to do it over me is, my dear, a waste of time. Don't misunderstand me, I love your dinners, it's delightful to come home to the smell of baking cakes. But Sadie, if that's what I'd wanted, I'd have organized it.'

Feeling like a chided child, Sadie scuffed her foot among the leaves.

Sternly, Leonie went on, 'What you're doing is all too plain. You're acting like a wife, to avoid having to do anything more positive. You're acting more like a wife, I'd lay money on it, than you did to Woolf.' She noted Sadie's wry little grimace. 'I thought so. But it won't do, you know. How are you for money? I'm not asking for any more than you give me each week, I don't mean that. But long term, you have never mentioned the position you're in.'

'The position I'm in is less than wonderful. You're right, you know, Lee, I'm trying to avoid thinking about what I'm to do. I'd planned to work things out on the boat. I put if off then, and I'm doing the same now.'

'So. Tell me.'

Sadie sighed. 'Well, I wrote to you about all that trouble with the Raphaels, you know about that?'

'All the business about the allowance if you lived with them?'

'Yes. Well, when I told them I was marrying Woolf, they naturally stopped my allowance. They'd paid the big debts Asher left' – she grimaced – 'they had to, really, there was no way I could find all the money, and it would have discredited them had I gone on owing.'

'Do they do anything for Esther?'

'Oh, yes. She has a very generous allowance – a hundred pounds a year. It goes up as she grows older, and then when she's twenty-one there's to be some sort of inheritance for her: it's all taken care of in Moritz' will.'

'So selling the house in London is your only way of getting your hands on any real money at the moment?'

'I suppose so. I'm giving Annie some, though. There was a long period when she worked for me for almost nothing, and I'm going to give her enough to feel secure. I thought about £250.'

'Is Woolf paying you anything?'

Sadie looked down. 'No.'

'What?' Leonie was clearly put out. 'Why in heaven's name not? Didn't he keep you when you were his wife?'

'It was always an odd arrangement, you see.' Sadie spoke apologetically. 'We never really did talk about it, Woolf and I. It was my house, I think he felt. He'd give me what he thought was a suitable amount . . .'

'And you struggled to make ends meet?'

'More or less. It usually worked out well enough. And then when I was working, of course, it was easier.'

'But you're not working now.'

'No.'

'And Woolf's not helping you in *any way*?'

'He offered to but I said no. I felt he didn't owe me anything, Lee, I didn't want to be beholden to him.'

'I think,' observed Leonie tartly, 'that was both understandable and foolhardy. What on earth are you living on? Esther's money from the Raphaels?'

Unhappily, Sadie nodded.

'But you can't do that indefinitely. It won't go far enough. It won't keep you when you're on your own.'

'I know. I *know*. I thought I'd have to get some sort of work.'

Shrewdly, Leonie regarded her. 'Such as?'

Helplessly, Sadie started to giggle. 'I could always be a cook. Or a housekeeper.'

'Don't be ridiculous,' Leonie snapped. 'I'm trying to help you, don't make fun of this.'

'I'm not, I promise you. But what on earth can I do? All I

know about is hospital administration, so I suppose it'll have to be that. If anyone will have me. What do I know about American hospitals?'

They had reached a low wall overlooking the water and stood watching a few disconsolate ducks fluffing up their feathers against the cold grey ripples. Leonie leant her elbows on the wall and stared into the water. Thoughtfully she said, 'I believe I may be able to help.'

Two days later Sadie accompanied Leonie to Broadway, to the New Amsterdam Theater. In the morning sunlight the elaborately decorated façade looked absurdly lavish. Great posters advertising 'Ziegfeld Follies of 1921' showed the attenuated figure of Fanny Brice holding a looking glass. The stage door stood open to the sun and an elderly cat draped itself across the step, eyes slit against the light.

'Morning, Tom.'

Sadie thought Leonie was addressing the cat until a rotund man in his shirtsleeves leaned out of a cubbyhole in response.

'And to you, Miss Leonie. Himself's inside, and they're making him some coffee.'

'Bad as that, is it?'

'Worse I'd say. He's shouting already and it's still not ten.'

Nervously, Sadie followed Leonie into the dark passage-way, through several doors and out into what she thought was the foyer of the theatre. It was a blend of painting, sculpture and architecture such as she had never before seen: exquisite art nouveau carvings and mouldings in the most delicate reseda green finished with dull gold. Leonie opened another door, parted a velvet curtain and peered into the space beyond. Sadie could hear voices raised in dispute, then the sound of a piano and tapping feet on a stage. Leonie hummed to herself and closed the door.

'We'll go over to the office and give him fifteen minutes. It never lasts long.'

'It?'

'The temper.'

Following Leonie back into the warren of passages, Sadie remarked, 'I feel thoroughly intimidated.'

'Of course you do, dear. And imagine how you'd feel if you actually worked for him. It's a very effective method of getting what you want.' She led the way into a room crowded with people. Two girls, one on either side of the same desk, were using what appeared to Sadie to be four telephones simultaneously. A lithe young man was telling them, crossly, that it had to be lilac tulle or nothing, so for God's sake get on with it. A third young woman was busily crashing away on a typewriter, seemingly impervious to the din around her. The walls were decorated with huge drawings of curvaceous girls revealing what seemed to Sadie daring expanses of bare skin. Leonie waved laconically around at everyone, opened a door on the far side of the room, and ushered Sadie before her. 'Flo's office,' she said in explanation.

The room held two desks. One was large, leather-topped, and boasted a crystal ink bottle and a collection of little elephants, their trunks erect, fashioned from jade and porcelain, gold and silver. 'Flo's good luck elephants,' offered Leonie in explanation. The other desk, at which Leonie seated herself after waving Sadie to a chair, was equally large but less opulent, and covered with her own haphazard clutter. Swatches of material were piled high, newspaper cuttings overflowed a deep tray. There was an untidy assortment of manuscripts and a slightly more orderly one of sheet music. Leonie started glancing through a pile of newspapers.

'Keeping an eye on the opposition,' she said in explanation. 'Not that there is much. No one can touch the Follies.'

She handed a sheaf of designs over the desks.

'See which of these you like best.'

Sadie leafed through them, fascinated. The sketches were

313

slick and skilful, of elegant figures in fabulous costumes, under floating feathered head-dresses. As she was looking at them, the commotion in the outer office ceased, then began again even louder. Then the door burst open and a man backed into the room, pursed by clamouring figures. Leonie hurried to the rescue, shepherded out the besiegers, and firmly closed the door. The man threw himself into his chair and fanned his face with a well-manicured hand. 'Thanks, Lee.'

He noticed Sadie in her corner, and gave her a quick, professional smile. Then he smiled again, properly this time, and said, 'Ah yes, Mrs Lander?'

He clambered to his feet and she held out her hand. 'It's good to meet you. Lee said she was bringing you in.'

He was, Sadie thought, the most arresting man she had seen for years. Tall and slim, his dark hair parted in the centre and brushed back, he wore an immaculate three piece suit and high white collar. Leonie, watching her face with amusement, asked, 'Now then, are you as intimidated as you thought you'd be?'

Sadie replied carefully, 'I think I'll reserve judgement,' and Florenz Ziegfeld Junior laughed.

'There you are, Lee. A lady as astute as yourself. Never show your hand, Mrs Lander. That's it, isn't it?'

'Flo's one of this city's gamblers,' Leonie offered in explanation. 'He'll bet on anything, won't you?'

'Anything,' he agreed, cheerfully. 'Cards. Dice. Croquet.' He stopped, and peered across at Sadie. 'The colour of your eyes.'

Disconcerted, she glanced away.

'Right,' Ziegfeld announced, a moment later. 'Let's see how they're getting on without me.'

He rose and pulled aside a short curtain on the wall which Sadie had not noticed. It revealed a window, and she found they were right next to the stage. The room was completely sound-proofed and the troupe of dancers on stage moved to an unheard rhythm, immaculately timed marionettes.

Ziegfeld watched carefully. 'That's it,' he said half to himself, 'that's better.'

'Round here,' Leonie commented from the other side of the room, 'we're only interested in perfection.'

Ziegfeld shot her a quizzical look. 'A hundred and seventy-five dollars a week per girl says I pay for it.'

'Most chorus girls,' Leonie said to Sadie in explanation, 'get around thirty on Broadway. So Flo pays a fortune and works them mercilessly.'

On the silent stage, the line of dancers twirled dizzily. When they stopped their outspread arms and legs resembled a giant flower. After a moment, apparently without moving, the flower started to open, and Sadie realized the dais on which the girls were posed was parting, dividing into two and sliding away across the stage. In the centre a platform was rising, slowly. Posed on it was a tall girl in practice tights, her hair hidden under a turban.

'She's one of the feature girls,' Leonie explained. 'Gladys Glad.'

Ziegfeld drew the curtain again. 'Right, Mrs Lander. Now Leonie tells me you could do with a job. What can you do for me?'

Sadie told him briefly about her hospital job, ending, 'It could hardly be more different from anything you might want. I feel something of a fraud.'

Ziegfeld tapped a pencil meditatively against his teeth. 'So basically, what you can do is collect and organize material? You can operate a file system and find what you want?'

Slightly surprised, Sadie said, 'Yes, of course. That's exactly what I did.'

'Then I think I have just the job for you. Leonie, what's Harwood going on about out there?'

'I gather he can't get hold of enough lilac tulle. Apparently Joseph commandeered the first order for the Arabian night set, and Erté wanted to match it. But the re-order came up in a deeper shade. He waved his arms about a lot and said it wouldn't do.'

'Harwood should have realized what would happen.' Ziegfeld turned to Sadie. 'Joseph Urban designs the sets here, as Leonie will have told you. He is marvellous,' he kissed his fingertips in an extravagant gesture, 'an artist. And this year Erté is doing some more costumes for us. He is also an artist . . .' Ziegfeld shrugged his shoulders. 'So naturally there are clashes. What we need is some sort of co-ordination, someone who'll be at rehearsals to hear what's needed and who can pass it on to costume designers and set designers as they work. Someone who has an efficiently organized indexing system, and can find what's wanted without all this frenzy. In short,' he spun rapidly round on his swivel chair, and pointed at Sadie, 'in short, Mrs Lander, you.'

'Heavens.'

Aware that her response was inadequate, disconcerted by the quizzical eyebrows Ziegfeld raised at her, Sadie said, helplessly, 'Do you think I can do that? I don't know anything about lilac tulle, you know. I've never been to a rehearsal in my life. I'd love to try, but . . .' Ziegfeld again tapped his teeth, ruminating.

After a moment, he said, 'It's a small gamble. If it works out, fine. If not . . .' He shrugged. 'But I'm sure you could do it.' He paused, and again flashed that charming smile. 'And Mrs Lander, if ever you were needed, you're needed in this madhouse.'

Sadie started work the following week. The salary was only reasonable – fifty dollars a week – but it made a vast difference to her state of mind. She worked conventional hours, from ten until six. Leonie, who always took the afternoon off in preparation for the work of the evening, would fetch Esther from school and keep her company until her mother arrived home.

That first month saw Sadie in a state of perpetual panic. New faces and the constant frenzy Ziegfeld generated around him combined to make her feel she would never find her way. The demands she daily received were bizarre: a stuffed tiger for use in the jungle scene; twenty-four red bicycles; six white baby grand pianos; three thousand yards of dark blue satin to drape the entire stage and enough white satin to dress all the Show Girls like candles on a gigantic cake for *Just Sweet Sixteen*. Eventually, with constant advice from Leonie and a considerable amount of goodwill, she felt, from everyone else, she began to make sense out of the jumbled files and telephone numbers, the names of theatrical suppliers and fabric warehouses. During the second month she found from somewhere enough confidence to make appointments to visit all the suppliers the New Amsterdam used. Nervously she took cabs to see costumiers and wigmakers, shoemakers and florists. She came to know Broadway and the forty or so theatres that stretched from Twenty-third Street to Fortieth, and spilled over into the sidestreets. Magical names: the Metropolitan Opera and the Knickerbocker, Hammersteins and Palmers, Wallachs, Weber and Fields Musical Hall.

As the Follies reached their zenith they became more opulent and costly to produce. A show would cost two hundred thousand dollars to put on, and tickets went for a hundred dollars a pair. Sadie would find notes in Ziegfeld's scrawling hand – he sent them to everyone in the theatre, and to those outside it he sent telegrams which could run to thousands of words – on the desk in the cubicle she shared with the wages clerk. *Need iceblocks for igloo scene. Two Roman vases ten foot tall.* One comical request, on a scruffy piece of paper that had passed forward and back between them, she framed. *Want ostrich please soonest*, it read. Underneath in her handwriting, was the query *Stuffed or imitation*? and Ziegfeld's testy reply, *Dammit. Live.*

Even when a production was running smoothly there

would still be occasional alterations, improvements and innovations to pep up routines Ziegfeld considered tired. There was never time to catch up on paper work, it seemed, for if she had an empty moment in which to attempt to bring order out of chaos, there would be a telephone call from Ziegfeld at home in his massive bed at Burkely Crest which sent her scurrying off on another errand. When a show was in production he would work eighteen hour shifts, and his staff, revolving around him, were drawn into this furious activity. At such times, Sadie did her best to keep out of his way, for the cool image he presented in public vanished entirely as he shouted his instructions and hurled pencils across the room. And then, once the show had opened successfully, he would be prone for days with a prolonged bilious attack.

Despite all this the work at the New Amsterdam provided for Sadie an anodyne more effective than any she had yet discovered. Weeks and months disappeared without giving her time to reflect or worry about herself. Satisfied that Esther was content, enjoying both her independence and her new-found knowledge of the city, it was only rarely that she gave a thought to the situation in London, where Woolf had now filed for divorce.

She and Esther continued to live with Leonie. After the first few weeks of a regular salary Sadie had started to look for an apartment she could rent. Everything within her price range had been depressingly uncomfortable: cold-water walk-ups if they were in the areas she wanted, impossibly distant if they were reasonable. The problem of Esther's afternoons was insoluble, it seemed, if they moved too far from Leonie.

After visiting such an apartment, Sadie would be cast into gloom for hours. One morning, Leonie tapped at the door of her office. 'What on earth is wrong? You look positively drowned.'

When Sadie explained about the search for a home, Leonie was frankly horrified. 'But what do you want to leave

Fifth Avenue for? Don't you like it?'

'Lee, it's not that. But I've been around long enough, it's time I found a home of my own.'

'But I love having you both. Isn't that obvious?'

Sadie looked at Leonie. 'Of course I know we've been welcome, but time's going by . . .'

Leonie sat down heavily, and said, quietly, 'Sadie. Please don't continue with this. I really need you, you know. You and Esther. I hate being alone.' Sadie saw that her eyes were red.

'I know,' Leonie went on. 'Successful, high-powered ladies with their own homes are naturally happy, right? Well, I'm not. I've never had much of a family, but that doesn't mean I don't want one. Having you here has made all the difference to me.'

Stunned, Sadie said, 'But I thought everything you wanted was here.' She gestured round the room. 'When we were in Manchester, this was all you ever talked about. Now you've achieved it and you seem so . . .' she hesitated. Certain of yourself, she meant, but felt reluctant to put it into words. 'So assured,' she finished, and gave Leonie a small, apologetic smile.

'Well,' Leonie grimaced. 'I ain't. So for God's sake, love, don't you walk out on me too.'

'Too? You mean you were . . . you had . . .' Sadie found herself fumbling for words.

Leonie had never mentioned any emotional attachments of her own. Now she laughed at Sadie's discomfiture. 'It's all right. You can say it. I *had* a lover. He done me wrong, as they so frequently sing.' She looked down at her long, immaculate nails. 'I haven't been totally honest with you, you see. I know everything that's happened to you over these years, but I've told you nothing, have I?'

Slowly, Sadie shook her head. 'You don't have to, Lee. I'm not even sure I want you to.'

The other woman laughed, without humour. 'Don't

worry, I won't subject you to dark secrets. There have been men. Several men. More men,' the old Leonie suddenly smiled at Sadie, 'than either of our mothers would have believed. But none of them lasted long.'

'I'm sorry.'

'Don't be. I didn't want that. If I had, it wouldn't have been difficult to arrange.'

'But Lee, you say you're not happy . . .'

'Nor am I. Only I'm not such a fool as to think a man is the answer.'

They looked at each other. Sadie sighed. 'Perhaps you're right.'

That conversation haunted her for a long time.

She pondered on it for days. It wasn't so much what Leonie had said, though she herself had not realized to what degree Leonie counted on her presence – as the surprising pathos in her voice. Sadie was unused to feeling pity for Leonie. Rather, she had always envied her the determination, the certainty she had possessed since she was seventeen. In their present positions, the envy had been intensified. Uprooted, uncertain, soon to be unmarried, she thought dolefully that her life, which had shaped itself round Asher and then less comfortably round Woolf, was now pointless. At its centre was her adored Esther; when she thought of her, contemplated life without her, she could quite literally feel a pull at her heart. Esther was everything that mattered. But the child could not fill the mother's days nor answer all her emotional needs. During those strange four years of war and the separation from Woolf, the situation between mother and daughter had been apparently the same. The difference, Sadie saw now, was that everyone else shared her situation. Women were left with their children, there was nothing to be done about it. Then she had the support of Mark and Zipporah, even old Mrs Lander. Now she felt isolated, displaced.

Sitting there in her crowded office, its walls covered with

photographs, bits of material, posters of vaudeville acts, she sighed and stretched her arms high above her head till she heard her muscles stretch. And all this time she had assumed that whatever her own failures and errors, Leonie had some sort of answer in her single-minded pursuit of success. Now she thought that the surface gloss was nothing more than that. No one wanted to be alone.

The following week Leonie gave a dinner party. 'Look,' she had said to Sadie, 'I haven't been entertaining while you've been here, but now you're staying, I'd like you to meet some of my friends. I'm sure you'll like them,' she added, with an odd defiance in her voice.

Sitting at Leonie's table, nervously pleating her napkin between her fingers, and smoothing it out again upon her lap out of sight, Sadie thought she understood the defiance. They were a curious group of people, even by her own now rapidly changing standards. She knew that New York and Ziegfeld between them had introduced her to a more bohemian world than any she had glimpsed in Asher's company, but she was still unprepared for Leonie's friends. For one thing, there were few women. Leonie had never had many women friends, Sadie remembered, and those present tonight reminded her of Aunt Zipporah. One or two of them were married – though the men accompanying them did not appear to be their husbands – and they were all *soignée*, with the quick New York humour Sadie had grown to enjoy. They wore gold jewellery, and one woman in particular gleamed darkly with more garnets than Sadie had ever seen together. But there was something they all had in common – a knowing, racy smartness – that she instinctively disliked. The man on her right noticed that she was talking very little and set himself to entertain her. He was a corpulent man with florid cheeks and a habit of stroking the side of his nose when he laughed, which he seemed to do all the time. She tried to be amusing, but found it an effort. She had had a long day at the theatre, and they had not even started eating until ten o'clock. By the time they reached the dessert Sadie, who had refused most of the proffered wine, felt her head whirling.

She saw that Leonie, opposite her, was flushed and laughing, more animated than Sadie had seen her. The tall man on her right leaned near her bare shoulder, his moustache brushing her skin. Leonie swayed slightly towards him and Sadie hastily looked away.

When the meal was over a card game started, while Leonie played Gershwin on the phonograph. Sadie, by now aching with tiredness, sat on one of the long cream sofas and tried hard to keep her eyes open. Her fatigue combined with the cigarette smoke and the over-sweet perfume of the women made her feel slightly sick. A lamp burned on the card table, the four players had removed their jackets and pulled open their bow ties. Someone turned the lights down and the dancing couples drew even closer. Sadie got to her feet and tried to make her way discreetly to the door. Just as she reached it a blurred voice spoke behind her.

'I'll see the lady home.' It was her neighbour at table. He followed her through into the quiet of the hallway and pulled the door behind them.

'Thank you.' Sadie spoke decisively. 'But please don't trouble.'

'No trouble. No trouble at all.' He burped gently.

'I live here. Now if you'll excuse me . . .' She made to pass him but he blocked her way.

'You live here, do you? Well then you must let me see you to your room.'

She sighed. 'You're most kind, but that will not be necessary.'

'I am kind.' He was propping himself on the wall beside her and now he unexpectedly lurched towards her and placed the other hand on the wall. Imprisoned, conscious of the smell of brandy and bay rum, she stood for a moment backed up against the wall. Taking her stillness for compliance he said, wheedling, 'And I can be kinder still when you know me well, so what d'you say?'

His breath was warm against her throat, and she could feel the hardness of his chest pressed against hers. She closed her eyes, not to see him, and to her amazement she felt herself wanting him. Scarcely knowing him, not even liking him, but welling up in her she experienced a lust as simple as his own. Wanting someone. Wanting anyone. She opened her eyes, looked at the soft, slightly silly face, the carefully groomed hair. He stroked her wrist with pudgy fingers and as he moved she slipped under his arm and ran down the passageway.

Behind her, fuddled by Leonie's excellent brandy, he gazed at the wall, swaying slightly, trying to see where she had gone. She locked the door of her room, checked that Esther was asleep in the dressing room beyond and started to undress. After a minute or two he knocked very quietly on the door. She held her breath and waited. The handle was turned ineffectually a few times and then he said, half to himself, 'Lady, you don't know what you're missing.'

Sadie lay in the darkness, shivering slightly despite the overheated room, in the grip of an immense sadness. That was just the trouble. She knew exactly what she was missing.

When Sadie had been in New York for almost eighteen months, she received a letter from Lena. She saw with a slight sinking of the heart the thick black ink on expensive vellum. Her sister-in-law had been in New York two months before, and had said she was worried about her father's health. Never a good correspondent, she had already written the previous week. Anxiously, Sadie tore open the envelope, scanning the scrawling, generous handwriting. Her father, wrote Lena, had had a stroke. He had lost the use of his left arm and leg and was confined to a wheelchair. Sadie sat at the breakfast table, the meal forgotten in front of her. Poor Moritz.

'Mummy, Mummy, your coffee's getting cold.' She jerked herself into activity, and hurried Esther to school. On the way to work she sent a wire to Lena: *Does he want to see me? Will travel immediately if so.*

The telegraphed reply came two days later. Moritz was dead. It had happened without any further warning, and no one had even realized it was coming. Rose and Lena had been sitting with him in the bedroom, and he had simply stopped breathing. The funeral had already taken place.

'He was so lucky,' Lena wrote to Sadie on black-edged paper – a letter which reached her shortly afterwards. 'He would have hated to go on living as a cripple, and he has been spared that. And now neither of them will be alone.'

Sadie read the last sentence over and over, in a pain so intense she thought something inside her would break. It was only hours later that she cried, walking home from the theatre, wandering along the sidewalk with her eyes streaming, bumping blindly into passers-by. Finally she could go no further. She was in Fifth Avenue, which seemed endless, and she halted outside Bergdorf Goodman. Behind the lighted windows were several evening gowns, carefully posed on life-sized dummies on pedestals. Above their upholstered bosoms the faces were smooth and impassive. Through her tears Sadie stared at them, trying to regain her self-control: she must compose herself before Esther saw her. She thought she would never forget the immovable figures before her. She wished to God she could go through the rest of her life like that, emotionless, untouched. She leant her forehead against the glass, spent and weary. Moritz was dead.

But it was not Moritz she mourned.

The shock of her father-in-law's death precluded all practical thoughts until the next letter with a London postmark arrived. This was from the Raphaels' lawyers, the firm she had visited the winter of her pregnancy. Almond,

Pearson and Rose wrote a civil letter. They hoped she was well and enjoying New York. They were writing on executor's instructions, regarding the will of their late client, Mr Moritz Raphael. Sadie read on hurriedly. Then she put the letter down and tried to summon a smile for Leonie and Esther, who were watching her anxiously.

'Everything all right, love?'

'Yes, yes, it's just a formality. Something I have to sign.'

She handed the letter over to Leonie. After a moment, she glanced up, nodded at Sadie. 'Mmm. Shall we share a cab to the theatre today? I need to be in early and we could drop Esther on the way.'

In the cab, Sadie let her concern show. 'What am I going to do? This is awful.'

'Was there any hint of this?'

'Not really. After . . . after Asher Moritz really lost a lot of interest in the business. He felt it would end with him, so what was the point? But I thought Rose had managed everything. It seems incredible that all that wealth should have dwindled away. But of course the war . . . no one was buying pictures, I suppose.'

'But there will be something for Esther, won't there?'

'It looks like it. But really, just enough to continue the present allowance. I'd hoped for the lump sum that was promised, so I could invest it for her, and we could use the interest to pay for college and clothes. I'd counted on it, I suppose. Silly of me.'

'But how will it affect you?'

'I can't work it out. I think what it'll mean is that Esther's allowance won't increase regularly, the way it had been planned. There'll just be about the same amount for her every year. Only she'll need more. I'd banked on that for everything, really. I can't do anything much for her myself.'

Comfortingly, Leonie patted her arm. 'Don't worry about it. There's nothing to be done, and Esther's a bright enough girl. And good-looking. She'll make it without a fortune

325

behind her, you wait and see.'

'There's not much alternative, is there? I can't believe it, you know. A few years ago, I seemed to have everything. And now Esther's facing exactly the future I faced when I was growing up. No father, no security . . .' Sadie let the sentence trail away, and stared out at the sidewalk. Leonie, for once, could offer no comment.

Over the next few weeks, Sadie determined to work harder and get a salary raise. It proved more difficult than she had thought. Ziegfeld, like all the other impresarios, paid out where he needed to, to the girls and the artists he hired. But behind the scenes there were plenty of people anxious to work for him. He could pick and choose. Sadie got her raise, with an apologetic smile, but it was for less than she had hoped: twenty-two dollars a week.

She started to fall into the same grey misery that had plagued her after Esther's birth. She could hardly haul herself out of bed in the morning, and her life appeared a limitless colourless desert. She knew this was not so; she had a stimulating job, there were Esther and Leonie. But no amount of reasoning seemed to make any difference. She tried to hide it, to make herself appear at least presentable, to join in the banter around the theatre, take Esther out. But alone, she would sit slumped and dejected. I can't be too bad, she thought, if I can still pretend to be all right. She knew, though, that she was slipping deeper and deeper into a state of uncaring.

Flo Ziegfeld had just started to work on his next production; 1924, he declared to the assembled company from the stage, was to be the most ambitious Follies yet. Evelyn Law and Lupino Lane would star, Urban and Erté would design and costume. Everything was to be of top quality. One set, for example, was already drawn, a country scene entitled 'Road to the Inn' and this was to be strewn nightly with real flowers.

326

'Roses,' ordered Ziegfeld. 'The best.'

'What sort?' Sadie raised a nervous finger.

'American Beauty.'

'But they're the most expensive,' she objected.

'No problem. I want fifteen dozen every night.'

Later, Leonie told Sadie the estimated cost of producing this show.

'Three hundred thousand dollars? I don't believe it!'

'You'd better believe it,' Leonie pinched her cheek affectionately. 'By your own account, you'll need most of that for roses.'

As the weeks went by, Sadie had to admit that Ziegfeld's massive ideas worked. The show already looked good, in the early stages of rehearsal. Sitting in the stalls one morning, watching the Show Girls parade and posture, she thought that she had always been aware of the perfect bodies posed nightly upon the stage, the slender thighs and concave stomachs, the pert breasts. Perhaps, she mused, she'd just never bothered to look at their faces. Seeing them now without the heavy theatrical makeup, she noted the smooth, unworn skin, the shiny eyes. My God, she told herself, they don't look much older than Esther. When she got back to the apartment that night she made a point of looking at herself carefully in the bathroom. Leonie had a theatrical mirror there, with naked bulbs set round it at intervals. Sadie, embarrassed at the professionalism of it, never used it. Now she did. She sat in front of it for a good fifteen minutes, touching her skin carefully, peering at the corners of her eyes. If ever you had a sense of humour, she told herself, you need it now.

Quite simply, she looked neglected. This face, she told herself sternly, was painted by Sargent. Yes, she added, but then someone loved it. She remembered how she and Asher had decided there were different kinds of beauty. There was pure beauty, possessed by those women and men whose features and bodies were so composed that they need make

327

no effort at all to achieve their effect. They had simply to gaze out from those privileged faces, not bothering to be amusing, or intelligent, or even to smile. Their regard was enough to enchant the watcher.

Some women assumed beauty under the gaze of others. The very fact that they were observed gave them vivacity. She was like that. Asher used to say that her charm lay in the changeability of her face, and she knew from the response of others that some days she did not have that curious extra allure. She had not had it for a long time now: no one she cared for was watching her.

All evening she brooded, and in the morning, before setting off for the theatre, she went to 15 East Forty-ninth Street. The *Maison de Beauté Valaze* boasted deep blue velvet walls and red fitments. The paintings that hung against the velvet were fine ones: briefly she wondered what on earth they were doing in a beauty parlour. While she waited for someone to see her (Madam has no appointment? Just one moment), she sat on a chaise-longue and leafed through a pile of new magazines. After about ten minutes a short dramatically dark woman hurried in. Her hair was drawn back tightly in a heavy bun and she wore pearls clustered at her throat and ears. Sadie knew Helena Rubinstein from the many photographs around the salon and watched her with interest. Madam Rubinstein acknowledged her smile, and then looked at her again, more carefully. She spoke to the receptionist and, clearly displeased with the answer, issued an imperious order. Then she bustled over to Sadie.

'Mrs Lander? Your treatment girl will be with you in a moment. Forgive me, but, I'm sure your face is familiar to me. Have we met?'

'I think not.'

'Curious. I know I've seen you somewhere. Ah, well. I hope you will be happy with your make-up.'

'Thank you. I'm sure I will.'

When she emerged an hour later, Sadie was still

wondering what on earth the conversation had been about. It was only then that she realized – Helena Rubinstein, famous as a connoisseur of paintings, must have seen the Sargent.

Sadie's new appearance was only a subtle change. The eyeshadow and mascara, the soft cream and the little rouge and powder, gave her face a definition that suited her. The only person who commented on the change was Leonie, who stopped in front of her and said, 'Aha, I see you've fallen prey to the tricks of the trade.'

'I just thought it was about time I brightened myself up.' But the improvement did not give her spirits the fillip for which she had hoped, and then something else occurred which made her feel even more dispirited. Leonie had been seeing more and more of the man Sadie had first met that night of the dinner party. Harold Werner appeared now many evenings at the apartment, either to accompany Leonie to dinner, or simply to sit for an hour or two. Sometimes they went to gambling clubs, and often she heard them return late, and from the sound of them slightly tipsy. On these occasions, Sadie and Esther would breakfast alone, then tactfully hurry out early. Leonie did not speak of him a great deal, and from this Sadie surmised the seriousness of her feelings for him. The relationship had been going on for a good five months when Sadie again raised the subject of finding an apartment of her own. This time, after the token objection, Leonie seemed to think it was a good thing.

'But are you sure, love? I don't want you to feel I'm throwing you out.'

'Of course you're not. I just think you're past needing a chaperone.'

'My mother wouldn't be pleased to know you were going.'

'And mine wouldn't be pleased to know I was staying.'

They both burst out laughing and Leonie promised to help in the search for an apartment. It was to prove as depressing as it had a year ago. For anything decent a considerable premium was necessary and Sadie could see no way of raising this quickly. Woolf was in the process of selling the house for her. 'You must be patient,' he wrote in his meticulous hand. 'I am anxious to obtain the best possible price for you.'

She knew he would ignore any pleas for speed, dismissing them as her usual impatience for instant results. But the urge to settle herself and Esther had become an obsession, and when she heard of an apartment to let on Thirty-fourth Street she was determined to secure it. She visited the bank, who were polite but unhelpful. Finally she wrote to Almond, Pearson and Rose in London. They responded with what Sadie described to Leonie as 'a most lawyer-like letter'. It would be months yet before their clients' affairs were sorted out, and until such time . . . they could not see their way clear to offering any hope of . . . Sadie's despair deepened. Then one morning she awoke knowing what she would do. Having made the decision, she could not imagine why she had not thought of it before. She would sell Uncle Mark's diamonds. She twisted the ring on her finger, buffed the stones against the palm of her right hand. She hated the thought of losing it, but the only other saleable items she had were the necklace and earrings of gold and coral that Asher had given her years ago. Everything else had gone in those frightening months before Esther's birth. And the corals would not fetch a tenth of the price of the diamonds. And anyway, she wanted those for Esther. No, there was no choice. The ring had to go.

She acted at once, before her resolution had time to cool. It was the first time she had entered Tiffany's. Such places as the exclusive jewellers were beyond her now, and she thought with pain that once she had been able to buy presents in Asprey's. Now, in her best costume – no longer as trim and elegant as it had been when she left London two years before – she confided to the deferential grey-coated salesman that she wished to sell, not buy. Certainly, Madam.

Would she care to take a seat for just a moment, the manager would be happy to see her. Sadie perched on a gilt chair and tried to keep her face calm. The lights were subdued and flattering, the wood panelled walls gleamed. On her left, an elderly lady was examining a miniature silver teapot and cream set, while her companion browsed among the cigarette cases in a glass cabinet. On the far side of the establishment, across the expanse of pale carpet, a man in a homburg was conferring quietly with a salesman.

Sadie sat on, lost in a reverie, feeling the unaccustomed lightness of her ring finger without the hoop of diamonds, which now lay in a morocco case in her handbag. She must go through with this, she must. She and Esther needed that apartment.

Without being aware of any approach, she was conscious that the man in the homburg was standing beside her. Absently she looked down: he was holding out for her inspection a case lined in grey velvet containing a single pearl on a gold bar.

'Madam, would you advise me? I know it is an intrusion, but I should appreciate a feminine eye, for my own taste is sadly uncultivated.'

She knew that voice. She raised her eyes.

It was Nathaniel Laurence.

Chapter Twenty-Three

They regarded each other. It seemed to Sadie that the whole of Tiffany's had become silent. She looked up at the man she had rejected half a lifetime ago and could find no words. She began to rise from her chair, and he put his hand beneath her elbow in a gesture she knew. Still neither spoke. She tried to smile, but it faded before it had begun. Nathaniel watched her with a look she could not read. There was pleasure in it, and pain, and a shadow still of the hurt she had brought him.

She saw that he was little changed. Older, more stocky, his hair thinning, but still the same shrewd, amused face. He saw in her a woman where he had remembered a young girl. The smokey eyes were more extraordinary in a face grown thinner. The arch of the brows, the wide mouth, were subtly emphasized by the grey hat she wore, hiding her hair.

He thought of that summer afternoon when they had sat on the grass and she had flirted with him from beneath the brim of a straw hat pricked with a myriad tiny holes that spangled her face with sunlight. And at last he spoke.

'Mrs Raphael. Sadie. I am so pleased to see you again.'

'Mr Laurence. I didn't expect . . . I never thought to meet you.'

She felt confused, taken aback, as nervous as she had been with him all those years ago in Bristol when she was still barely out of childhood. Under that intent gaze she dropped her eyes, embarrassed. Whatever happened, she did not want him to know why she was here.

'Are you visiting New York for long?' His manner was cordial, formal.

'No. I'm not visiting really. I – we – live here now.' They were still standing facing each other, in that moment of surprise. The tension between them seemed almost tangible.

On an impulse, Sadie put out her hand.

'Nathaniel. It *is* wonderful to meet you like this.'

He took her hand in both of his, held it firmly, then bent his head slightly. For a moment, she thought he was going to kiss her hand, but he relinquished it and when he looked up she could see by his face that he was moved.

'I never thought, you know, that I would see you again. I've not been back in England for years. And all the time you were here.'

'We've only been in New York for a couple of years. But,' she hesitated, then asked, 'how did you know I was Mrs Raphael?'

He lifted his eyebrows in a droll expression of surprise. 'You didn't exactly lead a retiring life, did you? The Sargent portrait created quite a sensation, you know.'

Feeling slightly foolish, she nodded. Just then a dapper sleek haired man coughed discreetly at her elbow.

'Mrs Lander? I wonder if we might . . .'

'Oh, I'm so sorry.' Sadie turned to him apologetically. 'I'm afraid I shall have to return another time, if you don't mind. An old friend . . .' she gestured towards Nathaniel. The manager bowed very slightly and turned away.

Nathaniel was watching her seriously. 'Mrs Lander, is it? I guess there's been a change or two in your life.'

'You could say that.'

He saw her eyes darken and regretted his comment. To divert the conversation he looked at the velvet-lined box he still held in his left hand.

'Well,' he enquired, 'should I?'

'Should you what?'

'Acquire this tie-pin.'

She took the box from him, and moved towards the elaborately chased wall-lamp. 'It's handsome. But you should ask your wife, not me.'

'*Touché.*' Now it was his turn to become grave. 'But I must confess, I do not have one to ask.'

In a rush of concern, Sadie said, 'You haven't married again? I'm so sorry.'

Pointedly, he asked, 'Are you?'

'Of course. I wanted you to be happy. It was just that . . .'

'It was just that you wanted to be happy too,' he finished for her.

'I behaved very badly.' Hesitantly she added, 'There is no apology I could have made then, or can now. I can only ask you to remember that I was seventeen years old.'

'So you were. Little Sadie.'

The affection in his voice drew her: it was a long time since a man had spoken to her like that. He turned, caught the eye of the assistant who had been showing him the tie-pin, and held out the box. 'I've finally reached a decision, thank you. I'll take it, if I may.'

He turned back to her. 'I'm sorry, I must have interrupted your business here.'

By a gesture she implied it was of no importance.

He went on, 'It's almost six, you know. They'll shut in a moment. Are you rushing off to meet Mr Lander?' She hesitated, and he added, 'Would you care to walk with me? I'd like to hear about you, if you have time.'

'Do you really want to? After . . . everything?'

'Oh, Sadie. A long time ago.'

She tried to decide what to do. She did not want him to know her situation. She needed time to think. And anyway Leonie was due to leave for the theatre shortly: she had to get back to Esther.

'I'm so sorry, but I have an engagement.'

The assistant waited with the package. Nathaniel drew out a crocodile wallet. At the doorway, he turned up his collar against the thin drizzle. 'It's not an evening for walking is it? Though I seem to remember you and I once walked together a good deal in the rain.'

She laughed, 'D'you remember that thunderstorm?'

'When you ran out of the park? Yes. But I see no reason

for you to get that wet again. May I drop you somewhere?'

She thought quickly. Fifth Avenue looked good by anyone's standards. She nodded her thanks, and Nathaniel turned to the uniformed doorman, who strode to the edge of the sidewalk, beneath Tiffany's striped canopy, and whistled shrilly. A cab obediently slid towards them from the stream of homebound traffic.

Nathaniel spoke first. 'The cab will only take a few minutes. Would you – and your husband, of course – do me the honour of lunching with me tomorrow. I return to Chicago next week.'

'I'm afraid that won't be possible.' Anxious not to appear rude, she added hastily, 'I work, you see. The middle of the day is difficult for me.'

'Do you indeed? What sort of work do you do?' Sadie told him about the theatre, and he did not conceal his puzzlement that she should need employment. Sadie did not enlighten him, nor did she refer to Woolf by name. When the cab drew up outside the apartment house Nathaniel accompanied her to the door. She did not invite him in: he did not press for an invitation. He started to say something, then stopped.

'Thank you for the ride, Nathaniel.'

'It was my pleasure.'

She felt sure that he would ask for her phone number, but he calmly bade her goodbye and returned to the cab. She stood irresolute in the doorway. She had implied that she was here with her husband. Did she expect Nathaniel to attempt to make an assignation? Yet she did not want to see him disappear. Before she could do anything, the cab had driven off. She lifted a hand in farewell and went inside.

For ten days she dressed with extra care, wore her best clothes. She did not know if she wanted to see Nathaniel again, nor what would be the point of meeting. But if it happened, she would look as attractive as possible. By the end of a month she had come to the conclusion that she had effectively repulsed him. She had spoken of 'we', without explaining that she referred not to her husband but to her daughter. She had deliberately misrepresented her situation, whether out of pride or self-protection, she could not tell.

She had not returned to Tiffany's: the following week, she had received a letter and a money-order from Woolf. He had managed to complete the sale of the house, had given Annie the £250 stipulated by Sadie, and enclosed the remainder.

It was less than she had hoped, but enough for the down-payment on the apartment on Thirty-fourth Street and some left to put away. Before Christmas she and Esther were settled. The new apartment soon acquired a personality: blinds and books, plants and pictures, a couple of pieces from the St John's Wood house; her little desk with the red silk pleated front, the Limoges mirror Asher had bought for her bedroom; Esther's rocking chair from Grandma Raphael. The apartment was small but suitable, in a modest block which ran to carpeted hallways and a live-in porter. Leonie was a tram ride away from Esther's school, and she was old enough now to take herself to Leonie's apartment each afternoon, where Sadie collected her. By January they were settling into a pleasant enough routine and Sadie's dissatisfaction with her life was partly mollified by having her own home again.

'I was a fool to be so long without one,' she wrote to Lena. 'I had not realized how misplaced I felt, among someone else's possessions. Even Leonie's.'

The Christmas spectacular at the theatre was occupying her every moment. The usual demands flowed from the insatiable Ziegfeld's office: 'Can you get Lester's "jungle number" material in by next week?' 'How quickly can we arrange the Louis Quinze wigs?'

She was dashing out to check the last request at midday one cold February morning, and pausing at Tom's cubicle for a cup of coffee in lieu of lunch, when she saw Nathaniel again. He was standing in the relaxed attitude of a man who

336

has been waiting for a long time, propped against a wall, hands deep in his pockets, fur collar up round his face, watching the stage door. Tom saw her glance across, and peered out. 'Guy's been hanging around more'n an hour,' he volunteered. 'Didn't want to bother you, he said.'

'That's ridiculous. He must be freezing.' She downed the last of the coffee, thanked Tom, and went outside. Seeing her, Nathaniel straightened up, and came towards her. 'Good morning. Is this inconvenient?'

'No, of course not.' She gave him a sidelong smile. 'Not inconvenient at all. Merely unexpected.'

'I stand corrected.' He turned down his collar, offered his arm.

'May I accompany you to your destination? I'll disappear tactfully if you'd prefer it. Only I had no address but the theatre for you – I've already spent two afternoons standing in Fifth Avenue to no avail: I couldn't find your name on the residents list at Number 506.'

'No, we were staying with Leonie.'

He raised his eyebrows.

'Not the girl I used to send your letters to in Manchester?'

'The same. That's how I got my job – she's Ziegfeld's co-ordinator. We'd been staying with her all this time, but now I've got my own apartment.'

They were walking towards Eighty-fifth Street past a delicatessen with salami hanging in the window next to a great barrel of pickled cucumbers. Nathaniel suddenly stopped.

'Say that again,' he ordered.

She stared. 'What on earth d'you mean?'

'You said, "I've got my own apartment." You didn't say "we".'

'No. It isn't "we". I'm alone here. Except for my daughter.'

'I think, Mrs Lander, you have some explaining to do.' He glanced up at the shop front. 'Can we get lunch here?'

'Of course.'

She pushed open the door and led him up the narrow staircase. At the top was a small kosher restaurant. Six tables were packed together in the narrow room, simply laid with white cloths, the minimum of cutlery and a large carafe of water. The proprietor, a man so large he could hardly push his bulk between the tables, greeted her as an old friend.

'We come here much of the time from the theatre,' she explained to Nathaniel. 'Mr Wienberger is famous for his *kreplach*. But,' she added in a low voice as he moved away, 'he's more famous for his bad jokes.'

'In that case, I'll let you handle the ordering.'

While they ate pastrami on rye, Sadie told Nathaniel about her life with Asher. She faltered when she told him of the accident, and hurried on to explain the marriage to Woolf and the birth of Esther immediately afterwards. 'And now,' she finished, 'he's in London with his mother again, and I'm here waiting for the divorce.'

'It sounds a bit bleak.'

'It feels that way,' she admitted ruefully. 'But what can I do? I couldn't decently let him ruin his prospects. After all, I have to admit he was inveigled into marrying me.'

Nathaniel shot her a sudden, pained glance. Clearer than words, it reminded her of her repudiation of him. He let the conversation tail away, and when the waiter brought their coffee Sadie stirred it thoughtfully, 'Why did you come to the theatre today?'

'I told you. I didn't know where else to find you.'

'No, I meant, why today, when we met three months ago? I expected to hear from you then. I'd thought you decided not to bother with me again.'

He kept his head lowered, not looking at her, tracing patterns on the tablecloth with his knife-point. 'Honestly, I don't know. It seemed like fate, somehow. I thought I wouldn't do anything deliberate and then if we met again it was meant, and if not . . .' he shrugged. 'After all, you appeared to be settled, a married woman. What right had I to force my way back into your life?'

He looked up from his invisible doodling. 'You always did ask a lot of questions. I'd forgotten. Well, I was back here on business, and I suppose I obeyed an impulse.'

Warmly, she said, 'I'm delighted you did.'

She glanced at her watch, and failed to notice that he had made no reply. He left her outside the costumiers who were providing the wigs, and it was only when he had gone she recalled he still did not know her new address.

Nathaniel Laurence walked to his appointment at the offices of Lowe, Arden, Ackerman to discuss their proposed new skyscraper office block. It took him forty-five minutes and when he arrived and found himself before the receptionist he realized that he could not remember a single incident for the whole of that time, so engrossed was he in his thoughts. As he took off his tan leather gloves in the foyer, waiting for Ackerman to send down a minion who would show him to the conference room, he looked just what he was: successful, self-assured, used to authority and decisions.

Although youthful for his fifty years, his face bore unmistakeable lines of experience and sorrow, and they deepened as he recalled his meetings with Sadie in that green park on Bristol's Black Boy Hill. He had been drawn by something he sensed in her, some promise of the woman she could become. It had pulled him from the emotional lethargy he had assumed as protection after the death of his wife. He thought he had won Sadie, he counted on it; he let his love expand to fill his days – and then, suddenly, she withdrew herself from him. Thinking of it now, he drew a deep breath to steady himself. He should have explained better to her what he had been through. But what difference would that have made in the end? He had gone back to Chicago, worked harder than ever, and had once more gained his equanimity. He had not spurned feminine solace, and there were many women who had consoled the young widower. One or two came near to him emotionally, but never near enough for him to risk disturbing the life he and his daughter had made for themselves. So why, now, was he jeopardizing that hard-won contentment by seeing Sadie again?

A voice broke in on his reverie. 'Are you the gentleman from Adler and Sullivan, sir? The Board are waiting for you now. If you'd care to come this way.'

Slipping a folder from his leather case, Nathaniel composed himself for work.

Over that winter Nathaniel and Sadie established a new relationship. When he was in New York – about twice a month – they dined together. After six or seven occasions Sadie asked him home for a meal, which she prepared as nervously as if she had never given elegant dinner-parties in St John's Wood. She began to look forward to his visits, to plan what she would cook, what she would wear, what flowers she would buy. To her pleasure Esther, too, welcomed Nathaniel. He enjoyed talking to her, treating her with all the serious attention he gave to adults.

He would bring a small gift for Sadie – a bottle of wine, chocolates – and there was always something for Esther. When he discovered that she had a doll's house, he arrived with minute pieces of furniture to fit it: a rocking chair with a patchwork cushion that delighted her ('It's just like mine,' she cried gleefully), a piano exquisitely carved in a dark wood. When Sadie exclaimed over this, he confessed that he had carved it himself. 'It's something I've been doing for years. I started it for Alice, making things for her dolls, and now it's compulsive.'

Then one evening Nathaniel took her to dinner with another couple. It was a pleasant occasion. The husband was an architect, the wife a fabric designer, and Sadie reflected that it was the first time she had seen Nathaniel with his own friends. When they parted it was still only just after eleven.

'We'd better get back. Your baby-sitter won't like us.'

'There's no hurry this evening. Esther's staying with a schoolfriend tonight.'

'So you're enjoying the heady taste of total freedom? I thought you seemed unduly lighthearted.'

Sadie nudged his arm affectionately. 'You fool you. But I must admit it's rather nice to have no responsibilities for one night.'

'What shall we do to celebrate your momentary independence? We could go somewhere and dance?'

'No, we couldn't,' Sadie protested. 'My feet have had me standing on them all day, I'll have you know. And you must be tired too.'

'Well, look, we're almost at East Fifty-Sixth Street. Let's go back to my hotel for a night-cap.'

'Are you trying to lure me, sir, to your boudoir?'

'As you will see, the bed is narrow enough to discourage any improper thoughts, much less actions.'

The Surrey was a fifteen-storey block of tiny rooms. On the ground floor a coffee-shop was empty of customers, the peach-uniformed waitresses tired and white-faced. They walked through the deserted lobby to the elevator. The operator took them up to the ninth floor and bade them goodnight.

Sadie remarked, 'You may not believe this, but I find myself in a totally novel situation. I've never actually done this before.'

Nathaniel gave her a broad grin. 'You and me both. Well, anyway, not here.'

His room was as narrow as he had warned. Beside the bed, with its tapestry coverlet, there was a bureau, an uninviting looking wing chair and a table with a pewter based lamp on it.

'Will you take the chair? I'll sit on the bed.'

Nathaniel poured a glass of lemonade into a toothglass, and handed it to her. 'Have I read you right, or would you prefer some illegal gin?'

'No. Thank you. This is fine.'

He leant back against the headboard. 'I've been coming here for years now. I don't actually like it, but on the other hand there's no positive reason to dislike it. And I'm really here very little, except to sleep.'

'I've only ever really stayed in hotels in Europe. When Asher and I went on our honeymoon trip.' She had never, after the first explanation, spoken of Asher to him, just as he never mentioned his dead wife to her.

'The one advantage of European hotels,' he observed, 'is the quality of their coffee. The stuff they serve downstairs is unspeakable.' He paused. 'I'm sorry things haven't turned out the way you wanted, Sadie. I really am.' He reached out and took her hand between both his own.

Soberly, she pointed out, 'I wouldn't be sitting here with you if they had, though.'

'True. And that's worth a very great deal.'

Still holding her hand, he got to his feet, and stood beside her chair, 'Change places with me.'

Puzzled, she obeyed and he sat and then pulled her unresisting on to his knee.

'Haven't sat like this for years.'

'I weigh enough for you to regret it pretty soon.' She laid her head on his shoulder, and rubbed her cheek against the texture of his jacket. 'This feels very old-fashioned.'

'I'm an old-fashioned fellow. Didn't you know?' He put his arms firmly around her back, and held her head close to his own. 'Are you ready for this?'

She giggled. 'I'll just have to take that risk, won't I?'

Very softly, he said, 'I've told you, haven't I, that you ask too many questions?'

The kiss was tentative, a soft exploration, experimental, slightly apprehensive. Sadie caught Nathaniel's face between her hands, and whispered urgently, 'Why did you wait so long?'

For answer he tightened his arms around her, and kissed her again. She closed her eyes, and folded herself closer.

For a long time they remained locked together, before Nathaniel pulled away. 'And now I'm going to take you home.'

'No. No, you're not. I want to stay.' There was a note of entreaty in her voice. 'Please, Nathaniel, let me stay.'

'I want to. But I can't.'

She slowly brushed her hair back where it was escaping from the knot on top of her head, hurt and bewildered.

'I can hardly explain myself.' He looked strained and tense.

Hurriedly she broke in, 'You don't have to explain anything. I'm free to do as I wish, and I promise you that you don't have to feel committed in any way. Only let me stay tonight.'

She faltered and stopped. His face contorted and he banged a fist into the palm of his other hand. 'Sadie. For God's sake don't go on. I don't want to hear it. I don't want to hear you tell me that. Can't you see that I *want* to feel committed? Are you so unaware of me as a man that you don't see my needs?'

He saw her dismay, but his pain prevented him from responding to it.

'I . . . I'm sorry.' Her voice shook. 'I didn't think, I just didn't think.'

He had his back to her now, staring through the half-open curtains at the neon lights flashing their semaphore across the streets. 'It's not your fault. I remember what you experienced – I've been there too. You have to think of yourself first, you've had to do that for years, just to survive. I see that, I'm not blaming you for it.'

He swung round to face her. 'Only I ask you to remember that we've been through this before, you and I. You made me a promise, and you broke it. You made a me a gift, and you took it back.'

343

His voice dropped. 'I will not make love to you, and comfort you, and be told that you are free and I am uncommitted. I cannot give you any more of myself, not until you too are prepared to risk your emotions. Now, let's get you home.'

Without speaking she gathered up her handbag and gloves and moved to the door. He followed. As they stood together waiting for the elevator to arrive, he turned to her. 'There is one thing I want you to know, and I don't believe I have told it you.'

'What is it?' Her voice was almost inaudible.

The elevator arrived, and the operator drew back the wrought iron gates and stood back as they entered. Side by side they descended, watching the brilliantined back of his head above the maroon suit. After interminable minutes the doors opened again. When they were alone in the dim lobby Nathaniel said, 'It's only this. I have not ceased to love you.'

For twenty-four hours Sadie locked herself in her thoughts. She stayed away from the theatre, and while Esther was at school she walked endlessly around the city she had begun to think of as her home. That evening, she put through a telephone call to Nathaniel in Chicago.

Next morning, she gave in her notice at the theatre. When she told Leonie, she was met with exactly the reaction she had anticipated.

'You're mad. You're out of your senses. Sadie, you've got your own home, a job you like. I don't understand how you can give all that up.'

Sadie looked at her with affection. 'Lee. I've tried to be like you, but I'm no *good* at it. Living like this,' she gestured round at the cluttered desk, 'I know it's amusing, and I love it here. Only it feels like filling time. It's not what I want to do.'

Sadie shrugged apologetically. 'Something you despise. I want to be a wife.'

Leonie groaned. 'Haven't I made you see any sense in all this time? Two marriages, Sadie, and you haven't had enough? I thought you were running your own life now.' She sat down, heavily. 'And all the time you were just waiting for another man. You're incorrigible. Do you know,' she shot Sadie a speculative look, 'I think you only really live through men. You see yourself as part of them, you don't feel whole on your own.'

'Don't I?' Taken aback, Sadie considered. It was true, she supposed, though she could never have put it into words. Now she said, 'I'm only doing what women have always done, aren't I? Women want a man, and babies. What else is there?' Hastily she corrected herself. '*Most* women.'

Unmollified, Leonie snapped, 'I've been trying to show what else there is. There's independence, Sadie, and achievement.'

'You're very critical, Lee. But I notice you aren't exactly sending Harold Werner on his way, are you?'

'I'm not denying normal feminine instincts, you know.' Leonie's exasperation brought her to her feet and sent her walking swiftly back and forth across the small room. 'I'm not saying you mustn't love, or that you don't feel desire, or that you can't cherish someone. All I'm saying is, that doesn't have to be *all* you do.'

'But I don't see those things as part of my life, Lee. I see cherishing someone as a full-time occupation. I want to be in Nathaniel's house when he goes out in the morning, and in it when he comes home at night. I want to send Esther to school, and walk home with her when she leaves. I hate rushing around the way I do, fitting her in when I can, trying to make time for her when I know I should be doing it the other way around.'

Sharply Leonie asked, 'And so you're going to marry Nathaniel?'

'I suppose so.'

'What d'you mean? Either you are, or you aren't. If you're

leaving to go to Chicago, presumably matrimony is your intention?'

'It's not quite as straightforward as that. For one thing, I'm not free to marry yet, remember. And for another . . .'

'Go on,' Leonie prompted her after a moment.

'He . . . we . . . I haven't been asked.'

'A technicality that doesn't appear to have deterred you in the past, from what you've told me.' Seeing Sadie's hurt look, she softened. 'I'm sorry. That was a hell of a thing to say. What on earth is going on, then?'

'I'm just making a gesture, I suppose. I think Nathaniel feels – no, I know he feels – that I let him down once, and he fears I'd do it again. So I decided I have to show him I'm prepared to risk what I have for him. He'll help me with an apartment there, and I'll take a job and put Esther into school. It won't be nearly so difficult this time.'

'What about Esther? Does she want to go?'

Sadie smiled. 'She's the least of my problems, bless her. You know how she loves Nathaniel.'

Leonie sighed. 'What else can I say? If you're going to do it, then that's it.'

'You know, Lee, you said to me, over a year ago, that you wanted a family too, that you were lonely?'

'I suppose I did.' Leonie went to the door. 'It was a momentary lapse, I guess. I'm not changing anything for Harold Werner, and he's changing nothing for me. That way, no one gets hurt?'

'No. No one gets hurt. But Lee, you can't go through life protecting yourself from unacceptable emotions.'

Leonie's eyebrows rose. 'Can I not? And just why can't I?' She moved away from the door. 'By what law do I have to expose myself to the whims and vagaries of any man's behaviour?'

'Lee, it isn't like that. Nathaniel's right. I told him he needn't feel committed to me, and he was furious – he said he

346

wanted to feel that, it was necessary to him. Surely it is to everyone, even to you?'

'No. Don't put your needs on to me. I don't need to feel committed – it would kill me, it'd be stifling, horrible. I've come too far alone to let anyone else tamper with what I've achieved for myself. And I thought you were beginning to feel the same. I'm sorry I was wrong. I'm disappointed in you.'

Soberly, Sadie said, 'You won't go against your nature, and I can't deny mine. You're right about me. Only I don't think it's weakness to need someone. It's not admitting failure to know you're unsuccessful alone. You seem to see it as a disaster to be vulnerable. To me, it's a sort of achievement – to be open to emotions, not closed up on yourself. Of course it hurts, sometimes. Certainly it's inviting some unhappiness. It's a risk worth taking, though, for the joys of having someone of your own.'

Leonie shook her head. 'Sorry, love. I tried, and I told you what happened. Never again. But if that's what you want' – impulsively she kissed Sadie on the cheek – 'then I hope it works for you.'

Chapter Twenty-Four

Sadie and Esther went to Chicago on the Twentieth Century Ltd, the fast and luxurious train which took only a boasted four-and-a-half-days to reach its West Coast destination.

'You must travel on it,' Nathaniel had insisted. 'The glass enclosed Observation Car is unbelievable.' As they tore through the vast and awesome stretches of Pennsylvania, Ohio and Indiana, Sadie was filled with delight at what she saw, and panic at the sheer size of America. She suddenly realized just how urban she was; at home in the streets of Manchester or London, she had found New York over-powering with its straight, endless thoroughfares and far horizons. But this daunted. She stared for hours out at the dizzying tracts of land, the rivers and mountains, and doubted that she had made a wise decision. But when at last they alighted, handed down the high steps to the platform where Nathaniel awaited them, she was soon reassured. If New York had intimidated Sadie, Chicago invited her: the ugly, blustery city, throwing up buildings apparently at random, the aggressive self-confidence of its inhabitants. 'It's so provincial,' she exclaimed to Nathaniel after less than a week. 'It feels just like Manchester.'

He roared with laughter at this. 'Your mother is amazing,' he informed Esther, who was squeezed between them on the front seat: they were driving back from the Illinois Institute of Technology, where Nathaniel lectured on the techniques of building with steel at the School of Architecture. 'You'll have to keep her under control,' he went on. 'Chicagoans may know they are living in the second largest city in America, but they hate to be reminded of it. The word "provincial" is not spoken here, and everything is the biggest, whatever it is.'

Esther and Sadie giggled and Nathaniel went on, 'I'm serious. For one thing, it's the world's biggest inland port. It's the biggest railway centre – it's called the Crossroad of the Continent. It's also known as "the city of big shoulders".'

Puzzled, Esther asked, 'Why? Because the people are large?'

'It's a reference to cattle – this is where all America's meat is brought to be killed. We have acres of stockyards here, miles of them, one after the other. You can smell them all over the city in summer.'

Sadie shuddered.

'However,' he went on, 'I'll take you one day to the Grain Exchange – which is, by the way, the biggest anywhere, and you can see almost all the world's cereal food being purchased and sold.'

Sadie grinned at him, 'Is that all? What else can you show us?'

'The birthplace of the skyscraper. The Chicago River, the only one in the world which the engineers have managed to make run backwards, out of Lake Michigan instead of into it.' He turned to Esther. 'Or shall I, instead, show you a splendid hotel for lunch?' Nathaniel acted towards Esther as if she were his own. They had met his daughter Alice, and spent a cheerful day together. Sadie had found to her pleasure that the young woman looked and behaved very like her father.

Those first months in Chicago were not without difficulties. Sadie and Esther lived in an apartment which Nathaniel had found for them, while the courtship continued, and Sadie found herself increasingly anxious about her daughter. The child was now thirteen and looked extraordinarily like Asher, lithe and dark. She had inherited his sudden changes of mood, and Sadie knew very well the look that would suddenly shadow her face. Esther herself found it harder than her mother to adapt to Chicago. She had established

349

herself in New York, and though she could not put it into words, she felt instinctively that her mother had rushed them both too hastily towards a new way of life. Like her father she had mercurial moods but a great need for stability in her surroundings. She found her new school daunting, so became difficult and obstinate, refusing to leave her room in the evening, regularly failing to do her homework.

Sadie did not hide her anxiety. She tried to encourage Esther to talk, alternated with gentle bullying. Neither made any difference. Never outgoing, always slightly shy, a little detached, Esther seemed to be turning from a peaceful child into a sullen young girl. One day, tidying her room, Sadie came across a locket, one that Lena had sent her niece for a birthday present. Idly she opened it. To her surprise – surely she had not given the picture to Esther – it contained an old photograph taken years ago when she and Asher were in the St John's Wood garden. Her immediate raction was to snap the locket shut, to shield herself from it. She never looked at pictures of him, for even after all this time it still hurt far too much. But she forced herself to open it again, and then she saw that Esther had cut the photograph in two so that only Asher's figure was framed in the golden oval. The other half of the locket was empty. Slowly she put the locket back exactly where she had found it, then went and lay down on her bed.

Throughout the period of difficulty with Esther, Sadie's relationship with Nathaniel was altering. Where she had been – she could admit it now – unthinking, and he defensive, the gesture she had made in coming to Chicago had removed their restraints and they slid easily into an intimacy new to them. They became comfortable together, able to share companionable silences as well as argumentative discussions. They were immediately responsive to each other's moods and needs, and began to develop a number of private jokes that amused only themselves.

Slowly and so subtly that neither was aware of the process, they slipped into the mould of a happy marriage. The event itself, when it finally occurred, seemed to both to be something of an anticlimax. The only practical difference was that they moved formally into the house they had bought in the Old Town. At first Nathaniel had been eager to build for them, but Sadie had long before fallen in love with the Victorian houses where so many of Nathaniel's friends lived: the Old Town was full of writers and artists, and for Sadie it evoked the happiest years of her life. When she said this he looked at her oddly, and she quickly amended her remark. 'I don't mean I'm not happy now. It's just that it reminds me of London.' He patted her hand. "I know, my dear. You needn't explain.'

Nathaniel was a man with very few illusions left about himself. He knew that the two of them were well suited and for his part the new-found contentment was sufficient reward for the years of loneliness. But he was aware that for Sadie this marriage was a practical affair also. Certainly she loved him. Undoubtedly she needed him. It was she, after all, who had sought this more than he. Yet he was well aware that although he could give her everything she needed – companionship, conversation, comfort and consolation – there was one element he could not bring to their alliance. Deeply as he loved her, he could not inspire her with that sense of romance she had shared with Asher. They had talked of this once – their understanding allowed them to speak of such things – on a hot summer afternoon when Nathaniel had not returned to the University after lunch. They had eaten at the Stock Yard Inn at Forty-second and South Halstead, where Nathaniel had ordered steaks so substantial that Sadie, eating greedily, had protested that they would not need anything for the rest of the week. In the wooden booth, when Nathaniel had poured the last of the Beaune – he was one of the few Americans she knew who regularly drank wine with his meals, a habit he declared was

351

a piece of European decadence he was simply not strong willed enough to resist – she had said, idly, 'I wish you didn't have to work this afternoon.'

'Your wish is my command.'

'Is it now?'

Seriously, he had looked at her across the table. 'You know very well that it is.'

'Then don't work. Come home with me instead.' In their shaded bedroom, in the quiet house, they had made love slowly and considerately, each careful to please and accommodate the other. Nathaniel was always more conscious of her body than his own sensations, finding his delight in her response to him, and only in those last moments of inexorable and blinding pleasure did he finally abandon himself. She sensed this treasuring of her, and experienced a gratitude so immense she clung to him with ardour. He smiled down at her flushed face beneath him, for he read her better than she could herself. When they had finished and lay warmly intertwined, Sadie pulled the sheet over them and whispered, 'Shall we sleep? Have we time?'

'We have all the time we need.'

When she awoke the room was darker. She could hear the housekeeper's voice: Esther must be home from school. Luxuriously she stretched and opened her eyes. Nathaniel was sitting in the armchair beside the bed, smoking his pipe. 'Good evening, Mrs Laurence.'

She turned over, mounded a pillow comfortably and propped her head on her hands.

Nothing was said for a long time, then Sadie reached out and smoothed the silk dressing gown over Nathaniel's knee. 'I don't deserve you, you know.'

'You don't, do you? But luckily for you, we don't only get the things we deserve in this life, And I, you see, did deserve *you*.'

'I'm trying to pay you a compliment. Don't turn the tables on me.'

Suddenly grave, he caught hold of her hand and held it to his cheek.

'Thank you. I hope I make you happy. I want to, very much. But I'm not a fool, Sadie, and I don't delude myself. I wanted you and in the end, I've got you. But I don't have all of your heart, because you no longer have it all to give, any more than I do.'

She flung out a hand in protest. 'But I do. I do love you. I don't love you any the less because I loved Asher so much.'

'It's not a question of quantity. What I'm trying to say is that I think what we feel for each other is tempered by experience. I adore you – you know that – but I recognize this as a very different emotion from the love I had for Alice.'

'I suppose you're right. But perhaps this is sweeter because of it.'

'Like the last of the wine?'

'Or perfume when the bottle has been opened many times?'

'Or the one remaining spoonful of jam?'

'Or the dregs at the bottom of the gravy boat?'

They teased each other with amused tenderness. Then Sadie said, 'Heavens I must get dressed, look at the time.'

Nathaniel pulled her to her feet, and put his hands on her shoulders. 'I mean it though,' his voice was low. 'I know you can't feel for me that passion you felt for Asher.'

She started to speak and he pressed a finger to her lips.

'Let me finish. All I ask is that you give me all you can.'

'I will. Nathaniel, I do.'

He relaxed and patted her bottom. 'Right then. Into your clothes, woman, or Esther will think you spend your days asleep.'

Six weeks later, after an appointment, Sadie went into a florist. When Nathaniel arrived home, an apricot rose was standing in a narrow glass on his bureau.

'What's this? I'm the one who buys flowers around here.'

'I thought you deserved it.'

'Now why?' He pretended to think deeply. 'Is it your birthday I've forgotten? Or mine? Have I been asked to rush to Washington to take over from Coolidge?'

'None of those things.'

'I give up.'

She said, slowly, 'It's to congratulate you.'

'But on what?'

'On being about to become a father.'

He stared at her. When he spoke, his voice was hoarse with emotion.

'*What* did you say?'

'We're going to have a child.'

He put a shaking hand to his forehead. 'What are you telling me? Is it true, are you sure?'

She nodded her confirmation.

'I'd hoped, of course.' He looked dazed. 'But at my age . . . oh, my dear, it's wonderful.' There were tears in his eyes as she put her arms round him. He sank into the chair behind him, pulled her on to his knee, and buried his face against her breast. Somewhere in her mind the needle of memory jumped, and she saw again Miriam and Caspar in their small living room when Miriam was carrying their third child.

The months of her pregnancy were joyful, marred only by Esther's reaction. When Sadie told her of the coming child ('It'll be the brother or sister I always wanted you to have'), she had shrugged and her indifference seemed so real that Sadie and Nathaniel found it hard to convince themselves that the girl was uncertain how to respond. Gradually Esther appeared to come to terms with the idea, and Sadie took especial care to give her extra attention. She asked Esther's advice about buying baby clothes, and by the time they were ready to plan the room set aside to be the nursery, Esther seemed happy with the prospect of the baby.

In the June of 1928, when Sadie was in her thirty-ninth

year and Nathaniel fifty-three, a son was born to them. They called him David, and if Sadie adored him, he was the light of Nathaniel's life, the son he had never thought to have. He would sit for hours reading, with the swaddled baby asleep in the crook of his arm, and Sadie knew a sweet and certain happiness she had not previously experienced. She relished this baby, for she had begun to think perhaps she would be too old to bear another. As he grew bigger and more responsive she would listen carefully while he fed, committing every murmur to her memory, and he would gaze up at her with unwinking eyes, jaws working busily, humming with love.

Before David was two, Esther had left school, and though Sadie tried hard to persuade her to study art, she insisted on training as a stenographer.

'But she can't want that,' Sadie had wailed at Nathaniel. 'It's so – ordinary.'

'Better let her get it out of her system,' Nathaniel had counselled. 'And anyway, it might well lead to something more suitable. Don't let's come down on her too heavily. She's barely seventeen.'

The stenography course was a full-time one, and Esther apparently worked hard. She was now out most of the day, and seemed to be making plenty of friends. She was invited to parties most weekends, and Nathaniel would insist on collecting her at eleven. One day she said that a young man would be calling for her, and would also bring her home. Sadie and Nathaniel exchanged glances, and agreed. After that, Alfred Lewis appeared regularly at the house. He was a pleasant enough fellow, reported Nathaniel. He came from a good family, was training to be an accountant, 'and knows how to mind his Ps and Qs.'

So that when Esther announced that she and Alfred Lewis wanted to marry, Sadie was far from surprised. She made a token protest – Esther's youthfulness, her lack of experience. The girl countered by pointing out that Sadie too had married at eighteen. Unable to argue on that point, partly relieved at the apparently happy outcome of Esther's difficult years, Sadie set about planning the wedding.

Not until the night before did she lie sleepless beside Nathaniel, her fingers pleating and repleating the sheet, smoothing and pleating. Sleepily, Nathaniel grumbled gently at her. 'It's no good,' she whispered, 'I can't sleep. Sorry.'

He groaned and propped himself up on an elbow, feeling for the light switch.

'We'd better sort you out,' he observed, 'or you'll look terrible in the morning.'

She tried to smile. 'It's just that – I feel I've lost her. I'm suddenly terribly afraid she's only marrying Alfred to get away from me. I feel I've let her down. And that hurts.'

Nathaniel groped for his empty pipe and put the stem between his teeth to help him think. 'I see what you mean. Perhaps she does view it partly as an escape. But my dear, most children want to escape their parents, one way or another, and Esther's no different.'

Wretchedly, Sadie said, 'No. Only I've hauled her around after me, and I presented her with a new family at a difficult time for her – I've made things very hard for the child.'

'I think you're being unfair to yourself. You did what had to be done. I suppose you could have stayed in New York. I know she was happy there. But suppose she'd married at eighteen anyway? You'd have been left entirely alone then. As it is, you'll both have families. Surely the best thing that could have happened.'

'Half of me says you're right. The other half says that if I'd not worked, if I'd always been there when she came home from school . . .'

'You're going to make me very annoyed if you go on punishing yourself like this. You worked for money, didn't you? She was with Leonie when she wasn't with you – hardly neglected. And I take your point about marrying me, but look how well Esther and I get on. And if you think the birth of a baby has upset her, then you're mad.'

He put an arm round her shoulders, and drew her against him. 'Daughters are the devil. Didn't you know? Here you are on the verge of marrying her off and you can't just relax and enjoy it. She's only doing what you did.'

Lying there, he suddenly started to shake with laughter.

'What's so funny?'

'Oh my Lord, Sadie. I'm just remembering that terrible afternoon I came to tea at Locket Street to meet your mother. She was utterly and completely daunting, d'you remember? I couldn't say a word in my own defence.' He stopped laughing. 'Poor woman. She won that round, though, didn't she?'

'Yes. Only the absurd thing is, my life would have been a hell of a lot easier and happier, in the end, if she'd let me marry you straightaway.'

'Which is exactly my point. We'll have to let Esther marry as she wants, because we can't plan her fate for her.' He drew on the empty pipe.

'It's a pity Sophie wouldn't come for tomorrow,' he went on. 'I'd have liked her to see you now, with David. I think she'd be really thrilled with our fat son.'

Sadie sighed. 'I've tried everything. I even offered to go over and bring them back with me. But Flora wrote separately to say Ma really couldn't face the journey, not after that fall. Her shoulder is still very painful, and she finds it hard to move.'

'We'll go over there this summer though, I promise.'

'I told them that. It'll be strange, after this.'

'Could you sleep now, do you think?' He yawned. 'Because between you and me and the bedpost, I could.'

'I'll try.'

Obediently she settled down and he clicked off the light. Struck by a thought, he added, 'I'm surprised at you, you know. Worrying like this. You're the marrying kind, after

357

all, and obviously Esther is too. Now if she refused to marry, then I'd have expected you to lose your beauty sleep.'

'Don't ask me to be logical about this. It's just an emotional reaction. I know I'm being a fool. But, oh, Nathaniel,' she sought his hand in the darkness. 'I wish Asher could see her tomorrow.'

He didn't speak. For answer, the pipe was placed on the bedside table, and he took her in his arms.

Chapter Twenty-Five

He lay in a high, white bed. In the dim room she could just discern the rapid rise and fall of his chest to his shallow breathing. He was turned on his side, so pale and quiet that to reassure herself she reached out and touched his arm. He coughed gently, a dry little sound. She sat on, listening to the faint sanatorium noises filtering through the closed doors: rush of wheels and hurrying feet on the rubber floor, the occasional voice, a distant clatter of crockery. How long she sat there she didn't know. In the rush she had neglected to put on her watch and the room had no clock. Just the two beds, the second one unoccupied, a cupboard containing extra pillows, and against the far wall an oxygen cylinder and mask.

She looked down at him again, noting the slight sweat on his forehead, the rasp as he drew breath. She was gripped by a fear that felt like black water closing round her head, blocking all thought, all hope. She reached under the sheet and his feet were ice; she kneaded them between her hands, trying to warm him. I ought to pray, she thought, what are the prayers for this? All she could remember was the beginning of the *Shema*.

'*Shema Yisrael*,' she whispered, '*Adonai elohanu, adonai echad.* Hear O Israel, the Lord is our God, the Lord is One.' She lost the thread, and found herself repeating endlessly, 'Please, please. Oh, please.'

She closed her eyes. When she opened them again, she thought she saw his lids flicker faintly. Very softly she said, 'Hallo. It's me. I'm here with you.'

His head rolled from side to side, the first movement he had made for hours. His lips were dry, and she wiped them gently with the sponge the nurse had given her in the curved dish. Without opening his eyes again he said hoarsely, 'No. No.'

'It's all right, my darling.' She tried to soothe, to reach the distressed mind. 'I'm here. It's all right. Just don't worry.'

His head rolled again, and she heard the breath rattle in his throat. He moaned, and she pressed the buzzer above the bed as she had been instructed.

A minute later the door opened and the nurse poked her head round.

'He's awake. He seems to be in pain.'

The girl hurried over, checked his pulse and listened to his chest.

'I'll be back in a few minutes.'

When she had gone, Sadie held his hand tightly between her own and watched him anxiously.

He had opened his eyes now, and was looking at her with growing recognition. Then he realized he was in a strange place, and she saw fear as he took in his bare, white surroundings.

'It's all right, my darling.' She stroked his cheek tenderly with a finger. 'You've been very ill, and Dr Benson brought you here. You're much better now, but you must be very good, and not make a fuss.'

His eyes darkened with the effort to understand her, and faintly she heard, 'Daddy?'

'He was here all night with you. He's having a little rest, then he'll come back.'

'Daddy!' The anguish in the hoarse little cry made her choke.

'All right, my love, we'll get him for you. Only don't cry, don't cry, you must be a very good little boy.'

When Nathaniel arrived, looking haggard from loss of sleep and worry, the child sobbed, clinging to his father's hand with frenzied fingers. He started to cough and they could see him trying to suppress it, to stop the pain it caused. The two adults looked at each other across the bed, wild with despair.

'Oh God,' Sadie whispered. 'What shall we do? What are we going to do?'

Nathaniel was smoothing David's forehead, trying to soothe him.

'It's so cruel,' he muttered. 'Being able to do so little for him.'

The suffering she saw in his face was so intense, she couldn't look at him. The child's sobs were growing fainter, and he hiccuped.

Sadie bent her head until her forehead touched the edge of the bed. Nathaniel leaned over and stroked her hair. 'We've got to keep going,' he said, sharply. 'You can't give up.'

'No. We can't. But if only I could go through this for him – if only it was me, not him.' She was almost whispering. 'He's such a baby, so little, to be hurt like this. My little son.' Her breasts ached for him, and she sat up, wrapping her arms round herself to still the dull throbbing.

After a while the nurse returned, moving with a brisk purpose that Sadie and Nathaniel both found reassuring.

'We'll just give you this, dear,' she said, and lifted David's head against her arm while he painfully swallowed the proffered medicine.

'It's just an opiate,' she said over her shoulder in explanation. 'Dover's powder. Now I'm going to put a hot poultice on his chest – will you wait over there, please?'

As she rose Sadie saw her open the top of David's bedgown. His exposed chest was covered with overlapping cross strips of plaster. Alarmed, she asked what it was for.

'It fixes his chest, and it stops the pain. Dry pleurisy almost always yields to this treatment.'

Standing at the window, Sadie asked Nathaniel, 'Have you talked to Dr Benson since last night?'

'He came in about three hours ago, while David was asleep.' He got out a handkerchief and blew his nose hard to hide his emotion. 'He said dry pleurisy isn't the most serious form of the disease. It's inflammation of the membranes around the lungs.'

Fearfully she asked, 'Did he say how bad it is? What about his fever?'

'That will go soon, and he should be much better in a day or two. The real worry is what effects it might have.'

'But it was that awful cold that caused it.' Desperate to minimize David's state, she clung to this. 'Surely it'll all just clear up?'

'Apparently it may be accompanied by disease in the lung on that side.'

She caught her breath. 'What sort of – disease?'

'He didn't say any more, but he wants to see us both when David's home. By the end of the week he'll be back with us, and then we're to keep him warm and rested.'

'But it might come back.'

'I know. We must trust in God that it won't.'

'God.' Her voice was bitter. 'Four years old, and this happens. What god does that?'

'My love, don't be childish, please. It's hard enough.'

With an effort she pulled herself together. 'I know. Sorry. I think I'll go and get a cup of tea. Have you had one?'

'Not for me, thanks. I was drinking coffee when the nurse fetched me. You go, though.'

As she rose, David said, 'Mummy.'

'Yes, my darling.' She bent closer to him. His eyes were fever bright, the skin stretched like a fine paper over his face. His breath carried the faint, sour smell of illness.

'Mummy, don't be sad. It doesn't hurt, really it doesn't.' His breathing laboured with the effort of making her hear him. 'Mummy. I'll be good. Really I will. I won't cry. Only don't be sad.'

'No, darling.' She sniffed, too overcome to say more, and bit the inside of her cheeks hard to keep herself from crying. At the door she looked back. Nathaniel's head was on the pillow next to David, and he was humming the same song of comfort he had used when he held David as a tiny baby against the hollow of his neck. Her eyes blurred and she fumbled for the door-knob.

Dr Benson sat down heavily. He was a short, dark-haired man with blue eyes: he had once told Sadie his mother was Irish. Normally forceful, he now looked tired.

In response to Sadie's questioning look he shook his head slightly. 'I'm not at all happy with the way he's progressing.'

'But he's much better,' she protested.

'The pleurisy's gone, certainly. At least this time.'

He glanced across at Nathaniel who stood before the fireplace, his empty pipe clenched between his teeth. 'Have you mentioned the possible complications we spoke of?'

Nathaniel shook his head. 'I wanted to leave it to you.'

Dr Benson turned back to Sadie. 'The worry is, you see, that the pleurisy does have a connection with other forms of inflammatory disease within the chest. Pneumonia is one, and a form of bronchitis.' He paused. 'Another is tuberculosis.'

Sadie and Nathaniel watched him as he pressed the tips of his fingers together.

'Sometimes it happens that an attack of pleurisy passes off, as far as we can tell, and then returns. And maybe after several years it is eventually followed by tuberculosis.'

'But not always?' Sadie asked, hardly daring to hear his reply.

When it came, it was scarcely reassuring. 'No, no, of course not. But the risk is there. David's so small, that's the trouble. If he'd been a bit older, even six or seven, he'd have had the stamina to weather this. But at four it's an uphill struggle. Now he's still not eating, and the colds he's had this winter have weakened his chest.' He pursed his lips. 'I don't like to make predictions, as you know, but David's a delicate child. I don't want him to become a permanently sick one.'

363

'What should we do?' Nathaniel spoke with a calmness Sadie knew he did not feel.

'There's only one thing I can suggest.' Dr Benson took out a cigarette case, glancing at Sadie for permission. Nathaniel leant forward and offered him a light, and Dr Benson sat back in his chair. 'There's just one thing that would help. Get him away from Chicago. This place is so damned inclement. I've been here half a lifetime and I've not got used to it. Sub-zero temperatures. Icy winds screaming off Lake Michigan. And the worst thing about it is the way it changes – look at January, 65 degrees one minute and then nearly two foot of snow before the day's out.'

Nathaniel asked, 'Where would we need to take him? And for how long?'

Dr Benson drew on his cigarette, then he glanced at Sadie, who was pleating and smoothing the edge of her dress against her knee. 'The answer to the second part of the question is, for as long as you can afford to. For good, ideally. Just leave Chicago and set up somewhere else.'

Stunned, Sadie asked, 'Where?'

Dr Benson shrugged. 'Why don't you take him some-where like Texas. Or the West Coast. Anywhere that will give him a good deal of sunshine and not expose him to these terrible winters.'

'What about the South of France?'

Sadie looked at Nathaniel in surprise, but Dr Benson considered for a moment and then nodded. 'Why not? Winters can be cold there too, you know, you'd have to watch that. But on the whole I think that should do very well.'

He rose, and collected his case of instruments. 'Anyway, you'll need to talk it over. Let me know if you can arrange something. Then I'll get in touch with someone good in that area for you.' He turned to Sadie. 'And try not to let David see your anxiety. It won't help him to know how worried you are, and it might hinder his recovery. Just treat him as normally as possible.' Sadie nodded and did her best to smile. 'I'll try. Thank you, Doctor.' Nathaniel saw him out. When he returned, he filled his pipe from the leather pouch he always carried and sat down opposite Sadie. Very softly he said, 'Christ.'

She gave him a wan look. 'I think I need a cup of tea.'

'Me too, please.'

When she returned he had a pad on his knee and was making notes. She poured two cups from the silver teapot and added milk to her own, a slice of lemon for Nathaniel.

'What do you think?' Her voice was uncertain.

'There's not too much choice, is there? We'll have to move. The only question is, where to? I think we might prefer the West Coast to Texas.'

'That's a fair assumption.'

'I've always wanted to take you to San Francisco,' he went on. 'And this might be the time to go.'

'Why did you ask about the South of France?'

Slowly, he sipped his tea. 'It's just something I remembered when Dr Benson started talking about climate. We've been approached by Danziger again – d'you remember that hotel we put up for him a couple of years ago?'

'Yes, of course.'

'Well, he's very keen to move into Europe. Claims that more and more Americans are going there, and that the Cote d'Azur in particular is becoming very fashionable. Reckons he'd like to cash in on the popularity, offer them a home from home, as it were.'

'I should think they go there for the French hotels, wouldn't you?'

'Oh, it'd be a French hotel, all right. Just his money and his design.' Nathaniel laughed. 'Or rather, my design. He wants me to take it on for him. He's been after me for months.'

'You haven't mentioned it before.'

He pulled a face. 'What with Alice's wedding and all, I

didn't think much about it. I just told him I'd do the design but that I wouldn't be available to oversee it for him. We'd send someone else. And that's where it's been left – you know how long these things take.'

She looked thoughtful. 'But you *could* accept?'

'Indeed I could. It'd take maybe three years from start to finish, and perhaps longer. Danziger wants me to design everything for it, you see, down to the washbasins. It's a huge task.' He was beginning to get excited. 'The thing is, when I work it out, there doesn't seem to be any reason why I shouldn't do it all over there. I mean, normally I'd see the site, design the building, then we'd appoint a French contractor to oversee most of the work while I sat in the office back here and designed the interiors. But it would be far better to be on site – I'd just have to return here occasionally for conferences and so on, perhaps twice a year.'

She watched him with hope in her eyes. 'So we could go soon. And have at least three years there?'

'Sure we could. The sooner the better.'

She let out a long sigh of relief. 'That's incredible. *You* are incredible.'

Soberly he said, 'Needs must. The important thing is to get David away before February, if we can.'

'Do we sell the house?'

'Not necessary. We'll let it, shall we? Store our stuff and the family will keep an eye on things. That'll give us a small income as well, which will be useful. If I'm working there long term I expect the firm will rent us a villa.'

'It sounds better and better.' She jumped to her feet. 'You go and discuss it, see what they say. And if it's yes, we'll start organizing things in the morning.'

He rose and she slid her arms round his waist. 'One thing I forgot to ask.'

'What?'

'Can you speak a single word of French?'

'As it happens, Mrs Laurence, I was going to keep that as a surprise. I went to night school for a couple of years, when I thought I might want to work in Europe some time. So while I couldn't write you a fluent letter I can certainly carry on a reasonable conversation. Which is one of the reasons I think this plan of ours will work. What about you?'

Indignantly she said, 'Of course I can. Gateau. Camembert. Chanel. All a woman needs to get by.'

He hugged her more tightly. 'First thing we'll do when we get there is find you a teacher. And if you're using a language every day, you'll be sounding like a native in a couple of months.' She grimaced and he grinned. 'Oh, all right. Three months and every other Wednesday off. And if you're able to do the marketing by yourself in four weeks, I'll buy you a Chanel. How's that for an incentive?'

It seemed to Sadie that the next month's events took an inordinate time, but even she had to admit that Danziger could hardly have moved faster. Arrangements were made, meetings held, contracts drawn up – and they were free to go. Only one thing refused to be organized, and anxious as she was for David, Sadie was loath to leave Chicago until it was achieved: Esther's baby was due in six months' time.

'I feel torn in half,' she told Nathaniel, brushing her hair fiercely. 'We must get David away, and yet I can't be so far from Esther. The first baby – what if anything goes wrong?'

From the bed Nathaniel blew a stream of smoke into the air and said calmly, 'I've said it before, my dear, and I'll say it again. Nothing will go wrong – why should it, she's a healthy girl. And Alfred's with her. He'll let us know immediately the child arrives.'

'I suppose you're right. You usually are, God knows.' She watched him in the mirror. 'I like Alfred more and more, you know. He's been helping me organize things here while you were planning at the office. He found the storage people for me, and helped me decide what to take. I'm astonished, he always seemed so vague.'

'He's a very competent young man. Esther's a lucky girl. I hope she appreciates him.'

'Umm.' Sadie absently smoothed cream into her throat. 'I don't know. She's so wrapped up in this baby, and enjoying all the fuss, I don't believe she thinks much about Alfred.'

'She's a fool to herself, then,' Nathaniel stretched and put out his bedside light. 'Come on woman. Stop preening and get yourself over here.'

'It's all very well for you,' she mock-grumbled at him. 'Your lines and crinkles merely add charm. Mine are less advantageous, representing the passing of more years than I care to admit to. But seriously,' she put down the pad of cotton wool she was using, 'can I risk leaving Esther?'

'Can you risk David in this climate for an extra six months? What if he has pleurisy again?'

She shuddered. 'I'm a fool. Let's get away.'

Chapter Twenty-Six

At first they stayed in Cimiez, the ancient village behind Nice. The Hotel Excelsior Regina amused Nathaniel vastly. He would gaze around in mock amazement exclaiming in a voice Sadie sought vainly to quiet, 'Nothing can have changed since Queen Victoria's last visit.' Sadie enjoyed the view of the Baie des Anges and the sound of "*Funiculi, Funicula*' played in the gardens on a sweet street fiddle. After two weeks she began haunting local estate agents and visiting villas to rent. She must have seen twenty before she found the Villa d'Auban, and having come upon it almost by accident, it was as though it had been awaiting them for years.

One of the agents had offered it as an after-thought, noticing a crumpled piece of paper in a half-empty file. He flicked it with a disparaging finger. 'We have also, this. It has been available for some time, I am uncertain as to its condition.'

'What's wrong with it?'

'Nothing at all, merely that the situation is remote. Our clientele,' here he gave her a glance, 'are mostly anxious to be near the *plage*.'

'Could I see it?'

'I will make arrangements to take you to Corbès myself?'

Corbès was barely a hamlet: a clump of stone houses half-hidden from the road, a few scattered farms. The only shop was in the front room of the largest house. Meat and vegetables were brought to the door by the farmers and fish arrived twice a week from Nice on a battered truck. The shop was also the Bureau de Poste, and the only gathering place was the open stretch of ground where, in the evenings, the men played *boules*. Afterwards they would visit the Hôtel des

Voyageurs with its peeling paintwork and rooms redolent of tobacco and cat to drink their evening glass of *anis*. Sadie, as the agent explained all this, took in the hamlet with growing uncertainty. There was no sign of a house in which she wished to live. She was mistaken.

The Villa d'Auban was low, of apricot stone, set secretive behind a high white wall, garlanded with mimosa in spring, laden with laburnum in early summer. Sadie walked through the shaded, dusty rooms. She looked at the sun-faded wooden floors, the pale carved gilt of the age-spotted mirrors. She peered into the stone-flagged kitchen, opened the long windows on to the overgrown courtyard at the centre of the house. She stood in the master bedroom gazing out across the white road, down to the distant sea. There were bay trees in the narrow garden, lemon trees: she imagined how they would smell in the heat of deep summer, and how David would get well.

They took the house.

The three of them lived there in great contentment and with deep delight. As that first summer lengthened and grew somnolent the house filled with scents of the south: wild lavender from the herb-scented foothills around Grasse; their own ripening melons and tomatoes; olives and aubergines simmering on the black iron stove; nectarines and peaches piled in pottery bowls.

In that benign atmosphere David began to recover. Dr Benson had been insistent that they allow him to run around in the minimum of clothing. Where the children of expatriate British and American families wore white dresses and parasols, knickerbocker suits and solar topees, David spent his time in the hot courtyard wearing short trousers and little else. His skin turned golden and his hair bleached to the colour of flax, and despite the heat his appetite became voracious. They watched him thankfully, and the deep pucker of anxiety on Sadie's forehead smoothed away.

The last of their worries vanished when they received a

telephone call late one night from an excited Alfred Lewis: Esther's child had arrived, all was well. He told Sadie that they would call her Sophie, after her maternal grand-mother.

Now Sadie felt free to enjoy herself, and found she wanted to do nothing more exotic in those early days than stroll around Nice and Cannes, charmed by the bustling boule-vards and pavement cafés, the inviting little shops crammed with merchandise. The patisseries were irresistible. Flat open tarts filled with glazed raspberries, redcurrants, or whole apricots were presented under glass counters; feathery *mille-feuilles*; delectable delicacies of chocolate and choux pastry. Then there were the minute boutiques selling nothing but the crystallized fruits in which Nice specialized: plums and peaches, green figs and grapes encased in shells of spun sugar.

Sadie was ravished by the flower market in the Rue Saint-François-de-Paule, where under striped and faded awnings flowers were massed in great wicker baskets, filling the square with their singing colours. She took David there almost every day: they would spend about an hour choosing a small bunch of flowers, then sit outside to drink a *citron pressé*: however often they did it, the pleasure never palled.

Sadie wandered the balmy streets in pale, frothy dresses such as she had never worn before, for this shimmering heat was new to her. Sometimes Nathaniel would take her, in the cool of early evening, to the Promenade des Anglais in Nice. They would stroll past the palatial hotels and watch the comings and goings at the Casino. Then they would visit a café for coffee with *marc*, the crude brandy that made Sadie cough and burnt her throat, but which she loved.

Both Nathaniel and Sadie resisted the encroachment of the outside world in a way they never had before. They had given up reading the newspapers since their arrival, taking only the local English paper, the *Menton and Monte Carlo News*, and this had the effect of distancing them from

America, and turning every day into a holiday. Nor did they particularly want a social life, since neither could bear to be away from David unnecessarily. They soon found that *hivernants* like themselves – those who remained on the Riviera all year – were very much the elite among the American and English who enjoyed merely the winter months there. They discovered, too, that increasing numbers were arriving for the summer. Many came to sail their yachts, more and more took to sea-bathing. The Laurences visited the Grand Hôtel du Cap at Eden-Roc and found the pool thronged with American film people sun-bathing, the lithe girls with bobbed hair and scarlet-tipped fingers daringly clad in loose bathing drawers and brassieres with midriffs clearly visible. Sadie carefully adjusted her shady hat and looked longingly at the lounging bodies.

'We're too old for such dottiness,' she told Nathaniel.

'Nonsense,' he replied comfortably, loosening his shark-skin waistcoat. 'There's not much point in being in this pyjama playground if you don't join in.'

After that, they regularly took David swimming there. Nathaniel was uncertain about sea-bathing, due to the French practice of dumping their rubbish a mile from the shore and he snorted with glee when Sadie reported that she had heard bathers were endangered by octopuses.

The most treasured moments of their day came in the evenings. When Nathaniel arrived home, he and Sadie invariably moved out into the courtyard, damp and pungent after its watering. They sat in low chairs beneath the purpling ribbons of bougainvillaea, speaking about small events, sipping their *pastis*. Above their heads pale plumbago flowers starred the dark wall. Where the days had been brilliant, skies brassy with heat, now darkness released myriads of tiny creatures from their hiding places against the sun. Filmy moths frilled vaguely towards the kitchen window, where Estelle prepared dinner, and bats slanted silently past. Beside the fountain a solitary frog rustled.

It was their private world, and Sadie thought that nothing could touch them.

The years that followed were prosperous. The Laurences became an established part of the American influx on the Riviera. The stars had been holidaying there since the twenties – Gloria Swanson and Charles Chaplin, William Powell and Ronald Colman, all arrived regularly, unaffected by economic hardships at home. As America recovered from the Depression, everyone who could afford it decided the Riviera was the smart place to be, and now the political figures were also in evidence, indulging in what they called 'swimsuit diplomacy'. The demand for hotel accommodation continued to increase.

Nathaniel finished work on Danziger's Hotel, which proved so successful even before it opened with advance bookings that he was asked to design and fit a second one. On the strength of this second commission he took on a local man who had been working for him part-time. Raoul Mabin had been a self-employed builder until a premature heart attack – he was in his mid-thirties – compelled him to stop work for a year, and to give up for good the stresses of running his own business. Mabin, bi-lingual and well educated, became a close friend, and spent many evenings with the Laurences. He was one of the few Jews they had met in France, and Sadie would occasionally make *Shabbes* on a Friday night for his benefit. It was at one of these meals that he asked, idly, why they did not buy the Villa d'Auban.

'I don't know,' Nathaniel had replied, half-surprised at himself. 'We planned to buy in France, but then we rented . . . and we just hadn't got around to it.'

He and Sadie commenced negotiations with the estate owning the Villa d'Auban. Eventually they sold their Chicago home and bought the villa. As Sadie said, 'We can always stay with Esther in Chicago now, and this place suits David.'

In Corbès they were known by everyone as Laurent. Their French had improved immeasurably and Sadie was now more than fluent. They occasionally even discussed whether they ought not to take French citizenship but nothing ever came of the idea, though they felt increasingly at home now in France. Twice Sadie made the journey to England, to see her mother and sisters, and all the family in Chicago came to Corbès for their holidays each year. Alfred and Esther brought little Sophie, and later her two baby brothers; Alice and her husband arrived every summer with, it seemed to the grandparents, another plump and shy toddler. And David continued to improve: the French doctor who now treated him pronounced his progress most satisfactory. But when he was seven years old he caught a heavy cold.

The doctor came on the second day. 'March is a treacherous month,' Sadie said bitterly to Nathaniel as they waited for him to finish examining the boy. Afterwards, Dr Péchin was less than reassuring, telling them they must expect the occasional setback. When, later that year, they visited Chicago and saw Dr Benson, he confirmed what they already knew: that the child would probably always be delicate. But, he added kindly, 'you're doing everything you can. Living where you are has given him the best possible chance. We must just watch him carefully.'

For the whole of that winter they carried the weight of their anxiety round with them. With the coming of the spring of 1936 he picked up again and for almost two years, with periodic check-ups, remained healthy.

One December evening in the winter of 1938 Nathaniel arrived home looking preoccupied. He hardly spoke during dinner and then he told Sadie he planned to attend a lecture at the Hotel Beaulieu in Cannes. 'Nothing much, my dear. I don't think it would interest you. I shan't be late.'

Sadie, who was occupied in making a patchwork cat for

Sophie's birthday, thought no more about it, merely asking how he had enjoyed the lecture and thinking little of his noncommittal mutter.

When his preoccupation had lasted for three days, she became anxious, asking finally, 'Nathaniel, whatever is it? You've hardly said a word for days. Is it the hotel? Are things going badly?'

They were in the middle of dinner. Nathaniel glanced meaningfully towards David, and said airily, 'Oh, I'm just having problems with Danziger. Wretched fellow wants more bathrooms than I've allowed for, and a swimming pool in what he calls an "interesting" shape. I'm sorry, I'll be all right.'

Later, when David had gone to bed, Sadie demanded, 'Well?'

Nathaniel packed more tobacco into his pipe and sighed. 'The lecture the other night made me think about something I'd put out of my mind.'

'What do you mean?'

'It was given by a Dr E. Wightman Ginner. It's the first of a series, and I think I'll go to the rest of them.'

'What are they about?'

Nathaniel lit his pipe, puffing steadily until the tobacco caught, then carefully waving out the match.

'About air-raid precautions. He's based the talks on measures now being introduced in Britain.'

Sadie said slowly, 'I was in London when there were those awful bomber raids. Towards the end of the war, that was. Over a hundred children were killed by a shell falling right through a school in the East End.' She shivered suddenly. 'I hadn't realized things had got so bad. Ma and Flora haven't said anything in their letters.'

'Well, your mother's an old lady, probably people aren't bothering her with it. I don't imagine Flora is too concerned.'

Why are they having the lectures here?' Even as she

asked the question, she knew the answer. 'Does it mean it's all going to happen again? I know there've been rumours, but somehow I thought it'd all blow over.'

'I think,' Nathaniel said, drawing on his pipe, 'that this time we're in for trouble.'

Urgently, Sadie demanded, 'Should we go back to Chicago then? It'd surely be safer there?'

'It's a difficult decision to make.' He got to his feet, and started to wander round the room, fingering pieces of china, touching chairs lightly. 'We're at home here, now, and I honestly don't want to go. We love it, David thrives here – and then there's my job. I'm contracted to do it, and after all, we don't even know anything will happen. We might be worrying for nothing.'

Sadie saw he was pretending an optimism he did not feel. She sighed. 'I don't want to leave either. Only nor do I want to take unnecessary risks. When I think of it, quite a lot of people we know have gone: the Unsdorfers left a month ago. And the Morgans went long before that.'

'Let's see how it goes, shall we?' He came over to her and planted a kiss on top of her hair. 'Don't worry. We'll be all right.'

She essayed a smile. 'Yes. But air raids . . .'

A month later, in January, they heard that in recognition of his achievements in preserving peace, the Place des Iles in Cannes was to be renamed Square Neville Chamberlain. It seemed a good omen.

That March, Germany extinguished Czechoslovakia. Nathaniel now took two newspapers everyday, *The Times* and the *Herald Tribune*.

The following month the Laurences, along with the other inhabitants of Corbès, went down to Nice to see the traditional military parade. At David's insistence they arrived early to see the French tanks and guns rolling past, the precisely drilled soldiers in their navy and red uniforms, the flags and darkly gleaming rifles.

Nathaniel watched in silence. They were sitting at the back of a stand along the route, with an excellent view.

David said excitedly, 'Look at those guns. Aren't they splendid?'

Drily, his father said, 'Splendid. If you're fighting the last war.'

'What do you mean?' Sadie was listening now.

Nathaniel shrugged. 'The equipment may be shining nicely. But look at it properly – it's mostly First World War stuff. There's almost nothing new here. The French haven't updated their army since their last battle.'

He was watching the crowds cheering, and then he turned to Sadie, 'I think I've just seen one man who'd remember First World War weapons. D'you see that Mercedes over there – the black one, parked to the side?'

Sadie looked at the large, highly polished but otherwise anonymous car.

'What about it?'

'Can you see who's in it?'

She peered again, screwing up her eyes against the bright spring sunshine. 'It looks like two people and a chauffeur, doesn't it? Do we know them?'

'That gross figure in the back: I'd heard he was on holiday in San Remo, but I hadn't thought to see him watching this shindig. I believe it's Herman Goering.'

Sadie, to whom the name meant nothing, was unmoved by this information.

That spring of 1939 was more beautiful than any either of them could remember, a soft and subtle prelude to summer. Already they could walk in the fields around the Villa d'Auban and surprise brilliant flights of butterflies like sequins in the grass. Even the palm trees, usually so dusty, were polished by the rain which fell every afternoon for an hour, only to give way to evenings mild enough for them to sit outside until dark.

It was a brilliant summer. The *Menton and Monte Carlo News* called it the gayest on record and the beaches were full of ardent followers of the new sports, trailing the mass of equipment needed for water-skiing and under-water fishing. At night they dined and danced to tunes by Artie Shaw and Jerome Kern, then later moved to the deep throbbing jazz rhythms of Louis Armstrong and Kid Ory. Sadie and Nathaniel took little part in all this, he remarking with some asperity that he had never seen so few people spend so much money, and she agreed. Nonetheless it was a mood she did not entirely escape.

One afternoon Sadie took the Citröen to do some shopping in Cannes, and came back with an elegant grey oblong box, and an abashed expression. 'I don't know what made me do it,' she explained apologetically as she rustled through the tissue paper. She held up a dress for Nathaniel to see. It was the colours of the tricolour, red, white and blue, but so delicately worked – a murmur of blue in the skirt, a glimmer of red on the bodice – that it was almost a reflection of colour.

Nathaniel said, 'It's a gypsy dress. It's beautiful.'

'It's Chanel. It should be. Do you mind? I've never spent so much on a garment in my life. But I won't buy anything else, I promise. I just had to have it.'

'Of course I don't mind. I want you to have pretty frocks. But,' he added, suddenly curious, 'why the intensity? You don't usually get so excited about clothes.'

'I don't know. I just felt I must own this. I think, you know, that it is the last spring when people will dance.'

She wore the dress one strange August night at the *Bal des Petits Lits Blancs* in Cannes. It was the sort of glossy affair they usually avoided, and it was only with reluctance that they decided to go: Nathaniel had invited a colleague from Chicago and his wife, who were agog to see what they described as 'the high life'. The patrons were the Duke and Duchess of Windsor, and Sadie found herself watching them with some pity: the strained, nervously smiling Duke, his glittering Duchess, swathed in white fox, her face set.

Sadie sat out many of the dances, for Nathaniel was in a sombre mood that evening. He slumped, twirling the stem of his glass morosely, hardly speaking. Sadie, sensitive to his feelings, said nothing, but George and his wife tried to jolly him out of it, urging him to dance. Finally George said, 'I don't know, Nat, here you are living the life of Riley and not a word to say for yourself.'

Nathaniel gave a thin smile. 'Sorry, I don't mean to be depressing. But all this . . .' He gestured round him, at the tangoing couples, the expensive wines, the three orchestras, 'seems so trite. So futile, when you think what might happen any day now.'

George was silenced, and Sadie thought, He's right. She remembered the hushed waiting of that distant Bank Holiday in London before war was declared twenty-five years before. This was different, wilder, the last frenzied fling before night came. She felt suddenly very cold.

While the revellers that night were still enjoying themselves in Cannes, Russia and Germany signed a pact of non-aggression. Sadie had a letter from Lena. 'Everything is in chaos here,' she wrote. 'They are sending women and children out of London. I won't go, of course, but Betty and Mother are taking all the children to Brighton. We have all been issued with gas masks. That is the most worrying thing of all. Should you not go back to Chicago? France is in hazard, even more than here.' Sadie received that letter on the first day of September. That evening, they heard the news: Germany had invaded Poland at daybreak.

Two days later, it transpired, Lord Halifax handed a note to the German chargé d'affaires in London. 'Since no German assurances had been received regarding the non violation of Poland's independence,' he wrote, 'I have the honour to inform you that a state of war exists between the two countries as from 11 A.M. today.'

On the morning of 4 September Nathaniel went to work as usual. By lunchtime he was back, ashen with anxiety, to tell Sadie of the reports that a German submarine had attacked the *Athenia*, a British liner on her way to Montreal. One hundred and twelve people lost their lives, and Europe was plunged into war.

Chapter Twenty-Seven

For many months the Laurences, in their fastness at Corbès, were untouched by the distant thunder. They knew that the sons of their neighbours had disappeared into uniform, but for a while there were few other signs of war. Food became more expensive, then clothes. Nathaniel's construction plans for the new hotel were halted because so many of the workmen were called up, and he advised Danziger that it would be better to wait before risking any more money. He and Sadie considered returning home but, reluctant to face Chicago's winter with David, they waited.

In the depths of November the Russians invaded Finland and for three months fought to subjugate that icy country. When spring came there was a breathing space, and Sadie and Nathaniel sighed with relief and thought perhaps they would not return to America just yet. In April the German armies landed simultaneously in Denmark, which they overran in a single day, and Norway. The Laurences planned to leave for Chicago the following week, but two days before their departure David became ill with a high temperature, and they were unable to move him. So again they waited.

Early in May the advancing Germans took Holland in four days and Nathaniel told Sadie, more to still his own fears than hers, 'They say the Ardennes are impassable.' Behind the Ardennes, the French troops were massed in Belgium. On 11 May they heard that the Germans had thrust through the mountains and were forcing back the French army towards France. Nathaniel said, 'We've waited too long. We shall have to stay.' The following day the Germans crossed the Seine: two days later Paris was declared an open city. By late June it was all over. The

German army held France as far south as a line marked by St Jean de Luz, Bordeaux, Clermont Ferrand and Grenoble. Beyond this line France was unoccupied and the government installed itself at Vichy. Nathaniel said, 'I think we shall manage well enough here,' and put the plans for the new hotel into a drawer.

For a few months more they lived quietly, grateful for the little fortress Corbès gave them, perched high above the towns of the coast. Nathaniel did not seem to mind the loss of his work. He was busy round the villa: he did much of the shopping with Sadie, took up his wood-carving again and went fishing with David after school.

Sadie became increasingly aware of the changes occupation was bringing to France. Because petrol was now scarce, people were using sidecars attached to bicycles to form rudimentary taxis. Outside food shops long queues formed to buy meagre quantities on their coupons. Coffee was almost unobtainable and the family in Chicago began to send welcome food parcels. Their cook's powers of invention were tested in the kitchen. Almost the only vegetables available during the winter months were swedes and turnips, and she showed Sadie how to cook the latter with duck, insisting that it was the greatest delicacy in France.

The Laurences found that many people had left the Cote d'Azur. All the English had long gone, either back to England, or, in the case of the elderly and impecunious, to Monaco, to the protection of its frail neutrality. In their place came an influx of French Jews who had fled from Paris and central France as the Germans approached. Their presence made Nathaniel uneasy, and several times he asked Sadie to take David and go back to Chicago. 'After all,' he said, 'David is a Jew because you are one. Neither of you is safe here.' Sadie always refused, confident in the security of her American passport and her Episcopalian husband.

Nathaniel began to form closer friendships with some of the Corbès men, particularly with a farmer who lived above them in the hills. Combarnous was a stocky, taciturn man with calculating eyes. Visiting Madame Combarnous one morning, cautiously evading the geese which ran hissing towards any stranger in the farmyard, Sadie had glanced across a field and seen him sitting in a tree, lopping off the branches with a vicious machete. 'To feed my goats,' Madame had explained. Sadie knew the pretty brown and white flock which grazed in the field around the Villa d'Auban, their wooden bells clanking in the bee-hung silence. She liked to lean in the doorway of the whitewashed dairy, watching Madame stir and strain the curdled goats' milk, moulding the cheeses which she placed to dry on washed vine leaves.

Sometimes, in the evenings, Nathaniel would play *boules* with the village men, and afterwards Combarnous would invite both him and Sadie for a drink. They would be entertained in the kitchen, sitting round the long oil-clothed table on hard, straightbacked chairs, for the Combarnous' life was all work: they rose at dawn and finished at dusk, and there was no time in their day for occupying easy chairs. Nathaniel and Combarnous drank homemade *marc* and conferred in low voices.

Early in July, the Vichy Government broke off relations with Britain, and Sadie became increasingly concerned about her family there. Sophie was now permanently bedridden and, Flora wrote, they could not get her down to the air-raid shelter unless someone carried her. In August they heard on the wireless about the heavy all night bombing raids over London and the terrible death toll. Sadie had a letter from Woolf describing the devastation in the East End which she could hardly bring herself to read.

On the night of 22 December there was an air raid on Manchester. Sadie heard of it over the wireless the following day: what she did not learn until days later was that Flora, hurrying in to Sophie's room on hearing the sirens, had found the old lady beyond waking. She had died quietly in her sleep, Flora wrote, and the end had been easy. 'You are not to worry. I am staying here for the present and when this is all over I will go and find somewhere to live near Miriam.'

Although she had anticipated this for months now, Sadie felt the loss of her mother sharply. Part of herself had gone beyond recall. She experienced wild grief, then guilt. 'I should have been there,' she told Nathaniel. 'I shouldn't have neglected her.' Nathaniel, sensing her need for self-recrimination, did not argue. One effect of the news was to rouse in them both an anger nothing previously had kindled.

One afternoon they travelled into Nice by bus, to conserve what little petrol they had. Sadie was staring out of the window, watching the road without seeing it. On an impulse she turned to Nathaniel, trying to make herself heard above the rattle of the bus.

'There must be something we can do. We can't live in the middle of this and not take some part. America isn't at war with Germany, no one's bothering about us. What can we *do*?'

Nathaniel glanced round at the elderly women in the seat behind them and pressed her arm for silence. When they reached Nice they got off near the harbour and seated themselves on the stone wall behind which the rowing boats were beached in neat rows. Nathaniel knocked the tobacco out of his pipe and cleaned the bowl before packing it freshly from his leather pouch. He puffed a few times to make sure it was well alight before he spoke. 'Are you serious? About doing something in this wretched war?'

'You know I am.'

'Well, my dear, I am doing what I can. And now I want to involve you.'

'*Nathaniel*! What have you been doing?' She took his hand. 'Is this why you've been out so much?'

'It was Mabin who started it, really. I met some of his friends, Jews from Paris who'd fled from the Germans. They knew they hadn't gone far enough, that they needed to leave France. But you can see how difficult it is to get away now.' He shrugged and added simply, 'So I've been trying to help.'

'*How*?'

He laughed and pulled her back down on the wall beside him. 'Don't stand there looking petrified, woman. My native caution hasn't deserted me. These people need money. With money you can bribe people, acquire papers. So – I've been providing it.'

'But how do you get it?'

'I've got quite a nice little organization going: I'm rather proud of it. The money comes through my bank here, just as it's always done, only considerably more of it.'

Puzzled, Sadie asked, 'Is it yours?'

'No, these are hefty sums. The money originates from American Jews who want to help, and Danziger funnels it through the hotel account.'

'But don't you have to explain the sudden increase? Especially as there's no building going on just now?'

He held up his right hand, the first and second fingers crossed. 'No one's asked about it yet. They will, I expect, and I shall claim that I'm planning to start construction work here on my own behalf as soon as it's possible. I've got plans all ready for a hotel, and Danziger has agreed to let me buy a site in his name, if it should be necessary.' He banged her hand gently up and down on the stones. 'I've been lucky. I've done everything in the simplest possible way. No subterfuge at all. It's been so obvious, no one's noticed.'

'And what do you do with the money?'

'Mabin's friends need contacts, and they don't know who

to get in touch with if they do manage to get out of France. Sometimes they need fresh papers. I arrange things for them. With help, of course. The best man I've found is Combarnous.'

'*Combarnous*?'

'He's lived here all his life, he knows everyone. I get the money to him, and he provides the papers for me.'

She put her arms round his neck.

'But the risks.'

'Yes. The Milice are the worst.'

'They're the new French security police, aren't they?'

'Right. And they're bastards. Combarnous says they'd hand over anyone they caught without question to the Vichy authorities, who turn them over to the Germans.'

Slowly she said, 'You don't have to do this.'

'I've got a Jewish wife and son, haven't I? What better reason could I have? Though God knows what I think I'm doing, sending the wives and children of other men to safety and letting my own stay in an occupied country. I only wish you would listen to me and go.'

Sadie ignored the often-repeated plea and asked, genuinely bewildered, 'Why did you never tell me? I would have helped you.'

'I know you would. Only this was the one way I could protect you. If anything had happened to me, then total ignorance might have helped you.'

They sat there for a long time, before the chill drove them away. Sadie felt as if she were looking at a man she had never before known. Through the years of marriage her real affection for him had strengthened, deepened. She both liked and admired Nathaniel, but now she sensed in him reserves of will power and determination she had never suspected. In his late sixties he was undertaking hazards that would daunt a man in the prime of life. She thought, he's been doing this for months now, and I never knew.

And the love and gratitude she experienced for him overwhelmed her.

After that the Laurences divided the risk between them. Sadie started to lead a busy social life, making many new acquaintances among the Jews in the area, where she would drop in for a cup of coffee. Money and documents, she found, fitted easily into packets of dress patterns when she lent them to other women.

Then one afternoon in the May of 1941 Sadie came home after such a visit to find Nathaniel pacing the floor, an empty pipe clenched between his teeth, white with anxiety: David had not come home. The boy arrived two hours later, casual, unconcerned. He had stopped off with Maurice and a couple of others for a chat, was something wrong? When he had gone to bed that night, Nathaniel told Sadie that he wanted her to take their son back to Chicago.

'Please. Don't argue. Just go. I tell you, when I thought something had happened to David, something I didn't know about, I felt I was going mad. No . . .' He gestured for her not to interrupt. 'It's too dangerous here, I should never have involved you. You know as well as I do what we've been hearing these last months about Jews being deported and massacred in Russia, about the mass arrests in Germany. What if it starts to happen here? We're in France, for God's sake, almost the whole country's over-run. I'll never forgive myself if anything happens to you.'

Sadie sat down, heavily, 'What have you heard?'

'Mabin just learnt of Polish Jews being arrested, more than three thousand of them, all naturalized Polish citizens. It could be happening here next, to French citizens. Jews are not safe anywhere now.'

'But no one knows I'm Jewish here. You're not Jewish, we're both American citizens. Nothing will happen to me.'

Exasperated, Nathaniel spoke with unaccustomed sharpness.

387

'Don't be a fool, Sadie. For one thing, you look Jewish. And apart from anything else, there's a famous portrait of you, remember – "Mrs Asher Raphael". You can't sound more Jewish than that.'

'But I don't look like that any more, no one will recognize me. We'll say – I don't know – that I have a Spanish grandmother. That'll account for the way I look. Nathaniel, I tell you, I'm not leaving you, and that's all there is to it. I'm not stopping what we're doing, it's too important.'

They argued for nearly an hour, and finally Nathaniel acquiesced in the face of her determination. But on one point he would not yield.

'We must get David away. He's got his life to live. We can't expose him to danger any longer.'

Reluctantly she said, 'You're right. We should have sent him back to Chicago before.'

The following morning Nathaniel contacted the American Vice Consul in Lyons. It was arranged that David should be sent back to Chicago in the company of the wife of an American embassy official. They would not know until a few hours before when the flight would be.

Sadie and Nathaniel viewed his going with a good deal of pain but David, at fourteen, already competent enough to handle the situation, was elated by the prospect of change. In the event, they had only six hours' notice of his journey.

'And keep warm,' Sadie warned him as they waited in the makeshift departure lounge at the small airport outside Nice.

'Mum, I know . . .'

'Promise!'

'All right, I promise.' He winked, a conspiratorial, masculine signal to Nathaniel. Sadie laughed and thumped him lightly on the chest. Already he was nearly as tall as she.

'Don't you go thinking you can pull the wool over my eyes, young feller-me-lad. I have spies everywhere. And do what Esther and Alfred say, won't you? We'll be there as soon as we can.' She stopped talking, longing to hug him, knowing how self-conscious he had become about public displays of affection. To her surprise, he flung his arms around both of them, squeezing them hard, unable to speak. Then he took his case, slid a hand in his jacket to check his passport and ticket, and hurried to the departure doors.

For six more months Sadie and Nathaniel quietly went about their self-appointed task, discreetly avoiding too much discussion about their son, who had ostensibly returned to Chicago for his schooling.

Early in December Nathaniel returned home as Sadie was preparing to go to bed. He told her that the Japanese had attacked Pearl Harbor, with dreadful casualties; he feared that America was now committed.

She had been removing her jacket as he spoke and now she halted, her arms still in the sleeves.

'What will happen to us then?'

He shook his head. 'Who knows? As American citizens, I imagine we'll be under some sort of detention?'

'Here? In the villa?'

'That's unlikely, I would think. Most probably they'll put us in that camp for the British near Grenoble.'

Sadie sat down very suddenly.

'But that's . . . We can't.'

His face was grim.

'Don't you believe it. We can, and we almost certainly will.'

'Isn't there anything else we can do? We might be separated.'

'Or worse.' He sat on the edge of the bed beside her, and they put their arms around each other.

'We've got one chance, but it carries risks of its own. Do you want me to get false papers? I've been talking with

Mabin. He suggests that we work up a story that fits in with our accents, which he says,' Nathaniel smiled despite himself, 'are somewhat *singulier*.'

Sadie, amused by the affectionate mimicry, asked with hope, 'What sort of story?'

'One that more or less fits the facts. That we both come from French backgrounds: my parents took me to the States from Toulouse as a small child, and your father was a textile worker who went to the north of England when you were only a baby. Then both our lives can be told exactly as they happened, except that when we got the chance we both returned to our native country, ten years ago, so we could retire here.'

After a moment's thought she said, 'It sounds convincing enough. What will we need?'

'Apart from documentation – no problem there, the mayor of Nice supplied all the British who stayed – we require only the ability to pass ourselves off as French under ordinary circumstances. Anyone checking on us casually should be convinced, and with luck we won't excite too much interest. Anyway, we're still in the *zone libre*. We should be all right for a while.'

She shivered. 'It's a big step to take.'

'I know. But one good thing is that the story will fit in with everything people here know about us. Except for Combarnous, and we know he won't be talking. Mabin will supply all the little details – street numbers, grandparents' names, you know the sort of thing that makes a story convincing, just in case.'

'Just in case.' She echoed his words as she went across to her dressing table. The woman who looked back at her was tired and drained, her skin washed of its colour by worry. She watched the reflection of Nathaniel in her glass and smoothed her hair. 'Oh well,' she said, forcing lightness into her voice, 'in for a penny, in for a pound.'

Their false identity papers came through a few days after

America entered the war. They were in the name of Laurent, by which Nathaniel and Sadie had long been known locally. For several hours they sat at the kitchen table, the documents spread out before them, familiarizing themselves with the new details. There was the buff *carte d'identité*, fingerprints in the top right hand corner; the *autorisation de circuler* branded across in red, with details of their motor; the *permis de conduire les automobiles*, the pink card bearing the same photograph as the identity card. Carefully they checked the recorded facts: *titulaire, departement, profession, domicile, taille, cheveux, moustache, yeux*. Satisfied at last, Nathaniel wrapped all their American documents carefully in oiled brown paper and placed them in a tea caddy. He sealed the lid with hot wax and later, when it was almost dark, buried the container beneath the small palm tree in the garden.

For the early part of 1942 they carried on their activities, though with increased anxiety. This was mainly due to the issuing, by Himmler, of the *Nachy und Nebel* decree. Where in the past any offences against the occupying German forces were punished with hard labour, this was now considered a sign of weakness. The only effective deterrent, which the SS practised, was death. Those caught were transported secretly and without trace to Germany; no information was given to the family.

Nathaniel asked Sadie, 'Do you want to go on? The Germans aren't here, it's true, but this will make the Milice more active than ever. And we're involved now: we're not bystanders any more.'

'What do you think we should do?'

'I can't take this decision for you. I wish I could. I want to continue: it's all the fighting I can do. But you need not take all these risks.'

She was making a blouse on her old treadle machine, and she let the material slip through her fingers while she reflected. 'I don't want to take unnecessary risks,' she

answered slowly, 'because of David. He's my main
responsibility. But he's well looked after: there's all your
family, as well as Esther and Alfred. And the people we're
helping are completely defenceless. Perhaps we really can
make the difference between life and death for them.'

Nathaniel watched her as she bent over the machine, and
pressed the needle down on a new seam.

'So,' she went on, 'I don't see that there's really a choice.
If one person is saved from death because we took a
chance, then that would be justification enough.' She
paused, and swore to herself as the thread pulled taut and
snapped. When she had re-threaded the machine she gave
Nathaniel a sudden glance of affection. 'And anyway,' she
finished, 'if you're going on, then so am I. What happens to
you happens to me.'

Throughout the spring and summer they continued to
pass their unofficial packages to Mabin's contacts. Then,
one hot July day, they drove the Citröen into Cannes and
bought red mullet fresh from the nets to be grilled on a bed
of dried fennel branches from the garden. In the flower
market, far smaller than usual, they chose some flowers for
old Madame Brusset, ailing and dispiritied since her son
had been taken into the German army. 'He's fighting and
killing in a German uniform,' she had whispered to Sadie.
'I'm ashamed, ashamed. His father died fighting the
Germans last time, and now look at his son.' She had
rocked herself in her misery, sitting outside her front door,
her face stiff in its rejection of her only child. Sadie thought
the flowers might please her and she carried them carefully
back to the Citröen. As Nathaniel turned out of the square,
into the deserted avenue, a vehicle travelling the other way
hooted at them, and stopped.

'It's Mabin.' Nathaniel drew to a halt and got out
hurriedly. Always a tired-looking man, with his deep set
eyes and thinning curly hair, Mabin now looked drawn and

haggard. He and Nathaniel talked for a moment, then walked across to Mabin's Renault. In the passenger seat an elderly woman sat, her eyes closed. Sadié joined them. Something was evidently wrong.

'I don't believe you've met my mother,' Mabin said.

The elderly woman looked at Sadie and nodded. She had obviously been crying. On the back seat were rugs and cushions.

Nathaniel said, anxiously, 'I wish you wouldn't go. I fear for you.'

Mabin shrugged.

'There is no question. We must. We could not live with ourselves not knowing what had happened. And who else could try to find them?'

Sadie said, 'What's happened? Where are you going?'

Mabin pushed a narrow hand through his hair, dragging back the skin of his face in a gesture of great weariness. 'Something terrible has happened in Paris: we scarcely know what. It seems that three days ago the Germans rounded up hundreds of people – thousands – and herded them into the Vélodrome d'Hiver.'

His mother said, in a low voice, 'Children. Almost all children. And their mothers.'

'Jews?' Sadie asked.

Madame Mabin could only nod.

'Can it be true? How do you know?'

'Oh, it's true,' Mabin answered. 'My cousin sent a message with a driver who brought a consignment from the building depot in Neuilly. But it was very garbled, we scarcely know what to make of it. It seems that my sister and her two children were taken. No one knows where her husband is.'

'But that's unbelievable. In *Paris*, how could they do such a thing? That stadium is open, there can't be any water for them.'

Mabin shook his head. 'We dare not think what might be

waiting for them. But if we make it to Paris we may not be too late.' He touched Sadie and Nathaniel lightly on the shoulders and got back into the driving seat. Nathaniel went round with him and asked a question. Mabin answered so low that Sadie caught only one word: *Drancy*.

When they had gone, and Nathaniel and Sadie were silently returning home, Sadie asked, 'What is Drancy?'

Without turning his head, Nathaniel said, 'It's a camp at Le Bourget. It's the assembly point for the concentration camp at Auschwitz. Mabin says there are rumours . . .'

'My God.'

When they reached the villa, they gave the red mullet to Estelle the cook and sent her home early. Then they sat in the courtyard for hours and talked.

It was several days before they heard anything from Mabin. He arrived back in Cannes with his mother, and Nathaniel went to see them as soon as he learnt of their return. It seemed, he reported to Sadie, that they had only been able to get as far as the outskirts of Paris. They had gone to the house of a friend and discovered that they were too late. The Vélodrome had been emptied. On the fifth day the mothers had been taken and then, later, the children were sent to Auschwitz. Apparently, said Nathaniel, his voice completely without emotion, there had been no food at any time, and almost no water. People had gone mad inside that stadium, and many pregnant women bore their babies lying on the ground. And then, Nathaniel added, those children, alone, terrified, had been pushed on to trains . . . Four thousand children . . .

For a very long time, when he had finished telling her all this, Sadie sat silent. She became aware that she was rocking forward and back, forward and back. Like old Madame Brusset. Like her own mother.

It took the Laurences three weeks to make new plans. At four o'clock one morning they set off in the Combarnous' rickety van. Nathaniel wore shabby trousers and one of Combarnous' more disreputable jackets, and Sadie had borrowed from Estelle a grey dress and a scarf which she wound round her head. Both wore espadrilles. Under the dashboard, muzzled and mutinous, curled the farm's Alsatian, an animal Sadie particularly disliked, the more so since she was occupying his preferred seat, and he clearly expressed his displeasure. 'He'll convince any interfering bloody *flics*,' Combarnous had remarked cheerfully as he shoved the dog in, 'to leave well enough alone.' In the back of the van were piled baskets of eggs and vegetables held firm with piles of sacking.

'Here are your papers,' Combarnous had said, leaning in at the window, 'all the necessary permissions for your deliveries. Now I'm going to be sick in bed all day as an alibi, and it'll be the first rest I've had for years.' He grinned at them. 'As delivery men you are *magnifique. Bonne chance.*'

Nathaniel pointed the van towards the Marseilles road. Before he reached it, they stopped once.

When they arrived in Montpellier it was lunchtime and the roads were thronged with factory workers on bicycles making their way home for lunch. Nathaniel parked on the Rue Bousairolles. He and Sadie sat silent for a moment, then he spoke loudly.

'We're about three minutes' walk from the hotel. We'll check first, then I'll return alone to collect you. I'm leaving the dog here – he's muzzled, don't worry. When I get back I'll be humming *Frère Jacques*, so if anyone else attempts to open the back, don't move.'

A man's voice replied softly from under the sacking, '*Bien.*'

Nathaniel locked the van and took Sadie's arm. They walked down the street and crossed by a *boucherie chevaline*. The façade of the Hôtel de Paris was uninviting; peeling paintwork and decayed wrought iron. Above narrow balconies torn awnings flapped. Inside it was little better. Beneath a glass roof the reception hall was dingy, thronged with moth-eaten chairs in which no one sat. At a desk in the entrance, screened by ornate scrolled glass, sat an elderly woman in black with a white peasant scarf over her head. Nathaniel moved towards her.

'Madame la Patronne? *Vous permettez* – I have some eggs for you and two parcels which I believe you are expecting. From Hippolyte.'

The woman regarded him with an expressionless face. '*Vraiment.*'

Nathaniel added, speaking very distinctly, '*Pour l'anniversaire.*'

She gave him a brusque nod.

'*D'accord.*'

Relieved, he answered, '*Merci, Madame.*'

Motioning Sadie to wait, he hurried out. The hotel seemed deserted. Flies buzzed lazily in the dusty air and from the street she could hear women hurrying past, their wooden soled shoes clacking on the pavement, their voices strident. Madame Pirie smiled at Sadie, but did not speak.

Five minutes passed, six, then Nathaniel entered. He was carrying a box of eggs. Behind him came a young couple, also carrying large boxes containing vegetables. They seemed exhausted, their clothes crumpled. They did not look at Sadie. Madame Pirie greeted them formally. When they had put down their boxes, she pushed the hotel register towards them and gestured for them to sign. The man looked at her questioningly. '*C'est bon,*' she said firmly. 'I will provide documentation to go with the signature. It is all taken care of. Now I will show you to your room.'

Sadie and Nathaniel waited while they ascended the stairs to a long gallery and disappeared from view. When Madame Pirie returned Nathaniel asked, 'Is there anything else for us to do?'

'I think not. Be careful. The Vichy police are everywhere and where they are not, they have eyes.' She held out her hand. '*Au revoir.* I will see you again.'

Back in the sunshine, the Laurences looked at each other with relief.

'I hope they're all right.'

'Now what happens to them?'

'They'll be collected some time within the next twenty-four hours and taken on to Narbonne. After that, they may have to walk, though with luck there'll be a boat.'

'I wonder how long they'll be safe in Spain.'

'God knows. I keep thinking this business can't go on for ever, but it seems to be doing just that.' He stopped by the car. 'Right. Now before we start back, I think we've earned ourselves lunch. Let's find somewhere shabby enough to accommodate us.'

Early in November the Germans broke their armistice with the French and seized unoccupied France. The Vichy government was obliterated and soldiers poured down into the South. Sadie and Nathaniel, driving into Antibes before any troops arrived, passed through deserted streets. Food shops were almost empty. In a motor showroom Nathaniel pointed to two highly polished cars. A maroon Bentley and a cream Rolls Royce stood in isolated splendour, each bearing a GB plate, obviously sold in a panic as their owners fled home.

Within days, Italian troops had been brought up from beyond Menton, and for the first time Sadie and Nathaniel, and their French friends, knew what it was to live in a defeated and occupied country. Homes were requisitioned for their use, and dispossessed families left to fend for themselves. Dark green uniforms were everywhere: in the streets and government offices, in cinemas and parks.

Nathaniel said to Sadie, 'Well, one good thing about the Italians – they don't seem so keen to harass the Jews as the Vichy police were. Thank God for that.'

Among them were the first German personnel to travel beyond Vichy. Officers, mainly, taut and military in their black and grey, whose staff cars commandeered the centre of the roads, and whose quarters were in the best hotels. They frequented the casinos, and after a while, Nathaniel observed caustically, their money appeared to be most acceptable.

One afternoon, when Sadie was in the kitchen with Estelle, the bell rang. The two women exchanged a glance, then Sadie slowly took off her apron and went across the courtyard. When she opened the outer door, she had a shock. The man who stood there was an Italian soldier. He handed her an envelope, saluted and remounted his motorbike. She watched him roar off down the hill before returning to the kitchen. The envelope was addressed to Nathaniel. She put it on the mantelpiece and she and Estelle carried on working in silence.

When Nathaniel arrived, she hurried to him with the letter. He opened it, then relaxed. 'It's what I'd been hoping for. An invitation to dinner. Tomorrow night. Is that all right?'

'Why the mystery? And why the soldier delivering it?'

'The invitation,' said Nathaniel thoughtfully, 'is from a man I met a couple of nights ago at the Casino. While you were talking to the Girards. It seems he'd like to get to know us better. The thing is, my dear, you'll have to be very discreet. He's a German officer.'

Sadie felt as though he had slapped her. Nathaniel said mildly, 'Don't look so amazed. They're all over the place, after all. And this fellow is really rather nice. He's an architect, and you know how keen I am on Gropius.'

'For God's sake.' Sadie's voice was bitter. 'What are you talking about? Are you suggesting we should associate with a Nazi because he's really a kindred spirit?'

Nathaniel looked at her without answering. Just then Estelle knocked on the door, called '*Bonne nuit*' and hurried out to her bicycle. When the house was quiet, Nathaniel spoke gently, 'Can you think of a better cover for us than

398

friendship with the enemy?'

So the Laurences went to the Hotel Negresco, and in its opulent eighteenth-century interior, beneath the chandeliers hung with bunches of glass grapes, they awaited *Oberleutnant zurzee* Richard Scherrer. He greeted them with a tense formality. Sadie felt so self-conscious that she could hardly look at him, aware that many eyes were watching this overt act of collaboration. She and Nathaniel had discussed the wisdom of making this so public and dangerous a gesture.

'I think we must,' he had decided. 'If we're to go on with this, the more like *collaborateurs* we look, the easier it'll be for us. The people who matter know what we're up to.'

'That's all very well,' Sadie had argued. 'But the dangers of conversing for a whole evening with a German officer . . . Dare we take such a risk? Would it be better for you to go alone?'

'That really would look suspicious. This man's in military intelligence, he's not out looking for Jews. And as for conversing, we'll be talking English.'

'*What?*'

'Don't panic. He knows no French. We have no German: I was actually introduced to him because I speak English. We've already been over all that stuff about my being educated in the States.'

'Did he seem suspicious?'

'Not at all. He was interested but not surprised.'

Sadie had relaxed slightly.

'Well, I suppose we could chance just this one evening.' In the event, her initial nervousness made conversation difficult. *Oberleutnant zurzee* Scherrer spoke excellent, if stilted, English.

When they had ordered, he turned to Sadie.

'I am so very pleased, Madam Laurent, that you and your husband were able to come tonight. Military conversation leaves much to be desired.'

'We . . . were happy to come.'

'Your husband told me that you also spoke good English. If I may say so, he did you less than justice.'

Sadie felt Nathaniel's knee press her own in reassurance beneath the table.

Smoothly she answered, as they had rehearsed, 'I spent much of my life in England, *Oberleutnant*. My first husband ran an art gallery in London.'

'So? And which painters did he exhibit?'

While she answered, Sadie studied him for the first time. He was not at all her idea of a naval lieutenant. He was rather taller than Nathaniel and somewhat stooped, in the way of a man accustomed to spend long hours reading. His aquiline nose was emphasized by the thinness of his face and he was losing his hair. When he noticed her glance he smoothed it self-consciously and she saw that his hands were beautiful, narrow and strong, with the spreading, spatulate fingertips of an artist. His physical appearance she found totally at odds with the uniform of formal white tunic over blue-black trousers which he wore. Apart from the brass buttons and sleeve stripes the tunic was plain and oddly familiar. With a slight start Sadie recognized it as almost identical to that of the British Navy. Even the cap on the chair beside him, with its white tropical cover, was similar to the one she knew except that the front rose high like German army caps. The badge was the eagle spread above the swastika and she noticed also a little white disc with red on it, surrounded with gold oak leaves.

Aware of her scrutiny the *Oberleutnant* ran a finger round his collar and said, half under his breath, 'I find uniform a trifle constricting. I must be too old for it.'

Nathaniel asked politely, 'Have you been wearing it long?'

'For two years now.'

'Might one enquire how you came into the naval intelligence?'

The *Oberleutnant* shrugged slightly. 'During the last war

400

I served as midshipman in the U-boats. I was brought into the *Abwehr* because Admiral Canaris wanted men here with Italian. I learnt mine in Florence, where I spent several years. So I liaise between the Italian troops and military intelligence. Officially I am attached to the Italian army.'

Curious, Nathaniel asked, 'What were you doing in Florence?'

'I was studying under Pier Luigi Nervi.'

'No!' Excitedly Nathaniel told Sadie, 'Nervi is *the* concrete engineer architect, absolutely the best.' He turned back to the German. 'Tell me about your work, what you were doing,' he gestured towards the man's uniform, 'before all this.'

There was a long silence. Then the German said, heavily, 'Nothing.' Abruptly he changed the subject, questioning Nathaniel about the problems of life in the area. Nonetheless, before the evening was over the Laurences learned a good deal about *Oberleutnant zurzee* Richard Scherrer. He was in his late forties, a native of Leipzig, where he lived with his wife and three children. He looked older than his years, he ate sparingly and – Sadie alone noticed this – he surreptitiously slipped a small tablet into his mouth when the meal was finished. For his part, he knew they were comfortably middle-class, well-travelled. Much like his own friends. He knew, too, that he had not spent so pleasant an evening for many months. He despised the situation in which he found himself, that of the invader. He had visited France before, on his honeymoon; he knew England slightly. He had colleagues in the United States and before the war broke out he had been planning a trip there to see the work of American architects, particularly Frank Lloyd Wright.

Now he found that just to talk of work again was a rare pleasure: by the time they were taking brandy he and Nathaniel were well into an argument about the elaboration of the Continental modern style. When the bill arrived he continued talking, patting all his pockets absent-mindedly. Finally he found his glasses, put them on and carefully checked the figures. When he said goodnight to them, formal and courteous, outside the hotel, he raised his hand. It could have been '*Heil* Hitler.' Or merely the brushing of his fingers to the brim of his cap.

Driving home, Sadie asked, 'Do you think it will work?'

'Of course it will.' Nathaniel reached for her hand in the darkness.

'I'd like to wait a couple of weeks, then we'll ask him to have dinner with us, at home. Before we do, I want to get the new housekeeper settled.'

She glanced across at him. 'Is that wise?'

'I hope so. Time's running out. I collected the documents this morning.'

'I'll miss Estelle.'

'I know. But it really is getting too much for her, the house and the journey on her bicycle. She says she's ready to leave as soon as we've replaced her. Will you tell her tomorrow? And we'll need to get a couple of rooms ready for the Meyers.'

Three days later Nathaniel collected Georges and Arlette Meyer and their small daughter from Combarnous' farm. They had been brought up to Corbès in his van with the empty vegetable baskets. While Sadie made coffee they all sat round the long kitchen table and Nathaniel dealt out their documents like so many playing cards.

'Identity card, work permit, tobacco card . . . Here's your medical certificate, Monsieur. We've had to make you an epileptic, I'm afraid, but if it keeps you out of forced labour in Germany it'll be worth it. And I've a driving licence for you also.'

Madame Meyer, a plump, talkative woman, broke into rapid French.

'*Monsieur, Madame, quelle gentilesse, quel courage . . .*'

Sadie patted her shoulder, watching the child gaze round the strange room. She opened her last tin of American candy and offered one to the little girl, who glanced at her mother for permission. Nathaniel was talking quietly to the husband.

'So you'll stay with us for a few months. You'll need to do some work around the garden, and perhaps help your wife in the house: keep busy, that's the thing. Everyone in Corbès knows Estelle has not been well, so no one is suspicious. Then we'll see about moving you on to Spain. I've got contacts there, families who will take you in until all this is over.'

The man nodded.

'Anything. We'll do anything we have to.'

'There's just one thing,' Nathaniel continued. 'We should warn you that we occasionally entertain a German officer. Only one, at the moment. This is done for all our protection, so try to be as normal as possible when he's here. The chances are that he will not notice you at all. If he says anything, just answer pleasantly. We'll take care of the rest.'

The couple nodded, and Sadie took them up to their rooms. When they had gone, Nathaniel gave Sadie a hug.

'We're lucky. They don't look noticeably Jewish, and the child's being blonde helps. If we can get them safely out of France in two months or so, we'll have done at least one thing to be proud of. And Madame Meyer is a superb cook: even with food the way it is at the moment, it'll be a recompense.'

Sadie laughed, and pretended that her hands would not meet round his back. Nathaniel had thickened appreciably over the last year, and his corpulence was a source of concern to him.

'That's what I like,' she said, putting her head against his chest.

'What do you like?'

'Men who are short and fat and heroic.'

'Like Napoleon.'

Judiciously she said, 'Mmm. I was thinking more along the lines of Donald Duck.'

'All right,' he mock-grumbled. 'I can take a hint. So I won't eat. I'll just sit and watch you, and pine away, like Augustus. Then you'll be sorry.'

She hugged him suddenly, fiercely.

'Don't do *anything* silly. Be careful.'

He caught her hand, turned it over and kissed the wrist.

'I will. *We* will.'

Over the next year they saw a good deal of Richard Scherrer. He took to coming to the Villa d'Auban once a week to dine, and would reciprocate by inviting them out in Nice, to one of the many restaurants which still managed to flourish with the aid of the black market. On one occasion, when he felt they knew each other well enough, Nathaniel returned to the question which had silenced Scherrer at their first dinner, and asked him why he did not practise as an architect. Scherrer thought for a long time before replying.

'Since *Hitlerzeit* I have not been permitted.' He gave a mirthless, barking laugh. 'I am suspect because of my training in Florence. That, combined with my well-known interest in Bauhaus, made me ideologically unsound.'

'Then . . . what have you been doing all this time?'

Scherrer's face hardened. 'I worked as a technician, merely. A draughtsman, copying the drawings of others.' He gave a bitter smile. 'So I was not displeased to find myself in the Navy once more, as you may imagine.'

Hesitantly, he asked, 'But what about your . . . affiliations, now? Don't they mind?'

'But no. As an architect I would not have been representative of the true, pure, Aryan spirit. As an Italian speaking sailor I am useful.'

'And what do you feel, doing such work?' Nathaniel's tone was sympathetic and Scherrer responded to it, his voice dropping.

'I should prefer not to be here at all. Since I cannot escape involvement, I would rather serve under Admiral Canaris than anyone else. He is a man of principle, a professional among opportunists.'

Nathaniel nodded his understanding and Scherrer went on, speaking hesitantly, as though compelled by his loneliness to answer the other man's unspoken questions. 'One of the reasons I made myself available to the Navy was that as a serving man I do not have to belong to any political party. Do you take my meaning?' He watched them both for their reaction and went on, 'The majority of Germans will succumb to pressure, sooner or later. They will all wear in their lapels the emblem of the Nazi Party.' He raised his hands, palms out, in a gesture of resignation, of regret. 'They join not because of their convictions, but because they have none.'

Sadie found she was almost whispering. 'But there must be many Germans who think as you do. Why then do they join? Don't they know what is happening? Haven't they heard of . . .' Out of the corner of her eye she saw Nathaniel make an involuntary movement of warning. She stopped speaking.

Scherrer nodded slowly, acknowledging what he knew she had been about to say.

'You would be wrong to suppose there is no opposition to what is happening in Germany. There are individuals, little groups, there are civilians and military men.' He lifted his shoulders expressively. 'But one cannot imagine what they will achieve against such odds.'

They were sitting in the courtyard before dinner, savouring the warmth trapped by the stones. Nathaniel was carving yet another toy for his granddaughter. Sadie was sewing, her fingers swift among the patches of bright fabric.

Watching them, the German felt a great and irretrievable sadness flood through him: it had been years since he had sat so, in his own home with his wife beside him. Even if he could return to Leipzig tomorrow he and Inge had lost those years beyond recall. He made an involuntary sound of protest at the thought and got up quickly to hide it, moving across to examine a vine clinging to the wall.

Richard Scherrer was a man who needed the stability of his family and his work. Over the last nine years this security had been eroded. He had been a successful architect until he was forbidden to produce any original work, and he saw his less talented but more acceptable colleagues promoted over his head. Then the outbreak of war had taken him from Leipzig and his roots. He had nothing with which to replace them: he did not believe in what he was so reluctantly fighting for. He found it difficult to recall that as a young man he had served in another war, had upheld the right of his country. But he had learned to be cautious in all his actions – the years of Nazi regime had taught him that – and he carefully hid his growing conviction that Germany deserved to be defeated. He carried out his duties with resignation and withdrew into himself as much as he could. He knew he was becoming increasingly nervous; he suffered badly from indigestion and found it hard to sleep. Never a violent man, his dreams were ferociously violent, and in them he was always the pursued, the hunted.

Scherrer had an acute mind. Well-read, well-travelled, highly literate, he had no illusions about his nature. He wanted desperately to unburden himself but there was no one to whom he could speak, no friend to turn to. He could not even hint of his state to his wife. To her, struggling with her own loneliness and ill-health, he was unfailingly encouraging. He knew he was behaving like a fool in seeking the company of Nathaniel and Sadie Laurent, but

406

he sometimes thought his conversations with them preserved his sanity.

Sadie, crossing the courtyard to where he stood, stopped on seeing his absorption. She observed, first amazed and then moved, as very cautiously, not to disturb the spider's web in which it had become enmeshed, Richard Scherrer was freeing a bee from the sticky filaments. When he felt her gaze and glanced up he smiled, apologetic, embarrassed.

During that year, Sadie and Nathaniel drove their housekeeper and her family to Montpellier and Madame Pirie at the Hotel de Paris. Another couple took their place. However, as Sadie confided to Scherrer, the wife was a terrible housekeeper, so her announced departure after four months to look after her sick mother was not too great a loss. Two days after she had made this remark, Sadie and Nathaniel again rose before dawn, and Nathaniel prepared for the journey to Montpellier. Travelling even with the Combarnous' van and the vegetables and meat had become far more hazardous over the last few months. The impossibility of obtaining petrol kept almost all cars off the roads. The only ones to be seen were the black Citröens with yellow wheels which belonged to members of the Gestapo, the occasional hearse – some business continued as usual – and a rare vehicle delivering essential supplies.

'Take care,' Sadie told Nathaniel urgently as they walked across the courtyard. He checked his forged documents, and she tucked in the muffler he wore against the early morning chill. They kissed, hurriedly, his just-shaven face warm against her skin: he smelled of coffee and tobacco.

She watched him go with love.

Chapter Twenty-Eight

Sadie stood in front of the house, peering into the blackness. She scuffed chalky pebbles underfoot as she walked across to the edge of the road, and leant against the low post which marked the drop. From here they used to watch the lights of Nice spread below them, twinkling and cheerful, and make out the town centre, the harbour. Now all was hidden in the blackout but the road winding away below was clear enough, and empty. To her left it glimmered white as it wound up beyond the house into the rounded foothills. She strained her eyes and ears, trying desperately to make out the motor. Nothing. Only the incessant soft twitter of the crickets, an occasional bleat from the belled goats in the fields behind the house, a plaintive shriek from one of Madame Combarnous' speckled guinea-fowl. She stood for a long time in the listening dark, then slowly moved towards the house. Waiting, she sat in the kitchen, comforted by faint odours of coffee and bread, the fading warmth of the wood-burning stove. Her head began to droop. She dozed.

Suddenly she leapt into wakefulness and looked at the wooden wall clock with a lurch of the heart. Four o'clock. Oh God, it would soon be light, and he not back. Hurriedly she wrapped herself in one of Estelle's old shawls and unlocked the door. She went through the courtyard and cautiously slid back the bolts on the heavy outer door. The unwieldy key squeaked in the lock. As she started to swing the door open, she thought she caught a faint smell of cigarette smoke. Alerted, she let the door drift closed and waited for a long time, perhaps five minutes, without moving. Silence. She decided it must have been someone passing on a bicycle – the Combarnous started work early –

and opened it again, stepping out into the road. No one. She moved forward. With a sudden start she saw the shadow of a motor parked a long way down the hill. As she looked at it, trying to decide if it was theirs, wondering why Nathaniel should choose to leave it there, instead of running it into the field as they always did, there was a movement behind her. With a gasp she turned, hope leaping – Nathaniel? A figure detached itself from the wall where the laburnum hung heavy and low, and moved towards her. Immediately she knew from the stride it was not him. The man flung down a cigarette end, paused to grind it beneath his heel, and in that second she saw the collar. A German. She pressed the back of her hand to her mouth, not to make a sound. Even as she did so, she recognized him. Scherrer.

He reached her side and saw how he had frightened her.

'It is all right, Madame.' He spoke stiffly. 'I am alone.'

With a gasp, she asked, 'What were you doing there?'

'I needed to think a little.'

'But at this hour?'

He put a hand on her arm. 'I believe, Madame, that we must talk. Shall we go inside?'

As they crossed the road, she determinedly avoided looking towards the hills. Nathaniel must not return while Scherrer was here: she must leave a sign, anything, to warn him. Desperately she tried to think. In the darkness, what would he be able to see? Ah yes. She shrugged the shawl off her shoulders with a casual gesture as they walked, held it in one hand. She contrived to linger slightly as they reached the arch of the doorway, and let it drop on to the road.

She gestured for him to go through before her, murmured, 'I'll lock the door.'

He moved ahead, then paused to wait for her. The key grated again in the lock. Relieved, she turned towards him.

'One moment, Madame, I think you have dropped your wrap.'

'Oh, have I? It doesn't matter, it's only an old thing. I'll find it when you leave.'

'No, I insist, let me get it for you.'

He passed her, reopened the door, found the shawl.

She thanked him, in despair, and showed him into the kitchen. She got out the grinder. 'Are you in a hurry? It's a bit early, but I'll make some coffee, it'll warm you up.'

He lit another of his hand-rolled cigarettes and sat at the kitchen table, not moving. She chattered on, scarcely knowing what she said, frantically wondering whether Nathaniel would be alerted if she turned on all the lights upstairs. Even as she tried to formulate an excuse to get away for a moment, Scherrer asked, abruptly, 'Have you any brandy left?'

Surprised, she answered, 'I think so, a little. Why?'

'I need something stronger than coffee, if I may. And I imagine, Madame, that you will too.'

Sadie felt she had been punched hard in the stomach. Scherrer was watching her with an odd expression. There was anger in it, and pity. She thought, he knows.

He got up, opened the cupboard where they kept the drinks and glasses, and without asking brought the bottle and two glasses back to the table. He poured them each a large measure.

'Here. Drink.'

Obediently, she raised it to her lips, gagged on the fumes, and drank.

He swallowed his at one gulp, and poured another. Only then did he speak. 'I must tell you, Madame, that we have your husband.'

Blankly, she stared back at him. *Say nothing.*

'He was picked up five hours ago,' Scherrer went on, 'near Tarascon.'

He waited. Sadie checked an impulse to lick her dry lips. Just how much did he know? Five hours ago meant eleven o'clock. Was Nathaniel just accused of breaking curfew?

'It was pure chance that I was present,' Scherrer went on. 'I happened to be coming back from a meeting in Nîmes. I stopped at the police station to see a colleague when your husband was brought in. Lucky for him I was,' he added grimly.

Faintly, Sadie asked, 'What happened?'

He shrugged. 'Nothing spectacular. Apparently there was a puncture, and while your husband was changing the wheel a patrol passed and asked to see his papers. All perfectly normal. Except that he should not have been there at that hour. The soldiers brought him in on a charge of breaking curfew.' He paused. 'And then they examined the van. And found his illicit passengers.' Scherrer's mouth closed in a tight line.

Desperately she wondered what had gone wrong, that Nathaniel still had the Gardons with him. Scherrer was speaking again.

'So then they started asking – a few questions.'

Dreading what she might hear Sadie asked, 'Do you mean – an interrogation?'

'It had only just begun when I noticed who he was. I stepped in, told them he was a collaborator known to me.'

'And then?'

'I brought him back with me to Nice under guard. He's in a cell down at the town now.'

'So – it's over?' He could scarcely hear what she said.

'Oh, no, Madame.' He spoke with sadness. 'Not over at all. It has not yet begun. We know what your husband has been doing. We know there must have been other Jews who gained freedom with his – connivance. We must have names and dates, contacts and telephone numbers, collection points and addresses. And we will get them, make no mistake about that. We will get them. Cost what it may.'

'What will happen to Nathaniel now?' Her throat was so sore with restrained tears that she could hardly make herself heard.

Scherrer fingered the stem of his brandy glass, rolling it back and forth, back and forth. 'Interrogation. Deportation. A labour camp, probably. Death, quite possibly.'

'Oh no. Oh no.' She wanted to shout, but it came out as a whisper.

Scherrer looked at her, his face unreadable. 'And what did you think, Madame?' He spoke harshly. 'What did you imagine would happen if he were caught? Is your life so charmed, you rich Americans, that you do not pay the price for *ihre fantasie*?'

Sadie shook her head, speechless, as she took in what he had said. She put her hands palm down on the wooden tabletop and closed her eyes. The surface felt grainy and warm beneath her palms, reassuring.

She took a deep breath, opened her eyes and asked, 'How long have you known that?'

Soberly he stared across at her. 'For months. Not at first. But then I had a feeling – things you said, things you didn't say.'

'I don't understand.' Bewildered, she pushed back her hair. 'Why didn't you report us?'

There was a pause, then he asked, with a faint smile, 'And lose my only source of conversation?'

'But . . . we are at war.'

'Indeed. But Nathaniel is an elderly man. This is not his war. And war is not the business of women. So,' he rolled the glass again, moodily, between his fingers, 'that is why I have not reported either of you for having false papers.'

Sadie tried to assemble her thoughts in the light of this. She could make no sense of it. Hesitantly she asked, 'Will you report it now?'

'If the papers stand up to examination – then no, I shall not speak. I have no proof, you understand, merely my own impressions.'

'But will it help Nathaniel if it is known he is American?'

'It would make little difference, I imagine, to the way he is treated. But for you,' he shook his head, 'it could be the difference between life and death.' Even as she half-turned to him, in that instant before he saw on her face the horror of realization, he knew that he had been right. Unable to sustain any pretence Sadie said, faintly, 'So you know that too?'

'That, also.'

She could hardly control her shaking voice as she asked, 'What am I to do now?'

He attempted a smile. 'Perhaps – the coffee?'

Obediently she rose, found two mugs, stirred the coffee and poured it through a filter. Scherrer looked harassed and preoccupied. With surprise she thought, he's hating this as much as I am.

She sat down, and repeated, 'What should I do?'

Meditatively he sipped the unsweetened liquid. 'It is imperative to keep their attention away from you. I might – *might* – be able to carry on with the pretence that your husband was working for me, claim that he infiltrated this clandestine smuggling operation to find out names . . . Yes, it might work.'

With conviction, she told him, 'Nathaniel will not give any names.'

'No. No, I don't believe he will. But a group of people have just been taken. Properly advised, I imagine Nathaniel will not mind mentioning the names of men already dead.'

Sadie shuddered. 'That's horrible.'

'It is the situation, nonetheless. And if you want to see him again.'

'Do you mean . . .' she could hardly believe his words 'Would he be freed?'

A look of genuine astonishment crossed Scherrer's face. 'That would not be possible. But I would hope I could get him sent to prison in France.'

Slowly, she asked, 'I really don't understand. Why should you want to do all this for Nathaniel? Why do you choose to involve yourself?'

He gave a short laugh that had no mirth in it. 'I scarcely know.' He slumped back in his chair and stared morosely into his coffee grounds. There was a long silence between them. Suddenly, he reached across the table to place his hand over hers. Her impulse was to draw back, but she checked it, letting her hand lie under his own: she must not offend him now.

'Yet here I am,' he went on, musing, 'at this time of the night, trying to find ways of protecting a man who is my enemy.'

'Nathaniel is no one's enemy,' Sadie interrupted. 'He sees what has to be done, and he does it. With him, it's not a question of politics or war, but of humanity. You said it yourself, this is not his war. But he would never let people die without struggling for them.' A thought suddenly occurred to her. Horrified at her selfishness, she asked, anxiously, 'The Gardons. What has happened to them? Where are they?'

'Nîmes, for the moment. After that, I imagine, they'll be sent to some camp or other.' He sounded vague.

She asked, sharply, 'What sort of camp?'

'Look!' He had her hand in his now, and banged it gently down on the table. 'There's nothing I can do for these people. Nothing, d'you understand? They're done for. Worry about your own. We must decide what is to be done. I shall have to be back at the station at eight, to make a report if I am to claim he is working for me. Is that what I am to do?'

He was watching her sombrely. Sadie thought, in consternation, is he asking for a bribe? Is this how it is done? Wildly, she tried to think what she could possibly offer him. It would take days to get hold of any large amount of money. Nathaniel's gold watch and chain? But he had that with him. She looked round the room. Could she offer him a painting? He was holding her right hand still. Glancing down, she saw, on her left hand, the dazzle of Uncle Mark's diamonds. She put her hands back on the table, palms closed, then opened the right so that the band of stones shimmered in its hollow.

At her movement he looked down, then glanced at her, puzzled. Very low, she asked, 'Will this be enough?'

She saw disbelief on his face, then growing hostility. She thought, I've done the wrong thing.

He was white, his lips compressed. And then the realization came to her that he was deeply upset. He rubbed his hands hard over his face, stretching his skin. She noticed his hair was receding. The high collar of his uniform hid the thin throat, the severe garments flattered his over-lean body.

In a tired voice he answered, 'No, Madame. I regret, you cannot buy his life with this.'

He reached forward and curled her fingers shut. There was silence.

He was the first to speak. 'You have always been kind to me, you two. I thought, perhaps, you had forgotten what I represented, and liked me for the man I am.'

She sat very still, her fingers pleating the thin wool of her skirt, smoothing it out against her thigh. She was drained. She had not slept all night. The shock of the discovery had sent her to the verge of panic. Now she felt so heavy with anxiety that she could not breathe properly. She focused more clearly on Scherrer and tried to think about him. He had removed his glasses so that for the first time that night she could see his eyes, and she understood with a faint pang that he was genuinely unhappy. It came to her that he was a lonely man, too intelligent to enjoy the company of aggressive young soldiers, too old to relish the challenge of war, wanting only to be with his wife and family in Leipzig. He had thought she and Nathaniel really liked him, that he was more than just a useful contact. And she had offered him a bribe as though he were any corrupt official.

415

Before she could give herself time to think she said quickly, with real contrition, 'Richard. I'm so sorry. I didn't understand. I didn't believe anyone would risk so much for us in the name of friendship.'

He was watching her intently, hopefully. She hurried on. 'I hope I have not offended you – I wouldn't want that. I want only to save Nathaniel. Will you really do as you suggest? Because if the risk to you is too great, then you must not do it.'

He continued to twirl the empty brandy glass. 'There is a risk, but I believe I can weather that. Of course I will do what I can. Surely my presence here, now, is proof of that. And,' he aded, looking away, 'I want no more talk of payment. If I help, it is because I choose to do so. I expect you to exercise more discretion, not to repeat this dangerous mistake. That is all.'

At the unexpected kindness in his voice, she felt her self-control sliding away from her. She could not yet fully comprehend that Nathaniel had been taken, and the realization that he would be a prisoner, at best, for many months seemed so terrible that her reaction was one of disbelief. She crossed her arms on the tabletop, and buried her face in them. Scherrer watched her, his face once more inscrutable. Then he said, abruptly, 'I will let myself out, Madame. *Gute nacht.*'

She did not know how she got through the hours that came afterwards. She could not bear to go to bed but wrapped herself in a blanket and huddled on the sofa. She was unable, despite her exhaustion, to lose herself in sleep for more than an hour. Then she awoke, damp with sweat, from a nightmare. She rarely dreamed now, but this was so vivid, so horribly familiar. She was looking out of a window at a distant hill, while someone, unseen, told her urgently that she must not attempt to go near it, or something terrible would happen. She lay, sick with apprehension and thought, I know this, I know it.

It came to her, after a time, that this was the same dream that had haunted her in the months after Asher died. The recollection was so dreadful that she got up and dressed, and went to do the shopping. Walking back up the hill from the village, carrying two bags of vegetables and bread, she brooded. She was carrying food for meals Nathaniel would not eat. She was desperate to talk to Combarnous, but she knew enough to keep away from him until she was contacted; she was almost certainly being watched.

As it was, the farmer arrived at the villa next morning as always on a Thursday with the egg ration. He stepped inside the courtyard, concerned at the sight of her, drawn from lack of sleep, her hair unkempt. 'You have been told?'

'Very little. Just that the van had a puncture and a patrol got him. But I don't know how the Gardons came to be with him so late. He was due to leave them in Montepellier at mid-day.'

'I know a little more. It looks as if the Germans arrested a man on Monday night. He was part of an escape ring centred on the Hôtel de Paris – you knew it was used regularly by agents? They must have taken Madame Pirie into custody and then filled the hotel with soldiers: your husband would have been walking into the lion's den. Something must have alerted him, and he attempted to travel home in darkness.'

'Monsieur, what will happen now?'

'I do not know. We had been afraid they would take you too into custody. We must not make any move: we can only hope.'

He shook her hand. 'I will send my wife down to see you later. She will bring some cheese. I must go now. Please come to the door with me and thank me as usual.'

She nodded, and saw him off with a heavy heart. It was as she had thought. No one could help her now.

There was only Richard Scherrer.

*   *   *
417

He telephoned at five that evening. 'Please be there at eleven. I will arrive when I can.'

He rang the bell precisely on time, his leather coat draped round his shoulders. Hurriedly he stepped into the courtyard. 'I left the car in a field a kilometre away. It's not much of a precaution, but I think it better if people do not know I am here.'

'What has happened?' she demanded. 'Where is Nathaniel? Is he all right?'

'He seems well enough, though we have spoken only briefly. He is being held for providing illegal documentation for French subjects. I have intervened and claimed he is working for me. I have done all I can,' he spread out his hands, palms upward, 'to ensure he will not be ill-treated. He will go before a military court next week. I think you can safely assume his sentence will be served in this country.'

She bent her head. 'Thank you.'

'And now I will leave.' Still he stood motionless in the courtyard. Sadie found herself inviting him in, desperate to talk further, for he was her only link with Nathaniel. The urgency in her voice surprised Scherrer.

He waited in the salon while she made coffee, stroking the polished flank of the wooden fairground horse Nathaniel had bought for David years before. When Sadie came into the room with a tray he fished in his pocket. 'I have taken the liberty of replenishing your brandy.'

He handed her the bottle. 'May I get the glasses?'

Then, he raised his to her, 'Your health, Madame. And your husband's release.'

'So there will be a release?'

'Oh yes. He will be given a few years. He will return to you.'

She let out a great sigh. 'We owe you so much. I am so grateful for your help.'

'It is not gratitude I need.' He spoke so low she thought she had misheard him. Then abruptly he pointed at the horse. 'This is a lovely thing.'

'Yes. It belongs to my son.'

'You must let me meet him one day. I like youngsters.'

At the longing in his voice she said, 'You must miss your own terribly.'

'They are not so little now. Almost grown. The eldest was about to start at university, but this war . . . she is nursing instead.'

'It must be lonely for you, being so far away from them. I hadn't thought until now.' She saw with sudden clarity that they were both now in much the same situation, set apart from those they loved.

'It is like having a limb amputated,' he answered, bleakly. 'I know they are not there, because I cannot see them. But I feel them all the time. And my wife has been ill,' he went on in a sudden burst of confidence. 'Nothing serious, but I cannot go to her for another two months, and then only briefly.' He shook his head. He looked haggard and Sadie felt deeply sorry for him. On an impulse, scarcely thinking what she said, she asked, 'Is there anything I can do?'

He got to his feet and walked towards the open window, looking out on the dim courtyard. The fountain splashed, and he heard the tranquil sound with pleasure. He asked, 'Do you mean that?'

'Yes. Yes, I do.' She thought, he's going to ask if he can come and have a meal here, even though Nathaniel's gone. But what Scherrer said was, 'It is so long since I felt close to anyone. So long. Would you – cherish me, a little?'

She imagined that his usually immaculate English had deserted him briefly, and that he had mistranslated the word he sought. She repeated, 'Cherish you? How?' Then, seeing the waiting stillness of his back, it dawned on her what he was asking, and she let out her breath in surprise.

419

'But – you can't mean that?' She was half-laughing. 'I'm – do you know how old I am? I'm over fifty. There must be dozens of women here who are young and pretty and available. Richard, you don't want *me*.'

He rounded on her, his face, impassive as ever, adding to the scorn of his words. 'I don't want them. What good would they be to me? I don't want a cocotte using herself for money. It is not merely pleasure that I seek, Madame. That is to be had for the asking. I want someone who is,' he paused, '*Liebeswürdig*. Worthy of love.'

'And you think I would be . . . *Liebeswürdig*?'

'I do not need to think, I know.' He spoke with certainty. She stared at him, stunned. It had never occurred to her that this might happen, she had no idea what to do. Helplessly she asked, 'But Richard, what about your wife? You've just told me how much your family means to you.'

He waited for a long time before he answered and when he finally did so it was in a voice heavy with despair.

'I have been away from home now for two years. We are at war. I may never see them again. Leipzig is bombed constantly. And I may be killed tomorrow; only yesterday the *Maquis* blew up one of our lorries on the road I travelled from Nîmes. Day after day, night after night, there is no consolation, no mitigation of the loneliness. Do you hate me so much you cannot grant me a measure of self-forgetfulness?'

She found herself saying, 'I don't hate *you* at all,' and she meant it. They had always got on well, the three of them. Richard's passion for theatre, his excitement over the paintings he saw in France, and particularly his knowledge of European architecture, made him easy company for Sadie and Nathaniel. But not hating was one thing. This . . .

She stared at his back, at the harsh lines of the uniform jacket. His unhappiness was obvious but she did not care. She supposed she should feel gratitude towards him for the risk he ran in attempting to protect Nathaniel from the full force of the vengeance that could so easily have fallen on him. Might yet fall, if she were not careful. She acknowledged nothing but her hard determination to protect Nathaniel if she could.

Scherrer was still staring out at the courtyard. Now he turned and she found she could not meet his eyes.

'What is your answer?' He was almost inaudible.

There was only one answer.

'Yes.'

He took a step towards her, then changed his mind and went to the table. He poured two glasses of brandy and with a formal bow handed one to her. Hesitantly she took it, thinking ironically, Dutch courage. He drained his at a swallow and looking straight at her tossed the goblet behind him so that it shattered in the the empty stone fireplace, the fragments glittering among the bowl of lavender she kept there. The uncharacteristic gesture, the sound of splintering glass, made her shiver. She set the brandy down untouched and turned towards the door.

That night was one of the strangest she had ever known.

She kept telling herself, this is nothing, it doesn't matter, it's not important. It is a thing you must do, to help Nathaniel. Undressing in the bathroom, putting on her nightdress, she reasoned that Scherrer was not repugnant to her, that she would remain in control of herself. After all, she was hardly an inexperienced girl. The thought made her smile. Fifty-three years and three husbands must qualify one for something. Only she had not imagined it would be this.

When she came out of the bathroom he was waiting for her in the light from the hallway. He had removed his jacket and tie, and his shirt was unbuttoned.

He asked, his tone tentative, 'Would you . . . prefer that we do not use your room? A guest room perhaps?'

She hesitated, wondering briefly why he should suggest this, then shook her head curtly. She needed the familiarity of her own room, the knowledge that it was Nathaniel's bed. She crossed the room to draw the curtains, reached for the lamp switch. He spoke, then. 'No. Can it be dark?' She left the door ajar, slipped off her dressing gown and sat on the edge of the bed, her back to him. She heard him grunt as he removed his shoes and felt the bed shake as he climbed in. She stayed very still.

I'm not going to make this easy for you.

When he touched her shoulder she waited a moment, then twisted to face him. He had taken off his glasses: she could see even in the half-light the indentation they had made on the bridge of his nose.

'Please.' It was an order, not a request.

Reluctantly she got into bed and pulled the covers high around her shoulders. His voice was mocking. 'I hope we may be civilized about this. I am not interested in rape.'

Sadie closed her eyes. She had never had intercourse with a man she did not love. Even in the bad days with Woolf he had been deeply familiar to her. This was a man she scarcely knew, an enemy soldier, a German: the very smell of his skin alien to her, foreign, threatening. Lying there, she thought of the Gardons, and her eyes filled with tears. She squeezed them back, afraid that Scherrer would notice and fearful lest she alienate him. Stop it, she told herself sharply, hold on, just get through this for Nathaniel's sake.

Scherrer heard her sniff and touched her face in the darkness. She wanted to shout, get on with it, for God's sake get it over, be done. He did not speak, but wiped her cheek with his finger. His unexpected solicitousness destroyed her last defences. If he had been uncaring, hard, brutal even, if he had ignored her feelings, she could have supported that. But his concern touched off the stream of tears and she began to sob uncontrollably, curled on her side away from him. She wept for Nathaniel, for the probable fate of the Gardons, for the fury at her own weakness. She cried until she was ugly, while Scherrer lay beside her, frowning. When finally she could speak she said, hiccuping, 'I can't help it.'

'Of course you can't. It is of no consequence.'

She had anticipated his anger and turned to him uncertainly. 'I thought I could do it.' She made a helpless gesture. 'It's just all been too much. I'm sorry.'

He eased closer to her and she found, against her will, that he had put his arms around her. She held herself tense, scarcely breathing, not wanting his body to touch hers. And then reason asserted itself. The German was the only person who could help Nathaniel now, the only one who could get them through this crisis. She gave a little gasp and buried her face against his shoulder. He thought it was assent, not knowing that she wanted only to blot out the sight of him. He started to stroke her back, hissing softly between his teeth like a man soothing a frightened animal. The rhythmic touch calmed her despite herself, and when her breathing had steadied he muttered into her hair, '*Est gibt ein bestimmt Verstandnis zwischen uns, nicht wahr*?'

'What are you saying?'

'There's an understanding between us, isn't there?'

He began to kiss her, small, dry kisses on her throat and arms. He asked, his voice pleading, 'Caress me.'

'I .. can't.'

'Please.'

She reached out obediently and her questing fingers found him soft and curled. She stroked him lightly so that his breathing grew hoarse. He shifted until he lay almost on top of her and pushed her nightdress hastily out of his way. He muttered, 'Help me,' and she parted her legs in false compliance. He started to move, forward and back, she could feel him against her. His movements became frenzied, his hands caught at her breasts. Then suddenly he groaned deeply and subsided, his whole weight upon her.

She lay rigid, stifling her impulse to wriggle away from his body. Without moving she finally asked in a whisper, 'Is it my fault?'

He exhaled heavily. 'No. Of course not. I'm an old man and didn't know it.' He gave his odd, abrupt laugh. '*Ich bin ganz doff.* I'm sorry. A bloody fool.'

Her mind careened madly. She thought, he'll be angry, he'll hate me for this. He's failed and I've seen his failure. Hurriedly she said, 'It doesn't matter. Don't worry.'

He rolled off her and lay on his back, eyes closed.

'This hasn't happened to me for years.'

'It's be all right, you'll see.' She hunted for words to console him. 'You're under a lot of strain, that's all it is.'

He made no reply, only opened his eyes to stare at the ceiling. Stiffly she lay beside him. Neither of them had said as much, but she was conscious that this night was her payment of a due debt. Richard Scherrer would help Nathaniel and in return . . . But there had been no return. The silence was now more ominous than any words could be. This man – she corrected herself – this German, this officer, had it within his power to decide, at least partially, Nathaniel's fate. On his word her husband might be dead or alive. She had thought she was buying his life but now perhaps it was more endangered even than before. Would Scherrer punish her for his impotence? Would he refuse to speak for Nathaniel, condemn him? In desperation she started to blame herself.

'It's my fault, I shouldn't have cried. Of course you couldn't go on, after that.'

Still he stared at the ceiling, his expression blank, the lines from nose to mouth etched black in the faint light.

Sadie watched him without appearing to do so, her head averted. Since this nightmare began she had allowed herself to think only of Nathaniel and how she might aid him. She had been prepared to do anything, and this had seemed a not unreasonable price. She was able now to imagine

Scherrer's feelings but the awareness aroused no softness in her, although later she acknowledged that he was, in that moment, pitiable. Lying beside the intruder in her bed she experienced only dismay and disgust so that she had to steel herself not to shrink from him. Instead she murmured, striving to make her voice gentle, 'Please, Richard, please. It doesn't matter, it's not important. We could try again, if you wish.'

Still he did not respond. After a moment he sat up abruptly, pushed back the covers and got out of bed. He gathered his clothes and put them on, then sat on the edge of the bed to ease on his shoes. For a moment he remained there, slumped forward, before pulling himself together and buttoning his high collar tightly. He went to the doorway. She leant up on one elbow, started to stretch out a hand towards him. He did not wait for her to complete the gesture. He made a stiff little bow and was gone.

Sadie fumbled with chilled fingers for the light switch. Huddled in her dressing gown she spent the remainder of the night half-sitting, half-lying, unable to sleep, one arm shielding her eyes from the lamplight and her terror.

Chapter Twenty-Nine

The trial was to take place on Tuesday.

All weekend she held herself in check, knowing that once she gave way she would collapse. Instead she cleaned. She scoured the villa from top to bottom, polishing the floors and washing the windows. She beat rugs in the garden and rinsed the curtains. In the kitchen she attacked the stone floor on her hands and knees. She dragged out all the beds, wiped all the pictures and pulled up every weed she could find in the courtyard. And still she could not sleep. Always, after an hour, she awoke from a dream of that haunting and horrifying landscape.

Curiously it was only in sleep that she panicked. Awake, it was as though her mind was frozen with fear. She remembered a bird that had trapped itself between the two panes of their sash window in the bedroom years ago. A linnet, it went wild at first, desperately hopping up and down, attempting to beat its wings and free itself. They could not get their hands down to rescue it, and two hours lapsed before the local handyman arrived to remove one of the panes. By then the bird had lost all hope. It crouched, passive and shivering in a corner, eyes glazed, beak slightly open. Sadie had felt certain it could not survive, but when released it was able, miraculously, to fly. She wished she could forget the pathetically huddled thing: it matched too exactly the way she felt.

On Sunday night, when it was dark, she sat in David's old bedroom at the back of the house, looking over the shadowy fields, hearing the occasional soft bleat from a goat. A bird startled somewhere in a bush, and she glanced to her left and froze: there was a shape that had not been there a moment before. It moved and she rose, quietly, and went into their bedroom. In the drawer on Nathaniel's side was his revolver. She had no idea how to work it, but she knew it was loaded. Presumably she just pulled the trigger. She went back to the window. The shadow had moved. Then she heard her name being called and she started to smile with relief: Combarnous.

Downstairs she opened a window and he climbed in, puffing with the effort, and grinned at her ruefully.

'Evidently I am no Pimpernel. The last time I did this was in the name of *l'amour* and that, as Madame may imagine, was many years ago.'

She was so pleased to see him she had to restrain herself from throwing her arms around his neck.

'Thank you for coming. I'm going mad here alone. The nights are so black.'

'We are not far away.'

'Far enough. Have you heard anything?'

'We know he is being held at La Turbie, a few miles from Monaco. The Fort de la Revère is used to hold British servicemen. It's on top of a hill and the security measures are strict. Even so, escapes have been managed from there, through the sewers, but we have not enough time.'

'I don't think Nathaniel could do anything dramatic. He's in no condition for wriggling through pipes. He's not a young man, you know.'

Combarnous nodded.

'It will not go easy with him at the court. I think he will be condemned to deportation, and that means death. Have you heard from your German friend?'

She thought of Scherrer's face as he left her bed and replied uncertainly, 'He says he will do what he can.'

'*Bien.* You are fortunate, Madame, to have such help available. I knew from Nathaniel the care you had taken to cultivate this man. Now you must use him.'

As he was leaving, Combarnous promised Sadie that on Tuesday he would take her into Nice by horse and cart. She

427

had no petrol, and he would be making his once weekly trip with supplies for the shops.

She was relieved to have something positive to do that day: it had been weighing on her mind. Sitting beside Combarnous in the early morning, wrapped up against the spring chill at that hour, she wished the day were less brilliant, less full of promise. It was too painful to think that Nathaniel was shut away from it. As they neared the town, and could smell the sea for the first time, she became increasingly nervous: she had no idea what she meant to do, only that she could not stay in Corbès. Combarnous drove straight to the Boulevard St Agathe and told her she had three hours.

'I will wait for you here. Do not be late. *Au'voir.*'

She walked aimlessly for a time, conscious as never before of the strain on people's faces, the unaccustomed hush in streets she knew as bustling and cheerful. She hailed a bicycle taxi, which she took for fifteen minutes, then walked towards the Jardin Albert-1, and stopped: across the Théâtre de Verdure, where she and Nathaniel used to attend open-air concerts, a great Nazi banner was draped, the crooked cross a stark reminder to the inhabitants that they were a vanquished people. Looking at it, an idea that had been drifting somewhere in her mind hardened into resolve. It was still only seven forty-five.

She knew that Scherrer's quarters were in the Hôtel Angleterre-Grande Bretagne, an irony which was not lost on him. She set off briskly for the Avenue Gustave V, not letting herself think what she would do when she arrived. She waited outside, on the opposite side of the street, for almost an hour. Then, conscious that she would attract notice, she moved off, discouraged. She had no idea where the court would meet, or where Scherrer worked. Disconsolately she started to look for a café. She was walking slowly, not thinking of her surroundings, when she found herself shouldered off the pavement into the gutter by the man beside her as he hurried out of the way. She soon saw why: coming towards her was a patrol of German soldiers, eight of them, footsteps ringing on the pavement as they tramped by. On the spur of the moment she turned and hurried after them. They turned sharply into the Rue de la Liberté and halted before another building draped with the black and cream banner. One soldier detached himself from the group and went inside. The building had sentries posted round it, and a glimpse of a uniformed figure at an upstairs window confirmed that she had stumbled across some sort of headquarters. She glanced at her watch. Nine o'clock. She didn't have much time. Opposite the German occupied building was a small public flower garden, nothing more than a crescent of flowers with a wrought iron bench at either side. She sat, gratefully, and began to wait. Even if he were not here – and she could hardly believe that he was – she had neither time nor energy to do more. She had been sitting for nearly twenty minutes when three German officers were driven up in one of the yellow-wheeled black Citröens used as staff cars. Scherrer was not with them. She was a fool: even if she saw him, he would be completely unapproachable. There would be a driver or armed soldiers. Dejected, she started to rise when she heard footsteps.

He looked preoccupied. In his right hand was a black document case. She stepped forward.

'*Oberleutnant*. Good morning.'

He stopped. That was all. He made no sign of recognition. Uncertain how to proceed, she instinctively reached out a hand. He took a step back.

'I'm sorry . . . I wanted . . . I wondered . . .'

'You will be informed, Madame Laurent.'

He gave her a brief nod and hurried away.

As the afternoon sun filtered through the half-drawn blinds of the Villa d'Auban, Sadie could feel dread like something tangible flowing through her body. Her legs trembled, she could not keep still. She had no idea when – if at all – Scherrer would contact her. He had looked at her in the Rue de la Liberté with hostility. She knew very well that normal German practice in cases like Nathaniel's were to keep all information from relatives and friends, and now she genuinely feared that she had misjudged Scherrer. He had taken against her because of that night, he was not going to help after all. She should never have gone into Nice, or tried to see the German. What purpose had she imagined her journey would achieve? Now, at the thought of Nathaniel's possible fate she was weak from despair. She thought, I need a drink, just to blunt the edges, just to get me through.

She found Nathaniel's last remaining bottle of whisky and poured herself a glass. It tasted terrible but she drank it neat, and after that another. Enough, she told herself, that's enough. Have something to eat. She went into the kitchen and cooked an omelette. She was very pleased with herself for getting the heavy omelette pan hot, and the oil sizzled before she remembered she hadn't beaten the eggs. She didn't seem to be able to find everything, and the eggs at first wouldn't break open. Then one did, the yolk slipping on to the floor as she misjudged the edge of the dish. She dropped a teatowel over it, cleverly thinking that if she didn't she would slip, and poured the unbeaten egg into the pan. It made a meal, of sorts, and just as she was finishing it, the gate bell rang.

Anxiously, she patted her hair, and hurried to the garden door. Scherrer stood outside. He said, 'Good evening. I should like a word.'

'Yes. Yes. Will you come in?'

She stood back with an elaborate gesture of welcome.

His eyes were fixed onto a point somewhere above her head.

'It will only take a moment.'

She held on to the door frame for support.

'I have to tell you that your husband has been sentenced to ten years' imprisonment. He will be held at La Turbie.'

She could not speak. The courtyard reeled around her. Scherrer stepped forward.

'I have done my best. I am sorry.'

'Ten years. Ten *years*.' Her voice was an unrecognizable croak.

She could not believe it. They were locking Nathaniel away for trying to save lives.

Desperately she said, 'But you can't let them do that. Nathaniel's sixty-nine. He's an old man, an old man.' She was sobbing now. 'He won't live. He'll die in there, I know it, I know it.'

Scherrer stood without speaking, his head bent. Her voice grew louder, she could feel the hysteria building, and did nothing to stop it.

'You told me you'd help. You promised to help. You said you cared for him. You bastard. You lying *bastard*.'

Wildly, she flung away from the doorway, tried to run out across the courtyard. Panic and the whisky impeded her and she stumbled on the cobbles and collapsed against the fountain. She caught at the rim to save herself, and the full bowl of water poured on to her arms and chest. Scherrer took an uncertain step forward then, as she remained half-lying across the pedestal, clearly unable to extricate herself, he hurried towards her. As she felt his hands on her shoulders she twisted away, soaking herself still more as she did so. Authoritatively he shouted, 'Stop it, Sadie. You're behaving like a fool.'

She stopped struggling then, and let him put his arms round her waist and haul her upright. He draped one sodden arm round his neck and half led, half carried her into the kitchen, and dumped her unceremoniously into a chair.

'A towel?'

She gestured towards the wooden maiden under the window. He caught at a dry towel, and started to dab ineffectually at her hair and shoulders. She had regained control by now: the shock of the cold water had seen to that. Weakly, she took the towel from him and started rubbing herself. She was shaking and Scherrer glanced at the whisky bottle and the glass on the dresser.

'You'd better have another of these. It'll warm you up.'

She took the glass, but her hand was shaking so much she spilled it, and it dripped down her chin.

'Here. Let me.'

He took the glass from her, wiped the drops with the palm of his hand, and held the whisky to her lips. She drank, shuddered, and said, hoarsely, 'Thank you.'

'May I have one?'

She nodded. She was beginning to feel better, although very uncomfortable. He said, 'You'd better get that dress off before you catch a cold.'

She got up, and started to walk to the door, but found she could not balance properly, and hit her shoulder on the door frame as she went through. Scherrer, looking anxious, followed her. She climbed the stairs very slowly, her legs feeling immensely long and far away. He waited in the hall. When she got to her room she pulled her dressing gown off a hanger and started to undo her dress. The zip was at the back and she couldn't get her arms round to undo it. As she wrenched the fastening, she overbalanced and fell again, this time properly. At the heavy thud, Scherrer called out, 'What's the matter?' and then, getting no reply, ran up the stairs to the landing.

Through the doorway, he could see her on the floor, inert. He hesitated for a moment, then entered. She was breathing heavily, but her eyes were open, fixed and staring.

'Pull yourself together.' He spoke sharply as he hauled

her up into a sitting position.

'Please,' he said more gently, 'undo your dress. You will make yourself ill.'

She did nothing, just stared at him with dull, uncaring eyes.

He clicked his tongue. 'Is there no one else to help you?'

Slowly she shook her head, and said bleakly, 'No one. No one.'

'Then you'll have to do it yourself.'

Still, she did nothing.

He sighed. Very carefully he felt for the zip and pulled it down. He pulled her arms out of the sleeves, and slipped the dress to her waist. Her petticoat was damp but not soaking.

'Help me get you up,' he ordered and pulled her to her feet. He sat her down on the edge of the bed and wrapped the dressing gown round her shoulders. The dress lay on the floor and he picked it up and found a hanger for it.

'Get into bed, please.'

He pushed her shoulders gently back against the pillow and pulled the eiderdown over her. Still she watched him blankly. He asked, 'Will you be all right now?'

She shook her head in desolation.

'I shall stay for a little while.'

Relieved, she muttered, 'Thank you.'

'Sadie, did you mean what you said out there? You know I tried to help, don't you? Surely you realize that without my intervention Nathaniel would have been deported to Germany like so many others.'

Wearily she nodded. 'I'm sorry I spoke like that. I knew this was going to happen. Then to hear the words, that's terrible. All those years – I thought it might be five. But ten years.'

He ran his hands down his cheeks in a gesture she had seen him make before. His voice was flat.

'It may not come to that. He will have to serve

something, of course, that is inevitable. But the war is not yet won. Do you understand what I am saying?'

'I . . . had not thought of that. The sentence sounded so irrevocable.'

He gave that odd, barking laugh that held no humour in it.

'As sentences are meant to sound. I do not want to make any promises. But you need not be without hope in this.'

She huddled deeper into the warmth of the eiderdown.

'Thank you. Thank you for helping. Both of us.'

'I'll try to get word to you about Nathaniel. You will have to be patient.'

'Richard . . .' she caught his sleeve, pulling him urgently.

Unwillingly, he perched on the very edge of the bed.

'In that park, in the Rue de la Liberté, you barely spoke. I thought . . .'

He shrugged. 'In the park, that was – not quite done.'

She added tentatively, 'I thought it was because of – that night. I wanted you to know it does not matter.' She closed her eyes.

Richard Scherrer looked down at her, at the woman who a few weeks before had charmed and amused him. Now she appeared drab and defenceless. A victim of circumstance. A victim, like her husband, of a rash attempt to oppose a system which brooked no opposition. And yet over the months he had learnt a good deal about her life, enough to know that she was able, without reservation, to do what she had to do in order to survive. She and Nathaniel had behaved with humanity and concern, and this was where it had brought them. And what would he have done, had the situation been reversed? Would he have been capable of the same actions, knowing the risk? Probably not. Experimentally, he stroked her cheek with his finger. At his touch she relaxed, comforted despite herself.

He said, in a voice she could scarcely hear, '*Ich lass dich nicht allein.*'

With an effort she opened her eyes and looked at him questioningly.

'I won't leave you alone.'

The Villa d'Auban became a closed world for Sadie, Richard Scherrer almost her only visitor. She turned to him as her sole contact with Nathaniel, the last bond with the man she loved.

Theirs was a strange alliance. There was nothing tangible between them save the occasional touch of a hand in comfort. She had said she would use the German to help her husband but she began to wonder whether there was not some more primitive urge to cleave to the oppressor. She perceived that Scherrer did not feel for her the emotions of a conqueror for what he has vanquished. He sought her because he was a man apart, and lonely, sickened by the act he was forced to play out, a civilized being in a barbaric role. Conceived not of desire but of despair, fashioned less by love than by longing, nurtured on unhappiness, sustained by mutual loss, their coming together nonetheless salvaged them both.

Nothing was said by either of them that admitted all this. Even so, their assumed relationship quickly became public property. The more sophisticated acquaintances had accepted the Laurences' association with *Oberleutnant zurzee* Scherrer as politic. It was common knowledge that in Paris especially the life of the intellectual élite continued almost undisturbed by the war. French and German sat down to luncheon together, discussed plays, reviewed books, organized translations and openings. It was only when it became a more simple arrangement, when it was merely a man and a woman, that eyebrows were raised, shoulders turned, doors firmly closed.

Among her neighbours in Corbès, Sadie had found the reaction less discreet. Covert hostility greeted her when she went out now. Nothing was ever said – or not loud enough to hear. No insult was ever proffered, no salutation ignored, for the German was an officer and potentially dangerous. But the dustmen neglected to call for weeks at a time at the villa. The vegetables she purchased at the shop would be even worse quality than the usual war rations, and the shopkeeper's wife would carelessly drop Sadie's loaf as she handed it over the counter, with only a graceless apology.

Monsieur and Madame Combarnous, the only people who knew the true state of affairs, were unable to say anything. They continued their clandestine work, and could not afford to reveal their knowledge of Sadie's association. And even there, she half-suspected, there was a feeling that she had betrayed too much. For a long time the couple would visit Sadie after dark, walking through the fields separating their homes to talk to her or share a meal. Gradually, they came less and less frequently, reluctant to condone what they did not understand.

They would have been astonished and disbelieving had they known how *Oberleutnant zurzee* Scherrer passed much of his time at the villa. He insisted on doing many of Nathaniel's odd jobs around the house and garden: mending a broken latch, clearing a gutter of fallen leaves. 'Let me just fix this,' he would say. 'Nathaniel hates things falling apart.' Sadie at first opposed him, feeling in some obscure way that he was trying to take over from her husband. But the German took such obvious pleasure in the small tasks that gradually she accepted his help with gratitude.

She accepted his presence, also, more and more naturally, so that the days when he did not appear were empty ones. In many ways he remained a mystery to her and it was with difficulty that she gained glimpses into his life. She knew, for instance, very little of his early background: he had told them only that his father was a schoolteacher who lived long enough to see war break out for the second time. Now Scherrer spoke of him to Sadie with respect and regret: the old man had watched the Nazi regime attack many of his former students teaching in the universities, and he died mourning the destruction of all he had worked for.

Once, when she was reading and Richard Scherrer had gone into the courtyard, she found herself inexplicably thinking of Manchester, of her home in Locket Street and of her father. With a start she found that it was Scherrer who had put them into her mind. He was singing to himself – she had never before heard him so spontaneous, so light-hearted – a song she had forgotten.

> *Rosslein, rosslein, rosslein rot,*
> *Rosslein mit der heide.*

She sat motionless, lost in recollection, listening to the deep voice caressing the melody out of her childhood. He was singing as a child does, in a monotone, absent-minded, and she thought with a pang, he is not so different from me after all. Perhaps he too grew up in rooms over-full of heavy carved furniture. Perhaps his grandmother played Schubert on Sunday evenings and fed him illicit bits of transparent pastry whenever she made a strudel.

It was as though a barrier had been lifted.

She understood that what drew her to Richard Scherrer were his inadequacies. Nathaniel looked after her, protected her, and she leant upon his knowledge and ability. But Scherrer needed her. He was on the verge of breaking down, unable to support the bleakness of his situation. He came to the Villa d'Auban seeking what only she could give him: companionship, a measure of peace. Despite their positions, despite his uniform and his power and her fragile safety, Sadie knew on some instinctive level that she would survive, while Scherrer might not. She recognized his weakness. She came to love it, because it made her strong.

She began to lose touch with reality: she could hardly remember, it seemed, her life in Chicago. Letters were heavily censored. David, sixteen years old now, wrote of his growing interest in music and a girl he had met. He appeared not to miss Sadie and by this she was both saddened and reassured. She could not write of what had befallen Nathaniel: it would have to wait until she saw the family and told them face to face. Perhaps because of this ignorance, Esther's letters were more self-centred than ever. Alfred had a desk job owing to defective eyesight and it seemed to Sadie that her daughter did not know what the war was all about.

She received one letter, heavily scored over in the thick pencil of the censor, that enraged her even in the midst of her artificial calm. Esther wrote that she was leaving Alfred.

'How can she, how can she do this?'

Sadie stormed through the room, holding the letter out to Scherrer. He took it from her. When he had finished reading it he commented mildly, 'You seem very incensed. Perhaps she has reason.'

'Reason? What reason can she possibly have that matters more than three children to bring up?'

When, four months later, Esther revealed that she was planning to marry again, that she had been having an affair during her marriage to Alfred, Sadie felt nothing but contempt. Her affection for Alfred, after her initial hostility, had been total. Now she considered that Esther's behaviour was cheap and careless. She remembered a lot of things about Esther: how round and affectionate she was as a baby, drooling with love, and how close they had been during the low years in New York when they had only each other and Leonie. She recalled the day she had found the photograph of Asher in Esther's room, with her own likeness cut away, and the difficult stormy years as the girl left childhood behind.

Sadie did not tell Nathaniel of the divorce. To him she wrote cheerful letters and prayed that he saw at least some of them. Scherrer started to make 'official' visits once a month, and then he would bring her a scrawled note from Nathaniel. The first was the most upsetting.

'I am in a daze,' he wrote. 'Caught, tried and sentenced in eight days, no chance to defend myself, and no defence to offer. Thank God you are all right – my only comfort.'

She was not allowed to send supplies of any kind to him, and this hurt almost more than not being able to see him. Scherrer had described the conditions in which he was held, and all too clearly she could envisage him sitting hour after hour with idle hands. She thought of him in the courtyard in the sun, wearing the shirt she had made for him of scarlet flower printed Provençal cotton, talking while she shelled peas and whittling away at a piece of doll's house furniture for his granddaughter. Now he did not have a book to read, he could never light a pipe. She took to carrying his old leather tobacco pouch in her handbag, and she would hold it for hours, sniffing the familiar odour with pain but unable to resist doing so.

Sadie asked Scherrer if he could possibly arrange for her to see Nathaniel. She raised the question with little hope, and although Scherrer was sympathetic, he lacked the authority to make it possible. He did do one thing, though. He took her to La Turbie. They drove along the Grande Corniche from Nice, the high road cresting the stony hills, and in the distance far mountains gleamed with snow. The Fort de la Revère, on top of a hill, was surrounded by a moat: it looked impregnable, although Scherrer told her that many of the prisoners held there – many of them British soldiers taken at Dunkirk, others captured airmen – had managed to escape.

'But not Nathaniel.'

'He must take no more risks, not at his age.' She sniffed back her tears, and without speaking Scherrer fished out a handkerchief and handed it to her. On their way back down to the town they stopped for a moment and looked at Monaco spread below, like something borrowed from a child's toybox. Only when they neared the sea could they discern the great rolls of barbed wire along the beaches, fencing off the water and any help that might be brought by it.

Her glimpse of Nathaniel's prison brought a new anxiety. It would be icy in the winter now fast approaching, and she knew that his age and the meagre food would weigh against him then. When she voiced this anxiety, Scherrer gave a mirthless smile.

'Germany now has yet another opponent,' he said. 'Italy declared war today. The winter will be a long one for us, but perhaps not so long for your husband.'

'You really believe Germany will be defeated, don't you?'

'Oh yes. I have no doubt of that at all. The lesson of history is that violent subjugation succeeds initially, but in the end the victims in their turn exact retribution.'

He was ready to leave, and he slapped a leather glove angrily against his leg. 'The only question is, how long will it take?'

She answered, 'Perhaps not so long – if men who believe as you do were prepared to speak out.'

He looked down at her, and when he spoke even his voice was grey.

'There is little point in using rational argument against the huge mechanism that used to be my country. It would do no good because there is no one to hear. And I have too much to lose. I have three children, my wife – I must protect them, and my principles must go to the wall.'

She let her hands drop open, helpless, in her lap. 'I know. I know. What's the use.'

As he was leaving, pulling the door to behind him, Richard Scherrer said an odd thing. He paused for a moment, as if making up his mind whether or not to continue, then, 'I was reading something the other day, I can't remember what, and I came across a phrase that haunts me. It applies to us both, I think.'

She waited, and he added slowly, '"We live all our lives with the dreams of yesterday."'

The truth of the words pierced her.

She had not let herself acknowledge that her life with Nathaniel was over. Her heart could not believe it and her mind would not. Even now, when the blow had fallen, she still did not feel its force, as though she were numbed by shock.

Yet this phrase did what months of loneliness and fear had failed to do. It sparked the recognition, hidden deep within her, that she and Nathaniel could never regain what they had lost.

Chapter Thirty

In the January of 1944 Sadie learned that Nathaniel was unwell. He was suffering from gout and found it increasingly difficult to walk without the aid of a stick. Scherrer had seen him twice in the space of a month, still ostensibly for information, and on the second occasion he realized suddenly how much the older man had aged. Shortly afterwards the German was posted briefly to Paris. 'I'll be back in about three weeks,' he promised Sadie, 'and I'll go to La Turbie as soon as I get back.'

He had been gone a fortnight when Sadie received an unexpected telephone call one morning. A subdued woman's voice asked for Madame Laurence. When Sadie identified herself the woman replied, 'My name is Soeur Beatrice – you do not know me. I am a nurse in the order of the Sisters of Marie Joseph. We work in the prisons.'

There was a pause. In a faint voice Sadie asked, 'How can I help you?'

'I should like, if I may, to speak with you. Could you come to our mother house? We are in Nice,' she gave the address, 'and I will be here all day.'

'Why do you want to see me?'

'I think than can be best explained in person. Please come, if you can.'

'Of course. *Au revoir.*'

Puzzled, Sadie stood in the hallway. What on earth could it be? A letter from Nathaniel, a message? How was she to get to Nice? She flung on a coat and hurried up the hill to the Combarnous farm. Madame greeted her with the formal correctness she had now adopted. Yes, the cheeses were going in this evening ready for market the following day. It would indeed be possible for her to travel with the cart.

So at six o'clock Sadie was ensconced in the elderly vehicle, while the Alsatian growled his disfavour. It was with immense relief that she was put down at the Rue Napoleon.

The convent was not at all what she had expected, but a tall town house with windows firmly shuttered standing directly on the street. The bell pull was an old-fashioned brass hook. She pulled it hard and waited for what seemed an interminable time. Then she heard footsteps, and after a moment a small trapdoor at eye level slid open.

Through narrow bars, part of a face peered at her. She said nervously,

'*Je m'appelle Laurent. Soeur Beatrice . . .*'

'*Oui, oui. Un moment, s'il vous plaît.*'

The opening was closed, bolts pulled back, and the door opened. In the gloom she saw a stooped figure in a dark blue habit. She followed her into an austere hallway, the walls bare, the wooden floor waxed to a high sheen. The nun opened a door and motioned her to enter. This room was also floored in wood. It held a table, two straight-backed chairs and an oil painting, in an unexpectedly ornate gilt frame, of a middle-aged woman in the same habit. Her face was lined, her hands crossed on a massive crucifix. Uncertain whether to sit, filled with trepidation about the meaning of the curious invitation here, Sadie waited for almost five minutes before the door opened again.

Soeur Beatrice was short, her skin ravaged by tiredness but her eyes grey and serene. She greeted Sadie, and when they were both seated she said, 'I have your telephone number from your husband, Madame. He asked especially that I contact you.'

'How is he now?' Nervousness hurried her speech. 'I knew he had been troubled by gout.'

'Yes that is right. We had been treating him for some time.' Soer Beatrice looked down at her folded hands.

'Madame. I have to tell you that he died early this morning.'

Sadie gripped the edge of the table to keep herself from falling. There were no words.

The nun said quietly, 'I am so very sorry. We did all we could for him. It was a massive heart attack. They brought him to the infirmary immediately, but there was nothing we could do.' In answer to the question in Sadie's eyes, she added, 'He knew what was happening. He was very' – she paused, seeking the word she wanted – 'very still. Very *tranquil*. We talked through the night, when he was conscious. It was then he asked me to contact you.'

She sighed. 'The German authorities take weeks to notify the family. Sometimes they fail entirely to do so.' Still Sadie waited in scalded silence.

The nun rose and came round to the front of the table. 'He talked of you a great deal. You and his son, and his daughters. You meant everything to him. You are a fortunate woman, to have been so loved.' She put out a hand, and touched Sadie on the shoulder.

And at that compassionate gesture the frozen moment broke and Sadie gasped with the realization that it must be true. If this woman was standing here looking at her with sympathy, then it must be true. He must be dead. And she had not seen him. For months she had not seen him. He had died without her, imprisoned, surrounded by strangers. The comfort of strangers. At the thought she gave a choking cry and covered her face with her hands.

As though reading her mind, Soeur Beatrice spoke. 'He had been in the infirmary before, you know, with gout. We knew what he had done. He was a good and a brave man, and we cared very much for him.'

Hoarsely, Sadie whispered, 'Thank you.'

The two women sat in silence for a long time. Then Soeur Beatrice asked, 'Will you come with me for a moment?'

She led the way along the passage towards the back of

the convent. She opened a heavy door and descended a short flight of steps. Sadie found she was in a chapel. Light filtered through stained glass windows, gleamed on the softly tinted figure of a Virgin and Child. There was a scent of bees-wax from the polished benches and another, sweeter, burnt perfume: incense. Soeur Beatrice took her arm and led her towards the simple altar. On the far side was another figure, this time of Joseph, his robe painted a deep blue. Before him stood a silver candelabra holding perhaps fifteen small candles. They were irregular and yellowish in colour: Sadie realized the nuns must make them by hand.

Soeur Beatrice lit a taper and turned to Sadie. She smiled sadly.

'I wanted to wait for you to see.'

She made an obeisance to the statue, stood for a minute with head bent. Then, very slowly, she touched each candle in turn with the taper. For a second each flame flickered and smoked, then the whole candelabra was aglow with their light. The dim chapel warmed and gleamed, the nun's face was illumined by their brightness. She turned to Sadie.

'For your husband,' she said.

She had known, for months she had known, that this must come. She had never been able to believe that he would leave that terrible place. But equally, she had not been able to envisage life without him. For so long he had been her mainstay, the firm and solid centre of her life, the pivot from which she could swing and spin, the focus and axis of her being. Even in his absence, this had remained true: she recognized that her emotions for Richard Scherrer were deeply affected by the depth of her need for Nathaniel. Without him she had neither aim nor direction, neither motive nor efficacy: she was a call which had no sound.

Endlessly she relived moments with Nathaniel: the winter

afternoon in King Street when he asked her to marry him; their laughter in that Bristol garden when her baby niece had sprinkled him with daisies; his face in the hotel lobby when he had said, 'I have not ceased to love you.' At that she broke down again, sobbing bitterly.

She did not know how she was to break the news to David, who so adored his father. She dreaded the letters she must write immediately to Alice in Chicago, to Nathaniel's brother. So for three days she did nothing. She cloaked her heart in mourning and gave herself up to grief.

When Richard Scherrer came back to Nice and, after his first day's work, to Corbès, he found Sadie with her hair wrapped in a turban polishing the floors. He let himself in through the courtyard door with his own key, and came up behind her so quietly she did not hear him and nearly jumped out of her skin when he remarked, 'Good evening.'

It was only when she turned to him that he saw something was wrong. She looked strained, but then she had been under great pressure ever since Nathaniel was imprisoned. It was something else. He could not work out for a while what it was, and it only came to him after a time that her eyes seemed to have lost that curious chatoyancy that so fascinated him, as their colour changed from grey to green. Now all colour seemed to have drained away, leaving them lucid as rain.

He asked, 'Something has happened, yes? What is it?'

She told him, then, of the visit to the convent and of Nathaniel's death. As she spoke, falteringly, Scherrer sank down on the stairs and sat with his hand over his eyes. When she had finished, and told him about the nun and the candles, she saw that tears dripped from between his spread fingers. Watching him, filled with gratitude for the depth of his caring, Sadie said, 'I don't think I knew how much I loved him.'

And Scherrer answered, simply, 'I also.'

He stayed that night at the villa. Neither slept; they were quiet for long periods, then they spoke of Nathaniel.

Towards morning Scherrer asked, 'What will you do?'

'I don't know yet. I've not let myself think: I've cleaned the whole place like a madwoman.' She sighed. 'And now I suppose it's time to decide. I know I want to get away, but that's hard to do at the moment. I'll have to stay here, but I feel so alone.'

He heard the desolation in her words. Rising, he peered out at the courtyard, now touched faintly with first light.

As he passed she reached out and caught his arm. 'I need you now,' she said, 'I really need you now.'

He stood rigid for a moment as though she had struck him, then suddenly got to his knees at her side. He buried his face in her lap, his arms about her waist, and groaned aloud. She looked down at the sparse hair, the narrow shoulders in the alien uniform. I should hate this man, she thought. He represents an evil force. He could destroy me with a word whenever he wishes. Whatever he says, whatever he secretly believes, he has perpetrated acts of violence upon innocent people. He is a marauding soldier, an invader, a killer, a German. Still, he clung to her. Hesitantly, reluctantly, seemingly against her will, her arms wound about his shoulders and she folded him close.

For the truth was, she could not care. It had ceased to matter that beyond the walls of the villa Europe still boiled with war. She had done what she could, and Nathaniel was gone from her because of it. The German alone had brought her solace in these last months. He was an individual caught up in the maelstrom; he needed her as she did him.

After the night when Sadie told him of Nathaniel's death, Scherrer continued to visit the Villa d'Auban. It was many months before they became lovers, since Scherrer's pride would not let him ask again for what he might fail to take.

So it was left between them, an unspoken word, until Sadie in her misery turned to him one day and said, 'Now it is I who needs to be cherished.'

The feeling she had for him was new to her. It was not the singing ecstasy she had known with her lovely Asher, nor the cautious ardour she had experienced for Woolf. He did not warm her like Nathaniel, with the steady reassurance of his caring. She knew only that Richard spoke to her in a voice she had not before heard. She was fifty-four years old, and thought that she knew men. Yet here was this German, younger than she, a tired and saddened man, uncovering springs of emotion she had not known existed. He came to her out of a void. He told her of no past, promised her no future. They did not attempt to load the physical act with emotional burdens; did not ask of each other fidelity or security. They shared only the moment, and the knowledge of its transience released in both of them a wild and sensual wanting. Sadie had never imagined that at her age she could experience raw desire, and the realization made her both frightened and ashamed. But that did not stop her. Nothing could stop her. She knew that the isolation in which she now lived intensified her emotions, but that made no difference to the power they exerted. She had sought this deliberately, that Richard Scherrer should aid her husband.

And out of it had come this violent and devouring passion of her life.

God help her.

She loved him.

Chapter Thirty-One

Richard Scherrer was again called briefly to Paris early in May 1944. He returned looking thinner and more anxious than ever. He contrived to get to the Villa d'Auban on his second evening back and they sat in the unlit salon, Sadie on the floor with her back against his knees. Neither had spoken for a long time when Scherrer said, out of his thoughts,

'I talked to a lot of people in Paris. Things are going very badly for us. Berlin is being bombed even in daylight now and we're almost finished in Italy. I don't think this war can go on very much longer and when it's over Germany will have lost. And then God knows what will happen.'

He paused and added in a low voice, 'And I don't want to wait around to find out. I'm getting out.'

She stiffened against his knees. 'Richard! What do you mean?'

He pulled her round to face him. Urgently he said, 'I'm leaving France. And I want to take you with me.'

She was stunned.

'But where will you go? Where is safe? If you were caught, you would be finished. They'd shoot you.'

'*If* I were caught. But I've got it all worked out, I've had this in my head for months. We can be in Switzerland in three days at most. I have friends there, we will be safe. Sadie, come with me. We can have a life together.'

Bewildered, she stared at him. 'What about your wife? What about Inge? She's waited for you, your family is in Leipzig. They all love you. You can't desert them.'

He was a careful man, a planner, a worrier, and now he pushed up his glasses and rubbed his hands hard over his face.

'I can't desert *you*. Don't tear me in two, for God's sake. I can take care of everything, of everyone, only I have to get away from here. I can't live out this farce any longer.'

She clambered heavily to her feet and it crossed his mind that it was the first ungraceful movement he had seen her make.

'Richard, I can't decide in a moment. You must give me time.'

'No. I must go now, and you with me.'

'Of course you must. But I cannot take you from your own family.'

His face set. 'Either we go together or I do not go at all. I am in your hands.'

'If we stay – what will happen to you?'

He gave his short, mirthless laugh.

'It depends. I could fight to the end, I suppose. Or surrender quietly. Either way I may die. Either way I will not get home.'

'I could speak for you, tell them how you protected Nathaniel.'

He stared at her. 'I don't think you appreciate the position you will be in, when the Allies arrive and the French are free. You will be treated as a collaborator for what you have been to me.'

She was shocked. 'But that's impossible! Look what we did, Nathaniel and I. Look what happened to him.' Her voice trailed away uncertainly as he shook his head. 'All that – will mean nothing?'

'I am very much afraid that one will not cancel out the other. After a war there is bitterness and suspicion, all the anger built up during these years of occupation will have to be released. Anything might happen, and you will be alone here.'

Sadie turned to the window. For long moments she listened to the splash of her fountain, obsessively pleating and repleating the folds of the scarf she held. She had not anticipated public repercussions for her private emotions, and the sudden threat was appalling and formless: she could not comprehend it, but Richard's anxiety was warning enough. She thought of Nathaniel in an unmarked grave where she could not even go to mourn him. She thought of her children: of Esther with her second husband, of David with his new interests, his shaping life. There was nothing to hold her here. With a decisive gesture she smoothed the material flat against her thigh.

'Let us go,' she said.

He did not allow her to do more than pack a single suitcase. 'Possessions do not matter. Nothing matters but your safety.'

He travelled in civilian clothes. She was startled by his appearance in the conservative dark suit, the soft-brimmed hat. He looked like a harassed businessman. His authoritative air seemed to have disappeared with the uniform and the expensive leather ankle boots. She reflected, as she sat beside him in the car, that she preferred him like this. He was driving her Citröen, for which he had managed to acquire a full tank of petrol and several spare gallons concealed in the boot beneath a rug.

'It may not get us there, but probably we can make it to a railway station fairly near the border. That's the best way to arrive – less suspicious.'

'How did you get all this petrol?'

He gave a grim little smile. 'You'd be surprised how many people owe me a favour.'

They talked very little as they followed the smaller sideroads across Provence towards Digne. Scherrer planned to get down to Grenoble, then head for Aix-les-Bains. From there they would try to board a train if any were running. If not they would drive or if necessary – he shrugged – they would walk. Sadie fervently hoped this would not be necessary. She had eaten very little over the

451

last two months and felt curiously light-headed.

It had been over a year since she was able to use the Citröen and the well-worn leather seats, the walnut dashboard, almost made her feel that life had slipped back a cog to deposit her where she had been before the war. In the darkness the figure beside her could have been Nathaniel. At the thought of him she made an involuntary sound and Richard reached for her knee, giving it a consoling squeeze. 'Try and sleep.'

His greatest anxiety was that they would meet a convoy of German soldiers moving position. It was unlikely, he knew, for they feared night attacks by the *Maquis*. It was a real fear and one he shared, but there was nothing to do but hope. He had doubts about meeting any French police but that should not present problems: a curt command, his papers, and they would assume he was an officer on an illicit *vacance*, and he did not think they would risk stopping him. As it happened they were fortunate. The Citröen slipped quietly through the countryside. No one apprehended them: the whole country seemed to hold its breath.

Throughout the night Sadie dozed in the enclosed haven of the Citröen, and wished the journey would never end. Suspended, encapsulated, protected, she and Richard Scherrer could be together always. Nothing hindered their happiness nor threatened their safety.

Just before dawn Scherrer said, 'You'd better talk to me. I'm getting sleepy.'

'Shall I drive?'

'We cannot risk that, I'm afraid. It would not be in character and if we should be stopped . . .'

Instead they talked of what they would do in Switzerland, where they would live. Richard had friends in Fribourg. They would go there and find an apartment to rent. He would obtain false papers as a Dutch citizen, perhaps, and there would be no problems about finding a

452

job with his contacts. His friends were sympathetic and of long standing; they would do everything they could, of this he was sure.

It all sounded feasible in the semi-darkness. Only when the sky began to brighten, and the fuzzy outlines of trees and fields assumed the clarity of day, did Richard fall silent. Glancing across, she saw his face was strained. He lifted his left hand from the wheel and wiped it down his cheek in his familiar troubled gesture. When they reached the outskirts of Grenoble they stopped. They left the car and walked a short distance to find a café where they gratefully drank coffee. Before they set off again, Scherrer consulted a street map of the town, and unerringly took them through Grenoble by the quiet roads.

Once, they saw a policeman; as they left the town a patrol of German soldiers tramped towards them, and Sadie found she was holding her breath. But they passed without a flicker of interest.

After that, exhaustion merged the hours together, and by the time the Citröen had climbed to Aix-les-Bains both of them were glazed with tiredness.

When they entered the town Sadie felt Scherrer stiffen perceptibly, alert to something she did not sense. As they passed the Sévigné Hotel he came to a decision.

'I don't like it,' he said abruptly. 'I'm not even going to look for the railway station. We'll drive straight through.'

Nervously she agreed: the streets did seem strangely empty for the time of day. It was only when the houses began to thin out that they came upon several people clustered by the roadside. Peering out, Sadie saw that a cyclist had apparently fallen.

Someone in the crowd called, '*Arrêtez!*' but Scherrer ignored them. Glancing in the rear mirror, he hurried on.

'Was that wise?'

'No. But we couldn't risk getting involved with an accident: they probably wanted the cyclist taken to hospital. We have our own skins to worry about.'

'Will anyone tell the police? Should we take a train as you said?'

'I don't think that's such a good idea now: I have a bad feeling. I think I'll try something else.'

They reached the shores of the lake of Annecy. Beside the water the undergrowth was thick. Scherrer drove into a wooded inlet and turned out the headlights, and for a couple of hours both attempted to sleep.

They reached Annecy in the early light which revealed the four towers of the twelfth-century castle dominating the town, and negotiated arcaded lanes and canals in the old quarter. There they found an open restaurant where the proprietor gave them warmed *brioches* while his trim seventeen-year-old daughter laid the surrounding tables and eyed Scherrer speculatively.

Afterwards, Sadie insisted on driving through the Haute Savoie, while Scherrer tried to doze beside her. When they reached the first signpost for the frontier town of Annemasse she woke him. He checked his papers and her own, and took over the wheel.

Twenty minutes later they were at the frontier post. It was raining heavily now, the peaks of the distant mountains cloaked in cloud, and the French *douanier* peered out at them from the warmth of his cabin. He emerged, pulling his collar high round his chin and took Scherrer's papers. He leant into the car and held out a hand for Sadie's documents, which she handed over together with the stamped card Scherrer had given her. A puzzled look crossed the *douanier*'s face, and he peered in at Sadie. Then he turned to Scherrer as though about to ask a question. Scherrer turned his head slightly so that Sadie could not see and made a furtive gesture with his right hand. The official gave a nod and turned back to the cabin, taking both sets of documents with him.

Sadie breathed, 'What?'

Scherrer mouthed, soundlessly, 'Police.'

The four minutes that Sadie counted were as long as years. A man with a raincoat over his dark blue uniform came to the door of the cabin and stared at the Citröen's numberplate. He said something to the *douanier* and both men laughed. Then the first one walked over to Scherrer, and with a wink of collusion handed the documents back.

'*Bonne vacance*,' he said, and Scherrer smiled stiffly. The *douanier* turned towards the border barrier and raised his arm. The two soldiers who stood there, rifles on their shoulders poking up beneath the dark rain capes, stepped forward and raised the white bars. Scherrer lifted a hand in salutation and started the car. Unmoving the soldiers watched them go.

Sadie let out her breath with a whistle. 'I thought they would stop us.'

'There are plenty of Germans travelling around Switzerland at the moment. The Gestapo have an active organization looking for *agents provocateurs*.' He gave his short laugh. 'We must avoid them, but at least we have something to thank them for – every French border guard is used to semi-official travellers.'

As they drove along the wide, tree-lined road it suddenly came to Sadie that they were in Switzerland.

It was almost dusk as they passed slowly through the broad avenues and formal gardens of Geneva, marvelling at the bright lights after the frightened darkness of France at war. They finally found a room at the old-fashioned Rivoli Hotel in the rue des Paquis. After a meal which they barely tasted they went upstairs, showered and collapsed into bed. Spent, they slept for many hours.

Waking, Sadie raised an arm to look at the luminous hands of her watch but she had neglected to wind it the night before. She had slept so deeply, so dreamlessly, that she had no idea of the time. She got out of bed, moving slowly so as not to disturb Richard, padded to the window and pulled the handle. The tall casement opened inwards and she pushed at the shutter beyond. It was still raining, the street was deserted. The soft, greyish light could have been eleven in the morning or four in the afternoon.

She turned back to the bed to try and see Richard's watch and found he was awake.

'I didn't mean to disturb you. I just wondered what time it was.'

'Time enough,' he said, and held out a hand to her. She moved in beside him. He was relaxed and sleepy, his arms warm around her. He nuzzled her throat and she murmured acquiescence, accommodating her body to his. In the unfamiliar surroundings she tried to recapture the happiness she had experienced driving at dawn through the wooded hills of Provence two days before; protected, enclosed, loved.

They knew each other with tenderness. Afterwards, Sadie opened her eyes and looked at her lover with an expression he could not read.

Later that day they found a garage and sold the Citröen. She insisted that Richard took half the money. He refused at first, then accepted gratefully: he had already told her that he had taken only his month's pay with him, for fear of arousing suspicion. Then they turned towards Cornavin Station, walking the short distance from the rue de la Servette in a fine drizzle which dampened their skin and left a faint sheen on their clothes.

Sadie changed some money at the *Bureau de Change* opposite the main concourse and told Scherrer she would get the tickets. It took her ten minutes, then she found him at the bookstall buying a copy of *Neue-Zuricher Zeitung* and registered the date printed at the top: 5 June 1944. Walking close together they crossed the station to the barrier. Sadie showed the tickets and they passed through. She tucked Scherrer's into his top pocket, and with it a small wad of notes which he failed to notice.

'Richard, that's my train over there.'

Uncertain, he glanced at her, then across at the platform indicator. It read Zurich.

'But we want Fribourg.'

Quietly she corrected him.

'*You* want Fribourg. I'm not coming with you, my dear. I'm going to Zurich. I have friends there, I can stay for a while and decide what to do.'

'What are you saying? What's the matter?' She swayed at the hurt in his voice.

'I wanted to be with you. I still do.' She paused, struggling to find the truth for him. 'But I know you have a wife you love, and people to take care of.' Her desire to touch him was strong: she moved closer and straightened his tie. 'So have I. We can't just run from our families. I couldn't do that to Nathaniel's memory.'

Scherrer closed his eyes, swallowing hard.

'It would be a mistake,' she went on. 'And in time we should regret it. We have had our moment, you and I. Thank you for it.'

She took a pace back and he moved also. He put down the cases and put his hands in his pockets, the material bulging as he clenched his fists. He said, quite simply, 'No. I won't go.'

'I – but Richard, I've explained. It's the only thing for us to do, you know it is.'

'I haven't come this far in order to be parted from you. I don't believe it's what you want either.'

He found himself remembering how he had thought once that she did what she had to do in order to survive. Uncertain for a moment he asked, trying to keep the pleading out of his voice and sounding, in the attempt, harsher than he felt, 'Did you come with me only to get out of France?'

She answered him steadily. 'No. It was you, remember, who wanted me to leave. I have not used you, if that is what you think. Though I will not deny that I did, once.' Her voice dropped. 'It seems as if a different person did that.'

Someone hurrying past jostled Sadie and she almost lost her balance. Scherrer put a hand on her shoulder to steady her. In a sudden gesture of weariness she rested her cheek on his hand for a moment and closed her eyes.

'So you love me, then.'

In the short sentence she heard relief, certainty, and a touch of triumph. In response, she put her lips to the back of his hand. He tightened his grip.

'Promise me something. Go to Zurich first. Then travel to Chicago, make sure everyone is all right. I will try to reach Inge and see what is to be done. Write down for me your American address and I will contact you there. Let us meet again in Zurich as soon as we can, as soon as things are calm again. Will you do that?'

'Could we? Is it possible?'

He shook her shoulder gently. 'All things are possible. You say I can't leave Inge, you speak of Nathaniel's memory. But for us, everything has changed. We can't go back to what we were before.' He released her and added, painfully, 'We are different, now.'

She listened to him with sudden, wild hope. It could happen, perhaps. That dream time on the journey from Corbès need not be the end of it all, as she had thought. Eagerly she responded to his request, hunting in her handbag for a piece of paper to write down David's Chicago address. As she handed it over, the engine beside them breathed a great sigh of damp steam. Through the drifting whiteness they looked at each other, reluctant to relinquish what they had shared for so brief a time, 'You will come?' Above the hiss of steam his voice was almost inaudible. She touched his lips with her own.

'I will wait for you in Zurich.'

After a moment she stepped back and unwillingly he loosed her. She gathered up her possessions and turned, heading blindly for her train, hurrying now to spare him her tears. Mounting the compartment steps she paused.

He waited where she had left him, still watching her. She lifted one hand, found from somewhere a smile. Gravely, he also raised a hand in farewell.

As her train pulled out she stood at the window, craning to see his solitary, still figure. After a moment the brightening sky caught the glass and she could see him no more.

Nothing was left but reflections.

Postscript

As she had promised, Sadie waited in Zurich for Richard Scherrer to come to her. She waited for a long time, unable to abandon the hope he had kindled that afternoon, the hope that they might, despite all odds, share a life together. The weeks turned into months, and the months to years.

They were not unhappy years. She lived in the luxury of her own small suite at the Dolder Grand Hotel, high on the Dolder Heights among pine woods and golflinks. Here she read and re-read the many letters he sent, telling her of his early problems when finally he was able to return to Germany, then of his wife's illness, later the news that next year he would be in Zurich. Next year . . .

Waiting, Sadie found a curious contentment. Cocooned by her surroundings, money and friends, she achieved a degree of peace that astonished her. Occasionally she would hold a small dinner-party, often she strolled round the city. She was known to all the antique dealers and art galleries although she never bought from them: for the first time in her life she had ceased to hoard.

She kept only her photographs. Sepia portraits of her mother and sisters. More recent ones of Esther and the grandchildren; of her son David with his young family.

Sometimes the French windows stood open and from the dining room below she could hear 'La vie en rose,' stringing remembrance through the warm nights. Then she would bring out other photographs. Of a young man with intense dark eyes; another stiff and solitary in a studio, light catching the gold rims of his spectacles; a third, older, smiling, generous face bent over the baby in his arms. And the last, a man with a high-bridged nose, a white uniform jacket hooked over his shoulder by a finger.

For a long while she would look at them without seeing: images of her past.

And wonder, for a moment or two, just what her life might have held if she had been, after all, a beauty.

Outstanding women's fiction in Panther Books

C L Skelton
Hardacre £2.50 ☐

Erich Segal
Oliver's Story £1.25 ☐
Man, Woman and Child £1.25 ☐

Nicola Thorne
A Woman Like Us £1.25 ☐
The Perfect Wife and Mother £1.50 ☐
The Daughters of the House £1.95 ☐
Where the Rivers Meet £2.50 ☐
Affairs of Love £2.50 ☐

Jacqueline Briskin
Paloverde £2.50 ☐
Rich Friends £2.50 ☐
Decade £2.50 ☐
The Onyx £2.50 ☐

Celeste de Blasis
The Tiger's Woman £2.50 ☐

Barbara Taylor Bradford
A Woman of Substance £2.95 ☐
Voice of the Heart £2.95 ☐

Alan Ebert & Janice Rotchstein
Traditions £2.50 ☐

Trevanian
The Summer of Katya £1.95 ☐

Raymond Giles
Sabrehill £1.95 ☐
Slaves of Sabrehill £2.50 ☐
Rebels of Sabrehill £2.50 ☐
Storm over Sabrehill £2.50 ☐
Hellcat of Sabrehill £2.50 ☐

Marcelle Bernstein
Sadie £2.50 ☐

To order direct from the publisher just tick the titles you want and fill in the order form.

All these books are available at your local bookshop or newsagent, or can be ordered direct from the publisher.

To order direct from the publisher just tick the titles you want and fill in the form below.

Name _____

Address _____

_____

Send to:
Panther Cash Sales
PO Box 11, Falmouth, Cornwall TR10 9EN.

Please enclose remittance to the value of the cover price plus:

UK 45p for the first book, 20p for the second book plus 14p per copy for each additional book ordered to a maximum charge of £1.63.

BFPO and Eire 45p for the first book, 20p for the second book plus 14p per copy for the next 7 books, thereafter 8p per book.

Overseas 75p for the first book and 21p for each additional book.